# SUPPING WITH THE DEVIL

Richard Elliot-Square

authorHOUSE®

AuthorHouse™ UK Ltd.
500 Avebury Boulevard
Central Milton Keynes, MK9 2BE
www.authorhouse.co.uk
Phone: 08001974150

Published by AuthorHouse 9/16/2013

ISBN: 978-1-4817-8356-9 (sc)
ISBN: 978-1-4817-8357-6 (hc)
ISBN: 978-1-4817-8355-2 (e)

*To my special friend, Lizzie*

# FIFTEEN YEARS AGO

There was a smell of medication and stale urine inside the room. For a once ruggedly handsome man, the gaunt face that had now replaced the matinee-star looks, with its taut, translucent skin, thin hair, and sunken eyes hidden within dark sockets in his skull, this was the last humiliation. He lay prone in his hospital bed, surrounded by drips of chemicals and saline, his skeletal frame accentuated by the loose, white linen sheet that covered his body. A full urine bag dangled below the mattress.

The cancer had come quickly and ruthlessly, a strain that was virulent and ever conquering. Cancer of the liver was the first diagnosis. He was a drinker among drinkers. And then, despite the endless hospital visits and consultations followed by one operation after another, he was told that he had cancer of everything else. He opted out of chemo, preferring to make the most of what life could throw at him. But he hadn't lasted more than three months. Self-indulgent, a bad drunk, a heavy smoker, and abusive to all that tried to get close to him, this thrice-divorced sinner had thrown sand in God's face, and now as he wheezed and coughed, he realized that he had perhaps gone too far this time. But he didn't care.

Only one person stood by his bed at that moment. He squinted at his visitor. His son, a good-looking young man of twenty, was looking down at the man who had abused him all of his life. The father who was jealous of everything he had, which he himself had possessed, but chose to throw to the winds. A man who had left the family destitute and a wife who never really recovered from the damage he had inflicted on her and their son.

"Is that you?" The voice belied the forty-five year old voice box that had been so sorely treated.

"I had to come." He paused. "How are you?" The young man drew closer in trepidation.

"I'm fucking dying," he rasped. "What a stupid question."

"Is there anything I can do?" He meant what his words said, but he didn't feel anything for this appalling man.

"Nothing! Why the fuck did you come?" His frail arms started to shake as he became agitated.

"You are my father, God damn you. That's why." A tear started to well up in his eye.

"Appropriate words indeed! Well, you can see that God has damned me. Thanks for telling me the obvious!"

"Father ..."

But the man cut him off. He tried to lift his head off the pillow without success, sinking back with a long wheeze. "Get out of here! Get the fuck out!"

"I came to see you ..."

"Die? Ha!" His pale, dry lips tightened. "I will not give you that pleasure! Get out now!" His emaciated fingers wrapped themselves around the nurse call button, which started buzzing in the distance. "And you know, Nicholas," he wheezed again, a hoarse dry sound that ended with a clicking sound from his throat, "I knew you were a waster, and I know that you will never achieve anything in your life. That is my paternal blessing! Go!"

The monitor flat lined, and his father was dead. The tears that streaked down his cheeks were not for this dreadful man but for himself. He moved forward and kissed the cold forehead. A teardrop fell from his eye and anointed his father's head, and then he whispered, "Goodbye, Father; you see what I do with my life! Just you see! I will never, ever be like you." He stood back and added, "I vow to rub out my memories and to prove you wrong. May God forgive you!" He turned, almost bumping into the two nurses that had arrived. "Too late! He's gone!"

Nick Adams left the hospital, and he was angry. He had heard what his father had said and made a silent vow.

# FIFTEEN YEARS LATER—MANHATTAN

The vein on the right temple of his head throbbed and complained mercilessly. He brushed his fingers across his face as if to smooth away the ache. The painkillers he swallowed with a slug of whiskey not thirty minutes ago had clearly not worked. Exhaustion had set in. He had nearly finished. He stood up and tried with great effort to straighten his much abused and neglected back, which had all but seized up from being hunched over his laptop keyboard for hours on end.

The tall, heavily built man had a deadline to meet, after which he could take it a bit easier, maybe go on a vacation with his long-suffering wife. Being the wife of a journalist, she knew the score. No matter how illustrious and well-thought-of by his peers he was, she indulged him and went with the flow. Most of the time. Howard was worth it. This was a big story, and from what she knew, it would cause uproar and discomfiture at the highest levels of government.

Howard Wayne retrieved sheets out of the printer tray, lit a cigarette, and moved into the sitting room, where he sat down and started to read his work.

He knew that the newspaper subeditors would top and tail and no doubt exaggerate and manipulate his words, making them more sensational, but his meticulous research deserved a wide readership audience, and the story had to be told. It would go viral on the Internet, and it would open an international nest of vipers.

A scandal in the financial world is harming many innocent naïve investors—

3

Howard Wayne sucked at his cigarette, asking himself whether the opening was strong enough, and conceded that the subs would edit his work to hell anyway and read on.

> a scheme that boosts the price of a stock through recommendations based on false, misleading, or greatly exaggerated statements. The perpetrators, who already have established positions in the company's stock, sell their positions after the hype has led to a higher share price. This practice is illegal, based on securities law, and can lead to heavy fines.

He flipped to a new sheet.

> The victims often lose much of their investment when the stock falls after the process is complete. This "pump and dump" scam is the illegal act of an investor or group of investors who promote a stock they hold and sell once the stock price has risen following the surge in interest as a result of the endorsement.

Ash dropped onto his jumper without him noticing.

> The stock is usually promoted as a "hot tip" or "the next big thing," with details of an upcoming news announcement that will "send the stock through the roof." The details of each pump and dump scam are different, but the scheme always boils down to a basic principle: shifting supply and demand. Pump and dump scams tend to work only on small and microcap stocks traded over the counter from companies that tend to be highly illiquid, whose stock price can move sharply when volume increases. The scammers increase the demand and trading volume in the stock. The inflow of investors leads to a sharp rise in its price. Once the price rise has peaked, the group sells their position to make a large short-term gain—at your expense!

Howard had a reputation as the poor man's investment guru, often drawing flack from the more conventional financial institutions in New York, London, and Frankfurt.

> On one stock I watched, the price rose from around ten

cents to nearly $5 in a one-week period, a massive increase. The stock had seen an average daily trading volume before the increase of less than 25,000, but during the scam the stock traded up to nearly one million shares on some trading days. The unsuspecting investors would have bought into the stock at around $1, watched it grow, dreamed of riches, then suddenly it was back to being a penny stock!

Blah blah.... It was time for bed. He would have to be up early, finish the story, and load it onto a flash drive before going to his newspaper. He smiled to himself as he added,

Always keep this investment caveat in mind: If it's too good to be true, it probably is. I am now going to expose the people and institutions that allow this contamination to go on without any retribution.

He stubbed out his cigarette, raised himself off the sofa, and left the sheets as they lay. He grinned as he thought of the faces of those who would see themselves spread all over the *Wall Street Journal* in days to come.

The cigarette was not completely out, and a spiral of smoke wound its way upwards to the ceiling. It heralded the careers that would soon be turned to ashes.

# NEW YORK

The client had given careful instructions. Half of the fee had been wired. The target had been chosen. This assignment was a walk in the park—simple, straightforward, with little danger. The time had come to put the meticulous planning into motion.

It mattered not that the actions taken that day would ruin so many lives and lead to a financial Armageddon that would expose corruption and greed on a colossal scale.

An assassin was on the prowl. She was in place, ready, waiting to pounce upon her prey.

# ZURICH, SWITZERLAND

"Another glass of champagne, Herr Adams?" The voice of the waiter jolted him out of his jet-lagged semi-slumber.

A dream? Not at all! After all of the shit in his life, everything had suddenly changed.

Boy, how it had, and in bucket loads.

"Why not? Thank you!" He sat up in the overly comfortable hotel chair, feeling not a little embarrassed. He smiled back at the waiter, glancing at the expensive watch that sat rather ostentatiously on his left wrist. It was new, an acquisition purchased that very same afternoon from Cartier on the Bahnhofstrasse. The waiter poured the champagne and placed the elegant glass flute back onto the table.

Not so long ago he could have lived for four months on the money that had been taken off his private Swiss bank-issued credit card.

"Six o'clock here," he murmured to himself while sipping the champagne, "that's 11:00 a.m. New York time." His BlackBerry flashed red, but he wasn't about to spoil his daydream by dealing with the usual mundane e-mails that hounded him 24/7. He needed this break. The next day he would be back in the States, and until then everything could wait.

He slipped back into the chair and reflected on the previous and present day's hectic schedule.

He had flown in the afternoon before. The hotel Mercedes had whisked him from the terminal building at Kloten Airport straight to the Park Hyatt hotel in central Zurich, where he was checked in and shown to his junior suite—all typically efficient in the true Swiss German style. He had gone through his usual routine of unpacking and activating his iPad and selecting the hotel Wi-Fi.

A quick check through his e-mails confirmed his appointment that evening. A shower reinvigorated him. He was unusually nervous. The next twenty-four hours would change his life.

At 7:00 p.m. he made his way down to the hotel bar, which was noisy and full of young professionals fresh out of their offices, middle-aged foreign businessmen, and a surfeit of stunning single girls, all with that East European look that made normally rational, sensible men shipwreck their lives upon the sirens' rocks, ultimately to be dragged through the divorce courts. He looked around at the faces, trying to identify his scheduled appointment for the evening. Despite the seductresses that smiled at him, he had important life-changing business to discuss. He found his man sitting in the shadows, seated at one of the corner tables, well away from the bar and the main source of noise.

"Mr. Adams!" He rose and offered his hand, stooping slightly as he tried to disentangle his legs from under the cramped table. "A pleasure!" The smile seemed sincere enough, Nick Adams observed as he pulled a chair back and sat down. They ordered two glasses of white wine, and the pleasantries done, started the business at hand.

"Because you're a US citizen,"—the man leaned toward him, trying to whisper somewhat unsuccessfully against the background noise—"normally we would not have been able to assist you …" He broke off and gestured at the futility of competing with the cacophony.

His fellow guest smiled and got up. "Finish your wine! Supper calls!"

The chic Italian restaurant, almost hidden in a cobbled side street lined with pastel-colored ancient buildings, with first-floor windows built out overhanging the neat shop windows and office doors, and just off the main shopping street, the Bahnhofstrasse, was above all quiet. The local Swiss citizens favored this restaurant in "downtown Switzerland," as publicists sometimes described Zurich.

The table had been reserved, and they were duly shown to it. "As I was saying, US citizens cannot have offshore accounts in Switzerland." He glanced around the restaurant. The light of the overhead chandelier flashed on the lenses of his rimless spectacles, but of course even had the conversation been overheard, the fellow diners who derived their very wealth from the work of this and countless other men such as him would have nodded their approval. "But as you know, we have a scheme that allows us to convince the back-offices of the local banks that you are not the beneficial owner. Therefore the authorities in the USA have no interest or jurisdiction!" He retrieved the veal that he had been pushing around his plate and put it into his mouth.

"Are you sure? The last thing I need is trouble with the IRS." A serious point made, but his grin gave him away. "I can see how you justify your charges!"

"Quite so." His dinner companion looked him straight in the eyes. There was no smile; money was to be treated with utmost respect. "Tomorrow will be a mere formality, I can assure you."

"Even though the account is in the name of the company your firm has set up, and the beneficial owner is not me, the bank will take instructions from me anyway?" He paused to allow a pretty waitress to remove his plate. "And they know that I own everything?"

"Oh, yes indeed, my friend." He put the wineglass to his lips and sucked red wine rather too noisily. "Everyone is doing it! Well, the rich in particular! And that covers you, even though you are not as yet über-rich; the banks like to mix and match." He smiled. "We have various parties who are clean and act as shadow beneficial owners. The banks check them out and accept them, even though they know that you really can take back control at any time, give instructions, and generally act as the sole owner. That way we all win!"

The lawmakers in the United States and the European Commission were forcing Switzerland to cooperate, whereby the Swiss voluntarily imposed a withholding tax on accounts held by the wealthy that banked within their borders. Switzerland had to strike such deals to try to preserve bank account secrecy, the cornerstone of its two-trillion-dollar financial services industry. But there were innovative ways around such matters, and Nick's newly acquired advisor specialized in such schemes.

They finished their meal. The bill paid, they made their way back to the hotel bar, which, if anything, had become louder. Most of the girls were now either not there, having found a temporary companion for the evening, or had found some father-figure friend eager to ply expensive alcohol through their Restylane-enhanced lips and down slender necks. Two drinks later, Nick shook the hand of his advisor in the hotel lobby. The next day would be an early start, and the young American had to be in top form.

He had hardly slept. Part of the reason was the international time difference, but it was mainly due to the excitement he felt coursing through his veins. It was 6:00 a.m. He called the front desk and cancelled his 7:00 a.m. alarm. After breakfast and a quick glance at the complimentary *USA Today*, he was off to his appointment.

The meeting room, one of many such rooms within the bank, overlooked the snow-capped mountains that loomed above the roofs of Zurich and the Cantons that stretched beyond, a timeless vista that had not changed for centuries.

His advisor, who oozed charm and professionalism through every pore, did the talking. He addressed the impeccably dressed banker seated on the other side of a table that had coffee cups, bottled water, and various Swiss chocolates neatly arranged in the center.

It was clearly a routine meeting between the advisor and the banker. For them this was normal daily business. A stream of Russians, Chinese, Greeks, Italians, East Europeans, Arabs, Africans, and exceptionally the odd Brit or American, all intent upon ringfencing their assets that had been obtained in various nefarious ways, walked into the very same antiseptic lobby of the bank, and if called, into one of many elevators that lead them to the very private levels where discussions and transactions took place in the utmost confidence.

"So, all is in order." The banker took back the newly signed document and placed it into the file that was in front of him. "The new account for Zen Holdings is open, and as we anticipated a successful outcome, we ordered a card for you." He smiled and slid an envelope across the table. "It's operational and has no limit, as it is secured by the assets held on the account with us, and is, of course, anonymous. We will make the payments for you as they are billed. There will be no paper trail. Just do not use it outside Switzerland." He stood up, towering over the American, and shook the hands of the advisor and new customer. More fees for his bank. Job done. "We welcome you to our bank, Mr. Adams! A long and mutually profitable relationship we hope?" Nick Adams, some nine million dollars securely lodged in the bank, gave the banker a broad grin. "Why not do a little shopping before you leave Zurich? Use the card! Enjoy!" Nick almost choked with amusement. Almost.

And that is exactly what the American did. He couldn't help himself. It was like being locked up in the most exciting toy store after it had closed. He would have to get used to this life. Already he was contemplating who might accompany him on the next trip. Or judging from what he had seen in twenty-four hours, maybe he would be able to source locally.

But there was still a tight knot in his stomach. It had all seemed so simple and straightforward. If anyone of his close colleagues found out, all hell would let loose. But they wouldn't. How could they? He had taken only what was his by right. It was his business, he had taken the risks, and now it was time to harvest. A cool glass of champagne would settle his stomach. Christ! The company even bore his own name! Then it would be back to Kloten airport and New York. The world was his now!

"Not bad, eh, Father?"

While the population of the municipality of Zurich is only some 400,000 strong, the chances of Nick Adams running into a certain notorious banker during his fleeting visit would have been just not only very bad luck but probably extremely dangerous. His actions during the trip would be deemed traitorous, and there would be no excuses accepted.

It would seem, however, that on this occasion Lady Luck had protected him. But for how long her bountiful largesse would be bestowed upon him, only time would tell.

# NEW YORK

A boisterous early morning wind snaked and spiraled its unpredictable way along the fashionable Manhattan street, weaving through the trees that lined the sidewalks. The heavy, glossed door of a townhouse slammed shut with a solid bang as the owner left for work. The noise startled a couple walking on the opposite sidewalk, who looked back sharply in the direction of the house. They did not notice a lone huddled figure lurking in a dark recessed gateway of the private residence and who remained undetected.

As was the usual case, at precisely 8:30 a.m., a black Lincoln 100 stretch limousine, bouncing on soft springs, glided to a halt outside a forty-five-story glass tower apartment building across the street from the townhouse.

Checking the time, the doorman greeted the now-familiar limo with a casual wave before retreating back to his concierge desk to continue reading his morning paper. The driver waved back, but rather than brace the bitter wind whipping up East Forty-Seventh Street, he remained in his snug cocoon and used his cell phone to announce his arrival.

The hidden observer watched and observed. Every detail had been committed to memory. Alongside the sidewalk, wide, well-scrubbed, shallow steps led up to the main entrance; to the curved zinc awning, its full expanse out of view of the doorman's post; and most importantly, to the location of stairwells and elevators within the lobby. Nothing had been left to chance.

She had been patiently watching there for almost forty minutes, leaning against a brick wall, hidden in its shadow. Dressed in full matte black, the hooded Brighton jacket concealing her smooth, milky face, a pair of mini binoculars were clasped in the palm of her gloved right hand. She occasionally threw furtive glances, looking for anyone who might disturb her.

Ten minutes later, the doorman, clutching his blue cap to his head, rushed through the center lobby door to the parked limo. The driver wrapped his scarf tightly around his neck, cursing the cold wind, and immediately stepped out of his vehicle and followed the doorman into the building.

A short window of opportunity presented itself. It was time to make a move. The hooded figure sprang out of hiding and sprinted across the street to the opposite sidewalk, each step exact in its stride, her body in perfect synchrony. She knew from her observations that the driver would have left the car unlocked. She opened the streetside rear door and threw herself into the dark, plush interior, shutting the door behind her quietly. Even though the morning rush hour had started to get under way, nobody seemed to have noticed her. This was New York, after all! Before entering, she had shut one eye, allowing her pupils to adjust quickly to the dimness inside, a proven and useful tool in her trade.

Her routine was basic instinct. Every morning for one week she had meticulously planned and practiced her assiduous work ethic to get practicalities and every detail right; and she never disappointed her clients.

The driver would remotely lock the doors after stepping into the lobby, where he would wait as always to greet his customer. She knew that the privacy partition between driver and passenger would remain shut, creating a completely soundproof cabin. With tinted windows throughout, passengers were kept well hidden from those outside, including the driver.

Uninvited, she crouched below the privacy panel between the console and rear doors like a wild cat waiting for its hapless prey, her back leaning against the bulkhead. She removed a heavy object from her coat, which she gripped tightly.

The passenger appeared in the lobby from the bank of elevators, followed quickly by the driver, and made his way out of the building to the waiting limo. The passenger door opened, thrusting chilly air into the car. Sliding heavily into the rear seat of the darkened limo, the passenger adjusted his crumpled coat, and the door shut firmly behind him.

The driver climbed in, looked at his mirrors, and slowly accelerated away from the building, joining the morning traffic. Seated comfortably and shielded from the chaos of New York City, the passenger's usual journey to work had begun. In recognition of his invaluable contributions to the success of the paper he worked for, and his seniority, he had the use of a company limo to shuttle him to and from the office. The usual stack of newspapers had been left for him on his seat. With reading lights on, he fiddled with ceiling-mounted controls to tune into a classical radio station before idly leafing through a copy of his own paper's early edition.

The unseen Valentina Vinogradov curled her gloved fingers around the gun's trigger and leaped with an athletic body from her hiding place. She lunged with impressive agility toward the passenger, ramming the cold steel of a silencer deep into his mouth, chipping one of his teeth in the process.

Terror-stricken, the passenger struggled in vain to shake the grip that held him. But Vinogradov straddled one leg around his arm and planted a knee on his chest to restrain him. Steel ground into her victim's teeth and he gagged.

"Shut up!" she hissed. "Do as I say or you are dead!" But the passenger squirmed and choked, refusing to give up the uneven fight. She twisted the barrel again and again inside his mouth. He choked up blood-slicked phlegm secreted from the mucous membranes inside his mouth, eyes watering as a trickle of blood slicked down from a cut on his lip.

"Be quiet," she spat. Eyes bulging, the victim stared, nodding frantically. Vinogradov removed the barrel from his mouth and thrust it against his left temple. Skin scraped off and more blood slowly oozed from a new wound.

"Tell me: where is your laptop?" Her Slavic inflections were becoming more apparent. She pressed harder with the weapon, searching the seat with her other hand. It wasn't there. She arched into a backbend to search the floor, still holding her victim in a vice-like grip. "You son of a bitch, where is it?"

"I haven't got it … I didn't need it today," he blurted out in fear, his mouth full of warm blood. The barrel dug deeper into his face. "What do you want? Who are you, for Christ's sake?" His gaze fixed on the wild, almost demonic eyes staring back at him.

"Answer me! The data sticks, your files. Where are they?" She threw the weight of her body behind her hand and smacked him across the face. "Give me the keys to your apartment, now!" she spat into his face.

Turning abruptly to avoid a cyclist pedaling illegally against the oncoming traffic, the limo driver had to swerve sharply as he approached FDR Drive, causing Vinogradov to lose her grip. The passenger, seizing the initiative, swung his fist with a powerful blow to her neck, screaming out to the driver, but the raised soundproof partition worked as designed. His pleas went unheard.

Vinogradov tussled vigorously with her victim to gain control again. The beast, just barely under control within her, forced her into squeezing the trigger. A muffled pop sounded, and a single bullet smashed through the passenger's left cheek spiraling into the soft tissue of his brain. A sudden odor of smoke and cordite permeated the compartment. A torrent of crimson blood gushed from his open mouth and the entry point of the bullet, his body slumped onto the seat. He let out a last strangled moan, then was silent.

"*Chyort voz'mi!*" Vinogradov cursed. She grabbed at his suit lapels and shook him. "That was not supposed to happen, you pathetic imbecile!"

With an angry grunt she let go of the inert body. Her orders had been clear and precise. All that was required was to scare the reporter off and get him to hand over the main tool of his trade: his laptop. Shit! She knew the bastard always carried it with him. Murdering an investigative journalist would only give credence to his story. The conspiracy theories would compound and complicate things for her client, whom she had quite unintentionally compromised. She could imagine the wrath that would be brought to bear upon her wide, muscular shoulders.

A few moments passed as Vinogradov lay still on the limo's floor, taking stock. Finally her mental faculties shot into overdrive, and she snapped out of her uncharacteristic depression and dark thoughts of retribution. There was a way to salvage the botched assignment. Vinogradov pulled the slumped corpse back into a sitting position, checked his pulse just to make sure, and skillfully searched his pockets. She found a set of keys and pocketed them.

They were fast approaching the financial district. She had little time. The traffic had moved faster than Vinogradov anticipated. She removed the silencer and returned it to her coat pocket, cleaned the murder weapon with her gloves, and placed the gun in the hand of the dead man, pressing his hand around it. Grabbing his right arm, she bent it toward the lifeless drooping mouth, allowing the limb to drop and the gun to fall.

As the limo pulled up to One World Financial Center, *The Wall Street Journal*'s world headquarters, workers scurried to shelter from the raging wind. Umbrellas were blown inside out. The driver stepped out of the limo. He pulled at the curbside passenger door handle, but the Russian had already escaped through the opposite door, quietly closing it unnoticed behind her. She disappeared, blending into the throng of pedestrians, her hood tightly wrapped around her face to avoid any video surveillance cameras.

The limo driver stood for several moments patiently holding the door for his customer. He bent down and glanced into the dark interior but saw no activity or movement. Leaning further into the car, he gently tugged at the passenger's coat sleeve.

"World Financial Center, Mr. Wayne … Sir." There was no response. The driver squinted into the back seat. "Mr. Wayne, are you okay?"

He reached out to touch Wayne's shoulder, but the body fell off the seat and slumped heavily onto the floor. His left arm dropped lifelessly out of the door and hit the sidewalk. A trickle of blood dripped onto the ground.

The driver's face morphed into complete panic. He jumped back, almost losing his footing. When his heart leaped back into his chest, he knelt down beside the motionless body. There was blood seeping from gaping wounds in Howard Wayne's mouth and head. Then he saw splattered blood all over the car's interior like an abstract painting. That's when he began to shout out for help.

In a surreal snapshot in time, a great gust of wind began to spiral out of control, swooping up pages of the rumpled *Wall Street Journal* from within the car and sucking them out, with pages flapping and dancing wildly like great soaring birds rushing upward through the air current, while others spewed out across the pavement like ghostly apparitions.

A crowd began to gather. Two women weighted down with shoulder bags and briefcases came over to console the driver, but he just gazed vacuously at the chaotic scene as he sat in disbelief on the cold sidewalk.

Then came the sirens, wailing in the distance. A fire department truck came roaring down West Street, lights flashing, bullhorn and siren blaring. Several police patrol cars were right behind them. In minutes, an ambulance with spinning red lights emerged from a side street, screaming its way through Battery Park. The NYPD pushed the bystanders out of the way and cordoned off the area. When the inevitable news hounds arrived, digital flashlights reflected and bounced off the car's windows. Forensic techs in white suits examined the limo inside and out. The medics transferred Wayne's body from the limo to a gurney, and the rubbernecking onlookers were rewarded with a clear view of the cadaver in a body bag.

Police officers took statements from the driver and what few witnesses they could find.

Valentina Vinogradov had seen all she needed to see. She had tried to make it look like just another New York suicide, but she had permanently silenced her intended victim, and now there was still a piece of unfinished business to attend to if the suicide theory was to be believed. She would get the second installment of her agreed contract fee only after she had secured the evidence that threatened to expose a number of high profile individuals and institutions, and after delivering Wayne's magnum opus to her client. That meant his files would have to be found and delivered, and only then would the job be completed. She knew she had to finish the job. She followed an ironclad code of honor, ingrained from her days at the Kremlin. She checked for Wayne's house keys in her pocket, turned around, and vanished. Those who saw her cold, steel blue eyes averted their gaze as though they knew instinctively that she was trouble.

The early morning sun was lower in the sky, and it was much colder, the temperature reflecting the time of year. The weekend had been a welcome but unusual bonus after Nicholas Adams's trip to Zurich, and he had made a snap decision to trawl the last of the parties in the Hamptons. He touched a switch near the armrest and shut his window. Immediately he was cocooned from the outside world, enveloped in the luxurious interior cabin, the rich smell of new leather still pervasive within the recently acquired BMW X6. He ran his fingers across the dashboard and adjusted various buttons and knobs as he selected the ambient temperature. He turned his head and saw the skyline of Manhattan gradually emerge from the early morning mist. It was going to be a good day. He knew it was going to be all right. Everything had finally worked out, and he was in control of his life. No more day-to-day struggle with money and decisions. Less work, more play. Behind him there was a blare of angry horns and shouting. His daydreaming was abruptly halted, and he pressed down hard on the accelerator and closed the gap that had opened ahead. Nick Adams raised his hand, nonchalantly acknowledging the driver behind him. He reached up and adjusted the driver's mirror, caught his tanned reflection, and smiled. He ran a hand through his thick brown hair and grinned again. Nothing would faze him anymore. He vowed that from now on in it would always be like this. No going back. It was history. Soon he would be back in his apartment, shower, breakfast, and then answer a few e-mails before dressing for the office. Back to the daily grind.

At about 1:00 p.m., Adams stepped out of a hybrid New York

Yellow Cab. With his iPad in one hand and a BlackBerry pressed to his ear with the other, he headed into his office building. He was late and hung over.

At just over six feet, he had the smooth gait and rugged good looks of a successful Ralph Lauren male model. His thick, dark brown hair with just a hint of invading gray along the temples complemented his genial, youthful air. Add the form of a natural athlete, and you had a rather striking, forty-something package, the envy of his not-quite-so-fit contemporaries. Indeed, Nick Adams was occasionally approached by magazine lifestyle editors for their "most desirable single and successful men of New York" columns. Women of all ages deemed him a great catch, and although he played down his reputation as a playboy, he insisted that he was no different from any other single man in his prime. But naturally he relished the attention; and now that he had the money, he would be able to play all the more. Life was good.

# WASHINGTON, DC

The monthly meeting ended. Those attending broke into smaller groups to discuss the various tasks brought up by the director. The world seemed doomed, according to everyone that had listened to him and his staff. The agenda ranged through terrorism, cyber-crime, murder and violent crime, bank robberies, kidnapping, crimes against children, fraud and white-collar crime, to criminal enterprises, which included drugs.

As an intelligence-driven and a threat-focused national security and law enforcement organization, the mission of those in that room was to protect and defend the United States against terrorist and foreign intelligence threats, to uphold and enforce the criminal laws of the USA, and to provide leadership and criminal justice services to federal, state, municipal, and international agencies and partners.

The long meeting table was littered with coffee mugs, water bottles, and legal pads. In front of each of the attendees a name card gave their details, including their particular government department. It was in this room deep down in the bunkers of the FBI building that world-changing decisions were made.

The director would meet later that afternoon with the president and debrief him as to what had been discussed; but now he had a task to allocate.

"Special Agent." He had approached a small group at the far end of the room and gave one of the men a friendly slap on the shoulder. "A word if you please?" He indicated an empty section of the room.

"Director?" Special Agent Dillon Rae wondered whether he had done something wrong.

"Dillon, I'm taking you off what you are doing. I'm setting up a new department and assigning a new team that you are to head up." The director was always succinct and to the point. There were few niceties. He had no time for distractions. "Tomorrow you will get some files on two individuals and their enterprises." He looked at his agent. "You will see just what they have been doing directly against this country's interests. These are international criminals. Enough is enough. Your task is to investigate and come up with a plan to crush them in the shortest period. I will be briefing you fully tomorrow after my meeting at the White House."

"But Director, what about the work in progress …"

"This is more important. Promote one of your team to take over temporarily until this is complete!"

"Okay. Is there a budget …"

"Our Bureau budget is almost $10 billion dollars a year. Start to use it and get me results!" The director caught the eye of another attendee and made motions to wind up the conversation. "Just one thing: these criminals are powerful and dangerous. They have friends in high places. Bring them down! I know you can do it. See you tomorrow." And he was off.

Even though he was tired, Dillon Rae was intrigued and also a little relieved. The director had singled him out. What did he mean by "criminals?" Terrorists? Drug barons? He couldn't wait to see the files.

After many years of being on the brink of financial oblivion, Nicholas Adams had hit the big time. He had finally built from virtually nothing a successful business that didn't have bankruptcy written all over it. And he had done it on his own. His innovation was a powerful financial software system far ahead of the standard-market packages. Rather prematurely in his mind, his financial backers had forged ahead with a hasty initial public offering, but the timing couldn't have been better. The public launch of Adams Banking Solutions Inc. was a triumph and lined the empty pockets of everyone on his team. The speed of the company's success was unparalleled and placed them all on the verge of realizing financial gain beyond the paper millionaire class. Nicholas Adams was king of his world, and there he wished to stay.

But if the truth were told, Adams Banking Solutions wasn't actually making money. In reality, it was hemorrhaging cash, paying for expensive programmers, costly PR, and marketing. In the year since the original and only backers at the time—a US–European based stock promotion company, Kersch & Co.—had supplied the initial capital, the company went through fifteen million dollars without any indication of a profit in the foreseeable future. Yet its shareholders remained elated over the company's potential because Kersch & Co.'s investor relations mouthpiece persistently churned out exciting news about Adams Banking Solutions being a sure bet. Shares surged ahead, with healthy daily volumes of trades drawing ever more investors. Despite its actual losses, Adams Banking Solutions occupied an upscale suite of expensive offices on Park Avenue at East Fifty-Ninth Street. Image was everything, and so the office was conveniently situated in Nick Adams's preferred playground.

The elevator doors opened, and Nicholas Adams stepped out into Adams Banking Solutions's corporate offices. Birdie Johnson turned to look toward the elevator, and a big smile spread across rouged lips.

"Hi, Birdie! You okay? Missed me?" A wide grin showed off his expensive dentistry.

Birdie was a stunning thirty-eight-year-old with big, expressive eyes and medium-brown skin that glowed like fine silk, a product of her New Orleans Creole ancestry. She was Nick's eyes and ears, and nothing escaped her unless it was intentional. Birdie was an indispensable part of his life.

Nick blessed the day he had lured Birdie away from her law firm. "Poached" would be a more accurate account of events. As PA to a senior partner, she often gave Nick special consideration, slotting him in at the last minute for meetings with the lawyers handling his various start-up interests. In those days the flirting that went on between them was legendary in the law firm. When Adams asked her to become company manager of a new venture that could potentially become the early retirement deal of a lifetime, Birdie had eagerly jumped ship. It was intriguing and exciting.

"Where on earth have you been, and why did you turn off your BlackBerry?" she said, staring at him in mock bewilderment. "I've been trying to reach you for over a week. Didn't you get any of my messages? Hiding out for some reason, are we?"

"Just stayed off the radar for a bit. A little detour down to Switzerland, then back here via the Hamptons. What can I say?"

Grabbing his arm, Birdie took Nick aside to tell him that the mood around the office was not good. "We've been subjected to even more of Erich's ranting and raving," she spoke in a hushed voice. Birdie had no time for Erich Kersch's temper, and too often made that quite clear to the major backer of ABS to his face.

"He's not just angry; he's furious about something you did and hasn't wasted a moment stirring up a serious firestorm. Nick, you are in a shitload of trouble." She wrinkled her nose as if detecting a particularly bad smell. "You've really pissed him off. What the hell have you done this time?"

"Nothing," he said, trying to sound as if he found the whole thing a joke. "The guy wouldn't feel like he was getting anything accomplished if he didn't have something to moan about."

"Well, maybe all those prescription drugs he keeps popping are beginning to affect his brain."

"No, it's just his ego. He probably found out that I've been screwing his wife." Nick grinned and winked at her.

"What?" Birdie shrieked. Her hand cupped her mouth in disbelief, pressing tightly on his arm for a moment before she could speak. "Oh—no, you didn't!"

"Yeah, she should be so lucky. Get real." Adams's mouth stretched into a mirthless smile. "It's a joke, though she is pretty easy on the eyes. Where is Erich by the way?" Nick Adams was riding so high on his horse that day that nothing the little pipsqueak was up to mattered.

"In his office in Phoenix."

"Good. I'll bell him later. What else is happening, Birdie?"

Birdie couldn't understand why Adams was acting so nonchalant about what she was telling him. "When Erich was here last week he spent an awful lot of time on the phone with that conniving snake Dale Peters in Spain. I heard some of their conversation. I think you need to know," she whispered, "they're up to something, Nick."

"Oh, so Mutt and Jeff are at it again. No surprise there. They're joined at the hip," he said, neatly deflecting her caution with humor. "Enough of this banter. Back to work." Adams quickly turned on his heel and headed back to the receptionist, who handed him a stack of messages.

"But we *really* need to talk, Nick," Birdie said, following him.

"Okay, okay. How about in an hour? Need a little time to return a few calls and get through some mail."

"Whatever you say." Birdie looked weary. "Oh, I almost forgot." Her tone shifted. "A girl called Luciana something with a really seductive accent rang earlier looking for you. As it was a personal call, they put it through to me."

"And?" He turned and faced her full on, grinning boyishly.

Birdie detected obvious excitement in his voice. Had she detected a faint coloring of his tanned cheeks? "She said that she forgot to give you her cell phone number. She sounds Italian. Okay Nick, tell me—who's Luciana?" she asked. "Another conquest, eh?"

There was a time when Nick had shown signs of possible romantic interest in Birdie. But Birdie had been uncomfortable, believing that office romances were wrought with career upheaval and personal trauma. So, of her own volition she had steered clear of taking it beyond their casual flirting, not wanting to risk putting their friendship on the line.

"I'll have to fill you in later," he said absently as he walked away. "And by the way," he continued, doing his best imitation of an Italian pronunciation, "her name is pronounced Loo-che-AH-na Cah-vah-LEE-nee."

Adams strolled along the corridor to his corner office at the far end of the suite, greeting staff who were talking into headset

SUPPING WITH THE DEVIL

mikes or sitting at their desks glued to computer screens and typing furiously. In no time at all he was back into the rhythm of the office again. For an hour, sitting comfortably in his leather swivel chair, occasionally sipping office-brewed coffee, he plied through piles of paperwork and e-mails, his BlackBerry endlessly emitting that familiar sonar beep.

"Mr. Peters calling from Spain on line one," the receptionist announced through the desk intercom.

Adams picked up the receiver. "Dale, my friend! How are things?"

"Great with me, not so good with you. Where have you been?" Without wasting time with any further pleasantries, Dale blurted out, "Erich's pretty hopping mad with you, Nick."

"Yeah? So what?" Adams sneered. "And I'm pretty hopping mad myself. What's he complaining about this time, Dale? He's been making a fortune off my back, and he still moans. What is it with this guy?"

"Fortune?"

"You and I both know he made a bundle on ABS, and all of the other small cap start-ups as well. All of which seemed to go bust pretty fucking fast. ABS is the only one that is working and is trading at a good price with a big daily volume."

"Look, Nick, if it weren't for Ravi introducing you to him, you wouldn't have a pot to piss in!" Peters sounded exasperated but paused briefly trying to regain his composure. "And what about you, Mr. Nicholas Adams?" His voice was cold and sarcastic. "You just made a small fortune yourself several days ago selling Adams Banking Solutions shares you were supposed to hold on to. So who exactly is calling the kettle black?"

"I wondered how long it would take for you to find out. It was fair game, Dale, and you know it," Adams replied categorically. "I sold because I found out a couple of weeks ago that you, Erich, and Kersch & Co. have been dumping ABS stock from the very start of our public offering, and while I can't prove much because of all of the offshore entities you have, I reckon from my calculations you have made over forty million dollars. Forty million, for Christ's sake! And nothing for the company.

25

If the share price collapses as a result, like all of the others, the shit will hit the fan. Big time." Adams stood up from his desk and shouted into the mouthpiece, "And from where I sit, it looks like you, Erich, and Kersch & Co. will walk away scot-free. Is this a pump and dump? It certainly smells like it. What the fuck are we—the people you leave behind—going to do when the SEC comes marching through these doors? Huh?"

"Hang on, now. Just you calm down!" Peters' voice rose to match Adams's. To Dale's evident surprise, he realized Adams had pieced together enough of the truth to threaten their position. "Nick, you're talking through your ass! You can talk it over with Erich when he gets to you tomorrow."

"He's coming here, is he? Good!" But Nick was surprised. Perhaps he had gone too far.

"His flight from Phoenix lands at LaGuardia around eleven."

"Okay, that's probably opportune, because I don't want to be the one left holding the bag at the end of the day."

"'That's not going to happen. Trust me," Peters said, trying to sound sincere. "Listen up. You really need to work all of this out with Erich. But a little word of advice, Nick: when you see him, I suggest you go well out of your way to be nice if you want him to get on your side and see things from your perspective. Do you get what I'm saying? Don't let the prickly burr get under your skin."

Nick agreed to try to keep it cool. The least he could do was show some respect to the man who had funded his venture. But no sooner had he hung up with Peters, a call came in from Phoenix, Arizona. Speak of the Devil!

"Mr. Kersch on line two," the receptionist reported sounding rather nervous.

Nick paused and sucked in air through his teeth. "Erich, what's up?" Adams answered wryly, trying to sound positive.

"Too busy to return my calls, Nick?" Kersch sounded almost menacing, while strangely and uncharacteristically calm. "You can afford to ignore your friends now that you've made it to the big hitters league, eh?" His words slowly snaked out of the receiver as if to grip Adams by the throat.

"You have a problem, Erich?"

Adams was trying to sound pleasant, belying his inner tension. Having ascertained from his Google searches that Kersch was a crook, he now loathed and despised the man, although he had never fully trusted Dale Peters either, for that matter. He knew he would live to regret the day he had ever met them. Kersch and Peters, neither of whom would have managed to get through the doors of any self-respecting bank or financial institution, had promised Adams the moon. He realized they were empty promises when his belated Internet searches showed that Kersch and Peters were charlatans and untrustworthy. But Nick had been an easy target. Although he may have suffered from a certain idealism that sometimes bordered on naïveté, he was brutally realistic about having been screwed. But he needed the money for his venture, and the normal funding routes were not playing ball!

"The stock will go into free fall, you stupid fucker. You'll ruin us all!" Kersch spat. "I was the one who suggested that you to hold some shares offshore, but not sell any of them without talking to me first! Damn it! Every market maker of Adams Banking Solutions's stock knows that the SEC is beginning to sniff around. And now *you*, trying to be so fucking slick, off-load your stock back to us! We thought the sale came from the market, so we bought it back to stabilize the price, you cocksucker!"

Adams remained silent, content that he had nailed Kersch precisely where it hurt.

"You'd better come up with something fast or you'll be back on the street in a blink of an eye. I'm flying to New York in the morning to deal with your shit. I'll be at the office by midday. Party time's over, guy! Go fuck yourself!" The line went dead.

Adams was left staring at the mouthpiece quizzically. Then he put the phone down. "Gloves off," he whispered to the empty air. "Keep cool!" An icy hand grabbed at his spine, and he shivered. Coffee! Lots of it.

The content of one of his old unretrieved voice mails hadn't helped matters either. The deep voice of Howard Wayne was instantly recognizable. The message was clear. He needed to meet Nick as soon as possible. He alluded to an article that was about to be published that might cause Nick some unintentional embarrassment. He wanted to explain and provide some comfort. Wayne rambled on, sounding tired and rather apologetic, and then suggested an evening with himself and his wife Kim to explain his actions. Nick decided to call him later that evening from home. Wayne was a sort of mentor to Nick, who valued his advice. He knew that he had been indiscreet with him, having had one too many drinks in a bar some weeks earlier, and had gotten into a deep conversation about Kersch and Peters and their activities. He had not known that Howard Wayne had prompted him to be even more forthcoming than Nick would have deemed prudent. He had vented his frustrations, and Howard had listened. It was the mortar that he needed to build his brick wall into which a number of parties would soon crash headlong.

After two more phone calls, Nick finally pulled himself together, standing for a moment to look out of the window at the construction workers across the street. He decided to take a break. He strolled down the corridor for that private talk with Birdie and noticed that the office seemed unsettlingly quiet. All the staff appeared absent from their desks.

"Where is everyone?" he asked Birdie as he approached her desk situated along the perimeter of a large, open-plan area. Servers hummed in the background, and flat screen monitors blinked, displaying the ABS logo on every desktop.

"They're all out," she responded, strangely nervous, her voice quivering, her trepidation evident.

"Out? Where?" he pressed. From a distance, Adams observed a senior programmer averting his gaze, as he made his way into an elevator and disappear. "Come on, Birdie, what the hell is going on?"

Loyalty bound Birdie to Nick, and she had no reservations in divulging everything she knew to him. She told him that when Erich Kersch had been in town the previous week, he had spent most of his time behind closed doors in a constant exchange of calls with Dale Peters in Spain and Gerhard Liebs in Switzerland. Liebs was a private and secretive banker. He was also their biggest shareholder through a network of anonymous offshore companies.

After Kersch had flown back home to Phoenix, he had arranged from his office a board of directors video conference call with everyone at Adams Banking Solutions on the following Friday morning. Kersch told all assembled that Adams would be forced to resign. That anyone who dared counter his dismissal would lose their bonuses, jobs, and all their prized options and warrants. And if the group as a whole stood up against Kersch's proposed plans, he would walk away and short Adams Banking Solutions's stock to pulp.

Adams lowered his head, completely defeated. His pulse began to build, shaken by what Birdie had said. She went on to tell how Kersch had warned of a potential investigation by the SEC, that if actions were brought against Adams Banking Solutions, they would all be disqualified as directors and at the very least fined. Everyone would be under fire if a line weren't drawn between them and Adams. Some tried to argue and even reason with Kersch, but to no avail. Altercations had erupted, leaving Kersch screaming obscenities and threats.

"Everyone who attended last Friday's meeting left the office half an hour ago to regroup at the coffee shop across the street." Birdie's voice sounded strained. "And they've left me to review a draft agreement that arrived this morning from our attorneys." She paused, her eyes noticeably watery. "It's your resignation letter, Nick."

A pain deeper than any knife or bullet could ever cause pierced his soul. He looked at Birdie, only to withdraw when she lowered her head. "Fuck Erich!" Adams shouted, slamming his fist onto the edge of her desk. Birdie nearly jumped out of her skin, startled by the abrupt uncharacteristic brute force. "Hell will freeze over before I give my creation up to these bastards!"

But Nick knew he had seriously undermined his own position by selling shares he was supposed to hold on to. It was now blatantly obvious that Kersch had told the others of his backdoor maneuver. The vicissitudes of fortunes in his previous incarnations told him that he had better claim what was his, sooner rather than later. He tried justifying his actions by convincing himself that he was simply recouping what was owed to him. Selling $9.9 million of stock may have been a bit greedy on his part, but he had no longer trusted Kersch to make good on his shares after what Howard Wayne had told him.

He had played lapdog to the thieves disguised as venture capitalists, and now they were trying to force his hand into resigning at a time when the business was on the brink of explosive growth. ABS had one very minor Caribbean bank in place, an introduction made by Kersch's Swiss banker, but in fact Adams Banking Solutions's pilot scheme was proving so successful they had fourteen banking institutions based offshore prepared to sign on.

Adams Banking Solutions could easily raise money for their rollout elsewhere while distancing itself from Kersch & Co. before the SEC came knocking. Besides, he had money now, and he could do it himself. It could very well be for the best, he thought.

But Adams was desperately trying not to give in to panic. A wave of angst surged through his body like a bolt of lightning, weakening his knees. He felt disorientated and faint. Had he done wrong? Was he strong enough to carry things through? The SEC would never find his money safely secured in an anonymous Swiss account. If they did, he would be in serious shit.

Birdie could only watch as she could see his mind racing. She could see his brainchild was being snatched from under him, his pride and dignity in ruins. He asked Birdie to give him a copy of the agreement so he could be prepared for what would be an all-out war with Erich Kersch.

The silence between them seemed to stretch for an eternity until broken by a call coming in for Nick.

"Mr. Adams?" the unrecognized voice asked. "This is Dillon Rae. I'd like to meet with you about something that concerns us both."

"I'm sorry, but I don't handle sales and marketing. And

unfortunately it's not a particularly good time at the moment. No one in that department is available right now. If you hold on a minute I'll transfer you back to the front desk to arrange an appointment with our sales group, or give me your number and I will get someone to call you back. I apologize, sir!"

"That won't be necessary, Mr. Adams. I'm a special investigator with the federal government," Rae lowered the pitch in his voice to assert more authority, "I am Special Agent Dillon Rae, and for your own sake it would be in your best interest to set aside some time for me."

"Wait a moment, I'll have this transferred to my office." It was a long walk. Deliberately, he took his time. Now he was scared. Special agent? Didn't sound good! When Nick picked up the line again, he listened quietly to Rae in a somber mood.

It didn't take much persuading by Rae to get Adams to cooperate. They arranged a meeting.

Adams replaced the handset, and immediately another call came through.

"*Ciao, tesoro*!" Luciana's silky voice oozed through his earpiece. "Thank you for everything last night, my darling, and for getting me a cab! Such a gentleman! So unusual. I am sorry I took so long to leave. Did I make you too late? *Voglio delle coccole.*" She laughed infectiously. "In Italian that means I wish to give you a hug."

"Oh … thank you. Yeah … me too," he said, trying to sound composed. "Look Luciana, can I check in with you later?" He wanted to talk to her so much—God, he really did—but he smelled trouble and had to concentrate. "I have a small firestorm raging. Where are you at the moment, darling?"

"At the office, of course." Luciana's intercom buzzed loudly, interrupting her. "My client has arrived. I need to go as well. Speak to you later; *tesoro, ciao,*" she said in a breathy voice. "Keep your strength, you will need it!"

"In more ways than you know, my darling Luciana!" But she had gone. The image of the stunning naked girl still lingered. Nick allowed himself a smile, but promptly shook off the vision to consider his next move.

*Who was Dillon Rae?* he wondered. *What did he mean by Federal? The SEC? FBI?* God help him if it's the IRS! If it had anything to do with all of the crap with Kersch and Peters, he knew he had nothing to worry about. If that was it, it was Eric Kersch and Dale Peters who would be in the quicksand, not him.

But there were warning signs: a full-blown crisis had arisen that couldn't be ignored. He had to extricate himself from any weak position quickly. Nick Adams was a loner, a team player only when it suited him, and he had only himself to glean advice from. He had to be decisive and not lose his grip on reality. But if the day so far was any indication, he was in for a very bumpy ride. It was up to him.

High above the city, just a few blocks away, sat the larger-than-life—in body weight and character—Harvey Milton III, reclining rather than slouching in a studded leather chair behind an overly ornate desk in his palatial and tastefully decorated office suite. Extensive art, part of a much larger collection, surrounded him on every wall, mixed with framed cuttings of past headlines and magazine articles, as well as photos of him posing with billionaires, multi-millionaires, iconic politicians, and powerful businessmen representing his vast international interests. Boats, planes, and properties featured large, and shouting über-wealth.

"Gerhard?" the robust voice drawled.

The elusive Swiss banker, Gerhard Liebs, was on board his yacht, *Cerise*, in Bermuda, the land of lush beauty, turquoise waters, and pink-sand beaches. Hamilton Harbor was the perfect location for the enigmatic Liebs. *Cerise* was eighty-two meters overall, sporting its own swimming pool and helipad. There were deck bars, salons of various layouts, studies, opulent suites, and all the toys that were now basics on such yachts. A whole deck above the water line accommodated tenders and a number of vehicles, including an armored-plated Maybach Saloon. A crew of fourteen highly-paid, trained, ex-special forces personnel ran the ship under the command of a recently retired Russian navy captain. This boat was not for charter, it was for one man's sole use.

"I've got some encouraging news." Milton spoke in full command of his voice and with controlled animation. There was always something of the politician in Milton's pompous expressions and sweeping gestures when he expounded on some vitally important, self-serving issue. "Since our conversation yesterday I did some research. I met with a few of my banking and broker contacts and casually asked them about ABS. The word on the street is that Adams Banking Solutions's capabilities are surpassing expectations, and potential clients are asking them to overlay more security and add-on systems."

Liebs reclined comfortably in his chair, sporting nautical attire, his thin legs crossed, with one foot perched on an elaborately embroidered stool, his dark blue, double-breasted blazer unbuttoned. He ran a gloved hand through his cropped gray hair, and he listened with increasing interest as Milton continued.

"I tell you, Gerhard,"—Liebs flinched at the American's exuberance—"you and I know you forced me into buying into ABS, and I admit it might well pay off handsomely, but you can't keep blackmailing me." Milton coughed, and Liebs took the earpiece away from his ear, his face contorted at the intrusion into his inner sanctum. "Gerhard, I didn't want any part of this deal, as you know, but you threatened me, and I now hear that the SEC is sniffing around the stock promoters involved because of the steep rise in the ABS share price." He lowered his tone. "I cannot afford to be linked into any investigation by the SEC. The only thing you need to do now," he said in a voice half-coaxing, "is to get ABS going on their second-generation system. Start incorporating more extensive global processing. That will prove any cynics wrong and justify the extraordinary stock valuation, which is patently absurd."

"Yes indeed, that would be a win-win solution. My bank, and of course you could benefit greatly," Liebs agreed, as if he hadn't already put certain plans of his own in motion.

"It's critical that ABS move forward immediately with potential clients, Gerhard. Grab the bull by the horns!" he said in a voice pitched an octave higher. "Look at it from my position. I own involuntarily, thanks to you, one of the largest blocks of Adams Banking Solutions shares. So I've got more to lose on this particular Kersch & Co. deal than anyone else, and I understand that the promoters Kersch and Peters have already made millions out of their stock. Time for us now, eh? We need some more announcements to get the stock trading and to get the SEC off the scent."

Liebs sat silent for a moment, as he pondered at what Milton had said. True, the SEC could come barging in before he was done with Adams Banking Solutions. He had to press the group to get a move on with its next phase. "No need to worry, Harvey. You must realize by now that I would have all the bases covered."

"Gerhard," Milton lowered his voice again shuffling uncomfortably, "I need to justify this investment in ABS to my board. It has to work or they will go crazy knowing that I have invested MCI's cash into a penny stock!" He knew that he controlled the MCI board, but he didn't need to spend his valuable time with such menial matters. "Let me know when you can place the stock elsewhere, I want it off our books ASAP, Gerhard."

A personal assistant entered the magnificent salon of Liebs's floating palace to announce that Erich Kersch was holding on another line, calling from his office in Phoenix.

"Harvey, I have a call coming in from Erich. Keep me posted. Good day to you!" Liebs waved impatiently at his PA, and the call was put through.

"The ungrateful bastard!" Kersch screamed, beside himself with fury. Gerhard Liebs flinched, and placed the call on speaker. "First we bail him out," Kersch continued. "We put up with his stupid ideas, and then we allow him to form an offshore identity that cloaks him from the IRS." Kersch spluttered. "And us!"

"But that was your mistake," Liebs interrupted quietly. He loathed all forms of any loss of emotional control let alone uncouth shouting.

"Yeah, but I had no idea he would try and place his shares so soon, breaking our pooling agreement."

"But he did, Erich." Liebs swiveled in his chair to look out across the bay at the small city of Hamilton. "And it cannot be undone. He simply made a killing, just like you and Dale. He should be congratulated, not reproached. Our boy has learned the game fast under your tutelage"

"I don't think the punk is that sharp." Kersch drew in a deep breath, clearly trying to calm himself. "But he could be a bit more on the ball than we thought, which is a big concern."

"He *is* clever at developing these powerful financial applications. Sharma said Adams had something worthwhile when he made the introduction. It was, and that's why we backed him, Erich."

Liebs knew without a doubt just how astute Nicholas Adams was. He had had a thorough background check done on him before giving the green light on his funding. Not only did he know everything there was to know about Adams, but he was also kept fully informed on all Adams Banking Solutions goings-on. Liebs also saw that, given the right opportunities, Adams Banking Solutions might well be a meteoric success, with richer pickings in the long term, with or without Adams. He sat up, reached for his rimless spectacles, put them on, and scribbled something on a white pad. "How many shares did he place?" He muttered. There was a short pause. You could almost hear the cogs of Kersch's brain grinding and whirring.

"Nine hundred thousand shares at an average of eleven dollars each," Kersch murmured.

Liebs stabbed at a remote and a Bloomberg screen came to life on one of many flat screens mounted on his desk. "Only eleven dollars? That was pretty senseless. The Bloomberg price is at fifteen, which is what it has been for weeks."

"He sold at a discount so it wouldn't disrupt the market," Kersch explained.

"Very considerate of him, but $9.9 million all the same!" Liebs bit his thin lower lip as it all became undeniably clear. *No wonder he was able to off-load so many*, he thought. "How many has he left?"

"Three million in his name and another three and a half or so in his offshore company."

"And who bought them, Erich?" Liebs inquired, even though he knew the answer. There had evidently been a careless breach. "Who, my friend?" he asked in a voice that never failed to unnerve Eric Kersch.

"Kersch & Co.," Kersch whispered hoarsely, his voice strained. Adams had secretly used an ingenious way to sell his shares without detection by the European Kersch & Co. salesmen. "We did, Gerhard," Kersch admitted, his voice quavering. "We bought the stock to stop it crashing. Our sales guys had no idea, as the trading was in small lots of twenty thousand shares at a time. His trader knew what he was doing and was obviously briefed well by Adams. We had no idea until all the stock had been traded."

"Quite so!" Liebs lost no opportunity to taunt. "A clever man is our Nick," he added. Liebs extended his emaciated, gloved hands and gently cupped them together, wincing. Under the white cotton finger sheaths festered a suppurating skin ailment.

"Too fucking clever. We need to clip his wings!" Kersch hollered. He had underestimated Adams, yet half admired him for being so devious. Regardless, Adams had made Kersch look like a fool, and the man was furious. "And I'll be in New York tomorrow to do exactly that. Where can you be reached if we need to speak?"

"Zurich. I'm flying back tonight to straighten out your mess," he said, his jaw tight. A calculated slur. Kersch fell silent. Admonished. Chastised. "But there is another matter I wish to discuss with you before you go." Liebs sipped some spring water, and turned his attention back to Kersch.

Kersch was calmer now and waited in silence.

"What I want to know is: where we are with the minister? Have we made any inroads on the oil deal?" Liebs queried, as he rubbed his gloved hands slowly together to ease the pain.

"Yes, we have," Kersch responded eagerly, relieved that he finally had some good news to report. "Great feedback from the meeting you hosted on your yacht. It turns out that the results were more positive than we expected. Dale assured me the deal is in the bag. The minister was very impressed by what you could offer in terms of future business and personal returns. Oh, and the entertainment arranged in his honor went down pretty well too. Just the sort of distraction he was looking for."

"Quite so!" Liebs said, his voice distant, preoccupied with plotting his next move, ignoring Kersch's obvious reference to some sordid activities that had evidently taken place on his vessel. He could never understand how men laid themselves out to possible exposure. He had retired long before the girls arrived in the vessel's tender.

"All we have to do now," Kersch continued, "is grease his palm with more tokens of our appreciation—monetary rather than sexual, if you understand." Kersch was almost salivating as he spoke. "Dale has already worked out which Kersch & Co. account the funds can be transferred from." Kersch tried to hold back his excitement on the prospect of making a shitload more money playing the oil game with Peters, who, through all his persistence in courting Eastern European officials and businessmen, had caught wind of a small "obscure" oil field in one of the former Soviet states that had somehow gone unnoticed. It was a golden opportunity to tap into the oil reserves of the Eastern bloc. The most attractive aspect of the deal was that oil distribution to the West, for the most part, had already been presold. The only potential problem they foresaw was the country's reluctance about resources going into private foreign ownership. But with Liebs's Eastern European connections, those concerns would never become an issue for them.

Liebs had sealed the deal by taking up the offering made by Oil Minister Marat Esdaulet, whose role would be as silent partner. Then he had insisted that a special account be set up for Esdaulet at Bank Schreiber Liebs as the depository for his share of the revenues. But the oil minister had stood firm against it and said that he wanted to use his own Swiss bank; otherwise it would be a deal-breaker. Liebs had reluctantly caved in, unusually for a man who always manipulated everything to his own cause.

Once initial funds were transferred, the minister would issue a license to a special purpose vehicle set up by the partners of Kersch & Co. and his own bank for the oil concession. Dale Peters simply had to wait until the license was physically granted before turning it into an asset. The asset would then be reversed into the special purchase vehicle. The new shell company and Kersch & Co. would in turn raise the money for the oil deal. It would be one of the many bulletin board shells they had created over the years. It was time for another pump and dump promotion.

Peters had also laid out plans for an elaborate money laundering scheme to be carried out through the oil transactions. The purchase would be a bonanza deal for them, with a probable investment return of hundreds of millions of US dollars.

"Good. Let's just keep it up. And, Erich, try not to have any loose ends slip through our fingers this time. And get that situation with Adams sorted out." Liebs hung up.

Liebs was pleased with Peters for having secured such a deal on their behalf. He had bigger plans in mind for his protégé, who was turning into a brilliant grafter, and one easier to manipulate than Kersch.

But as they would find out, such deals are not always as straightforward as they seem. Minister Esdaulet had certainly agreed to their participation, but he also favored another. He would wait for the highest bidder.

Esdaulet was the Minister for Power and Energy of his East European country, which needed financial backers from the West for the construction of an oil pipeline linking the Black and Baltic Seas, aimed at improving regional energy security and reducing dependence on Russian crude. His country needed assistance to make its contribution to the overall project that would precipitate the nation into the oil and gas boom, making it a force to be reckoned with, and opening up enormous and rewarding opportunities, not least for himself.

He had enjoined his country, knowing only too well that the coffers were bare, into an agreement, signed by other East European countries, including Azerbaijan, Georgia, Ukraine, Poland, Lithuania, and others. It would result in building a three-hundred-mile extension to an existing pipeline in western Ukraine northward to the Polish port of Gdansk on the Baltic Sea, securing supplies of Azerbaijan's crude from the Caspian Sea.

The estimated two-billion-dollar pipeline was a victory for East European governments, who were increasingly wary of Russia's nationalistic energy policy, and who were searching for both alternative energy sources and supply routes. Esdaulet knew that his country could not be left out and be at the mercy of the Russians. In the past, Russia had wielded its energy resources as a diplomatic weapon, punishing former Soviet satellite states for not toeing the Kremlin line. Russia had temporarily cut off natural gas supplies to Ukraine and Belarus, and permanently ceased oil deliveries to Lithuania and Latvia.

But with corruption accusations and a history of deals that had ripped off Western companies, Esdaulet knew he had few choices. His country had crude oil, but everything was so badly organized; and it was unclear whether it could commit enough crude to the new pipeline to make the project economically viable.

After the fall of the old USSR, it was a free-for-all in the "wild East" of the former Soviet republics. Hoping to cut prime deals with the new governments of the newly independent republics, Esdaulet realized that he had to offer a big incentive to any backer, which naturally would help himself.

To do a deal such as this he would have to deal with the C-list of potential partners. No major investor would contemplate such a deal for their reputational reasons.

Esdaulet had two contenders. One was through his private Swiss banker, who had introduced a fellow banker, Gerhard Liebs; and he had cautioned his East European customer that Liebs was not the easiest of people to deal with. The second was an international conglomerate that seemed to have no qualms about doing business with his country.

He had approached both separately with his proposition, and on the basis of total exclusivity. They had to raise the money for his country to perform within the terms of the agreement with the other nations. The rewards would be a large proportion of the revenues that would come cascading in once the pipeline was opened up, as well as rights to his country's crude oil in the interim, and the all-important oil exploration licenses, which would enrich them even more.

The minister would share with either of the eventual contenders in the deal. He had two horses running. He cared not who won.

# THAT EVENING—NEW YORK

Physically exhausted and mentally depleted from a brutal day, Nicholas Adams didn't suspect things could get any worse. He was sitting at his island counter in the kitchen with his friend and colleague Ravi Sharma, reading the evening paper, when he saw the heavy bold face headline leap out at him.

*The New York Evening Post*—Late Edition

**Suspected Suicide**
**Respected Wall Street Journalist Found Dead in Limo**

New York, NY—Howard Wayne, a Wall Street investigative journalist, apparently took his own life yesterday. Wayne, 54, was found by his driver in the back of a limo en route to his offices at *The Wall Street Journal.* The Coroner's Office states that he died of a single gunshot wound to the head and was pronounced dead at the scene.

Mr. Wayne was well known for his in-depth investigations into international securities fraud, tax evasion, money laundering, and mail and wire fraud. He also had a string of books and novels to his name, all focused on the darker side of the financial corridors of power.

As Mr. Wayne's family, friends and colleagues made tributes, Detective Lloyd Lee of the First Precinct NYPD said that investigations are underway, and that a preliminary examination of the deceased has indicated that the fatal wound may have been self-inflicted, but foul play had not been ruled out at this stage.

Wayne's death has come as a shock to his journalism peers, who described him as the consummate journalist. "He was in a class by himself," said a colleague. The outpouring of support was, according to another, "a true testament to his character."

During his tenure at *The Wall Street Journal*, Wayne won
numerous journalism awards. He joined the *Journal* after
retiring from the US Army. Although his regular columns
and features were somewhat controversial, Howard Wayne
never swayed from his convictions. Renowned for the kind
of writing that probed and pushed the edge of the envelope,
he never succumbed to shallow and sensational trivia, nor
did he adopt caution as a watchword. "Howard Wayne will
forever be remembered as the type of shoe leather legend
that's fast becoming extinct in the new world of journalism,"
said a former editor in chief of the paper.

Mr. Wayne is survived by his wife, Kim, a well-known New
York charity supporter and former model.

Nicholas Adams froze. He stared at the article, looking
blankly beyond its printed words. His tired, bloodshot eyes
reflected his turmoil, and total dismay registered across his face.
The newspaper he held dropped to the counter.

"Oh … shit!"

The news hit him full square in his solar plexus. He sat
paralyzed for several minutes. Then he re-read the article over
and over again in a daze as the impact sank deeper and deeper. His
mind tried desperately to process the shocking news. Stunned,
Sharma just slumped in his seat, and said, "The world has gone
mad."

"This is not good, Ravi; something is very wrong." Adams
jumped up to turn on the kitchen flatscreen TV for any news
coverage of the incident. "Howard left me a message to call him,
but I didn't," he said quietly. "Now I feel really bad. I've got to
call Kim." He picked up his cell phone and dialed Wayne's home
number while his eyes remained glued to the news channel. It
took several tries before Kim Wayne finally answered.

"Kim. Kim, I am so, so sorry. Christ, I just don't know what
to say."

"Howard—he's …" Her voice quivered, and Adams heard
her strangled wail. "He's gone," she choked. "Dead. He's dead!"
her uncontrollable sobs came hard and long. "My Howie is dead!
He killed himself. Why would he do that? A gun? He never
owned such a thing. Hated them!" Kim Wayne broke down

and gasped for breath. "Why? How could he do this to me? To himself? Nick, tell me! Tell me! My Howie!" Then the phone went silent.

Adams put the phone down and turned to Sharma. "Ravi, I'm going to her right now."

"Did Kim say how it happened?"

Adams cut him off as he strained to hear the live news report just coming in. The overly bronzed reporter swiveled his head to the best angle that suited him and gravely read the teleprompter in front of his desk.

"The tragedy happened at nine ten this morning," the newscaster said. "The New York Police Department has issued a statement saying that Howard Wayne took his own life with a single shot from a handgun while on the way to his Wall Street office."

Adams and Sharma watched in horror, unable to take it all in as the scene unfolded on the small plasma screen: the limo, its doors wide open; the gurney with Wayne's body; the crowd. "We'll have more on that news story right after the break."

"Oh, my God … I'll grab a cab."

"I'll come with you." Sharma rubbed his eyes wearily. "Things are just getting way too scary. My God!"

Nick looked at his friend, saw the pain, walked over to where he sat, and patted Ravi on his shoulder. "Listen, it's going to be alright." But he truly didn't believe his own words.

Nick always knew how to calm Sharma when he became rattled. For a long time Adams had been more accepting of his gay friend's sexuality than Sharma himself. Live and let live, he always told him. He had kept his friend's secret for many years and stood by him until Sharma had drummed up enough courage to come out and make the transition to the openly gay lifestyle he most craved, which would have been unthinkable among the Bengalis back in India.

"I'm going to her apartment. Come if you like." He stopped and suddenly remembered his date. "Shit, Ravi, do me a favor and stay will you? I forgot that Luciana is dropping by! When she gets here, fill her in and tell her to make herself at home.

Okay with you?" He patted him again. "I've got to get out of here now. Please look after Luciana!" So much was happening at the same time, but now he had found someone special, and he had to fence her off from the crap, or he would not even get off the starting blocks.

Although he had his own place on Fire Island, Ravi Sharma lived and worked out of Adams's apartment most of the week, and sometimes on weekends, depending on how much code he had to write. It had been their routine ever since his release from jail for hacking into and manipulating international bank security systems. Fire Island, which was free of cars and chaos, was a world away from its neighboring New York metropolitan way of life. The pristine beaches, without a hint of pretension, nestled in between the Great South Bay and Atlantic Ocean. It was back to nature, with biking, hiking, swimming, and surfing, all of which suited him and was so different from the monotony of the gym routine in New York.

Nicholas Adams arrived at the late Howard Wayne's building, hurriedly greeting the doorman as he entered. The doorman recognized Adams and rushed to hold the doors open as he stepped into the elevator. Alone inside, he dreaded his meeting with Howard's wife. He walked along the familiar, rather tired corridor toward their apartment. The door was half open, and he could hear voices from within.

"We're all very sorry, Mrs. Wayne," a tall African-American detective was saying with evident genuine sympathy. "But we still have to ask these questions—it's procedure." He looked up, away from the seated woman, and saw Adams enter the apartment.

Detective Lloyd Lee and his officers had been investigating the details of Wayne's death all day, and Lee was tired. Another suicide? It was an ever-increasing problem, although the rate in New York was surprisingly half the national average. Firearms were the chosen method in some twelve percent of the suicides, followed by hanging, jumpers, and death by trains, fourth behind guns. The senior detective had had many years of dealing with the apathy in the tough, cutting-edge, daunting city that was New York. But why on earth would a man at the top of his game want to kill himself? New York may be a whacked-out town, but he just wasn't buying it. He sat uncomfortably opposite Kim Wayne, his broad frame making the designer chair look like it was intended for a twelve-year-old.

Kim saw Nick and rose from the sofa and ran toward him. She grabbed him, buried her head in his shoulder, and burst into quiet sobbing. He stroked her short-cropped curls gently as she cried, her petite frame nestled like a child in his arms.

"A relative, Mrs. Wayne?" the detective inquired from a distance as he stood up, his notepad gripped firmly in his hand.

"No, just a friend," Kim responded. Without looking around toward the detective, Adams tightened his arms around Kim and began tenderly massaging her back. She stopped sobbing and looked up into his handsome face. Despite her tear-stained face and bloodshot eyes, you could still see vestiges of the former model who had been the face of popular cosmetic lines that had adorned the magazines and subway billboards. She still did the occasional assignment, but her real aspiration was to become an actress.

"Yes, a true friend, Detective Lee." Kim allowed herself a faint smile as she released Nick. Lee greeted Adams, taking his hand. There was strength in the man's handshake, Lee noted.

The police detective took Kim through a series of questions, with Adams prompting her at times. Nothing much was gleaned from the answers; and then came the business of returning Howard Wayne's personal effects. Forensic evidence had already been collected, so Detective Lee was able to release the items to Wayne's widow. He tipped the plastic bag rather unfeelingly onto the glass-topped coffee table in front of her.

"There is not much here, but could I ask you to sign this receipt for me, Mrs. Wayne? We've held back the cell phone for our forensics lab." Detective Lee held out a clipboard and pen.

Kim sat motionless, staring at the clipboard, sensing the finality of the whole affair once she signed the release on everything Wayne had carried the last day of his life. Noticing her hesitation, the detective placed the clipboard and pen on the coffee table. "I'm sorry, Detective," Kim said, snapping out of her daze. Despite her trauma, she managed a slight smile.

"Lee," he smiled back, "Lloyd Lee, Mrs. Wayne. No hurry. You can sign this when you're ready. He smiled. "There really is no hurry."

"I should have offered all of you coffee, something to eat maybe ... you look so tired."

"Not to worry." He paused and looked at the newly widowed woman. He had done this so many times before, but it was always so emotional, and he was still not hardened to the rituals. "Please understand, Mrs. Wayne, the procedure requires that you'll need to come down to the city morgue and make a positive ID."

A sharp involuntary sob escaped from her as again the reality set in. Kim gained her self-control and told the detective she would wait until her brother arrived in the morning on a redeye flight from Los Angeles, if that was acceptable. The detective agreed and gave her his contact information to call if she needed anything. As part of their investigation the team removed Wayne's diary, an address book, a few journals, and several other items from the apartment. "Oh, by the way,"—he had turned to face them—"we can't find any computer or other IT equipment, which is surprising." Detective Lee nodded, not wanting to cause any more stress, and he and his officers left. Nick and Howard's widow were left alone.

Adams decided to hang around for a while. He didn't want to leave Kim there all alone. She shuffled Wayne's items that were sprawled out on the coffee table. She told Nick that Howard was a good man, the perfect gentleman, and that although he had had a few bouts with alcohol over the years, she could not understand why he would shoot himself. "I don't get it, Nick, where did he get a gun?" she asked.

"I have no idea. I saw him a few weeks ago and he was happy, even excited about life, and even when he left me a message I didn't detect anything was amiss." Adams had grown very close to Wayne and his wife in the short time he had known them. The situation just didn't make any sense to him either. Why would a man with everything to live for self-destruct like that?

Kim went on to tell Adams that Wayne seemed perfectly normal when he had left for work that morning. They had dinner plans with friends on Thursday and a drive through the Catskills over the weekend to catch the autumn vistas while the leaves were turning gold.

"He planned the trip himself and booked a couple of historic bed and breakfasts along the route. Said it was a celebration." Kim allowed a smile to cross her face. "He had just finished an important story he was working on, and there was talk of a television show." Kim used a tissue to wipe her nose. "You know Howard," she said sniffling, "fighting for things like truth and accountability, as he often said. He never really confided in me with his work, but his latest story had something to do with small shareholders being ripped off. Damn it, Howard! Why?"

Her words jolted Nick, and a cold shiver ran down his spine, but he said nothing. The sickening feeling in his gut forced him to sit up and take stock.

The grief-stricken wife continued to shuffle languidly through her husband's personal effects: an old silver DuPont lighter; several assorted pens; a handkerchief; a Moleskin notebook; a black leather wallet; and odd pieces of scrap paper filled with scribbled notes.

"The keys," Kim looked again, poking her fingers around the items, "did you see Howard's keys, Nick?"

"Maybe they're still with the police," he replied. Kim looked back at him as he met her troubled gaze.

"Kim?" Then in a voice thick with anxiety, he said, unaccountably and completely out of character, "Did you hear Howard ever mention a company called Kersch & Co.?"

"No." She shrugged her shoulders. "Why?"

"Kim, I don't know why, but I have an uneasy feeling about this. Can I have a look inside Howard's study?"

"Of course. Do you think the keys are there?"

"Maybe," he lied.

At the far end of the narrow hall was a dreadfully untidy

room that called itself a study, with books, box files, papers, and printouts littering the desk, shelves, windowsills, and floor. Adams turned on the desk lamp to get a better look. He combed through files on Wayne's desk and shelves, rummaged through stacks of journals, books, and files on the floor behind the desk and below the window, looking for anything that might be at all relevant, when he noticed a particular file folder under a stack of newspapers. The label read "Kersch & Co., File 002, Initial Findings by Howard Wayne, *Wall Street Journal*". He turned around to make sure Kim was nowhere in sight, and pulled the file out, dislodging papers as he placed it on the desk. He opened the file, ran his finger down the indexed headings, and gasped. His brain seemed to be boiling and bubbling within his skull. He started to choke as he began to understand. He knew he was in the shit, but he hadn't known how deep until he saw it spelled out in black and white.

He randomly flipped through the report. Things were about to get really ugly! The cozy, unrealistic little world was about to be severely changed for many named in the documents, and that included Adams Banking Solutions and—obviously—himself. Adams had known that Howard Wayne was investigating Kersch & Co., but was shocked by the depths to which Wayne had also investigated him personally as well as Kersch & Co.'s interests in Adams Banking Solutions. Adams's eyes clouded over as he read. The file presented a succinct overview on the dealings of Kersch & Co. Wayne had been thorough. Too thorough. He felt let down by him and wondered what he was doing in the investigative journalist's apartment. Was Howard a friend or had he been used?

Adams closed his eyes to hide what he was seeing. His heart was skipping beats, and the veins in his temple began to swell. Then, reaching a moment of pristine clarity, he doubted the suicide theory.

Adams understood that the situation absolutely forbade complacency, and he decided to do something about it there and then. His business, his finances, and his future were clearly on the line. In a sudden realization, he searched for Wayne's computer, which he knew Wayne often hid behind the tall file cabinet. Not surprising that the police missed it.

"Are you okay in there, Nicholas?" he heard Kim calling from the kitchen. "I have a glass of wine ready!"

"Oh, go ahead, I will be a couple of minutes," he leaned out of the study doorway and added, "I will be right with you. By the way do you know Howard's password?"

"What are you doing Nicholas?" Kim sounded worried.

"I may have found something—please, do you have any ideas?" Nick didn't want to say anything that would lead to suspicion or more heartache for this woman.

"Howie always used my name. Try *happykimusa* ..." She broke off.

He found a random flash drive, powered up the laptop, entered in the password when prompted, and waited as the desktop screen opened. He found the folder "Kersch & Co.," searched through the files until he found "Kersch & Co. Final," and printed the file. There were other folders with some names that he recognized but there was no time to copy them. He placed the loaded flash drive in his breast pocket. He thought about wiping Wayne's incriminating files from the laptop, but instantly realized that any forensics expert could easily restore the data with date and time of deletion if he didn't perform a seven-level wipe, which in the absence of time and software was impossible. And then there was the issue of the hard copies. How could he possibly get those out of the apartment without Kim noticing?

"Kim!" he called out. "Kim!"

Kim entered the study with two full glasses of white wine. "Thought we could both use a drink."

"Thanks."

Kim raised her glass and they both drank to Wayne's memory. "Did you find the keys?"

Adams shook his head. Then he said, "You must get the locks changed as soon as possible, Kim."

"Really? You think that's necessary?"

"I do. And by a professional."

"Okay, I'll try and get it done in a couple of days. I just can't get my head around that right now. Besides, this is a secure building."

"You're not hearing me, Kim! Take this seriously. Howard's keys are missing and no one knows for sure what really happened this morning. You need a multi-point, deadbolt locking system installed immediately no matter how secure this building may be. Listen—why don't I just get it done for you? I'm sure I can find a twenty-four-hour locksmith somewhere."

"You don't need to bother with all that, Nick," she insisted. "My brother's on his way and I promise to get him on it as soon as he arrives in the morning."

"Swear?" It was a heartfelt call for reassurance.

"Of course."

"Good. Then it should be his first order of business when he gets here. Because, Kim," he said, taking hold of both her hands, "I have an awful feeling about this, and I hope to God I'm wrong." Kim's hands felt dead and clammy. They trembled as he added, "I just don't get the idea of suicide!"

Kim was clearly shocked.

Nick was running high on adrenaline. The veil on his business dealings was about to be torn wide open. There was no question as to what Howard Wayne was about to unleash. Not only was Adams's situation at the office about to be in complete shambles, he had now uncovered the possible murder of one of his friends— although he now really wondered about the friendship. He had been used. Unable to mask his anguish, and not wishing to upset Kim any further, Adams promised to touch base with her in the morning and left the apartment. He had to get out, get some air. Stifling dread was setting in. He felt his heart pounding, and he sucked in gulps of air. He was in panic mode.

As if on autopilot, Adams's quick strides carried him through the well-lit streets of the Upper East Side. He could have hailed a cab but chose instead to walk, needing time to clear his head and get a handle on the day's dramas. If his convictions were true about the demise of his friend, he feared he would soon be subject to police interrogation. Anyone with the slightest trace of intelligence would deduce he was somehow connected. With the details of Adams Banking Solutions's business practices laid bare by Wayne's report, he and his fellow compatriots would certainly face SEC investigations. If that happened, any share price suspension would not only seriously damage the credibility of his brainchild; it would put a major dent in his net worth.

"Fucking crooks!" he shouted to the street. He had confirmed that Erich Kersch and Dale Peters not only artificially inflated the price of countless companies and raked in massive cash rewards, but they had also targeted ABS. "Bastards!" Startled by his own outburst, he hurriedly crossed to the other side, oblivious of his surroundings.

Although seething with anger at how she had failed earlier, Valentina Vinogradov suffered no pangs of regret for Wayne's accidental termination. *He should not have put up a fight*, she mused coldly, then shrugged off her concern. One more stiff never made a bit of difference to her or her employer. The important thing was that she had little more than a few hours to secure what she came for. The police had been crawling all over the place, but now she had an opportunity to make good her contract.

The Waldorf had been her home base for the past week. Chosen for its size and volume of business, she was able to go about her business unnoticed, blending in with its scores of hotel guests, visitors, and conference participants.

Vinogradov worked diligently at the small table in her suite, a glass of neat vodka in her right hand as she searched through a dossier in front of her. To her left was an open bottle of American beer.

After reexamining the floor plan of the building for the umpteenth time, she leaned back, stretching her long limbs, and raised her glass, toasted those that she had disposed of in her long career, and downed the triple shot of her Russian "water of life" in one go, followed by the beer chaser that was all part of a ceremonial tribute to her heritage. "Vodka without beer is money thrown in the wind," she whispered absently. Once the sensation of alcohol hit her bloodstream, she got up and went to a cupboard in the bedroom to choose the outfit she would use as cover for the plans she had that very evening.

This cool Russian beauty was a master of deceit, and an impressive figure at five foot eleven, with high, tight cheekbones and long, platinum blond hair that draped over her shoulders, her complexion almost transparent, with glittering eyes and an unflinching gaze. Many had fallen for her striking looks, and she used them often and skillfully for her own ends.

The former KGB agent was a legend among her kind. Only the highest bidder secured her skills; but no one could ever outwit or dupe her relentless current employer when it came to monopolizing her talents, and so the union was sealed. Now she worked for him exclusively, for fees rivaled by none. She was never as busy.

Vinogradov pulled the curtains shut, obscuring the now lit-up skyscrapers that dressed the familiar Manhattan skyline beyond her window. She changed quickly and applied a touch of makeup just in case the evening called for some maneuvering around guards, handymen, and residents. On the bed lay a black suitcase containing the important tools of her trade. She unzipped the case and removed a leather pouch, unrolled it, and placed its contents methodically on the bed along with a bunch of keys placed to one side. She looked at her watch, muttered something in Russian and was as ready for her assignment as she would ever be. She sucked in air deeply before slowly exhaling. It was time.

The building was just a few blocks away from her hotel, and for the intruder dressed in black slacks, a dark turtleneck, gloves, and a full-hooded coat, gaining access to the building was child's play. A small duffle bag hung from her right shoulder. She tried a couple of keys before slowly opening the lobby door. She pulled her hood down across her face and hurried inside the building. The night doorman was patrolling his domain, as she knew well he would be doing at that time. He would be away for at least thirty minutes. A vapor trail from behind the main desk emanated from a Starbucks to-go carton. It might still be hot when he came back.

Off the lobby were four elevators with a stairwell situated on one side. Vinogradov took the stairs directly adjacent to the underground garage entrance, ignoring the elevators with their security cameras, and began to ascend the twenty-two flights.

The stairs were wide and shallow, with metal treads sunk into the edges of each concrete step. The landings were well lit, and she cast long shadows, heralding her strong athletic lithesome trek. Barely a sound could be heard as she ascended cat-like on her toes, silently approaching her destination. There would be no more blood this time; she would be in and out in minutes according to her earlier deliberations.

With blood pumping and breathing heavily, Vinogradov reached the twenty-second floor and cautiously opened the landing fire door. With no one in sight, she sprinted down the hall to apartment 22E. She quietly slipped two keys, one after the other, into each of the front-door locks, and feeling the door give, she slowly pushed it open, only to be thwarted by a door chain. There was a loud clunk as metal hit metal. But Vinogradov was prepared: she retrieved a mini molybdenum steel bolt cutter from an inside pocket, eased the head of the tool through the gap, and cut the chain. It sprang apart and fell against the wooden frame. She paused. Hearing no noise from within, she replaced the cutter into her duffle bag, eased herself quietly through the door, and moved into the shadows, carefully leaving the door ajar to ensure her departure was not hindered.

Her eyes searched the dimly lit hallway of the elegantly furnished apartment. She paused before switching on her flashlight. Nudging doors open, Vinogradov peered carefully into each darkened room. But when she reached the master bedroom she was caught unawares by the shape and form of the sleeping woman lying carelessly amidst crumpled bed linen. The sight left Vinogradov for a split second … breathless.

She stood in the doorway gazing at the beautiful naked body that was half-covered by the sheets that clung to her exquisitely curvaceous frame. Full blond curls concealed the woman's face. Her breasts were half exposed. Vinogradov's curiosity piqued, and she stepped into the bedroom for a closer look at the perfect symmetry of this vision of beauty. She couldn't understand her body's strong reaction to the woman lying there. "Perfection," she whispered, "absolute perfection!"

She tore her eyes away from the mesmerizing figure and rapidly got back to the task at hand. She left the room, pulling on the handle of the door until it was almost shut.

She located the study and entered immediately. The flashlight caught the dull silver casing of a laptop lying on a glass worktable covered with pages and files. She unplugged the lead, and placed the laptop into her bag. She pointed the flashlight at the other items on the desk when the beam caught a label on a file. She opened it, and identifying its contents, stuffed the documents into her bag and began rummaging through desk trays and cabinets, randomly selecting CDs, odd flash drives, and a few loose documents. In her thoroughness to get hold of all of the dangerously incriminating material, she failed to notice a lone figure moving slowly and quietly across the room.

The water-filled glass vase with white lilies crashed, sending shards of glass flying in all directions, but the blow was surprisingly powerful and accurate as it landed across her back just below her shoulder blades. Water splattered everywhere; flowers rained down, landing on the furniture and carpet. Valentina collapsed onto the Persian rug she was standing on, momentarily stunned and aghast, her body wedged between the desk and a chair.

"*Yobany stos!*" she cursed in anger. Pain shot down her spine. She deftly spun sideways in an instant, before her attacker lunged at her again, this time with the desk lamp. Her reflexes were far quicker than her attacker had anticipated. Vinogradov rolled under the desk, avoiding impact, and the lamp crashed to the floor beside her. From the safety of the desk she grabbed her assailant's ankles and wrenched her off her feet. The woman fell onto her back, breaking her fall with her right arm.

Gaining the advantage, Vinogradov moved forward and then caught sight of her attacker wrapped in a bed sheet. My God, it was her Sleeping Beauty, now evidently more than awake, her face illuminated by the beam of the flashlight that had become lodged in a small basket beside the desk. Vinogradov found herself staring into a pair of the bluest eyes she had ever seen. She broke her trance and within nanoseconds leaped up and grabbed Kim Wayne by the wrists in an iron grip to subdue her arms, and pinned her down on the rug, her legs wrapped tightly around her opponent's torso. She held both wrists down with one hand, and her other hand cupped Kim's mouth to muffle her cries. Nothing could hide the terror on her face as she struggled. Kim attempted to dislodge the offender's gloved hands, but she was much smaller than the tall intruder and knew she was at a frightening disadvantage. But still she continued her vain struggle to escape from the vice-like grip.

Those high, sculpted cheekbones. She was so strong, staggeringly beautiful, and very desirable. Vinogradov couldn't remember the last time she was so affected by anyone, and it could only mean trouble. Kim let out a short whimper, for she, too, was totally unprepared for the sensations that began to surge through her body.

"I don't wish you harm," Vinogradov said in a low, soothing tone. "I am just doing my job. Carrying out instructions, my darling!"

Even gasping and strangulated, the voice was quite clearly East European. Kim fixed her eyes on the steady gaze of the woman above, who looked at her with an intensity that practically seared through her flesh. And then a peculiar unnerving calm descended upon Kim and she ceased to struggle.

Valentina stared down at Kim, gently stroked her cheek, and then abruptly stood. The sense of urgency was palpable. She seized her bag containing the stolen items, and for just a brief moment she paused to look at the beautiful woman she knew she could never see again—and left. It was so uncharacteristic of this consummate expert and stickler to detail, for she had blown her cover. She could be at risk and that would put her employer in danger as well. But she reminded herself that there would be no more blood that day, and that she just knew that she could not harm that wonderful woman.

As for Kim, she wished she had been killed, as she remained shivering in spasms on the rug. She eased herself up, drew her knees in tight to her bare chest, leaned against the wall of the study, and sat there stunned, biting her bottom lip. Her every sense had completely shut down. She was in a living nightmare, a horror story that she knew she could never recount, as she grew cognizant of what had just occurred. But she was paralyzed in disbelief, unable to focus on anything else. Her first experience of female intimacy played havoc on her mind, and a sense of rawness overwhelmed her.

"Oh … my … God!" she cried.

Numbness soon followed. There were no tears. Her reservoir of tears had all but dried up from crying all day over her husband's death. She thought for a moment she had been dreaming it all.

Kim knew she had to report something to the police, but didn't know what exactly. "The theft," she thought, as a wave of confusion swept over her. She raised herself up and staggered to the phone in the hall. "I must call Detective Lee and Nick," she muttered to herself in a daze. It was 1:00 a.m.

Through the fog of deep sleep Nick Adams was woken abruptly by the intrusive shrill ringing and vibrating of his cell phone that was on his bedside locker, which he had forgotten to turn off. He had fallen asleep exhausted but satiated, lying languidly across Luciana, after drowning away the events of the previous day with alcohol and sex. Luciana mumbled something and rolled over. Adams turned his head to look at the time on the clock beside his bed. "What now?" he groaned, his head splitting from the excesses, and picked up his phone. "Yeah!" he growled, only partially awake. "Who is it?"

Kim Wayne spoke quietly, and although she was somehow coping, at that moment she was nearer to a breakdown than she thought. "Please come; please," she begged.

"Are you all right?" Nick asked anxiously as he sat up.

Luciana turned over, looking inquisitive. "What's going on, *tesoro*?" Her voice was husky. "Another lover?" Though sleepy, she managed a grin. Adams signaled her with his hand to wait.

"Don't worry, Kim … I'll be right over." He hung up and got out of bed.

"Something's come up."

"Again? You are insatiable." She nestled down into the pillow feigning total innocence and pouted those extraordinary lips. "Come back to bed darling!"

"Sweetheart, it's serious. All of this is turning into a total nightmare," he declared. "I can't believe what's just happened. I have to go out." He bent over to kiss his young lover. She pulled away with a faint look of mock anger.

"I'll go home then." She moved to get out of her side of the bed.

"No ... please, I'd like you to stay." Nick sounded a little desperate, and she noticed the change in her man whose exertion earlier was a new and exciting experience for her.

Nick stumbled around the bedroom and threw on the nearest articles of clothing and shoes he could grab. As he dressed, he explained what the call was all about. Luciana listened intently to the details of Kim's ordeal and became increasingly concerned. "I'll come with you," she said, leaping fully naked out of the bed.

"No, no, you don't have to." *Damn*, he thought to himself, *what a beauty she was, like a young colt, leggy and so sexy.*

"Are you sure? Another woman can be of great help in this type of situation, *tesoro*."

"I know, but she doesn't really know you. Don't worry; I'll get a handle on it. For now, just wait here and get some sleep. I'll be back before dawn. Please my darling?" His eyes almost pleaded.

Kim Wayne sat curled up on a sofa, suffering a maelstrom of emotions, dressed in jeans and a sweater, a mug cupped tightly between her hands, with her elbows resting on her knees. The policewoman beside her adjusted a blanket over her shoulders while Detective Lloyd Lee sat opposite in quiet dignity, making notes in his well-worn notebook. It was 2am.

The identity of the female suspect was unknown and investigators were following up on leads given by witnesses who saw a tall, hooded mystery figure leaving the building carrying a black bag. But there had been no further sightings. It seemed that the Lobby CCTV cameras were not aligned and the film showed merely a figure moving quickly across toward the stairwell with a view of the back only.

When Adams arrived, a technician was dusting the doorframe for prints. Nick's eyes fell upon the severed door chain, and he saw that investigators from the robbery task force and the forensics unit were swarming all over the apartment. He made his way to the living room to find Kim looking completely bewildered, her pale face stained with tears. He rushed to her side on the sofa, placed both arms around her, and pulled her into a fierce hug. Kim just leaned in, desperately seeking solace in his tight embrace.

"Who did this?" Adams asked apprehensively.

"I don't know …" She trailed off. "I … I … can't remember any distinct details apart from …" Kim cleared her throat, "that the woman was blond, wore dark clothes, a hooded coat, and had an East European accent, maybe Russian …" She trailed off again.

Adams had an uneasy feeling about the turn of events and wondered whether he should get any more involved in the matter than he already was. After all, his friendship with Howard Wayne had only developed because of Wayne's probing into his relationship with Kersch & Co. and ABS's involvement.

Adams noticed Detective Lee completely engrossed in thought while writing on his notepad. He would intermittently stroke the short, coarse, gray stubble that lined his jaw. Finally acknowledging Adams, Lee rose to his feet and moved to where Adams was seated beside Kim.

"Mrs. Wayne tells me that you were close to Mr. Wayne," he said, looking at Adams squarely. Nick searched the tired, bloodshot eyes that demanded answers.

"She tells me that you had some business together?"

"No," Nick answered quickly. "Not business, just research … advice."

"On what?"

"Stocks and shares. General business investment research and the like."

"Mr. Wayne was an investigative journalist, Mr. Adams. He

specialized in uncovering corporate fraud." He looked at his notebook. "Were you advising on that?"

Lee dropped his pencil and bent down to retrieve it. Adams moved the cocktail table to assist. The gesture seemed to help the pressure ease.

"Thank you. Even *I* read his columns, you know." Lee nodded pensively. "Yeah, I've played the stock market for years. Some you lose, some you win. It's like the track, always a possible hit, huh?"

"Bit of a day trader?" Nick grinned uneasily.

"Too risky. Too many guys in on the inside track." Lee smiled. He paused briefly. "This guy Wayne had a lot of balls, you know. Always taking on the big boys in his columns." He looked down at Kim. "I apologize Mrs. Wayne …"

"Yeah, he was pretty sharp and had more guts than most people I know." Adams began to show some discomfort with Detective Lee's manner.

Then suddenly Zeus let the lightning bolt fly from his hand. "You do something wrong … Mr. Adams?"

Nicholas Adams froze. In his deadpan seriousness Detective Lee had launched his weapon straight at him.

"Wrong?" Adams queried. "What kind of question is that?" He tried to sound affronted, but he strangled his words.

"Perhaps he was investigating *you*, Mr. Adams." Lee signaled Nick to join him at a small seating area in front of the bay window for a more private chat while the policewoman continued to console Kim.

Lee took a seat on the arm of a chair directly in front of Adams. "We did some checking from Mr. Wayne's diary and a recent journal. There were entries indicating meetings with you and comments written on what he needed to talk to you about." Lee looked straight at Nick. "A whole list of questions with penciled notes."

Stunned, Adams was about to interrupt, but Lee raised his hand, stopping him.

"We did a background check on you and found that you run a fast-growing public company with a share price rising through the roof, and that *you* are one of the main shareholders." He had to raise his hand again to stop Adams from speaking.

"But we're *more* interested in some of the comments and notes on the other names that we recognized, so relax man! Just tell me what you know." He looked candidly at Adams as he said, "Did Mr. Wayne die by suicide, and is this just a coincidental break-in, or are we onto something bigger?"

Detective Lee checked to see if Kim Wayne could hear them. Once satisfied that she was too involved in making her statement, he returned his focus back to Adams. Lee's steady, unflinching stare demanded an answer. Adams almost cowered, shifting uncomfortably, unable to mask his edginess. "Okay, Detective the fact is, I don't want to believe this and I've been trying really hard to convince myself otherwise, but every bone in my body is telling me that Howard was murdered," he responded in a hushed tone. "Howard was far from suicidal." Lee showed no reaction. Adams continued. "Did you know that after you returned Howard's personal effects, Kim noticed his keys were missing?"

"Yes, we determined that entry into the building—and the apartment, except for the cut door chain—was not forced. The intruder used keys."

"Christ, why didn't you advise her to change the locks?" Adams hissed angrily.

"We didn't know the keys were missing." The veteran city detective stroked his gray stubble again, as if he were sizing Adams up. "But if you were aware of that fact, why didn't *you* do or say something?"

"But I did! In fact, not only did I insist that she have them changed immediately, I suggested a multi-point deadbolt. I even offered to get the locks replaced myself, right then. But I think she preferred that her brother take care of it when he arrives. So what could I do?" A shroud of guilt crossed Adams's face. "I should've just gone ahead and called a locksmith the moment she noticed the keys missing. Was anything taken?"

"According to Mrs. Wayne, when she interrupted the attacker's search in the study, the only thing the perpetrator seemed interested in was the computer and some files. Funny we never saw a computer when we were here earlier."

The detective's words struck a deep chord, but Adams pressed hard not to be visibly rattled. "Damn it!" he exclaimed as his thoughts swung into sobering clarity. Now he realized he wasn't the only one interested in Wayne's files that threatened to bring everyone around him down. "All Howard's research and work was on that damn laptop," he blurted out. "Stories ... names, companies, addresses, facts ... a whole library of what takes place within the corrupt side of finance. And I'm pretty damn sure there would be many interested parties if they knew of that Pandora's box—people who would probably do anything to get their hands on it. Holy shit. Fuck; even murder?"

Lee lurched to his feet. "Come on, I need to show you something," he said, leading Adams to the study. As they walked down the hall, Lee shared with Adams what his unit had uncovered thus far. There was no indication of assault, he told him. Kim had apparently attacked the intruder with a flower vase, but the intruder got away.

A sudden chill made Adams shiver. The disarrayed desktop, the overturned desk chair, files scattered all over and papers strewn across the floor. Nothing looked as it had since his earlier visit. The Persian rug was wet and peppered with broken glass and cut flowers.

Lee spoke to the forensic technician working the study and gestured that he give them a moment. The guy muttered to himself and left. "A man of few words." Lee smiled, shrugged, and arched his eyebrows. He turned back to Adams. "When you look around this apartment you see some pretty valuable stuff. But none of it was lifted. In fact, Mrs. Wayne says her handbag was wide open on a table in the hall, and the thief ignored it." Lee shrugged his shoulders. "If the computer was the only thing stolen, then the intruder or someone else who maybe she worked for badly wanted whatever was stored on it."

When Adams added, "And maybe he was about to go public on something so sensitive that somebody needed him silenced," Detective Lee took a note.

Sizing up the situation, Adams now realized that the best position he could possibly take was to get Detective Lee on side. He resolved to cover his ass as best he could and play whatever game this was by the book. Although it meant opening a can of worms, he was fairly certain that anything Wayne might have written on Kersch & Co. would put him in the clear and deem Adams Banking Solutions a viable systems company. Christ, that little sojourn to Zurich seemed an age away.

"So he was killed and the suicide was just a cover," the detective deduced. "Not hard to believe when you think about it."

"Howard would have backed up everything from his computer," Adams offered, attempting to appear genuinely helpful. "He routinely backed up certain data and files on external drives and storage discs. It was almost an obsession with him," he said as earnestly as he could.

Adams pressed on, giving Lee the names of companies, including his own, that might have been part of Wayne's research. It took the pair just a few minutes to find an external hard drive and a cabinet housing a comprehensive library of CDs, each meticulously indexed. If Kim had not disturbed the intruder, Valentina would have found them. Lee called out to one of his men for assistance.

"Tell them to search for anything with the names on this list." Lee handed over a crumpled sheet that he had taken, to the utter surprise of Nick, from his inside pocket. "And in particular Kersch & Co. It'll save time," he told them.

"Well, Mr. Adams, it looks like we might have a murder inquiry." Lee jotted down further notes and looked up at Adams. "Thanks, man. You've helped a lot. Let's just hope it doesn't cause you more harm than good, eh?" he stated in his cool, systematic style. He turned around for a final look and left his officers to carry on with the search.

Nick remained, unable to move or shake the impact of Lee's words. Then he took a deep breath, gathered every ounce of nerve he had left, and went in search for Kim. He found her listening nervously as Detective Lee spoke. Lee asked if she would be willing to go down to police headquarters later that morning to help with a composite sketch of the suspect. She apprehensively agreed.

*My God*, she thought, *I could draw that exquisite body with my eyes shut. Those penetrating and tantalizing eyes that bore into me as we both struggled.*

"Howard was murdered, Nick," Kim whimpered as she got up and went to him.

"We can't be sure," he said quietly.

"They just told me they had possible evidence." Nick put his arms around her. Her trembling body became rigid.

Since the forensics team were still combing the apartment and collecting evidence, Adams offered to stay with Kim, at least until her brother arrived. But Kim assured him there was nothing more he could do that night, so he left, not a happy man.

Except for a few homeless down-and-outs huddled in the portals of buildings, the streets were deserted. Adams's frantic, uneven footfalls bounced off the buildings from all directions, echoing in his ears. Streetlamps gave the sidewalks a cavernous evil glow that seemed to remind him of the past fifteen hours, which were fast becoming a nightmare he just couldn't shake off. Everything that had happened bordered on the realm of the unreal, as if he were caught up in some bleak film noir. He spent the better part of his walk home lying to himself. He'd been through bad patches before and survived. Surely he could get past this one too. How long would he hold onto the cash in his Swiss bank? He arrived home and without undressing eased himself on top of the bed next to Luciana and tried to fall asleep. But a horrible weight had descended upon him. He would not sleep that night. His father would no doubt be laughing in his grave at the unexpected twist in his son's fortunes. Ha! Leopards don't change their spots.

Detective Lee, however, couldn't afford the luxury of going home to a warm bed. He had to further his line of inquiries. While forensics officials were left searching Wayne's apartment for clues, others in his team were at the station precinct checking phone records, backup disks, and e-mails. Printouts from Wayne's backup files littered Lee's desk. The Wayne investigation was well underway. To the detective, it was clear where they were heading.

Lee slipped off his coat, sank into his chair behind a battered steel desk stacked with files, and began to read, his eyes focused and deep, his eyebrows straight and a little forbidding, the steaming cup of coffee he had picked up from a 24/7 corner deli close at hand.

Hours passed before he finally rose from his chair. He stretched his fifty-six-year-old frame, pressing both hands into the small of his back. He removed his loosened tie and rubbed at his neck. It had been a long time since Lee had pulled an all-nighter like this, but it seemed from his perspective to have been a productive one. He sat heavily on the edge of his desk and absently observed his detectives through the broken and dusty blinds that separated them. He leaned across to his old Rolodex file, retrieved a telephone number, grabbed at the receiver, and made the call.

"Gavin Hart? It's Lloyd Lee," he announced, looking at his watch. "Is it too early?" The man fought to remain asleep, but Lee was insistent, having awoken him from his drink-induced stupor. Hart pulled himself up against his pillows, reached for a cigarette, flipped open the pack, and fumbled for his lighter.

"Christ, man," Hart grumbled, startled by the early call. He squinted to see the clock by his bedside straining to make out the time. "Did you say it's Lloyd?" He fumbled and put flame to cigarette, inhaling deeply.

"I've got an urgent need to see you," Lee grunted.

"Damn it, man. Don't you have a home or a wife?" Gavin Hart balanced his body on one elbow and coughed as the first of the day's smoke hit familiar territory. "What's up?"

"I'll tell you what's up." Lee spoke slowly. "It's Howard Wayne."

"Yeah, I know. Tragic loss, good man …"

"He was murdered."

"Murdered? You got to be kidding!" Hart choked and ash dropped onto his pillow. "Don't believe you," he said in disbelief

between the strangled wheezes. "CNN news said it was a suicide
..."

"Yeah, but I'm the fucking detective and I say he was
murdered."

"Well, I can't deny your career advantages man; maybe
you've got a point there. Bloody hell!" Hart sat upright in bed,
shuddering. Now he was fully awake. A wave of incredulity
swept over him as he realized that his old rival might have been
killed. "Who would want to kill Howard?"

"Don't know yet." Lee paused and then asked, "Does Kersch
& Co. mean anything to you?" Lee beckoned to an officer passing
by his office, pointed at his cup, made a pouring gesture, and then
gave him a thumbs-up.

"Oh, the clown show. It sure does, Lloyd. Where do they
feature in this?"

"Seems like Wayne was about to expose them in his column
along with a whole bunch of other scumbags. Then he planned
to break the story nationally on a TV investigative program."
Lee mentioned a few other names to Gavin Hart, who growled
in recognition at each. One name that Hart didn't know was
Nicholas Adams, whose name had apparently shown up on
several pages recovered from Wayne's backup files. Lee told Hart
that having met him he had the impression that Wayne appeared
to be a decent enough guy, but Lee had to find out the depth of
his involvement. "I need to get a handle on the cast of characters
mentioned in Wayne's files. Can we meet up for coffee?"

"It had better be more than that, Lloyd."

They agreed to meet in a couple of hours. Gavin Hart threw
the phone carelessly onto the rumpled bed, which slid off and fell
with a thud onto the floor, but he couldn't be bothered to retrieve
it, and he attempted to go back to sleep, but the unsettling news
rendered that impossible. Instead, he wandered aimlessly in a
bathrobe around his quaint time warp apartment mulling over
Lee's call. It had landed him a quite a jolt. Hart himself was in
the throes of an offshore tax haven story, but that was more of an
excuse to travel around the Caribbean investigating possible law
infractions rather than some personal mission. He and Wayne

had often exchanged information, but Wayne apparently and surprisingly kept this one all to himself. "Crafty old Howard," he muttered, causing his cigarette that balanced precariously off his lower lip to fall onto the floor. "An opportunity for me then. Perhaps I can take over what he left?" He stooped, grunting, and put the cigarette back between his lips. He fumbled for his lighter and relit it.

Hart was a brassy English expatriate, a freelance investigative reporter who trawled the mean streets of New York City, while the more refined Howard Wayne sought the prestige of a high-profile reporter and followed the path of stories that raised Pulitzer hopes. Hart, in contrast, operated assiduously beneath the radar and led a life investigating crooks and defrauders of every kind. Habitually, his face or other body part found its way to the back end of someone's fist or foot. Hart shrugged off those incidents as simple battle scars. But now he had cause for concern. He had been ignoring the recent rumors of contracts being taken out on him, and now that Wayne had been silenced for good, maybe he would be next. Was this a vendetta? Threats maybe, but murder? Gavin Hart stroked his once-blond hair, now tinged with orange, that still retained the style he had all of his life, and blew out a perfect circle of smoke. He had big teeth, stained with the years of tobacco, which sat between large, full lips. They were not exactly buckteeth, but they did alter his speech, which sounded as though he was sucking cotton wool.

"Kersch & Co.?" he muttered. *What have they been up to this time?* They were always on his radar, and he felt not a little miffed that maybe Wayne had encroached onto his turf.

He opened the French doors that were off his small kitchen, stepped out onto the tiny balcony, and lit yet another cigarette. The crisp, early dawn air didn't faze him. "Kersch & Co.? Well, well, well … our old friends Dale Peters and Erich Kersch surfacing again," he said under his breath. "Can't keep the buggers down!" He grinned. "Guess it's high time I had a closer look at you boys."

# ZURICH, SWITZERLAND

A molten, orange sun slowly rose over the mountains, melting the night gray away. The air was cool and fresh. Zurich stretched its arms, awakening from its slumber as her citizens made their way into work. Switzerland's largest city sits by a lake of the same name on the banks of the Limmat River. Renowned for its charm, the commercial capital never fails to impress with its architecture and works of art: the historic Fraumunster Cathedral, with stained-glass windows by Chagall; historic art galleries with Picasso, Matisse, and Miró paintings; its colorful clock towers and steeples. Gerhard Liebs often sneered at what he considered the city's minor collections. His private collection was by far greater, and in the last half-century it had not been seen by anyone other than himself.

The chairman and sole proprietor of the most secret private bank in the Swiss cantons eased himself from the rear of his maroon and black armor-plated Maybach. A few moments earlier, a black-windowed Range Rover had pulled up to the curb and parked. The security detail always rode into the city directly in front of his car. Three bodyguards climbed out and quickly took their positions. The Swiss banker stepped carefully onto the anally clean sidewalk, hissing orders at his driver. A black homburg fitted squarely on his head cast a deep shadow over a bloodless, gaunt face, and a thin, gloved hand held firmly onto its brim. He braced himself against the chilling morning wind and cautiously mounted the freshly scrubbed stone steps that led to a pair of vast, ornately carved wooden doors, which opened for him without so much as a pause in his stride, the staff already being alerted of the approaching fastidiously punctual Liebs. The morning routine had begun.

Gerhard Liebs entered the grand, gracefully elegant foyer and crossed the marble floor to an oak-paneled reception area adorned with tapestries and oil paintings. Crystal and gold chandeliers hung from the ceiling; an 825-year-old Roman fireplace graced a far wall. The sweeping marble staircase and the spaciousness emphasized history and grandeur. The only noticeable modern concessions were the imposing electronic entry, biometric identification, and camera surveillance systems. The message at Bank Schreiber Liebs was quite clear: if you aren't extremely wealthy, you do not cross this threshold. This was for the über-rich, not for the mundane high-net-worth customers that were catered for by the other private banks in Zurich.

Liebs carried himself with a long-practiced show of nobility that invariably put the fear of God into any adversary. He barely acknowledged the two overly ingratiating staff that welcomed the sixty-five-year-old banking tycoon with obsequious, stooping bows. Of slightly less than average height and physical stature, he seemed up close to be surprisingly scrawny for such a mythic figure. The bronze gates of the ancient elevator clunked shut and he was away from the irritations of the daily rituals.

Soon the banker was ensconced behind a huge, hand-carved desk that allegedly had been owned by Field Marshall Rommel during the latter days of World War II. It was one of many such "items" Liebs possessed in his eclectic collection. In the vaults of his Swiss schloss there lay works of Durer, Mantegna, Rembrandt, Van Gogh and Holbein. Paintings, drawings, sketches, and sculptures undisturbed and unopened, their Third Reich casings still intact. Most of his art had come from special dealings with Russians who had commandeered Nazi collections at the end of the war. It was one of the reasons why Liebs retained excellent relationships with ex-SMERSH operatives. Although it was claimed that SMERSH went out of existence, the funding and brilliant orchestration of their metamorphosis into hired guns, oligarchs, or so-called respectable business people bore the trademark of Liebs's mastery. SMERSH was Stalin's notorious Soviet organization, and never really went away.

A beam of light from the morning sun danced on the glass of a platinum picture frame sitting prominently on Liebs's desk.

It featured an image of the *Cerise* with its resplendent length mirrored in the crystal-blue Caribbean Sea. It was the only bright color in a particularly dark and gloomy oak paneled room.

The Swiss government has tried to rebuild the reputation of Switzerland's largest lenders, damaged by a near bankruptcy in 2008 and the unprecedented delivery of, until then, secret data about their affluent clients to the US to avoid a criminal indictment. Switzerland and its banks benefited from laws protecting secrecy. The inflow of foreign money seeking a haven in the country contributed for decades to lower interest rates, making borrowing and expansion cheaper for domestic companies, and boosting household wealth. The biggest shake-up Swiss financial firms have seen in eighty years left scars on the economy.

"The problem with any good thing is that it's too good to be true." Gerhard just knew that for him the writing could well be on the wall as he mused to himself, "If you have that for too long, there comes a day when it falls apart. And that's the case with bank secrecy." He muttered and made a mental note. He had plans. He knew that the pursuit of the major Swiss banks by the US tax authorities had opened floodgates to attacks on other Swiss banks that threatened to tear down the bastion of secrecy, and that included Bank Schreiber Liebs.

Switzerland is the biggest manager of offshore wealth in the world, with about a 27 percent share. Clients from Germany, Italy, Saudi Arabia, the US and France make up about 42 percent of all offshore wealth managed in the country. Then there are the Russians and Chinese. Should Switzerland abolish banking secrecy, it would risk losing as much as 700 billion francs ($768 billion) in the worst case, or about half of all money managed by Swiss banks on behalf of private clients not domiciled in the country

The Swiss financial industry has prospered from others' misfortunes. Two world wars involving neighboring countries made neutral Switzerland a refuge for people concerned that their governments and currencies weren't stable.

The bank's high-profile French clients enacted secrecy laws in 1934 after French police arrested top bankers of Basler

Handelsbank in Paris in October 1932 for aiding tax evasion. Police confiscated a list of clients and later seized more money of tax evaders at other private banks in Geneva.

A run on Swiss banks that followed threatened their existence, and stopping the money flight became a priority. Switzerland got rich through undeclared "black" money, which will radically change in the future.

One of the many phones to the left of Liebs's desk rang. Recognizing the displayed caller's name, he slowly picked up the handset with his gloved hand, and listened without so much as a greeting. It was more than evident that the caller was aggravated and angry. Liebs's face showed no emotion as he waited for the caller to pause, whereupon he began speaking quietly into the telephone. "I hardly think you're being very adult about this, my dear friend." The tone was condescending, the message delivered with a sneer. As Liebs spoke, his long-suffering PA briskly entered the office and gestured to interrupt Liebs's first call of the day. With a dismissive hand motion, Liebs waved her away, clearly irritated by now. The woman, accustomed to his abruptness, left the office without hesitation and returned to her own desk. "For a man in such an important position, I find this all too childish."

"Don't you fucking patronize me," the American voice responded angrily. "You think your heavy-handedness can cow me into submission?"

"That wasn't my intention." The banker swiveled on his chair and looked out toward the snow-capped mountains beyond.

"If you ask me, your nasty little threat was totally unnecessary. Thank God, the envelope was opened by me and not one of my staff." he stormed.

"Indeed, how very lucky. There you are, then," said the Swiss banker. "It just goes to show how very dangerous such things would be in the wrong hands." Conversations like these always struck Liebs like a broken record. *Why don't people just do as they're told?* he thought. "So many of your friends would look at you in a rather different light," he continued, "it would be most distressing for all parties."

"Haven't I done enough for you already?" the agitated voice boomed and spluttered, although now the temperature had subsided and he sounded deflated. "But you seem to forget who I am!" He knew it was futile.

"And to drive my point a little further, we ..."—it was almost the editorial *we*—"wouldn't want details of certain offshore dealings to be known to the US authorities either, would we? I hardly think that your government would look kindly on such activities from such a wealthy and influential soon-to-be statesman. I believe, my friend, that they would hang you out to dry." There was a slight pause as Liebs allowed such statements to sink in slowly. "Looks like you're somewhat compromised, Harvey ... from all positions." It was venom-laced spittle that trickled into the mouthpiece. There was no doubt as to who was holding all of the cards.

Gerhard Liebs spun back to face his desk and mused that it had been only the day before that he learned that the influential Harvey Milton III had turned down an offer, a proposal that really had to be accepted, to purchase a significant block of shares in yet another Kersch & Co. pump and dump moneymaking venture shell deal. But Milton had insisted this time, after his forced investment in ABS, that he wasn't going to invest in any more Kersch schemes.

"We still need you, Harvey," Liebs said, sounding genuine. "I will tell you when your contributions are no longer required." He licked his dry lips. "You are important to the early funding of such deals!"

"But we agreed Adams would be the last. And after all the other fucking things I've done for you!" Milton kept his voice down, but it was shaking with rage.

"Care now!" Liebs responded with a touch of menace in his tone. Milton knew that Liebs's threats were ignored at one's peril.

"Okay, okay, Gerhard," Milton said, now restraining himself, silently cursing the day he had chosen to use Bank Schreiber Liebs for a private Swiss bank account. "Guess I'll just have to go along for the ride. Like I have a choice." He was tempted to tell Liebs to take a fucking leap up his own scrawny asshole, but *There will come a more appropriate time for that*, he reminded himself. "But let it be the last; say we treat it as my swan song?" He detested negotiating with the Swiss scumbag, but he was reluctantly prepared to play ball, for the very last time.

"Either that or bring me a few new investors." Liebs smiled, "I'll guarantee them the best return they've ever had. And naturally, there'd be something in it for you."

"I'll take the swan song," Milton responded stiffly.

"Well then, we carry on with what we have agreed, my friend; and do keep in touch. Nothing changes, then, and no hard feelings, my friend. My very best to Abigail. Such a lovely woman." With his thin index finger the Swiss pressed the call-end button and cut Milton off. *Yes, indeed, your swansong*, he mused, looking down at the unpleasant blood stain seeping through his glove. *If you really knew just how important you are to me, the tables would certainly turn against me; and that just will not happen.* He stroked the outside of a heavy black file on the desk in front of him. The etched copperplate label clearly displayed the name of the prominent businessman with political aspirations: Harvey Milton III.

A clever but thoroughly careless and indiscreet man, no less. Such addictions uncovered by Gerhard Liebs would ruin him if he were ever to put the information and facts into the public domain. Should the American ever make high office, even the White House itself, Liebs would have extraordinary powers. "So predictable, Harvey," he said, emitting a high-pitched whimper that passed as a laugh, that ended in a rasping croak.

Liebs played the blackmail game expertly. He stood up and took Milton's file over to mahogany bookshelves to the right of his desk, and pulling at a row of leather-bound books, a false bookcase opened to reveal a concealed, fireproof, walk-in vault. Liebs entered a sequence of numerals on the entry keypad, the locking system deactivated, and the door slid open. As Liebs stepped in, his arm caught the handle of the solid steel door. Suddenly the file flew out of his hands, spraying its contents in a shower across the polished floor. He cursed inaudibly at the mess.

Stooping low, he grabbed at the papers, pausing only briefly to look at the sordid photographs that were on display. Not for him, the pleasures of the flesh. Anything that played on emotion or caused any kind of weakness had no place in his life. His only mistresses lurked in the wood-encased tombs that contained his collection of art. He returned the contents to its folder, entered the vault, and placed the file back on its shelf. "So many secrets, such countless cooperative friends," he murmured, amused as he looked around. "Ignorant fools!"

Bank Schreiber Liebs was the bank of last resort for those who failed the KYC or know-your-client requirements carried out by the regulated banks. Here there was only one requirement: massively obscene deposits of cash and realizable assets. The shelves in the vault were crammed with files ridden with documented errors of judgment made by countless powerful men and women who influenced the world of politics, business, religion, science, and other areas of importance. It was a veritable global who's who. These were sensible, sane individuals who, by some predilection or bizarre act in their otherwise perfect lives, put their careers, positions, families, reputations, and lives at great risk. In fact, none was a victim, he thought, just malfeasants caught up in situations brought on by their own greed and ambitions. These were individuals who, in their quest for power, ended up as his unfortunate puppets, his trophies of conquest and control, mere automatons functioning as cogs in his gigantic international empire.

Once the vault was secured, he returned to his desk, settled down into his mahogany-framed, red leather chair, and removed his spectacles. With the linen handkerchief from the breast pocket of his navy Savile Row suit, he meticulously cleaned his frameless lenses, occasionally squinting to check and recheck for any imperfections, any errant speck of dirt that might have escaped his attention.

Gerhard Liebs had amassed great wealth through careful and calculating diligence, hard work, and unprecedented manipulation. His bank, of which he was sole shareholder, controlled many different businesses and assets, including, amongst more usual private banking activities, a worldwide network of currency exchanges. It was he who owned the small, glass-fronted currency exchanges that were mini-banks seen in New York, Paris, London, Geneva, Zurich, and Rome. As his empire had grown, he added branches in Hong Kong, Sydney, Tokyo, Manila, and Bogotá, and then virtually every major city thereafter, including those in the new burgeoning Eastern Europe.

Liebs had set up his first *bureau de change* while working for the private banking arm of the Swiss bank Credit Suisse, the section that dealt exclusively with high-net-worth non-resident foreigners. The venture had proved so successful he had sought to open more locations, but couldn't secure the capital to fund such an expansion. Then he hit on a solution: he "borrowed" the money from several customer-numbered accounts at Credit Suisse. Overnight his *bureau de change* exploded faster than he believed possible. With the profits he set up his own bank with the help of his old school friend Heinz Schreiber, who lent his credible illustrious banking family name. Unfortunately for Schreiber, who had no idea of the tactics Gerhard Liebs would employ, he eventually succumbed to Liebs's threats, handing over control of the bank shortly thereafter. Schreiber protested in vain and eventually threw in the towel when Liebs made threats that would undoubtedly ruin the man and his family.

Deposits poured into the exclusive Bank Schreiber Liebs. But since very few accounts, by their very nature, were truly active, being really receptacles of wealth that were there to be fenced off from their own national tax authorities, Liebs had the means to expand even faster, primarily in offshore tax havens that ultimately became outlets for his massive money-laundering operation. He spent the next two decades building the largest private financial conglomerate of its type in the world.

Outwardly, Liebs was not the run-of-the-mill private banker. He belonged to no associations or clubs and was regarded by his peers as a rather strange individual who was unquestionably up to no good, but there was nothing that could be pinned on him.

He even entered into arrangements with certain Islamic countries using the hawala informal and therefore less traceable transfer system. By this means each payment was based on the performance and honor of a huge network of money brokers situated in the Middle East, North Africa, the Horn of Africa, and South Asia offering a parallel or alternative remittance system that exists and operates outside of the traditional banking or financial channels.

Liebs had never touched his own ever-growing capital, preferring the use of other people's money. The old adage PMA and OPM—positive mental attitude and other people's money—had stood him in good stead. Borrowing from client-numbered accounts had become the Liebs trademark. If ever an account holder questioned any discrepancies, funds were quickly transferred from another less active account owned by a third party to cover any irregularities. Apologies were profusely given, and all was well again. However, if the account holder made an issue of it, he simply resorted to blackmail. Early on, Liebs had brazenly set up a network of private detectives, paid informants, journalists, press clippings services, and personal trackers who spied on depositor activities. He kept coercion dossiers on anybody worth a damn, and those unfortunate enough to bank with Liebs had every reason to regret it as they became compromised to his every whim.

The intercom buzzed. Liebs poked delicately at the speaker button and barked at his PA. "I said no calls."

"But Herr Liebs, it is Herr Kersch from America." Habitually ignoring his rudeness, his loyal PA was proficient at screening his calls, knowing who, out of the scores of callers she handled each day, should be turned away.

"Ah, the ubiquitous Mr. Kersch." Liebs paused and then resigned to taking the call. He reluctantly picked up the handset. "Erich." Liebs's voice oozed with charm, masking his typically icy delivery. "Long time?"

"Yeah, sure. Listen, Gerhard: did you get my message about Harvey Milton turning down our new deal?" Kersch asked anxiously.

"Yes, I did. In fact, I had a call from him earlier. He just needed a little persuasion. I don't think you'll have any more problems. What's the time with you Erich? Isn't it the middle of night in Phoenix?"

"It is. But I need to know what to do about Harvey. He's not jumping ship then?" Erich Kersch was more than a little surprised.

"That son of bitch will walk when and only when we want him out. Understand?"

"But he's such a powerful guy. He carries a lot of weight over here, and as it so happens he has just made the latest Forbes billionaires list." Erich sounded genuinely worried. "He could make life difficult for us, just at the wrong time!"

"Public recognition—such petty concerns. Only lesser men seek acclaim."

"But he could be a problem. I don't think we want to piss him off."

"Enough!" Liebs hissed. "I told you that I have dealt with it!" He snarled. "He will not hinder us and we carry on as usual." The intercom buzzed, announcing Liebs's next appointment. When his guest appeared in the doorway, Liebs motioned to the person to enter and indicated a seat in front of his large desk. "Now, Erich," he continued into the mouthpiece, "let's talk about matters that concern you, namely the question of Adams Banking Solutions."

Kersch was growing bone tired of Liebs and increasingly uncomfortable with their association. Even the little time he spent with him face-to-face bore the resemblance of a visit to the principal's office. "I catch my flight to New York in several hours," Kersch reported as he cleared his throat. "Not to worry, I've got everything under control."

"I hope so, for your sake. Oh, and give my regards to your wife. She's such a pretty girl; we wouldn't want any nasty inconveniences upsetting her."

Liebs hung up and shifted his attention to his guest. Dark glasses, a tightly wound scarf, and a long, fashionable coat did little to disguise the beauty of the blonde who had entered into the inner sanctum and was now seated opposite him. Liebs raised an eyebrow and almost allowed a smile to crack his thin, worn face. "I am pleased to see you, my dear. Coffee?" She smiled and raised an elegant hand to decline the offer. "You have done well, my trust in you never wanes. What a woman you are. You have everything, yet you continue taking my instructions and carrying them out superbly. If only others were so obliging. There's so much more to be done, and I will call upon you again. But it is nothing that would be too difficult for you, Valentina."

# TURKS AND CAICOS

Despite the old, rusting air-conditioning units whirring noisily in the background, the small private aviation terminal was unbearably hot and airless. At only a short distance from the main passenger terminal, the building dissolved into unsightly pretzels of metalwork and shabbiness. Mildew and Lysol hung in the air as two waiting pilots began showing considerable anxiety, agitated by the amount of time it was taking to get their flight plan to the Caymans filed with air-traffic control.

The weather, to the unsuspecting eye, appeared tranquil. But the brief from the local flight service center revealed that severe storms were on their way, with conditions affecting all areas close to their intended flight path. So every second counted. But the operations clerk, as quick as a tortoise on Prozac, couldn't quite grasp the meaning of *pronto*.

As a routine trip that could only be scheduled last minute, the pilots knew there was no room for delays or overruns. Not alone in their frustration, in the lounge adjacent to an unmanned immigration desk sat their passenger, waiting edgily in the heat, his briefcase balanced firmly on his lap. A dusty soda-vending machine stood nearby with a heavily stained and dog-eared "Out of Service" note scotch-taped to the grimy cabinet.

Thirty minutes elapsed before the two men shot out of the pilots' reception area with flight plan in hand. They apologized profusely to the banker and escorted him out into the blistering heat for a short walk to a small private jet. One pilot carried the passenger's overnight luggage, but the man's briefcase remained clutched firmly to his chest. Short of handcuffing it to his wrist, on no account would the androgynous middle-aged man let anyone handle his prized possession.

A dry wind whipped around the small planes tethered to

concrete slabs resting on the tarmac. Clumsily, the banker climbed the few narrow, steep steps into the plane's low cabin. He bent his back as he stooped, moving awkwardly between the seats before settling more comfortably into a plush leather recliner and positioning his briefcase securely in the empty seat beside him. Advised to buckle up tightly, the man prepared for a bumpy ride. The vibrant blue early-morning Caribbean sky belied the dark heavy clouds fast approaching from the south. Their flight path would take them across Cuba and on to the Cayman Islands, a route plied by the banker several times a year in the course of his offshore banking business.

An air traffic controller bade them a safe journey, but the doubt in his voice did not go unnoticed. The plane took off, veering from right to left through the buffeting wind. The pilots struggled to wrest control, fighting the wind, and to maintain a constant airspeed. At ten thousand feet the small jet was being thrown about the sky in the turbulence. They continued their ascent, and before long, like a two-minute rollercoaster ride that leaves your stomach in your throat, the plane leveled out. The calm before the storm. For the moment the instability had abated.

Finally composed, the passenger settled in for the short flight. He reached for the well-kept bar, poured a glass of wine, and sat back. The skies ahead were clear, but the gathering banks of dark clouds were quickly rolling up behind them. Suddenly a rattle of thunder rumbled, and forked lightning tore across the sky. The passenger's glass fell from his hand, spilling its crimson liquid over his off-white linen suit. The storm raged with sheets of rain and gale-force winds. There was a rapid increase in both headwind and updraft as hailstones smashed against the windows. The jet jolted endlessly, falling in and out of air pockets that threatened to tear off its wings at any moment.

"Hold on, sir!" the co-pilot shouted over his shoulder. The banker gripped the arms of his seat as beads of perspiration appeared on his florid brow.

"We're trying to get out of this hailstorm and divert over Guantanamo Bay, sir," the captain announced over the PA system. "We've requested a deviation from our flight path to take us around the storm, but the Americans are being difficult."

Moments later the captain looked back out of the cockpit. "Please move the briefcase to the floor and secure anything that might fly around the cabin".

"Will we be okay?" shouted the banker above the clamor.

"Sorry, sir; I hope so, but we do have a serious problem." He struggled to make himself heard over the noise and glanced toward his co-pilot fighting with the controls. "The Americans won't let us into their airspace. They've threatened to send up a fighter to shoot us out of the sky if we make any attempt to fly over them or indeed make an emergency landing. Assholes."

"So what are you going to do?" The passenger mopped his brow with his wine-stained handkerchief.

"We have a possible category four hurricane spiraling to our south, and we can't make Grand Cayman because the hurricane is in our path."

"Then go back to Turks. Now!"

"Impossible, sir. Same problem. We have to make a landing north of this weather pattern."

"Where?"

"Probably Miami."

"Oh no, no! We can't!" the banker exploded. "Anywhere but the US!"

"We have no choice, sir. It's out of our hands."

The captain turned back to consult his instruments. The banker looked down at his briefcase and sank deeply into his seat. His worst nightmare was about to begin. That's if he survived the storm. Maybe crashing would be better for him; anything but landing in the States.

The new flight plan radioed through to Miami was rather quickly and surprisingly accepted without any hint of resistance. Given the circumstances and passport number of passenger Dieter Gruber onboard, Miami air traffic control was more than happy to oblige.

# MANHATTAN

Adams arrived early for his meeting at ABS, where he sat sipping at a caffè mocha in the conference room. Alone in his thoughts about Howard Wayne and his current predicament, he was almost oblivious to the others turning up and taking seats around the table. His mental mapping was soon interrupted when Dale Peters appeared on the teleconferencing video monitor.

"Afternoon everyone, how are you all?" Peters said amiably, his gelled, thick brown hair swept back from a bloated, once-handsome face. "Let's all hope this goes better than originally planned. Nick, did you get a chance to think about what we…"

With a noisy bang, suddenly the conference room door flung open, and Erich Kersch came storming in. He slammed his briefcase on the conference table and headed straight for Adams.

"Erich." Nick Adams pushed back on his chair and stood up. Despite his attempt to appear nonchalant, Nick fought to disguise his contempt for the man. "Good to see you," he lied, managing a crocodile smile.

"Fuck you. You're fired!" Kersch screamed with eyes blazing. "Get your things and get the fuck out! And before you go," he said, leaning in close to within inches of Adams's face, "get out your checkbook and write me a check for nine fucking point nine fucking million fucking dollars, punk!" Kersch looked at the shocked faces around the table in triumph. "Nine point nine fucking million dollars, you fucker!" he repeated, jabbing his finger in Adams's face.

The spittle landed on his suit lapel. He refused to budge, but the halitosis from Kersch's mouth made him almost gag. Adams was fit and years younger than the squat, pudgy Erich Kersch. He could take him out in one swift move, but for once he took back a semblance of self-control. He sat down again and calmly looked up at the man and smiled, but the look of amusement in his stare only served to fan the flames of Kersch's wrath.

"You think this is a fucking joke? Do you want to go to prison? A pretty boy like you?" With shaky hands he reached into his pocket and pulled out a white canister of pills. He unscrewed the lid and swallowed three whole, washing them down with a swig from a bottle of water on the boardroom table, and stuffed the container back into his pocket. "Pretty boys don't have such a good time in prison!" He spat out the words with a venom that had brought the room to a complete silence.

"Now, Erich, that's enough." Dale Peters' voice resounded from the video screen.

"Shut up, Dale!" he shouted, dismissing Peters. "Under these circumstances, I'll do and say as I wish!"

It took several more outbursts from Kersch before any sort of order was established. He singly reprimanded and regaled each director in the room for their own ineptitude. Even the lawyers and accountants that had been summoned to attend were subject to the rant and wrath.

"Sign this!" Kersch threw in Adams's direction a copy of the confidential document Birdie had previously shown him. It sailed across the table and slid off the edge onto the carpet. "Pick it up, now!" he said, as he ran his hand through his cropped blond hair, a triumph of the very latest hair transplant technology.

A soft-mannered man seated beside Nick picked up the document and didn't bother sparing a glance at it and placed it in front of him. "Sorry, Nick," the man said with profound sincerity.

"What's the problem, Erich?" Nick spoke the question, pretending not to know already. "I just don't get it!" As far as Adams was concerned, Kersch was several feet deeper in shit than he was, having already been given the heads-up from the Howard Wayne report that the SEC was mounting an investigation on how Kersch & Co. shares held in companies such as Adams Banking Solutions were being sold. He had read the blogs online that clearly showed what scumbags they were, and it was only because of his association with Kersch & Co., Kersch, and Peters that he was being tarred by the same brush as them in the first place.

"Problem?" Kersch spluttered. "Don't screw with me. I don't need this shit right now. No more talking," he said between clenched teeth, "It's all bullshit. Just sign where the stickers are, buddy!"

"You know what your problem is, Erich?" Adams retorted calmly. "You suffer from integrity deficit disorder." Gasps were heard from around the table. "You were furthering your and someone else's agendas while the rest of us were being taken for a ride." With everything in crisis mode, it seemed ludicrous not to let it be known that there was more behind the Kersch's antics than those present realized.

"Nick!" Hard-pressed, Peters quickly intervened. "Why don't the two of us talk on a private line, and I'll explain the way we see it." Peters began to dial. "I'll have reception put the call through to the conference room." Peters muted the sound from the video link so he and Adams could discuss the issues along with each item of resignation privately. Meanwhile, oblivious of the chaos he had caused, Kersch took a call on his cell phone and stepped out into reception to speak with Gerhard Liebs. The boardroom phone rang, and Adams took the call from Peters standing up. Ten minutes elapsed with Adams hardly saying anything at all. At the end of the call he replaced the receiver and went back to his seat at the boardroom table.

Peters brought the sound back up on the video link and summarized the deal in exact terms that he had expressed privately to Adams for all assembled so that nothing would be called into question later.

"So," he began, "you will resign as president immediately, Nick. Adams Banking Solutions acknowledges your contribution to its success and will appoint you as a consultant on a fair retainer, renewable every quarter. Your share options will be cancelled, and in return you will be allowed to keep the proceeds from the shares you have taken as more than fair compensation. The fact that you will be referred to as a consultant is purely window dressing. You won't be expected back in the office after today."

The boardroom doors opened, rather more quietly this time. All eyes quickly shifted to Kersch as he reentered the room. Peters continued his diatribe, his voice sounding metallic and remote. "The other members of the board of directors have all signed over their shares into an escrow account. This will assure that no more shares are placed in the market. And Nick, you will offer back all shares currently registered in your name …"—he paused—"that you have not already sold back to Kersch & Co."

Alarmed by what Peters was proposing, Adams interrupted, "Are you totally insane?" he blustered, and raising his voice he almost shouted, "They're trading at dollars each. I am not agreeing to this!" Adams couldn't believe the audacity and greed of Kersch & Co., which stood to make millions from his block of equity. They were asking him to just hand over more than six million shares he had between himself and his "associated company" Zen Holdings Limited.

"That's the deal, Nick. Take it or leave it." Peters sat back in the chair at his Spanish office, visibly fatigued by the whole ordeal.

"Well then, I'll just have to leave it, thank you." Nick replied.

There was a lot at stake for Nick certainly, but it wasn't just about the money. It was the principle. He was not so thick-skinned that he didn't know there was some hypocrisy in his situation. He prided himself on his ability to withstand intimidation and coercion. He had learned to rise to his feet no matter how pushed against a wall by an oppressor.

Without succumbing to the pressure, he rose from his seat. "Does everyone here think this fair?" The looks on the faces of his colleagues spoke volumes. It was evident that storm clouds against him had gathered, and that bothered him the most. Had Kersch gotten to them all? Sure, he understood, they had responsibilities, families, and mortgages, enough to let them go with Kersch, who had browbeaten the hell out of each one of them. Adams just shrugged his shoulders in defeat. "I see. Looks like I've been voted off the island. Well, maybe we should ask the shareholders," he looked around the table and saw, almost to a man, averted eyes. He looked straight at Kersch and added, "or perhaps I should appeal to the SEC for their opinion and support?" His words were firm and to the point as he watched Kersch's face turn crimson.

"Don't be such a fucking fool, you dipstick. You'll be shooting yourself in the foot, damn it. The shit will hit the fan and you will be ruined!"

"To hell with you, Kersch," Adams barked back. "I'll consult my lawyers and weigh my options." He grabbed his BlackBerry and made for the door.

"Sit down!" Kersch shouted, blocking his way out. "That's quite a threat!" Adams stopped in his tracks. Kersch lowered his voice. "Listen, there are wild stories circulating everywhere. Blogs are being posted all over the Internet about a problem between Adams Banking Solutions and Kersch & Co. If we don't sort something out now, we will all be in the crapper and we'll have no business left. Period!" Kersch turned back to the video screen. "Dale, talk some sense into this idiot?" he shouted, for that is what Kersch always did—shout and intimidate.

"Now, why on earth would I agree to let Kersch & Co. steal my shares to make yet another killing for you?" Adams glared.

"We need the money to eat the stock as it crashes, if you must damn well know. And crash it will, unless we do something!" Kersch sat down, his face drained of color. "We will provide the necessary support in the market until you turn over your shares to reduce ABS's exposure."

"And so alleges the coin-operated venture capitalist as he stacks the deck," Adams muttered.

"Can't you see that the spotlight will also be on you?" Kersch was almost conciliatory. "Nine point nine million dollars stolen by the president of a public company? Just imagine the headlines. Everything you've worked for turned to dust overnight. Your career incinerated."

"May you never grow old, Erich," he said angrily.

They had reached a stalemate. Adams sat down, ignoring

the constant texts and e-mails and the occasional call as he promised to listen. It took another hour of wrangling to finally reach an agreement. The deal changed in only one vital respect. Nicholas Adams's shares would be transferred to Kersch & Co. for a nominal $500,000. Both parties would then share fifty-fifty on any net profit. Adams could still become a very rich man. Although he let no hint of losing show, he felt crushed. Nevertheless, he forced a grin at Kersch and the others. Nick rose rather unsteadily to his feet and moved round the table shaking hands with his directors and lastly Kersch. He was happy to rid himself of the thieving prick, he thought as he left the room.

Nick walked home. It had been the worst couple of days of his life. A friend probably murdered; the friend's wife attacked; a forced resignation from the company he had worked so hard to build. One could argue that getting booted out was the best thing that could have happened, but to have his life's blood drained out from within him was shattering. It was easier to feel nothing than to feel the pain of his company being reduced to a sham, to be fuelled by greed rather than viability. He just knew that Kersch and Peters would start a pump and dump very soon at everyone's expense except their own.

He wanted to get away, anywhere, if only to step beyond the bounds of the madness for just a short time to think. He needed oxygen. Space. Maybe he could take a trip with Luciana somewhere. Maybe after Howard's funeral? In a muddled daze, he made his journey home, stopping once at a bar to bolster his nerves with a quick beer.

Kersch, however, stayed behind to speak privately with Peters on his phone. "We make him the scapegoat, and we keep our backsides out of the sling."

"You've got a point," Peters said, nodding in agreement. But the dastardly maneuver was actually Gerhard Liebs's plan to distance Kersch from the mounting inquiries, to be achieved by putting Adams out to pasture.

"But if that fucker thinks he'll get one cent more than the five hundred grand, he can kiss my ass!" Kersch blustered in defiance. "You should get the boys to pump and dump his shares starting at market open on Monday. And we *won't* be giving him any of the proceeds either," Kersch uttered emphatically, his voice quivering as his spoke, "not a dime, do you hear me, Dale?"

"Erich, I think you may need to watch your step." Peters' voice broke Kersch's tirade. "For Christ's sake, don't talk about such things on a cell! Are you insane?" Erich took out a prescription bottle and swallowed a few more pills. He slipped off his suit jacket, placing it on the back of the chair. Peters cleared his throat, and Kersch could hear him spit. "Nick's nobody's fool. He's sharper than you give him credit for. But if you really think you can get away with keeping all proceeds from the sale of his stock, fine. I'll back you one hundred percent," Peters added skeptically. "I just hope the fuck that you know what you're doing."

In a low whisper, Kersch asked, "And what about Gerhard, Dale?"

"I don't think he should get Nick's money either, if that's what you're asking. He's already taken the largest cut on this deal as it is," he paused to cough again, "as he does with every deal." Peters fumed. "Okay, Adams aside," he said, quickly changing the subject, "let's move on to more important matters". Kersch turned to lock the conference room door and paced the room.

"I think it's time we changed tactics on Gerhard," Peters grinned to himself. "We're going to play him at his own little game. I've put in motion an idea on how we can cut him out of the oil deal and still use Kersch & Co. funds for the purchase."

Thirty minutes later Kersch emerged from the conference room in an unusually buoyant mood. Breaking free from Liebs's claws was well in sight, a subject guaranteed to send any crook over the moon. He would cut the strings of the puppet master and be free and much richer.

Kersch handed Birdie a note giving instructions to get Adams's shares transferred to Kersch & Co. Birdie couldn't bring herself to look him in the eyes. What she wanted to say was, "into the hands of you, you sick, greedy pig!" But all she could summon up was, "Is this really necessary?" Detecting her lack of support, Kersch spun around on his heels, ignoring her, and left. He made a mental note that she would be next to go and strutted out of the office with every line of his body asserting his irritation. On the sidewalk outside the building he hailed a taxi to the Mandarin Oriental New York, where he was booked for the night.

After such a long day of plotting and betrayal, the double shot of whiskey seemed to improve his disposition considerably. It was only after he held his head and doughy cheeks under the cold tap for several minutes that he could pull himself together and gear himself up for the evening ahead.

Buying sex was the only way Erich Kersch could ever rid himself of his rage. He suffered from restless frustration and pent-up anger that remained relentlessly simmering just below the surface. Through word of mouth he had been recruited by an A-list escort service catering to power-broker businessmen, politicians, and showbiz personalities. Only those considered wealthy enough were accepted and given access to the service's secret website. It was a site that catered for all tastes and delectation, offering any sex for hire; and "any sex" meant all combinations of sexual orientation. No one of whatever persuasion was ever disappointed. Over the course of three years since joining the elite club, Kersch had enjoyed the company of a stream of glamorous women willing to have sex with him for a whole wad of money. For that evening's entertainment he would spend upwards of $20,000 on drinks, dinner, table dancing, and a night of one-sided passion. His tumescent manhood, boosted by blue pills, was primed. His credit card would be taking a hammering. Who cares? If he ran out of cash one day, which was totally unlikely, he would just go and steal some more. Simple. He had the perfect formula. Never failed.

Kersch dwelled on what lay ahead. He trembled while he changed into suitable attire. To the casual observer, his clothes were expensive, yet something never seemed right about them: his blazer too tight around his rotund waist, his trousers too short. Another person would have managed to look cool in his choice of clothes, but Kersch just looked very provincial and somewhat sweaty, like a short, little pervert. You almost had to feel sorry for the guy. He was weathered by innumerable crises spread over decades and had the look of someone who was certain the world owed him everything. He was eternally ticked off with life and determined to take whatever he could. And if it meant he had to be dishonest, then that was hard luck on the pricks who got in his way. He popped a second Viagra, and with a brush of his salivating mouth with the back of his right hand, he was off.

# MIAMI

A haggard Dieter Gruber shifted uneasily and winced at the pain as he sat in an uncomfortable metal chair with three pairs of eyeballs fixed on him. He cowered and shivered, a sign that the marathon interrogation was taking its toll. He had lost count of the hours since being picked up at Miami International Airport. He hadn't even gotten to the immigration desks when he was approached by four burly, non-talkative men and escorted away from the lines of rubbernecking tourists toward a waiting vehicle. The Speedcuffs cut into his wrists as a large hand pushed heavily down on his bald head, and he was bundled into the back of the unmarked car. There was no indication as to whether the men were police or FBI or from any other of the myriad agencies that existed in the US. Not a word had been addressed to him until he arrived at a nondescript building at the other side of the airport complex.

No one in the stark, cold, concrete building had told him who they were or whom they represented. But by their callous demeanors, they appeared to be more than just the local police. Whoever they were, they were certainly expending a hell of a lot of energy on the Caribbean banker. The light from a desk lamp made his eyes water as he squinted to see the two men who sat opposite him and who threw question after question in his direction. They demanded answers. Over and over again they pummeled his brain with demands. He knew he was finished. He knew why they held him. His worst nightmares always had this as a theme. But he refused to give in. He had to protect his clients. It was a matter of honor.

"We're in," said a woman dressed in an unassuming navy pants suit. She sat at a separate table, glued to a computer screen. Various cables and electronic devices were scattered around the surface.

The silent and apparently more senior of his interrogators pushed himself away from the wall where he had been leaning. He moved slowly toward the desk and approached the heavily perspiring hapless center of interest. The interrogator signaled with his fingers as he approached, and the two agents got up from their seats, moving away from Gruber to join the woman, where the captive's laptop rested, surrounded by the paraphernalia of decryption. The desk lamp beamed a cylindrical ray of intrusive light on the one person seated beneath it.

"Well, well! Finally! Now that wasn't too difficult, was it?" His voice was gravelly and that of an obvious smoker. "Thank you for nothing! You just couldn't give us what we wanted. All we asked was for the password, Mr. Gruber," said Dillon Rae, sounding exhausted and frustrated. "A simple matter, but we cracked it anyway. But time is at a premium these days, and I, for one, have wasted enough of that precious commodity on you." He lit a cigarette, flouting the rules for the building, and blew a perfect circle through the stream of light, watching the smoke spiral toward the ceiling. "This is not good for you, not good at all!"

Gruber shifted again in his seat, staring blankly at the man standing in front of him. He knew the gamble of travelling with the one tool that could put the anonymity of his bank's customers at risk by exposing their identities and beneficial Ownership. But when making "special" visits abroad, access to the bank he presided over was vital. However, the unfortunate detour had landed him on the unwelcoming shores of America. His laptop had fallen into the wrong hands and would now turn into a high-potential mother lode for meddling financial regulators who, in his opinion, had nothing better to do with their lives.

"You will now cooperate fully." Dillon Rae leaned forward; his eyes blazed down at his cornered prey. "If you don't, I'll have you sent down to the Federal Courthouse for arraignment on charges of conspiracy to commit securities, mail, and wire fraud, and for aiding and abetting US citizens to commit tax evasion. You will not be given bail, and I will personally hand you a one-way ticket to a Federal penitentiary."

The intimidated Gruber acknowledged defeat, lowering his head in complete submission. He clutched the edge of the table to brace himself. "What do you want from me? Please?" His right leg started to shake uncontrollably, and he held onto his knee in a vain attempt to stop it.

Special Agent Dillon Rae and his team were operating within the terms of the government's decree, given free rein to take whatever action they saw fit against an escalating epidemic of private individuals and multinationals banking offshore. Scores of government agencies had been granted unconditional authority and unlimited resources to meet those objectives. His orders came from the director of the FBI himself.

The feds at Bureau headquarters had made full use of this new carte blanche directive that gave sweeping powers by setting up a special task force for the sole purpose of entrapping offshore banks and rooting out their clients, assigning a maverick FBI special agent to head up the new agency, the Taxation Repatriation Unit, codenamed TRU. Although based at FBI headquarters in Washington, Dillon Rae preferred to use a Miami field office as his nerve center for this new agency. The wretched Gruber was just one piece of the jigsaw.

The TRU unit had already scored their first major coup, having seized large sums of untaxed offshore funds by going after Americans who had undisclosed offshore corporate bank accounts. Quite a few small-time private account holders had been caught. But the agency had merely scratched the surface. They were out to bag the owners behind offshore holding companies, the banks concealing them, and the brokers handling their trades. With the capture of the unfortunate banker Dieter Gruber, Rae's trap could now be set for higher stakes. They had finally nabbed a linchpin who would be forced to hand over all the intelligence they needed to accomplish their goal. Catching Gruber was a very lucky break for TRU. The chance of capturing this notorious Caribbean banker was nothing short of a miracle. But there was much to do. Within the hour he was onboard the agency jet, bound for New York—exhausted, but elated nonetheless.

# NEW YORK

The shock was almost too much. Framed in the doorway was the man he least wanted to see. His first overwhelming impulse was to slam the door in his face. But Ravi saw the look in the eyes of the quintessential hard-ass standing there.

"Are you mad? What are you thinking about," he almost whispered, "turning up like this?" Sharma was frightened and suspicious; there were no plans for another meeting for at least a week, and certainly not at the apartment. "We had an agreement," he said hoarsely in a strangled low whisper.

Dillon Rae ignored Sharma's look of trepidation, sidestepped him, and walked in. Sharma took a deep, shuddering breath, closed the door, and followed.

"What are you doing here?" Sharma asked anxiously as Rae wandered around the apartment, taking mental notes.

By any conceivable measure, this was a man on a mission, one who had successfully recruited scores of informed and reliable people, but none more so than Ravi Sharma. "Relax," Rae almost smiled. "It's not you I have come to see, my friend." Finally Rae revealed his arrangement to meet Nick Adams at his apartment, and told Sharma that for his own sake he should make himself scarce before Adams arrived.

Unwittingly, Ravi Sharma had found himself in an unsolicited role, courtesy of the FBI. It was cloak-and-dagger and caused him considerable anxiety, considering his relationship with Adams. He never would have intentionally betrayed the man who had helped change his life, but Dillon Rae had made it clear that he had no choice but to cooperate. This was government business. He had no choice in the matter; that had been made very clear.

Manhattan was a far cry from Ravi Sharma's youth in southeast India, and certainly beat the hell out of living the life of a wet rice farmer in the Tamil Nadu state. Like most aspiring people from his area, Sharma was highly ambitious and had left home for Chennai, the big city formerly known as Madras, and had never looked back. While there, he had ended up doing a myriad of jobs for a wealthy family who were so bowled over by his genius that they helped him secure a scholarship to the Indian Institute of Technology Madras. Several years later Ravi met some American backpackers and followed them to Goa, where he met Nicholas Adams, who was travelling through India during a gap year between his undergraduate degree from Harvard and a planned post-graduate degree at Stanford. A unique friendship formed, and the two headed to Mumbai and joined a think tank of young programmers and system developers. Eventually Adams helped Ravi get into Stanford, where Adams received an MBA in finance, and Ravi a master's degree in computer science.

As things turned out, and with utter shame, at a particularly difficult point in his new career in his newly adopted country, Sharma became strapped for cash while developing his own operating system, and began hacking into banking systems, siphoning off funds to pay for, among other things, equipment he needed. And eventually he got caught. He was arrested, tried, and thrown into jail. But after only a few very scary months in prison, Sharma was miraculously released. Someone with influence had intervened.

Out of jail, on the street, and out of a job and a place to live, he reluctantly contacted his old friend. He had let him down and was totally devastated by his extraordinary behavior that was based on pride and his need to prove himself without any help from anyone.

Adams offered him a place to stay for as long as he wished. For Nick, Ravi's predicament was easily arranged. Although he was angry and hurt that Ravi had not told him about jail, as he would have visited him, their friendship would not be tarnished. But there was also an upside. Ravi was brilliant. Adams badly needed his skill set. Between them they came up with a mutually acceptable way to move forward. Ravi agreed to write the code for Adams's rich-in-concept but floundering new venture. It was difficult, and took far longer than they thought, but from Adams's apartment, together they designed Adams Banking Solutions's very first proprietary software.

There was one serious problem. Ravi's conviction for fraud would have to be kept under wraps. What bank would entertain any form of software built by a thief, a proven hacker?

One month after Sharma's release from jail, Erich Kersch, who claimed to represent the sponsor who had rescued him, made contact with a surprised Sharma. Kersch told Sharma he had been plucked out of prison on the condition that he work for Kersch & Co., Bank Schreiber Liebs, and their international *bureau de change* as an IT consultant.

Much as he could have used the money, Sharma wasn't keen on taking an offer from such an obviously contemptible character. But Kersch threatened that if he didn't accept the offer, he would be sent back to prison to serve his full five-year term. Such lucrative job offers from business sectors were commonplace for infamous hackers after serving their prison sentences, although not proffered with such strings attached. It seemed that Ravi had to compromise himself again, but he reluctantly took the consultancy job. Not that he had a choice. It was in the course of his work with Kersch that he naively got Kersch & Co. interested in the small company that he and Nick had founded. ABS then required serious funding. Kersch had access to money, but it would come at a heavy price.

After Adams Banking Solutions had its successful public IPO, thanks to the support of Kersch & Co., Sharma, because of his prison record, remained working behind the scenes. He had too much of a sensitive role within the organization to make it public knowledge, and no mention of his name was in the company's prospectus. Ravi Sharma's shares were lodged in an offshore anonymous corporation, safe from the IRS and the ABS shareholders who had funded the company. Ensconced in Nick's oversized third bedroom, he had established his own high-tech software laboratory, helping Kersch & Co., and backing up Adams as a shadow development director. The arrangement suited them both.

After everything Adams had done for him, the last thing Sharma wanted was for Nick to find out about his secret meetings with Dillon Rae. Sharma exploded. "Man, I can't do this anymore! This situation has gotten way out of control!" he shouted. "Nick is my mate. I am not going to let our relationship go down the toilet."

Rae grabbed Sharma's arms and shook him like an errant child. "Calm down, for God's sake! He's not going to find out. I know what I'm doing." When he released him, Rae said, "Tell you what. Let me give you a heads up." He smiled at Ravi. "Let me spell everything out and fill you in on what takes place from here. Then you'll know you are doing the right thing!"

Rae didn't have an aversion to gays, although their sexuality made him feel uncomfortable, so he was never quite sure how to conduct himself in their presence. Although he preferred dealing with John Cemach, more commonly known as JC, another programmer from Kersch & Co. he had managed to cajole into assisting him, Sharma was the real genius and had the necessary personal connection to some of the pieces of the jigsaw that were missing. Rae calmly gave Sharma an outline of the grand plan, assuring him Adams's interests would be safeguarded. All Adams had to do was play ball, which was why he was there to see him. "Ravi—" Rae looked him straight in the eye and in a low threatening tone said, "you know all of the reasons why you will help me, don't you? On any one of the misdemeanors I've listed, you would be going back to jail for a long, long time!"

The front door opened and Adams entered carrying a brown paper bag containing a wine bottle and groceries. Sharma rushed out into the hall.

"A Mr. Rae is here to see you ..."

"Oh, yeah," Adams said, rolling his eyes up and sighing. The day could only get worse. "Sorry, Ravi, I forgot to tell you." Sharma relieved him of the bag and headed for the kitchen, ignoring Rae, who had walked into the living room and was looking at some of the pictures that were placed about, mainly of Adams in some exotic location and involving cars, boats and planes, and always sunny. There were a few that were obviously his parents, but none of any woman who might be deemed to be a girlfriend.

"Mr. Rae," Adams said, entering the living room, extending his hand to greet him.

"Drink, or is it too early? *I* could certainly do with one."

Rae shook Adams's hand and took a seat as Adams poured a whiskey for a tired Dillon Rae. He poured a glass of wine for himself. "Ice?"

He saw Rae shake his head. "So, what can I do for you?" He had meant his voice to sound nonchalant, but his throat wasn't playing the game, and the question was choked.

Dillon Rae took a good hour to go through his task force operation and to explain to Nick just how difficult and delicate the situation was. He explained how efforts had kicked into high gear since the death of Howard Wayne, and that the file containing details of his searing, potentially devastating exposé were stolen. He also warned that no mention of their conversation could ever be made, not even to Luciana Cavallini, or the whole operation would be in serious jeopardy.

"Lu?" Adams sat upright on the sofa looking puzzled. "How on earth do you know about her?" The dark thoughts running through his mind were nearly as numbing as the idea of Howard being murdered.

"That's my job—it's what I do."

Rae stood up, glass in hand, and drained the last drop of his Glenfiddich. "Call me," he said, handing Adams his card. "Think about what I said." As Adams walked him to the door, he added, "I can't promise immunity, 'cause those guys at the SEC are a different department and are rottweilers, but I'll do what I can. In the meantime, if I were you," he moved in close to Adams whispering, "I would spend a quiet weekend mulling over everything said here. Ponder on my offer, or on Monday I would get my affairs in order and find myself a damn good lawyer. I mean it!" With that he turned and made a quick exit into the hall and through the front door, which slammed shut behind him, giving Nick yet another jarring jolt.

# MARRAKESH, MOROCCO

Like a shimmering silver dart, the private jet streaked effortlessly across the bright blue North African sky. High above the arid desert, the red, phosphate-rich plains leading to Marrakesh stood out for miles. As the plane decelerated for its runway approach, a glint of brilliant early-afternoon sun flooded the cockpit with a warm glow. Once it touched down along the bumpy tarmac, the co-pilot switched on the intercom and offered the usual address to their employer and his security detail of two.

It had been a long journey, and although physically tired, Harvey Milton III was full of anticipation. He stayed seated in the custom leather armchair in the sumptuous bespoke cabin and waited patiently as the plane taxied toward its position, guided by the "Follow Me" sign on top of a bright yellow, slightly rusting 4x4. The Gulfstream bypassed the main terminal building of Menara Airport and proceeded with engines humming toward a cluster of vehicles at the far end.

With temperatures hovering at around ninety-eight degrees, droplets of sweat popped up on Milton's brow from the moment he stepped outside the private unmarked jet. The heat slammed into him. Intermittently, he wiped the perspiration with a handkerchief as he made his way the short distance to a stretch Mercedes waiting on the tarmac thoughtfully parked in the shadow formed by the private terminal building, its air conditioning set on high.

There was always something intimidating about Milton. He exuded an intense measure of dignity, an aura of command. With a full head of carefully groomed silver hair, he stood broad at six feet four inches and carried far more weight than he should. Perhaps it was his imposing physical stature that kept people cowed when meeting him for the first time.

Within minutes Milton was safely inside the limo, seated beside a dapper Minister of the Moroccan government who had greeted him warmly, planting a kiss on both cheeks of the American.

"Habibi!" He threw a half smoked cigarillo carelessly out of the car window. "You are looking well despite the long flight!" They waited while special airport staff handled customs and passport control details for Milton and his crew. As was always the case, it was a mere formality. Milton was a frequent and welcome visitor.

The minister was pleased as ever to see the illustrious American again, who was always great to do business with. A particular wire transfer had already hit the minister's account in Zurich that morning. Early prepayment of commissions typified an act of good faith in all his business dealings. If there was any question of integrity, it was only to do with Milton's private addictive predilections, which the minister always made certain were catered to, no matter how bizarre and corrupting. Who was he to judge?

The Mercedes followed behind its police escort as it entered a stream of traffic at the chaotic Boulevard el Yarmouk, just below the walls of the Old City. Traffic policemen whistled and waved white gloves at all sorts of modes of transport: calèches, petit and grand taxis, bicycles, motorbikes, and donkey-drawn carts, all of which seemingly conspired to deliberately halt the smooth progress of the minister of state and his guest. There was much shouting and cursing by the police escort as they weaved a path through the great unwashed masses. The Mercedes and security vehicles finally arrived at the gates of the luxury La Mamounia Hotel.

Again, there were no check-in formalities. Milton shook hands with the minister of technology, who bowed, placing his right hand against his heart, and bid him farewell until the next morning. Marathon meetings were scheduled for the next day, concluding with signed contracts between Morocco and Milton's ever-expanding global private investment group. They were in negotiation on a new nano-semiconductor factory that would employ thousands of nationals, offering cheap and grateful labor.

Escorted by three senior hotel staff, Milton stepped across the opulent marble hall and into a waiting elevator that glided silently to a penthouse suite equipped with a personal butler waiting to serve him. No creature comforts had been overlooked. Ceilings dripped with silks; sumptuous fabrics and pillows abounded; baskets of fruit and bouquets of flowers adorned every table. It was intoxicating. This had been Sir Winston Churchill's favorite hotel, and was now fast becoming Harvey Milton's as well.

Milton dismissed the staff with the exception of his private butler. His bodyguards and crew had been allocated rooms on the floor just below, and the hotel provided a seated guard along the corridor.

After being presented with a glass of champagne, Milton strolled over to the stone balcony to take in the dramatic setting and magnificent vistas. Despite the heat and long flight, he felt eager about his sensitive meeting with Marat Esdaulet, who had flown in earlier that afternoon, and the prospects of his evening plans. He stood gazing above an extravagantly large swimming pool and manicured gardens below. The snow-capped Atlas Mountains formed a backdrop farther in the distance against the brilliant sun. "Exquisite," he said out loud, and mopping his brow, he turned back into his suite.

Marat Esdaulet was also booked into La Mamounia and was paid the same courtesies as Milton when he arrived. Over the years, Esdaulet and Milton had developed a relationship of great personal interest. They had met on one of Milton's many visits to Eastern Europe during the Yeltsin days. With the help of Milton's political ties, Esdaulet became a survivor and also a beneficiary of the economic scramble in post-Soviet years. Esdaulet had secured the position of oil minister of his small, oil and gas rich, but cash poor country and had begun seeking foreign investment. Milton, like Liebs, had chased lucrative opportunities in Eastern Europe, but his friendship with Esdaulet had actually paved the way to penetrating that market in pole position.

"My oh my, you're looking the part," Milton said, meeting his friend's hand with a tight grip. Having changed from his usual black business suit, he wore a tailor-made jellaba of fine linen and intricate needlework, with tiny silk knots that were the buttons that lined the length of his tunic. "Come on in."

"Is all okay with our deal?" Esdaulet inquired as he finger-combed the coal-black hair that fell over a commanding forehead.

"It will be. Let me get you a drink," Milton said motioning to the butler.

"Harvey my friend, such a pleasure meeting you in Marrakesh. It's a perfect place for business and pleasure, is it not?" Esdaulet made himself comfortable on a silk-covered sofa and crossed his legs. Milton smiled. "Our meeting last time was far too brief. So I've made special plans for us this evening." The butler presented Esdaulet a glass of champagne. "We'll have an early dinner here at the hotel, and then I've arranged for an enchanting creature to join us for cocktails. After dinner she will take you on a most unforgettable journey. I myself have other arrangements, so you'll have to excuse me after the main course." Esdaulet grinned revealing the whitest of teeth. "Here's to the land of irresistible charm." Both men raised their glasses in a toast.

"And when night falls, let the Moorish magic begin." Milton leaned forward, slightly out of breath, and clinked his glass against the other man's; they both laughed loudly. His full lips were now wet, not from the champagne, but from drool, for he knew what lay ahead that night.

To hell with the business, Esdaulet's deals with Milton were not nearly as important as his special connections and services that now had made the important American a dangerously addicted law-breaker. Esdaulet knew that in the US Milton would be completely ruined if he were ever found out. He had kept Milton up to speed as regards to Liebs's interest in the deal. He wanted him to know that there was another contender to ensure that neither he nor Liebs made any last-minute changes to the reward package. Milton knew, but Liebs would never know of Milton's involvement.

"Harvey," Esdaulet said enthusiastically, "I have some news

that may be of interest—a surprising development principally with Kersch & Co." His East European accent was completely at odds with the drawl of the American.

Esdaulet had been secretly keeping Milton abreast of Kersch & Co.'s plans, how they were to structure their interest in the pipeline, and the production projections.

The minister had only one concern: How much money would be paid and when? He cared not that he was playing everyone against the other, whether it be Milton, Liebs, or Liebs's less-than-loyal partners, Peters and Kersch. Whatever the deal, he would run with the money. Everyone in his opinion was entitled to a lick of the spoon, but the pudding was his alone.

Milton sat back and placed his glass on the side table. "Tell me," he said, sounding irritated. "What are that unsavory duo up to now?"

Esdaulet sensed the corpulent American's mounting anger, something he had seen many times before. "First, thank you for the warning on Bank Schreiber Liebs. You were totally correct." His voice grew louder. "Liebs did try to force my hand in using his bank, without much success, I must say." He sipped at his champagne. "I made it quite clear that he was not in a position to negotiate on that point, and if he felt uncomfortable with my choice of bank, I would be forced to do the deal with another interested party." He looked out through the high French windows and sighed. "Liebs was very intimidating, but I am used to threats from my own compatriots who, believe me, are far more persuasive."

Esdaulet's aggressive tone and uncompromising egotism brought an intense look of satisfaction to Milton's face. "Well done, Marat!"

"Wait, it gets better. A few days later I receive a call from Dale Peters. Dale offers me a side deal," he clicked his fingers together, adding dramatically, "with a significantly larger stake than Liebs had put on the table. Of course I accepted without hesitation." Milton tried to interrupt him but was overridden as he continued, "Dale has somehow managed to fund the purchase through Kersch & Co., and has cut Liebs out entirely. How that is possible, I do not know." He smiled. "I really do not want to know. God help the man if he is found out!"

"What? Has Dale lost his mind?" Milton said, shaking his head emphatically in disbelief. "The man is more stupid than I thought. Good God, he is a dead man walking, Marat! The thing about Dale is that he's delusional when it comes to Liebs. He thinks he can do no wrong. Well, I've known Gerhard for a long time and I think Dale is in for a rude awakening if he thinks he can outsmart him."

"As long as I receive my share of the proceeds, their battle of wits is not of my concern; nor indeed yours, my good friend. Besides, earnings from the transaction will be a mere pittance compared to yours and mine."

"And, of course, my investors." Milton had assembled a consortium of international investors to buy into the pipeline and develop one of Esdaulet's larger oil fields. His interests were not only financial, but also politically motivated. "Oh, yes, let me tell you the news from my side," Milton said, as he motioned for more champagne. "We've had some promising new developments too. Let me fill you in."

By 8:00 p.m. Milton was back inside the Mercedes, alone with his designated driver. The two motor escorts kicked their bikes into gear, and the small convoy moved rapidly into the traffic, away from the hotel, toward a prearranged destination organized for the American guest.

The tinted window framed the familiar brightly lit Katoubia Mosque that dominated the buildings around the Old City like a moving travelogue. Many stared at the stretched vehicle that arrogantly steered its course through the cobweb of streets leading to the center of the Old City. The streets were wide enough for only a single lane, but somehow all modes of transport managed to pass in either direction without as much as a scratch. Farther down the side streets, a deluge of activities was underway. With horns blaring, they soon reached the Jamaa el Fna, a vast open-air marketplace surrounded by shops, cafes, and stalls. The place was crammed with Moroccan tradesmen plying their goods to tourists who flashed fat wads of cash. Dancers and acrobats, musicians, snake charmers, and storytellers commenced their timeless performances, as they had for centuries, as dusk fell over the square. Muezzin chants from mosques called out in mysterious dissonance above magnetic ghaita pipes vying for attention.

The Mercedes eased its way through the mélange without protest from the crowd and glided to a stop just below the Terrace Panoramique that marked an entrance into the labyrinth of the largest indoor souk in the world. The driver leaped out and opened the rear door while the escorts dismounted and shielded Harvey Milton from inquisitive onlookers.

The driver handed over his important consignment to a dark-skinned Arab wearing an expensively tailored jellaba, a fez crowning his shaved head. The Arab bowed to the Westerner and beckoned him to follow. Together they walked quickly through the covered walkways of the Souk Sammarine, ignoring the enticements of traders. They hurried down corridors, passing tanneries and dyers, apothecaries, caged falcons pecking at the heads of dead chickens, snakeskins, and ocelots hanging from hooks, endless barrels of spices, and metalworkers beating and forming metal with their crude tools. The scene was timeless.

They arrived at two twelve-foot-tall, hammered-brass-covered cedar doors and entered into an air-conditioned carpet and tapestry shop. Three browsing tourists were abruptly shown out of the emporium, and the massive doors were quickly closed behind them.

The guide gestured to one of the carpet salesmen, who scurried to a massive carpet hanging from the high ceiling and covering a large part of the crumbling, plastered wall. One of the carpet salesmen pulled back its outer edge to reveal a small, tenth-century, arched and bolted wooden door.

Milton's head swam in delight. He felt strangely at ease as he began to cool down from the outdoor heat. But perspiration still caused little rivulets to ooze their way down his spine. He entered, his tall, corpulent body ducking through the low door. Although he was familiar with the surroundings, he still paused for a moment, awed by the sight that greeted him. The walls on either side of the long walkway opened to the night sky above and led to a turquoise-and-green-mosaic pathway that seemed to hover over a moat ten feet wide on both sides. Candles and hibiscus floated on its black oil surface while incense burned at each corner. Milton moved along the path toward another door, his heels landing heavily on the tile floor. Cleverly positioned mirrors added to the *Arabian Nights* fantasy. Another Arab dressed in a white caftan complete with silk turban swung another door open. Evidently Harvey Milton was expected.

It was the same now-familiar ritual. First, the quick and expert hands of silk-masked attendants disrobed him. It was so familiar, yet so unutterably exciting. The evening's program consisted of a steam bath, a rubdown with coarse straw, followed by an oil-and-herb massage. While fingers played along every inch of his body, Milton strained to contain his excitement.

Once the spa treatments ended, he was dressed in a white-silk robe and led to a room laden with draped tapestries and candles, floors strewn with exotic cushions, and low tables offering coffee with cardamom seeds and mint tea. Darkened, small, discreet, curtained alcoves along the room's periphery hid their occupants.

As Milton stepped into his own alcove, a North African band burst into rhythmic patterns of Moroccan music, cueing the entrance of the belly dancers. Swaying hips twisted and turned; arms and hands flailed. Silk veils covered faces, showing only dark, sultry eyes. Woven costumes revealed no body flesh, but these were not the common or garden belly dancers that danced for the easily pleased tourists of Marrakesh.

The music grew hypnotic, and Milton went wild. He beckoned to one of the dancers who had moved across to his alcove, and the dancer slowly, tantalizingly, lifted the headscarf to reveal an breathtakingly beautiful face. The dancer winked, acknowledging the regular patron. Milton could hardly contain the strained hardness beneath his robe. The other dancers moved on to the other alcoves, leaving Milton alone. Milton beckoned his private dancer to join him. The young dancer obliged and sat closely beside him on the kilim cushions and silken throws. While toying playfully with the folds of the robe that now hung loosely from Milton's large frame, the dancer hummed a serenade along with the hypnotic music, sending Milton straight to dizzying heights of euphoria. The dancer's eyes shone bright as his fingers caressed Milton's thighs. Tonight the young man would be paid well ... far more than a year's wages.

# MARBELLA, SPAIN

It was not the largest, but nevertheless it created a stir everywhere. Newly launched in Italy and collected by its proud owner, with bright white upper paintwork and marine blue hull, one hundred and twenty feet in length, with a flying transom, eight full-time crew, mainly female and beautiful, this boat made the statement the owner craved.

Cruising the Mediterranean coastline of the Costa del Sol, Dale Peters was relishing in the comforts of the southern Spanish coastline, a setting close to ideal, with its beautiful beaches and impressive mountain backdrop. Not far from his Spanish home, it was the perfect place to enjoy his new motor yacht.

Peters was lounging on his sundeck, barefoot and with a glass of expensive white wine in hand (there would never be red wine on board for fear of staining the pristine decks), and amusing himself with a couple of young statuesque East European girls he had brought along, he felt on top of his game. For a shallow, greedy, self-centered man, the fruits of his labor were the standard-issue business tycoon boys' toys. Designed not only for luxury, his yacht was equipped with a full-range, satellite communications and radar system that allowed him to conduct business outside the realm of the authorities when he took it out into territorial waters.

Earlier that day, Erich Kersch had joined Peters on a Skype video conference call to discuss progress on their scheme to get out from under Liebs's thumb. Peters had every intention of letting Kersch know about the boat, knowing it would irritate him. And as he talked, he moved the camera lens of his iPad to capture images of the vessel. "Our amenable oil minister has agreed to sidestep Liebs for a larger stake," Peters reported. Kersch stared back at Peters in disbelief; his body thumped with an adrenaline charge. Neither man could hold back their elation, but both knew the prospect of what that particular maneuver might bring down upon their heads if discovered. "Liebs has already sanctioned the release of funds for a down payment on the purchase, so altering its source location and the amount retrieved won't set off any red flags." Peters sat down and grabbed at his wineglass. "As far as Gerhard knows, the monies never left Kersch & Co. when we eventually tell him Marat Esdaulet awarded the purchase to another party." He poured himself another glass of wine and toasted Kersch. "The full purchase amount will be taken in a single transfer from a concealed account I've buried in several layers of dummy corps within the group. No one knows of its existence or the sums held there. Esdaulet's initial fee will be handled separately and paid in cash from a private account I have in Hong Kong."

"What do you need me to do?" Kersch asked eagerly. He knew Peters's plan was a dangerous game to play, but Kersch had really had enough of Gerhard Liebs, so threw caution to the wind and agreed to go along without hesitation. The seriously rich pickings were a big enough incentive.

The two spent the better part of an hour going through the details of the devious plot Peters had instigated. The Wi-Fi connection was intermittent and annoying, but at least it obviated the need for long-distance travel. With such a complicated plan, involving all sorts of deceit, Peters had Kersch sift through the fine points, item by item, laboriously checking and rechecking every detail. Their motivation matched their level of effort, necessitated by the activities of a man who had become a big-ass thorn in their sides. Several sequences of events were formulated until they were confident they had a scheme that was absolutely airtight.

Dale Peters didn't care much for either Erich Kersch or Gerhard Liebs. He never did. Kersch was simply a valuable pawn in his game. Peters, who owned one the largest share-pushing pump and dump networks, had been implicated in several share-rigging scandals and was under investigation by the US SEC. He needed Kersch because he could no longer step foot on American soil without being picked up by the FBI.

Liebs had conned him out of his rightful inheritance. Back in the 1980s, Dale Peters and his older brother lived a full-fledged, self-indulgent lifestyle, so uncharacteristic of their Dutch background. It was all about greed back then and they were excessively consumptive in their pursuit of wealth. The market at the time was over-speculated, and the Peters brothers' share promotion operation had gone through tough times. But when the bottom finally fell out in the crash, they were left untouched, having already bankrolled their profits, leaving a few small brokerage houses crippled and investors suicidal. But the elder Peters had a habit of stuffing his head into bags filled with cocaine, and eventually died of an overdose, leaving a share-pushing, money-producing machine all ready to gear up again. The brothers had hidden their wealth with Gerhard Liebs. Although it took a certain amount of arm-twisting, the younger, less talented, and rather naïve brother, Dale Peters, soon succumbed to Liebs's Machiavellian ways. In a blink of an eye Liebs managed to wrestle voting control from Peters without so much as a thank-you. Dale had become a servant of Gerhard Liebs, although he had been richly rewarded with considerable crumbs that fell off the Swiss banker's table.

While their reasons may have differed, both Peters and Kersch had the same goal: they wanted out of the game and out of Liebs's control, and in the process here was their opportunity to outwit Liebs and pull off the scam of a lifetime. It was their retirement plan. So Peters naïvely trusted Kersch to play his role impeccably. Out of the frying pan and into the fire.

The screen went blank and Dale Peters got up and decided that he had talked enough.

He walked onto the quayside. Tourists parted in awe as he made his way to his new Aston Martin convertible coupe. He touched the start button, exaggeratedly revved the engine, and moved slowly through the crowds, until he got onto the main road, where he could ignore traffic restrictions. He gunned the beast down the highway toward Malaga. He found a bar, had a drink, and lapped up the admiring glances at his car. Thirty minutes later he paid the bill and strolled to the Aston Martin. Smiling, he adjusted his sunglasses in the vanity mirror. He started the engine, and with a deep growl pulled away from the curb and aimed back to the marina some miles away.

Wearing only a scant bikini bottom, one of the girls stepped onto the deck to alert Peters of an urgent call on the private phone in his cabin. She wiggled behind him and followed him to the owner's stateroom, which was styled in lacquered and hand-polished fine woods, and leaned seductively against the wall. Her silicone-enhanced breasts were freshly massaged with suntan oil, her young nipples pert.

"I need to take this call in private," he said coolly, ignoring her flirtation, his hand capped over the mouthpiece of the telephone. "Why don't you join your friends for a dip in the pool?" With her beautiful young lips pouting, the young girl turned, shrugging her shoulders, and left to rejoin her friends back on the sundeck. Frankly, she preferred the company of her girlfriends but her monthly allowance more than compensated for putting up with the boorish Dale Peters. When the time came she would jump onto another ship and restart the process of seduction with someone richer and more appreciative. She lay down beside the sleeping girl on the foredeck, rolled toward her, gently brushed her lips across her cheeks, and giggled.

Below decks, the news was not at all good. The thought of an oversight made Peters extremely apprehensive. There was a possible blip in his well-thought-out plans. He had to act fast. Within the hour he was on his way to the airport to pick up a private jet bound for Bermuda. A fallback maneuver had to be set in motion before all was lost.

# NEW YORK

"This is all very constructive, Oscar," Harvey Milton said flatly, "but there's no real meat here; it's all gravy." He looked up at his assistant. "Don't get me wrong, you've made a good effort," he said, leafing through several pages, "but where is the Achilles' heel?"

Milton's assistant and general counsel, Oscar Randell, was sitting with Milton in his office, poring over a complex and lengthy report. Randell looked dejected. He thought his work had been exemplary, but Milton was berating him like a disgruntled parent disappointed in the inadequacies of his son.

Harvey Milton had arrived back in New York from Marrakesh. Now he was at the usual Monday-morning meetings at Trump Tower. Ostensibly one of his private residences, the apartment had evolved into the natural headquarters of Milton's holding company. The apartment's grand, formal foyer accommodated the company receptionist, security staff, and personal bodyguard posts. The receptionist sat at an eighteenth-century desk; the guards and security took positions at antique tables on either side of the main entrance door. The foyer opened onto a large hall, with two wings splitting the penthouse into office space and private living areas. Every inch of the sprawling penthouse clearly affirmed the billionaire's wealth and influence.

"We both know he's been playing treacherous games for a very long time now. That greedy little Swiss shit needs taking out!" There was so much venom in his words. "So, where is Liebs's weakest point?"

Randell couldn't answer, and instead rubbed his brow, looking genuinely bewildered.

"Okay, then, let's find out." He was increasingly irritated. "That's clearly what I want," Milton growled, tapping a finger firmly on the cover of the thick report. "Oscar: the whole point of this exercise is to get that arrogant son of a bitch *off my back*." He paused and added, "I need something much more detailed. I want to know what time he gets up in the morning, what time he has a dump, when and where he pisses, everything that he does, to what time he goes to bed, who's on his payroll, the names of all his hatchet men and emissaries, the names of all the people he's screwed over the years, medical reports, his vices, the women in his life." He paused. "If he has any, of course. Can you imagine fucking that weasel? I want every speck of dirt we can muster on Herr Gerhard Liebs. We may need to stoop to his depths, and if so, so be it." He liked the sound of his ranting. "Spend whatever you need to get people talking. But above everything else, get me his whole net worth statement!"

Randell was stunned. Milton was behaving way out of character. It was painfully obvious that Liebs had finally gotten under his skin. "He's too private; he has too many legitimate holding companies interlaced with numbered accounts. Trusts and nominees, different jurisdictions."

Randell quietly watched Milton thumb through one of the many statements again. "You estimate, based on the information in this report, that his tentacles stretch across the world, and that his assets could be worth over $14 billion!" This was truly a formidable valuation, and Milton shook his head slowly and added, "With a turnover of $32 billion last year. It's unbelievable! You must be including all of the customers' accounts?"

"Yes we did include that information, based on banking estimated statistics gleaned from other typical and comparable secretive private banks in Switzerland. And after all, we already know that Liebs treats all of the accounts at his bank as his own!"

"I have no idea how you got this stuff, but it looks like someone in Zurich may have cooked the data. I would venture that your figures must be well off the mark, but let's say you're right: you'll still need to keep digging deeper, and in due course we'll find our silver bullet to blow his evil bank and all its interests to hell!"

So the debate continued. They explored wild theories centering on the manipulative Swiss banker. They had a full afternoon of work ahead of them, with a charity dinner for Milton in the evening to follow. Milton's PA poked her head in to ask if lunch would be taken in Milton's office. He nodded to her and turned his focus back to the task at hand. The two were left huddled over pages of documents, issuing instructions to a steady stream of employees who were summoned into the inner sanctum of the office suite while his private chef prepared lunch.

Some hours later, Milton moved from his office and crossed the wide hall to enter his private apartment, where he poured himself a whiskey and made for his dressing room suite to shower and change into black tie, occasionally taking calls on his BlackBerry. Dressed, he waited for Abigail to appear. The women in Harvey Milton's life served as a smokescreen for his dangerous and perverse appetites, which, if discovered, would be ruinous both to his business and—more importantly—his political ambitions. High-maintenance women put up with his erectile dysfunction and non-intercourse sex by accepting cash, charge cards, and other negotiable items such as jewelry, trips abroad, cars, and—for some—exclusive pads. Abigail, his current girlfriend, was a well-connected socialite and perfect partner. Milton's wealth and charm worked for her, and it soon became apparent to them that their open relationship suited them both. Within the closed society they mingled with, they were an exciting couple, envied by one and all.

Milton and Abigail were joining friends and attending a gala fundraiser at the Pierre Hotel that evening. Senators, socialites, bankers, and power brokers were expected, along with a sprinkling of A-list celebrities. They would mix with the best and brightest of the social elite—three hundred of their closest friends. The paparazzi would love it.

Tall and willowy, the blonde American appeared, looking even more stunning than usual. Her effortless glamour complemented her classic WASP features, and she knew just how to show them off. Her carefully straightened hair cascaded over her bare back and shoulders onto a bright-red evening gown that revealed the seductive curves of her carefully honed bottom. The diamond necklace and bracelet Milton had bought her sparkled against her perfectly tanned skin. Abigail knew the secrets of Botox and collagen injections: just enough to deter detection, and never overused. Her pert breasts were her greatest triumph to date. This latest sculptured pair was the brainchild of her new plastic surgeon, and apparently a huge success, judging from all the admiring glances and discreet propositions she received during her usual daily routine of gym, shopping, and girly lunches (where she nibbled at salad leaves and sipped at a rarely finished glass of white wine).

"You look so ravishing, my dear," he said, kissing her proffered elegant hand. Harvey Milton III was the perfect gentleman. And the ladies loved him. "You'll be the envy of every woman tonight." He wished that he had a real sexual desire for her, but a futile attempt it would be, requiring an injection into his penis to achieve even a semi-erection. Shaking off his frustrating thoughts, he extended his hand. "Shall we go and join our friends, darling?"

The glitzy fundraising event was in full swing, with all of the fashionable society people and influential movers and shakers. The refined and well-heeled patrons were definitely A-list. Men in black tie along with the most elegant women you'd ever want to see. Milton and Abigail spent the first half-hour after they arrived greeting people with exaggerated formality. The well-known, charismatic Milton, with his wide grin and chiseled pre-War film star looks, was a living caricature of an aspiring politician. He shook hands and patted backs like someone already scavenging for votes. Luckily, there were no babies to kiss. Since most of his business dealings involved other people's money, and these were investments strictly by invitation only, he found time to chat privately with a few associates and some investors involved in his successful hedge funds that invested across a broad range of sectors. For the men, such gatherings were an extension of business. But on this occasion, Milton took the opportunity to meet with several of his oil consortium cohorts, who were keen to hear of the news from Marrakesh, and to lie a few nagging concerns to rest. Milton glad-handed his partners and placated them, telling them that an important telephone call to the oil minister was scheduled for later that night.

The evening rolled along with a distinguished lineup of celebrity speakers who were given briefs instructing them to point out certain distinguished guests as they worked the audience, with Milton's presence being acknowledged as a major coup. High-end frivolous holidays, exotic trips, dinners for two at the most exclusive restaurants, Sir Winston Churchill's cigar, autographs, and the rest, all generously donated by sponsors eager to seduce, were auctioned. If conspicuous consumption was no longer fashionable, these guests had clearly never received the message.

Nicholas Adams had heeded Dillon Rae's warnings and had taken time out to get a handle on his precarious predicament. He had agonized for hours on end with little rest until coming up with an action plan. Next on his agenda was to let Luciana know what was going on and to explain how he had ended up in such a mess. If their relationship was to have any hope at all, he owed her an explanation. A romantic evening at home might soften the blow, and he could be assured of privacy, so he got busy in the kitchen preparing supper before she arrived back from work. His cell phone vibrated and flashed, but he ignored it. Tomorrow would be soon enough to deal with the calls he knew were very important.

Nick Adams had met Luciana Cavallini at an end-of-summer party at one of the vast mansions littering the prime beachfront of Southampton. Long on looks and incredibly graceful, her seductively sensual Italian accent had set her apart from the usual Hamptons crowd. There was something intriguing about her, and the cultured new girl strangely moved Adams. Was it the way she brushed away his initial advances? *Was she playing hard to get, or just shy?* he had wondered. He knew that a woman like Luciana probably had a million guys gunning for her, but there was little evidence of any boyfriend around as he scanned the room.

While brunching at a beachside restaurant, toying with a Bloody Mary that he reckoned would help his self-inflicted raging headache, he saw her enter with some other girls. She stood out, being almost totally opposite to the more typically American girls who were making a noisy entrance, making their presence felt by everyone who was already seated. A striking beaded sarong made of mesh so sheer you could see the three metal rings on the bikini squeezing her hips enhancing her gentle, slim figure. She seemed not to have noticed him, but her exaggerated movements as she talked to her friends gave her away when she turned and glanced hypnotically over her shoulder, staring directly at Nick's table, smiled, and turned back almost at once. Nick had clocked the look. He had seen it so many times before from women. Suddenly his head cleared. He pretended to read the messages on his phone, but he couldn't help himself as he looked up and stared at the girl in the queue.

It was during a date he had engineered through a mutual friend that Adams became utterly captivated by her. He found out a lot more about the girl. She spoke five languages, had travelled extensively, and worked as a corporate attorney in Manhattan. The sharp mind her pretty head contained made him catch his breath. They had been together ever since.

That evening Adams hoped to impress Luciana with his culinary skills. So for dinner he prepared a Mediterranean bouillabaisse infused with saffron and capsicum, and six different kinds of seafood. Women love men who cook. Though most women know men do it to impress as a way to get into their knickers, and even so obviously, women never seem to mind the seduction.

Adams put a bottle of champagne on ice and dimmed the lights to reflect the dramatic Manhattan skyline seen through the large plate-glass window running the length of his living room. The finishing touch: a little music preselected for the evening from a playlist on his iPad, which he had played countless times before under the same sort of circumstances. He had lost count of the women who had been entertained in his apartment, but something about Luciana had clicked with him, leading him to start questioning his rather selfish lifestyle and wonder whether he had found someone he really wanted to be with.

With everything perfectly arranged, Adams retreated into his bathroom. The textured natural slate felt soothing under his bare feet. He placed his head under the powerful water jets and stood motionless, hoping to wash away all of the turmoil. But the events of the past few days began to crowd in, wholly absorbing his mind. Howard's murder. Kim's attack. Detective Lee's piercing, accusing, brown eyes that still bore into him. His forced resignation. And people like Kersch hovering with an axe, just waiting to deliver the coup de grace. He tried to console himself with a litany of self-deception. Giving up the futile fight to make up a clear picture of everything, he stepped out of the shower. His body was toned, with not an ounce of fat. He toweled off his wet hair vigorously.

"And Dillon Rae," he thought to himself. "What an incredible proposition had been made. It was inconceivable that a government agency could get involved in such a venture. It was like being part of a movie. What was also very disconcerting was how did he know so much about his relationship with Luciana?"

At the other end of the landing, Sharma was ready for a night out with his newly acquired boyfriend; for Ravi it was a welcome respite from all of the unpleasant recent events. Vivacious and stereotypically too pretty to be straight, Sharma never had a problem pulling whomever he wanted. That night it was two tickets to an off-Broadway show followed by them both going to his favorite gay haunt in the Village near Christopher Street. He took a final look around to make sure everything was perfect for Nick's evening, teased the flower arrangement on the hall table, and left the apartment.

The doorman buzzed to announce Luciana's arrival, and almost at once his cell phone rang in the kitchen. He didn't recognize the voice on the other end, but before he could make an inquiry Luciana was at the front door, ringing the bell. He placed the caller on hold. Luciana threw both arms around him as she entered, almost knocking him off his feet. The smile that lit up her face could lighten anyone's darkest day. Noticing the cell phone in his hand that jabbed into her ribs, she asked, "Were you on the telephone?"

"Oh, God—yes." Nick pulled free of Luciana's embrace, grabbed her overnight bag and briefcase, and led her into the living room, pointing to an open champagne bottle in the ice bucket.

"Another woman?" Luciana teased. Nick met her questioning gaze with a boyish smirk.

"Hello?" Nick cupped the phone to his ear.

"Nicholas Adams?" the stranger asked.

"Yes, speaking, sorry about that," he said, still smiling at Luciana, who kicked off her shoes and poured herself a glass of champagne. "I have a guest who just arrived."

"Guest?" Luciana shook her head. "*Merda*, girlfriend!" she cried out and turned away, pouting her lips.

"My name is Gavin Hart," he announced and took a deep drag from his cigarette. "Could we meet up for a chat tomorrow? We have a mutual friend, Dillon Rae, who suggested that we do."

"Meeting?" Adams froze. "What about?" he responded apprehensively, caught off guard by the unexpected request.

"I'll fill you in tomorrow. All I can say to you is that we may be able to help each other."

Although deeply skeptical, he reluctantly acquiesced. "Okay, how about breakfast, eight o'clock at the Lotos Club?" Adams's membership at the elegant members-only club would provide the perfect setting for a private meeting. It was one of Manhattan's most handsome private retreats, with a well-established power scene and dining facility, and being on his own territory, could offer him a degree of protection and a more level playing field.

"Lotos Club it is." Hart picked up a pen to jot down the time.

Noticing Luciana's animated gestures, Adams quickly retracted, "On second thought, make that 10:00 a.m. for a late breakfast or coffee. I have something on earlier."

"Ten will be fine," Hart said, relieved. Eight in the morning was far too early for him, no matter how important the task. "See you there."

When Hart hung up, Adams stood bewildered for a moment.

"You let me down, *tesoro*," Luciana said, pretending to sulk. "First I am a guest and then you arrange a meeting so early in the morning; I think perhaps that you are not interested in lounging in bed with me in the morning."

Nick placed the phone on the table, and stretching out his arms, pulled up from the chair and held her close to him, nearly squeezing the air from her body. Her dazzling eyes were green and amber, both colors vying for dominance, offset by her olive complexion and jet-black hair that fell loosely over her shoulders. He kissed her lips, and clasping her tightly, expertly drew her down to the sofa, their shadows thrown onto the wall behind the sofa by the flickering scented candle on the coffee table. He kissed her again. How could anyone's lips be so soft? A gentle probing, then with bold strokes against her tongue, he reached farther, deeper, trailing a line of kisses across her slightly flushed cheek and jaw and down along the nape of her neck where he brushed his tongue across the fine hairs of that beautiful neck, breathing in the intoxicating scent of Luciana.

"Let's go upstairs." His voice was strangled and low. He coughed and cleared his throat.

"What about dinner—will it spoil?" Luciana knew he made a special effort.

"It can wait." He grinned at her. "Besides, we need to work up an appetite."

Luciana slid down from the sofa onto the rug, rubbing her body close against his, the firm mounds of her breasts protruding above her tight cardigan.

"Do you need to take me upstairs?" Luciana teased, grabbing his crotch. "Hmmm, I don't think so! Bad boy!" She giggled and squeezed tighter.

Nick gave an unconvincing cry of pain. "I guess not."

By the time they were ready to eat, the couple had stirred up an insatiable appetite. Luciana devoured everything Nick placed before her. She stayed with the champagne, while Nick worked steadily through a bottle of red.

"Who was that on the phone earlier?" Luciana asked.

"God, you girls never miss a trick" he smiled, his lips stained red from the wine and the excesses of their kissing. "Who needs a backup disk when you can recall everything!" He gazed at her lovely, unblemished face and praised his God for bringing her into his life. "For your edification, it was some guy named Gavin Hart."

"The guy who does all those TV exposé shows?"

"TV?" Nick raised an eyebrow. "You know him?"

"You must have seen one of his shows. All tacky but quite brutal; no one escapes unblemished." She took a sip from a water glass. "Darling, this guy is an investigative journalist," she ran a hand through her long black hair and looked seriously at her lover. "He exposes crooks." She looked at him circumspectly. "But why would he want to meet with *you* darling?" She hesitated. "Are you involved in something?" Luciana leaned in toward him and reached for his hand.

Nick gulped down a mouthful of wine and pushed his plate away. "Let's talk," he said, standing up. "It's way overdue." He stood and took her hand and led her back into the living room. "I have got myself into something and I think I may need some help, some sort of advice."

"What sort of advice?"

"It's a really stupid story and makes me look like a real fucking loser."

"Is it to do with what happened to your friend Howard?" she asked, assuming the problem was related to Wayne's terrible death. Luciana put on her attorney's hat and listened intently, while Nick told her the story. The tale came gushing out like a personal exorcism, the whole sequence of events: starting with the $9.9 million he had made on the sale of his shares; being on the radar of the SEC; his forced resignation; how he thought that the NYPD, led by Detective Lee, was on his trail; how he could face a possible murder investigation; his conversation with Dillon

Rae; and now that night's strange call from Gavin Hart calling for a meeting.

"I had no idea that my boyfriend was so rich." She smiled at him, looking surprised at this revelation about his sale of shares. "If I had known sooner I would have succumbed to your charms much faster—even if you had been ugly!" She was teasing him, but her smile was gone.

Her face looked paler as questions started to formulate in her mind. "How did you make that money so easily when your company isn't making any money?" She tried to tread carefully, gauging his state of mind. "ABS has a great idea and no doubt will be a fantastic success, but how can it be so highly capitalized at such an early stage? After all, you are really a start-up small cap business," she spoke calmly and rationally. "Or have I got it wrong? Forgive me, my darling, but I am a cynical lawyer!"

"Look, I know how it must look, but the junior markets in the US are really one big lottery with so many hopefuls trying to make the big time. It's impossible to raise working capital for new ideas, no matter how good they may seem, and most of us have to rely on people like Kersch & Co. to raise the funds." He looked at her to see if he was making any sense. God he loved her. "Kersch and his partner Peters are pretty sleazy. You would hate them, but we didn't have any choice. I did some due diligence …"

"So did I, darling, and they are all over Google and stock blogs …"

"Yes, I know, but they did get the money, and that has got ABS to where it is, with solid partners and even a bank that trusts our software. And soon we will be able to stand up on our own and leave the promoters and maybe attract proper funding from institutions …"

"But your share price is up and down all over the place, and that must scare the shit out of you …"

"Darling, you're right. I sold some of my stock just at the right time and caught Kersch & Co. unawares because they didn't know it was me, so they had to eat the stock themselves."

"Eat the stock?"

"Yes. It means they had to buy the shares offered to keep up the share price. Otherwise there could be an investigation by the SEC if it collapsed." His words sounded hollow, and the more he spoke the more he realized just how the thin the ice he was skating on was. "They now know what I have done and want me out. Well, I have just played their game."

He sat up and took another mouthful of wine. "You know, I remember when I talked to Kersch about him losing out on the ABS shares if they fell into a hole, and I asked him what he would do. His answer was quick as a flash: He told me that if it all went tits up, he would just have to go back into a new business to make good the loss. Stupid bastard!"

"Yes, that's what all the blogs were about ..."

"I know, God help me. Fuck, I know he is scamming small investors and shorting stocks. I'm also guilty."

"How do they get investors? Christ, it's difficult enough finding them for proven businesses." Luciana almost scoffed, but it was a genuine question.

"By promotion. These guys force a company like ours to issue good news, which we put out as a press release. Then they send that to potential investors by e-mail, faxes, and cold calling in the few countries that still allow this sort of selling." He shook his head. "Naïve investors hoping to hit the next big one buy into the story. If they buy at say ten cents and it goes to twenty cents, they double their money!" He looked directly at Luciana. "Some of these investors make small fortunes, but most are caught up in pump and dump deals that leave them with nothing."

"But your share price is not a penny stock, is it? How did it get so high?"

"We made announcements particularly about our relationships with a couple of banks, which was enough to show the real promise of ABS. But now I wonder about everything."

"Nick, enough self-doubt. Things will work out, but please, darling Nick," she held out her hands, "please, please be careful. I will love you just the same with or without lots of money." She detected a slight watering in his eyes and tightened her grip on his hands.

Nick stroked her hands and leaned back. "Do you know this guy Dillon Rae?" he asked her.

"Should I?" She was truly shocked by the revelations, but strangely pleased that he felt he could open up to her. Despite being lovers, they were virtually strangers, and she had no idea where things were going, but she knew this man was more complicated than she had reckoned and could see that under the tightly controlled exterior there was a greater depth to him.

"He seems to know about you."

"That's weird," she responded. "Take my advice. Try to keep a level head and don't become too suspicious before you get all of the facts."

"They want me spy for them," he blurted out.

"They?"

"The government. Dillon Rae propositioned me in this apartment."

"The government? Dillon Rae is with the government?"

"Yes. The FBI."

"Really? You have to be joking with me. How do we know he's with the government?"

"For the moment, let's assume he is." He paused. "I have an idea: do you think you could do some checking through your firm?"

"Sure. I'll do that tomorrow." But without mentioning anything to Nick, Luciana made a mental note to ring her father, Franco, in Italy. His contacts across the globe were extraordinary. It amazed her. "No problem. Perhaps you would you also like me to join you at your meeting with Gavin Hart?" She allowed herself a smile. "I could be your attorney, your own very special legal representative."

"That's a great offer my darling, but if he's involved with Rae, I'd like to get a fix on what they really want before bringing you into this fucking mess. I don't want to piss anyone off by turning up with a lawyer." He looked deeply into her eyes. "Anyway, you would give half the Lotos Club members a heart attack if they saw you!"

"Members?" she inched toward him. "There is only one

member that matters at the moment." Nick laughed out loud and leaned in to her welcoming arms.

They chatted in between the kisses about their immediate plans and ideas, which included a possible quick trip to the Caribbean to get away from it all. But eventually the kissing took its effect, and the talking ceased, and they settled for one idea that was simple, straightforward, and without complication: bed.

On the street below a light glowed from within a nondescript late-model Ford. Parked in the shadow of a tree outside Nick's apartment building, its color was difficult to discern. The sole occupant's face lit up briefly as the lighter flared and burned the tip of a cigarette. It was his first night on duty. He flipped open a file and perused its contents. His orders were to monitor, and if necessary, protect.

# TRUMP TOWER

It was a short trip back to the apartment. After being dropped off, Milton instructed his driver to return to the Pierre Hotel and look after Abigail before clocking out. He never enjoyed spending too much time glad-handing at these charity events. It was more important that he reach Marat Esdaulet in Eastern Europe than staying till the end, so he had made a quick exit once the dinner was over. He would leave Abigail to enter some head-turning bids in the charity auction.

Untying his bowtie, Milton headed directly for his study, dialing Abigail's cell phone. Of course it didn't answer and went into voice mail. He apologized again for having left the party so soon, and left her a message that he had placed his driver at her disposal. In fact, Abigail didn't mind his early departure from the party at all. She was having a great time being entertained by many of the other guests, especially a rather smitten congressman. Milton knew there was no need to wait up for her.

Milton checked for phone messages and had received one he had been expecting. "Call me as soon as you can," the voice said. There was no salutation.

A smile, a little forced perhaps, and a feeling of alcohol-induced well-being swept through his large frame. He telephoned Esdaulet back immediately. "Marat … it's Harvey. I just received your message. Hope it's not too early in the morning for you."

"No, not at all. I've been up since five."

"You have news for me?"

"All has been agreed as planned." The voice was low, but the words were precise. "How did you make out on further commitments?"

"Very well, I must say. Actually somewhat better than

expected. I am happy to report that we have the funding for the new pipeline in place."

"Harvey, you never cease to amaze," Esdaulet said, clearly impressed.

"It's good my friend, very good indeed!"

"Tell me the details, please."

And so he did.

Nicholas Adams awoke to the smooth texture of a feathered down pillow beneath his cheek and the gray light of an autumn morning filling his bedroom. The talking clock that was supposed to make waking easier shouted in a mechanical female voice that the time was 9:30 a.m., and what the outside temperature was. "Oh, shit, I'm late!" He looked anxiously around and saw no trace of Luciana. Grabbing a robe, Adams rushed out of the bedroom, down the stairs, and almost collided with Luciana and Ravi. Luciana was preparing a breakfast tray to bring up for him.

"Well hello, Nico! I see Sleeping Beauty has decided to join the land of the living." Ravi was just too campy. He turned, coffee mug in hand, and left for his study. "Some of us have work to do. Hi, ho, hi ho, it's off to work we go …"

"Thank you Ravi, always the comedian!" Nick couldn't help laughing as Ravi stopped singing and broke into whistling the same refrain.

Fully dressed, Luciana looked every inch the very able corporate attorney that she was. "I thought you would need something to help put back some of that energy you burned off last night. *Ti amo, tesoro.*"

"I've got to be at the Lotos Club by ten." Nick's words came out in a nervous rush.

"Gavin Hart rang earlier to ask if you would mind if he made it eleven." She took a cup from the tray, filled it with coffee, and handed it to Nick. "I told him it wouldn't be a problem." She smiled. "You were sleeping so peacefully, I didn't want to wake you."

"Thanks for that. Guess I needed the extra sleep." A grin played across his lips as he remembered.

"I must go, *tesoro*, I have a ten thirty conference call. Call me after your meeting." She kissed him on the forehead and stroked his cheek. *Ciao* "

By ten thirty Nick was out the door and on his way to the Lotos Club.

Nick did not notice the man who shadowed him among the morning crowds almost to the footprint.

Gavin Hart's briefing from Dillon Rae was running behind schedule. Unofficially the two men had had several meetings over the previous days talking through Hart's offshore tax haven investigations, and now the story had taken on much wider implications. On the heels of Howard Wayne's death, Rae accelerated TRU's timetable and restructured his operation to include Hart as part of his team.

They had known each other over the years and had cautiously exchanged information that had mutual benefit, but this time, much to Hart's annoyance and irritation, it seemed he had no choice but to take orders from Rae. Hart had met Rae years before, when he worked as a freelance investigative journalist exposing corrupt government officials. Hart loved probing into the bowels of human foibles, especially if the target in question was some empty-suit politician. During the course of one of his investigations, he stumbled upon a story concerning a certain US senator, a story of greed, corruption, framing people, and possible murder—all to further that senator's ambitions. The investigation had taken Hart deep into the underbelly of American politics and economics. But the incumbent White House had needed the support of that senator and couldn't stomach another public witch hunt.

Dillon Rae had been brought in at that time to put the squeeze on him. Hart had begun receiving anonymous threats. Then the threats turned into harassment, including IRS audits relating to tax returns going back well over ten years. Rae's campaign of persuasion and intimidation had been as bad as those Hart had sought to expose. Hart finally relented; the senator had escaped investigation and lived to fight another day.

Although Hart had been forced to lay off the senator, Rae had secretly kept close tabs on the ignominious politician from that point on. When the appropriate time came, the senator was finally thrown out of the administration for a series of misdemeanors, including misappropriation of funds, alleged financial misconduct, public corruption, and sexual harassment. It was a fait accompli in Dillon Rae's typically egregious style. Hart, who had done all of the groundwork, deserved a medal, but Rae later rewarded him with only a drink.

In Rae's new campaign, however, Hart became a prodigious supplier of intelligence and informants. They compared notes and drew up charts showing ties between certain multinational entities and individuals regarding money laundering, drug trafficking, arms dealing, and other sources of great profit for the corrupt. And although some links were yet unproven, a convincing sublevel began to emerge. Dillon Rae came to the point, and Hart realized that with his help they were structuring an extraordinary entrapment plan, which was loaded with great potential liability and ramifications. Rae had pressed the *On* switch, and the timer mechanism had started to tick. There would be no stopping him in his mission.

Setting up men such as Harvey Milton III and Gerhard Liebs was a precarious and hazardous business. Milton, after all, mixed socially with the establishment and media moguls who owned a good chunk of the TV and newspaper groups Hart worked for. And Liebs, for the most part, was untouchable. In their own distinct way, the two men wielded extraordinary influence all over the world. Hart was amazed at just how close he had gotten to the real truth about the two during his past investigations after exchanging his notes with Rae. Many of Hart's investigations into corruption and financial abuse turned up a surprising number of individuals who seemed to have some connection with either

Milton or Liebs. It truly was an intriguing web of deceit and had undertones of evil.

Rae had to ask Hart to shelve his offshore exposé story for the moment, thus preventing any leaks to the media. Given this chance to break the most sensational story of his career, Hart was now only too glad to oblige.

With Hart being cooperative and agreeing to working closely with TRU, Rae was now able to cast his net wider. TRU's new geared-up operation integrated interagency cooperation with the SEC, several prime local agencies around the country, and because of the Howard Wayne connection, the NYPD.

Finally, Rae coached Hart on how best to engage Nicholas Adams's cooperation before he left for the arranged meeting at Lotos Club. He suggested that Hart use a friendly but authoritative tone, since he believed Adams would try to opt out of any commitment to assist. The two men parted, and Hart made his way to his next meeting.

Gavin Hart entered the Beaux Arts mansion at Five East Sixty-Sixth Street, just off Fifth Avenue, across from Central Park, to find Nicholas Adams standing in the grand, white-marbled entrance hall, flirting with the two receptionists anchored in their places behind a small window. It was from here that members and guests were registered, and the dress rules were enforced. The receptionists did not recognize the casually dressed Hart without his TV makeup and razzle-dazzle that came part and parcel with *The Hart Files* But Adams intervened, saying, "It's okay, he's my guest. Gavin Hart, I'm Nicholas Adams." With his accustomed smile, Adams extended a hand and Hart shook it.

"Good to meet you," Hart responded. In the palm of his hand he could feel the heat from his partially extinguished cigarette butt. "Excuse me, I need an ash tray ..."

"Oh, yes, Mr. Hart." The receptionist smiled and lifted a waste bin from behind the desk. "We didn't recognize you, sir. May we offer you a tie for your sports jacket?" Realizing he was inappropriately dressed, Hart graciously accepted the addition. "Please come this way, gentlemen." Hart took in his surroundings as he followed the receptionist, the eclectic and unusual furniture catching his eye. The two were led to the library, which was furnished with heavy leather sofas and lined with dark wooden paneling and shelves of bound and engraved books. Portraits and sculptures completed the ambience of the high-ceilinged room. Within an impressive stone fireplace set into the wooden mantelpiece surrounding it, a fire burned.

The two men sat down, ordered coffee, and looked at each other closely.

"Sorry about changing the time."

"No problem," Nick responded amicably. He noticed that Hart was forever rubbing his hand through his spiky orange hair and drumming his fingers on any flat surface, rather a force of habit rather than being uneasy.

They sat at a table alongside a painting by James Montgomery Flagg, a former member. An hour went by; the coffee and mineral water was replenished several times. Appreciating that Nick was understandably shaken, Hart excused himself to give Adams some space and time to take stock before he closed in for the kill. He took the corridor down to the men's room.

Adams now realized what a snake pit he had fallen into when he met Erich Kersch and Dale Peters two years earlier; and now having taken stock of his situation, he concluded he should have chosen bankruptcy as the preferable alternative. But whatever had happened he also knew that without Kersch & Co., he wouldn't have millions sitting safely in Switzerland. And his shareholders, who had been duped into buying grossly overvalued Adams Banking Solutions stock, were now about to buy a whole lot more from the pump and dump pair of shysters. His conscience had never been challenged until now; he had rationally convinced himself that although he was moderately rich, he deserved to be. After all, his company would soon justify the means to the end and be very successful, and he could leave this particular distasteful part of his life behind.

Gavin Hart had made it quite clear as to how dire Adams's situation was, pointing out that that as an American, having undeclared funds over ten thousand dollars outside the US was a criminal matter, and that he knew just how much he had sequestered away. It was his job to find these things out. To make matters worse, Adams was now being asked by Hart to go along with everything Erich Kersch had demanded of him recently and not create any more waves. Nick leaned forward, put his head in his hands and groaned, without realizing the attention he was drawing to himself. An older member seated at the next table looked up, mildly irritated.

When Gavin Hart returned he said, "So, my friend." He sat down, poured more coffee, and leaned forward toward the visibly shaken younger man. "You know where we stand, and we need your help," he whispered. "We actually demand your cooperation and will not entertain any negativity from you." He paused and added, "What we want is a mole."

"What you mean is that I should spy on the Kersch crowd? Oh, good," Nick said in mock relief. "I thought it might have warranted something really difficult." He sounded cynical.

"As you wish," Hart responded. "Nick, you must understand how important this is. You've been dragged unintentionally into the treacherous web of one of the world's nastiest offshore conglomerates. We know where the two main spiders are lurking, and we must exterminate them. And joined at the hip with those tax-dodging culprits are a ring of drug barons, arms dealers, warlords, fraudsters, and murderers. The illegal earnings and tax evasion run into billions." Hart felt genuinely sorry for Adams. And it would have been naïve of him to expect Adams to agree wholeheartedly with his extraordinary proposition and jump in without a fight. "We need an insider with your particular skills, and we don't have the luxury of time on our side."

"Look … I'm just a guy who got lucky."

"Oh, yeah, on other people's money."

"Caveat emptor."

"Damn the *buyer beware* crap. You people make me sick to my stomach." Hart leaned in toward Adams. "Don't you get it? Kersch & Co. has screwed you, your company, and its shareholders. For fuck's sake, they cleared more than twenty times what your company made in working capital. That's one hell of a brokerage fee." He looked at Adams squarely. "You knew all of this. Don't kid a kidder. You found out about how they made their money; then you recoup some of what you feel they owe you by selling your shares behind your own employees' backs." Hart's eyes bore into Adams. "That, along with your conveniently already-established offshore accounts, makes you fucking guilty too." Hart took it home: "And, as I have told you, a number of parties at the SEC, IRS, and FBI already have the heads-up on you. So if you don't play ball with us, you stand to lose everything. End of story."

"Fuck you." Adams leaped to his feet. "How do you get off? Why don't you go find someone else to do your dirty work?"

The man at the next table almost choked, and then exaggeratedly shuffled the broad sheets of the *New York Times,* pretending not to notice the dispute.

"Look, Nick," Hart said, "the mind is like a parachute. It works much better when it's open. Come on, sit down." He smiled reassuringly at Adams. "We're on the same team, you know. What do you say?" He pushed his coffee cup away and laid his hands flat on the tabletop. "If you cooperate, you will be bullet proof and can walk away to enjoy all of your money."

"You have to admit it's all a bit overwhelming and confusing." Adams sat down, but he still didn't want any part in the scheme. "I'll have to sleep on it. Sorry, that's the best I can do."

"Forty-eight hours okay?" Hart asked.

"I have a funeral to go to that day. Howard Wayne's." He saw Hart nod sympathetically. "How about Friday?"

"Almost forgot about Howard's funeral. Guess I'll be seeing you there." Hart wouldn't dream of not paying his last respects to his one-time adversary.

"That's right; I forgot you were sort of rivals. You would know him, wouldn't you?"

"Howard and I go way back. He was an old friend. Sure, we fought on the same turf, but we kept our distance. Sometimes we shared information, but he was much more old school than me." Hart's lips peeled back in a wolfish smile. "Don't make it any later than Friday. We're on a very tight schedule. You know who I report to and ultimately who he's accountable to."

"Yeah, yeah," Adams sneered, "all very mysterious." He was deeply unhappy, and his mannerisms betrayed his uneasiness. Hart knew he had unnerved the young entrepreneur.

"Of course," Hart continued, "you should go about your business as usual. Pretend you don't know anything." His comradely tone suggested how relieved he was to be finally getting through to Nick. "Remember, you have to make up with Erich Kersch as soon as possible, mend your differences, and start working closely with the team at Adams Banking Solutions again. I should also tell you that money is no object. We will cover whatever you need." Hart continued without waiting for a response. "And a word of advice from someone who's been operating in the thick of it for some time: always look after numero uno."

Adams pushed past his trepidations and concentrated on the positive ramifications of the proposition. To begin with, he stood to make several million more from the fifty-fifty resignation deal. With that and his cash in Switzerland, it was possible to bail out from under Kersch & Co. for good. He'd pay owed taxes on the shares in his name, since it would get the IRS off his back, and preserve Zen Holdings as is, which was already fenced off and fire-proofed by his advisors in Zurich. And if Adams Banking Solutions found itself stuck deep in the mire, only Kersch and his crew would get the blame because Rae had promised him indemnity. But the notion of being Rae's mole to bring down Kersch & Co. scared the living hell out of him. All he could see were two eighteen-wheelers bearing down on each other at breakneck speed, and he was standing hapless in the middle of the road between them. He would be crushed to a bloody pulp.

The FBI wanted him to use his software and finance skills to come up with what was clearly the ultimate sting. It was ingenious. It was a dangerous plan in which, if Nick understood it correctly, the ultimate loser would be Gerhard Liebs and all of those that serviced this evil and troubled banker. Nick signed the bill. They left the library, made their way through the club and out onto the sidewalk in silence, walked the short distance to Fifth Avenue, shook hands warily, and parted company.

An uneasy alliance between the two had begun. But Adams was determined to work to his own timetable and would not be coerced into any crazy life-changing scheme unless he was completely sure it would work.

He would, however, test the waters with Kersch and see if there was actually any chance of mending fences. The dice had been thrown, so Adams had to seem to be cooperating for the moment, where necessary, for the sake of immediate collateral damage control.

Adams walked the nine blocks to the ABS offices. He had nearly reached his destination when his cell phone rang. It was Luciana, agitated. Breathlessly and clearly upset, she told him that she had put out inquiries on Dillon Rae, using nearly every contact she had, and had just received an irate phone call from the very man himself asking why she was checking him out. It must be a matter of some urgency, he told her, to put her through so much trouble. Although he delivered his point in a cool, even tone, she didn't underestimate the threat behind it.

"What did you say?" Nick asked anxiously, straining to hear her above the traffic noise.

"I lied," Luciana said, composing herself. "Maybe unconvincingly, but I told him that you had lost his business card and asked me to find his number."

"Ingenious. What a gifted liar. I'll have to watch myself with you." Nick laughed but felt distinctly unsettled. "How did you leave it?"

"He gave me his number and told me that I should stop causing any more inconveniences." Luciana went silent.

"You still there?" Nick thought he had lost the connection.

"He made me feel really uneasy. Who the hell is this guy?"

"Trouble." Nick Adams murmured inaudibly. A fire truck went by, sounding its deep bullhorn, adding to the difficulty of hearing her. "It's okay, I can deal with him."

"Okay," she replied, but she trailed off. "On a brighter note, I've e-mailed you flight details for Antigua, darling." Her mood quickly changed and her voice became less strained. "It's going to be wonderful. I can't wait."

SUPPING WITH THE DEVIL

"Sounds good."

"You could try sounding a little more excited."

"Sorry, darling, I was lost in thought for a moment. I'll take care of the arrangements today, promise. Listen, I'll catch you later." He entered the lobby of his building smiling at the receptionist. "I'm about to get into the elevator." Adams banked on getting out on Friday regardless of what they expected of him. It would give him time to think, far away from the clutches of Rae and Hart. They would just have to wait. Their dastardly plan would be put on hold. It would just be a temporary delay.

A car pulled into a space outside Adams's office building. The 24/7 surveillance on the target continued. Inside, the driver took off his headphones before typing into a log on the government-issued laptop. Within moments his bosses would know about the Antigua weekend.

# BERMUDA

Gehard Liebs had flown back to Bermuda from Zurich. He was tired and irritable, despite having flown there in his private jet.

Curious locals in sailboats and motorboats floated around the *Cerise* to get a look at the megayacht moored just outside Hamilton Harbor. But three manned Rigid Inflatable Boats, one complete with a centerline-mounted helm station, patrolled within a hundred yards of the yacht to fend off any boat that got too near. Half an hour earlier, divers had carried out their painstaking routine survey of the hull, with the aid of underwater cameras, to identify anything attached to the underside, forever reminded by their boss about being particularly diligent, given the latest tiny explosive devices on the market, and of his being a target of those that he had double-crossed.

The Italian-built yacht was originally built for an Arab sheikh, with the facilities of a five-star hotel, but Liebs had the vessel completely renovated in Malta. His floating fortress was equipped with a garage for several water and land vehicles, a helipad, and helicopter hangars for quick getaways, a submarine garage integrated into the hull, highly sophisticated security, and underwater-surveillance systems. The yacht also carried anti-missile devices and an armaments room of weapons, including small machine pistols and sonic Air Zulu weapons capable of deterring the pirates of Somalia and the Caribbean. *Cerise*'s living quarters were protected by bulletproof glass, and meeting rooms were equipped with white noise emitters to disrupt undetected bugging. The yacht was opulent to the point of indecency, with eighteen staterooms, a massage room and gym, a twenty-four-seat movie theater with reclining couches, a wine cellar, an indoor pool, and a deck that hydraulically extended over the water. With a permanent crew of thirty-three, including a helicopter pilot,

Liebs's every demand on board was met, and every whim catered for. Even the oligarchs famed for their megayachts were in awe of this Swiss banker.

In his lavish suite spread over two decks, Liebs sat plagued by visions of himself as some circus performer spinning plates on spindly wire poles. He had spent the last two decades building the largest private secretive financial conglomerate in the world, but the very foundations were becoming unstable due to global financial problems and disappearing tax havens. While playing the volatile international markets; plugging holes; and managing precipitous activities in a game where blackmail could backfire at any time, any one of his plates could crash to the ground he stood on, causing a catastrophic collapse.

Grim reports filtering in from the field suggested that authorities were achieving considerable success at cracking down on some of his more lucrative trades. His high-speed boats that chartered courses from Colombia en route to Miami by way of Turks and Caicos usually fanned out in different directions to confuse predatory drug-enforcement agents. But their detection rate was on the rise, causing enormous losses to Liebs and his credibility with his associates. Drug barons in Bogotá had expressed concern over the situation and threatened to return to dealing with historical partners such as the Mafia. There were also reports that delegates purporting to work for Harvey Milton had been seen at meetings in some of the fortified haciendas in the Colombian hills. Although it was Liebs who had encroached on Milton's drug business and inflicted considerable damage, his efforts didn't seem to have had any effect on Milton's preexisting relationships. Clearly the Columbians were playing them both against each other. It was business after all. No emotion.

By Liebs's calculations, Milton controlled a great many businesses, most of which were out of the public domain. Milton was almost as secretive as himself. He also learned that Milton's businesses were not only growing at a far greater pace than his own, but they seemed less highly leveraged. Liebs was in need of a lot more "loyal" allies to pull off the scores of deals he had in the pipeline—deals he needed to complete to avert the hemorrhaging of his capital reserves.

He reflected on the days when he could use information on Milton's sexual appetites to control him. But now, no matter what he did, Milton fought the coercion. A few deals even had to be scrapped due to Milton's lack of cooperation. Then, certain sources in high places told Liebs that Milton had recently launched an investigation on him, warts and all; and for the first time in his life the puppet master felt threatened.

As the plates spun, his annoyance festered. His nefarious naked short selling schemes that flooded markets with nonexistent stock drove down share prices on his carefully targeted companies, only to maneuver takeovers and acquisitions on the cheap. Legislated against by US authorities and banned entirely by multiple governments in Europe, the illegal practice of short selling shares normally allows traders to borrow a stock, or determine that it can be borrowed, before they sell it short. Liebs was a past master due to the various loopholes in the rules, and discrepancies between paper and electronic trading systems. His ability to naked short sell continued, but it was getting much harder, so the naked shorting route was not to be relied upon anymore. The hedge funds he controlled were not to be such a massive source of capital.

Even moving cash around proved more difficult with each passing day. Electronic banking systems were not infallible; large sums were always questioned by regulatory authorities, even in most of the tax havens; and the US government was increasing its surveillance on accounts suspected of money laundering and racketeering.

Liebs's *bureau de change* and global electronic payments-processing empire, once a stable bridgehead, was also facing scrutiny from authorities, placing his licensing at risk. The messy Euro currency handling, his *bureau de change*'s stock in trade, offered less cover than it had previously enjoyed from its illicit activities. Since an organization took longer to recover from losing cash than intercepting actual drugs, authorities had begun confiscating cash from known currency exchange networks.

Certain questions the US, EU, and Australia were asking led him to believe he had a whistle-blower in his network, and Liebs was not about to let his empire be at the mercy of an imbecile. He would be found and then Vinogradov would receive another task.

As more damning reports had come in on other possible traitors, assignments were being dispatched to the already overworked Valentina Vinogradov. Liebs's light-starved fingers tapped a speed dial code to arrange a sizeable wire transfer just to oil the wheels for what could be Vinogradov's busiest time yet. He needed her confidence now more than at any other time in their long and bloody relationship.

# NEW YORK

Nicholas Adams strode out of the elevator to find the loathsome Erich Kersch in the ABS reception area, engaged in an excessively loud and animated conversation. Kersch was half-sitting on the arm of a sofa with a cell phone parked on his ear, the mouthpiece of which was suffering an onslaught of spittle and decibels, when in mid-sentence he spotted Adams from the corner of his eye. The look on his face was one of genuine surprise. "Hold on." He almost spat into the cell phone. "What the fuck are you doing here?" The hairs on the back of his neck prickled, and he wrapped up his conversation and cut the connection. "Are you deliberately provoking me?" He had stood up but was considerably shorter than Nick, which annoyed him even more. "You've got ten minutes to do what you have to do and then you leave this building, or our deal is off and we'll leave it to the lawyers."

Birdie, who appeared carrying a file, stopped dead in her tracks when she saw the two adversaries. Without saying a word, she proceeded toward reception and waited quietly, not knowing what to expect, stunned by Nick's presence. An awkward silence permeated the room. There was no sudden hush or collective whisper. With the exception of telephones ringing down the hall, the office was peacefully quiet.

Adams felt anxious. He took a deep breath and faced his foe.

"Eric, I have come to apologize. I have been out of order." He tried grinning, but his face contorted fighting the hatred he had of this odious little man. "Can we shake on it?"

"Well, well!" Kersch seemed to change his mood almost at once. He became curiously friendly and in a far better mood. He

140

moved forward and placed his hand on Adams's shoulder as if they were old friends, and led him to his old office.

"Sorry to hear about your friend Howard Wayne. How are you holding up?"

"It's been a shock." He cursed Rae and Hart. All he wanted to do was head-butt the bastard. Now he was playing a role he doubted he could perform.

Birdie was more than slightly intrigued. She had never seen Kersch that courteous toward Adams. Was it a prelude to another potential blow-up? There was something strange about Kersch today, but she couldn't quite put her finger on it. Nick felt Birdie's eyes burning holes in his back as he walked away, sharing pleasantries with his avowed enemy.

The sunlit office was motionless, the air still. Everything in Nick's office lay untouched since his forced resignation. His desk chair remained facing the window, a pen lying on a stack of work orders ready to be used. His door locks hadn't been changed, nor were his personal belongings packed up in boxes. How very uncharacteristic of Kersch. Perhaps they had had a change of heart after all.

Kersch smugly walked over to Nick's desk and deliberately sat down in his chair. Ignoring the affront, Adams sat down on the adjacent sofa. He refused to give Kersch the satisfaction of sitting in one of the visitor's chairs that fronted his own desk.

"How's it feel to be even richer, Nick?" Kersch said, grinning and spinning from side to side, relishing the discomfiture of the handsome man sitting down in front of him.

"Richer?" Was he being sarcastic?

"Of course. You will have amassed a nice little nest egg once we sell your shares. I'm told sufficient buyers in Europe and the Far East are all lined up." With hands folded, Kersch leaned back and gazed at Adams from beneath his heavy eyelids, a cunning smile crossing his face. "We're getting a press release out, and then we'll start a promotion to sell your shares." He nodded slowly and grinned. It was out of character. "Pretty good feeling, eh?"

Adams regarded the insincere grin as something that came

with a painful price. Kersch was about to do a pump and dump promotion. "Sure … sounds great, thanks."

"By the way, Nick," Kersch seemed relatively nonchalant considering the news he had to impart, "the fucking goons from the SEC have been on the phone. They're asking questions." He raised his eyebrows in mock shock.

"Questions?" Adams's breath quickened, but he resisted the urge to respond harshly.

"You know, just a few bureaucratic clerical questions. Nothing we need to worry about right now." Kersch folded his hands behind his head. "Maybe you could contact them, talk to them as president and tell them everything is progressing according to plan." He took his pudgy white hands off the desk, leaving a damp patch that dried almost at once, and gesticulated toward Adams. "Tell them that development and expansion targets are on track, performance-management systems are in place, and that shareholders are supporting your new business model." Kersch cut off an incoming call and continued his instructions, for that is what he was issuing. "But I don't think it's a good idea to mention you've resigned. There will be time later to issue such a press release."

He felt sick. Recalling what Hart had said about the FBI wanting him to play along with Kersch, Adams agreed. "Okay, whatever you say. But they'll find out when my stock is sold."

"We can cover that by not clearing the share certificates into shares that trade electronically for a while. See, we've thought of everything. Nothing will be seen by these fuckwits!"

Adams simply shrugged his shoulders.

"Another thing, Nick … I want you to convince Ravi that you and I are now friends again. Even though he's been relegated to the backwaters of your apartment, he's a valued member of the team here, and I don't want him bailing out on us while the new applications and interfaces are still in development. Can you do that, buddy?"

Then Adams realized why Kersch was being so nice. *Perfect*, he thought. *Kersch had just played right into the hands of the FBI.*

Nick would just go along for the ride with Rae and Hart, but in his own time.

Adams spent the whole day at Adams Banking Solutions meeting with people and sorting out his affairs. Everyone, including Kersch, seemed more solicitous than usual. Maybe being ousted was a blessing in disguise. Actually, he wasn't bothered at all by his prospects; he had the money and wherewithal to start over again if he had to, with or without the shares about to be placed through Kersch & Co.

Back in the safety of his soon-to-be-relinquished corner office, he retreated behind closed doors, mulling over the brief laid down by the FBI. Although he was convinced that what they were proposing was totally unworkable, he felt strangely inspired by the plot and decided to take a stab at it. He began to sketch several diagrams on a yellow legal pad. He wasn't concerned about anyone entering while he worked. The awkwardness around the office was enough to keep everyone away.

As he toiled, ideas began to take shape. He discovered that given certain precise conditions, it might be possible to carry out the plot after all. With Sharma's help they could create a program that would make the extraordinary plan, which was tantamount to vacuuming or siphoning vast amounts of cash out of many different accounts, potentially viable. But persuading Sharma to jump onboard, and soliciting cooperation from a number of other players were different issues. He doubted whether they were likely to be party to such a scheme. Clearly they would question their own positions and survival in its aftermath.

Satisfied with his preliminary calculations, Adams decided to call it a day and pick up again when he returned from his trip to Antigua. He placed his work in his office safe and keyed in his secure code. Slamming the door with a metallic clunk, he retrieved his jacket, and after a cursory inspection of his office, he left.

Dillon Rae retrieved the latest transmission reports of the cellphone conversations over the last twenty-four-hour surveillance while in his Washington office. His anger flared as he learned of

Adams's defiance. Furious, he immediately initiated measures to halt the Antigua trip.

A speed dial button patched him through to an office in New York.

"Yes," the voice answered, crisp with impatience.

"Dillon here."

"What's up? Anything new?"

"Our bird might fly on Friday," Rae said, exasperated, "and we need to clip his wings."

"Okay, how much clipping?"

"Until it hurts. Do the usual things. Now."

"Got it."

"I'll leave it with you. Don't fuck up!" Rae hung up.

# GENEVA

The helicopter started. The blades slowly rotated and started to beat the air. The morning sun glinted off the aircraft fuselage.

With the potential blip in his plan miraculously gone, Dale Peters couldn't believe his luck. This share-pushing maverick had just completed the biggest coup of his life. It was a very significant transaction, and he was thrilled to the point of hyperventilating. Not only had his side deal with the oil minister gone off without a hitch, it had worked out far better than even he could ever have envisaged.

Peters had secretly created and intermittently channeled Kersch & Co. cash into a private slush fund for several years. The small amounts skimmed off stock transaction funds were such that discrepancies in share sell prices would be unnoticeable. Every time a trade had been done he conducted a private kickback deal with the traders. His mad money, as he called it, had grown to a substantial figure. Buried deep within the labyrinth of overseas accounts, the trail was so convoluted that it would take a rocket scientist to uncover it, least of all Liebs. No forensic teams would be able to uncover the trail of deceit. He had transferred proceeds from the slush fund to purchase an oil field under the ownership of a separate shell company he owned through an offshore entity. The oil field would now become an asset owned by him and him alone. To hell with Liebs and Kersch. He owed them nothing.

To sever the Liebs connection, Peters sent a message informing Liebs that the oil deal was off, that Marat Esdaulet had decided to sell to another party. Since Esdaulet's fees were to be handled under a separate cover, Peters planned to deliver Esdaulet's finder's fee personally in cash, to avoid any wire transfer and delivery trails.

It was time to get the show on the road. He stood on the tarmac beside the helicopter near the storage compartment, stooping and bracing himself against the downdraft from the swirling blades. Casting a surreptitious glance behind him, he carefully examined the two Zero Halliburton attaché cases, which earlier had been filled to capacity by his Geneva bank with US dollars in the highest denomination bills. The impenetrable aluminum cases, equipped with drawbolt latches, ensured that no interloper could gain access to the contents within. He took time securing his precious cargo within the luggage compartment. These cases were his ticket to freedom from the tentacles of Gerhard Liebs.

For the first time, Peters knew he had outsmarted Liebs. He knew when he first had the idea that his plan was insane, but the tall Dutchman was closer to Liebs than anyone on the team. Peters wasn't completely imprudent. He was well aware that Liebs kept him near only because Liebs kept an eye out for anyone who might try to steal control of his lucrative share-pushing business. And as far as Peters was concerned, his alliance with Liebs was purely an affair of expediency; it was his route to the billionaire caste that Liebs belonged to and which Peters aspired to. It was simply a case of the robbers robbing each other. It was Liebs who had taught Peters how to be a complete bastard with no emotional feelings whatsoever. This time Peters had had to outthink his tutor, make off with all the money, and then blame the oil minister for reneging on their deal. Peters had always vowed to beat Liebs at his own game, and the oil deal had presented him with the perfect opportunity.

Peters stepped aboard the rotorcraft Jet Ranger helicopter and sat comfortably on plush cream leather seats, brushing his oily black hair back into some sort of shape with both hands. Abandoning the task, he took out a comb and ran it through his hair. The pilot prepared to lift off. Flipping a few switches on the ceiling-mounted console, he slowly lifted the powerful helicopter above the ground, hovered, and waited for clearance. They were headed to a destination chosen by Esdaulet, where the money would be handed over.

As the helicopter swayed slowly, hovering a few feet above the helipad, a female engineer wearing a baseball cap quickly slipped alongside its frame. Crouching, she released a panel latch to reveal the luggage compartment containing the two cases. The two men on board did not notice as she removed each case and dropped them onto the tarmac below. Neither did they notice the small package that replaced them. She closed the compartment door, and crouching, backed away from the helicopter. At that moment her baseball cap blew off and struck the window by Peters before tumbling away across to the grass verge nearby. Peters turned and saw the cap and made a sideways glimpse out the window. He saw the girl, her blonde hair being blown over her face, and saw his two cases beside her on the ground.

"What the fuck!" Peters screamed out. The helicopter engine was far too loud for the pilot to hear. He increased the power and lifted the helicopter higher, continuing to climb, and turned into the wind. He couldn't possibly have heard Peters screaming. Even when Peters grabbed him, clawing at his back, the pilot still couldn't understand the reason for the commotion. The helicopter rose higher and higher toward the mountains above the airport.

Suddenly a deafening blast was heard over the low hills below the mountains overlooking Geneva. The mysterious explosion rattled the windows of the farmhouses on the Alps below. The fireball increased in size, then flattened at the end of its trajectory, whittling into a fiery trail. Soon a black plume of smoke formed at the crash site, and streamers of fragmented material fanned out, scattering metal debris and body parts across the ground.

The Swiss rescuers found two bodies, too badly charred to be identified immediately. A call to the Geneva police who checked the flight plan and tail registration number of the helicopter soon provided the names of the disaster victims. There was not much to go on, and the investigation would no doubt be lengthy. There were few witnesses. The police investigators did not rule out the possibility of foul play, but it was too soon to say with any confidence.

Liebs glanced at his watch. It was over. A flicker of a smile creased the Swiss banker's colorless lips. He was sitting in the lavish main salon of his yacht. Millions of dollars in cash were no doubt already en route from Geneva to Zurich by train and would soon be safely stashed in the vault of Bank Schreiber Liebs. Peters was now added to Liebs's trophies of war. No one could double-cross him without expecting total retribution. He did not feel a flicker of remorse for the hapless helicopter pilot.

As for Erich Kersch, the Swiss banker mused, as a shaft of bright light moved across his gaunt face shining through the cabin window as the *Cerise* moved at anchor, he would know what had happened soon enough. Kersch had certainly lost the plot. How the American could have gone along with Peters's absurd plan to rip him off was beyond Liebs's comprehension. Evidently a share of one billion dollars hadn't been a sufficient incentive for these idiots. Peters had been dealt with like all troublemakers: punished in a way to remind all others of his powers.

# CENTRAL PARK, NEW YORK

Central Park was now the chosen location for a clandestine early-morning gathering. Fortuitously for those invited, the weather was on their side. The low sun had slowly eased the chill from the air as it cast long shadows across pathways and the green spaces. They had arranged to meet on the eastern edge of Park at the steps of the Metropolitan Museum of Art. The crowds of residents and tourists assembling in front of the neoclassical facade waiting for the Met to open would deflect attention away from the group of men.

Gavin Hart stood leaning against a tall column, listening to Dillon Rae with a growing sense of apprehension. "Are you sure about that, Dillon?" Hart massaged his eyes to wipe away his early-morning fatigue. It was cold enough to make his eyes water, and he constantly dabbed his cheeks with a handkerchief.

"Yes. We've got to play it that way." Dillon Rae talked quietly. "No need for their direct involvement until everything's in place. We're proceeding on a need-to-know basis. We'll let the NYPD in on the full deal nearer to the time of implementation—but not today. When's your meeting with Harvey Milton?"

"Friday afternoon."

"I trust you didn't run across any obstacles getting in to see him. I put in a few calls to pave the way." A tight grin gleamed from the corners of Rae's mouth. "But remember: Milton has powerful friends in Washington, so it's important you exercise caution."

"No worries, I've got it covered," Hart said, raising his hands. "I get it! I've been dealing with guys like him for a very long time. It's the function of my profession."

"I know that," Rae growled. "Don't forget: show him the money. He'll never refuse that incentive."

"This is going to be one hell of a deal for him. How could he possibly pass it up?"

"Let's hope he doesn't." Dillon Rae moved closer and looked him straight in the eyes. "For all our sakes."

The two men spotted Detective Lloyd Lee hurrying toward them and descended the museum steps to meet him. Lee and Hart shook hands. Rae greeted Lee and led the two men into the park. They walked down a path that ran alongside Fifth Avenue, and then turned right onto another path just before Seventy-Ninth Street. Rae paid for coffees at a vending kiosk and did most of the talking while they walked deeper into the park. Fifteen minutes later they reached Turtle Pond, at the base of Belvedere Castle, and claimed a bench facing the water. Hart and Lee sat while Rae remained standing and resumed holding court.

"And I'm pretty certain we'll have everyone we need on board to see it through. That includes both the bait and our target." Rae gathered the coffee containers and placed them in a nearby trash bin.

Questions shot out like darts from the two men, which Rae expertly handled with wit and efficacy. Rae's cell phone rang, and he motioned to Hart to take over as he stepped away to take the call.

"To be honest with you, Lloyd, it's not exactly clear to me what's specifically required of you at the moment, but it's obvious that your assistance is vital."

"I don't know, man," Lee said. "I'm getting an ugly feeling in my gut. How can you expect my department to be party to a deal that might lose us our jobs?" He looked into the distance and looked thoughtful. "The end of your career is what a person is usually judged on, you know. And Rae is asking me to put my neck on the line." Lee stood up and looked toward Dillon Rae, who was lost in conversation on his cell phone. "How well do you know this dude Rae?"

"Known him for about as long as I've known you. Frankly, I have nothing to lose," Hart said nonchalantly. "And at the end of the day, no matter how you look at it, we win." He craved for a cigarette.

Rae finished his call and walked back to join them.

"What if we say no?" Lee questioned, addressing Rae squarely. Lee was never keen on interference from another government agency and didn't want the FBI's agenda overshadowing his case. He shifted his weight from one foot to another, swaying like a boxer ready to pounce.

Rae's eyes narrowed as he moved in close to Lee. In a lowered voice, he said, "You don't want to play ball with me, Lloyd?" He stabbed at Lee's chest with his finger. "Aren't you planning on retiring soon? Well, how about if I get your pension revoked and put you to work for five more years? Maybe on traffic duties?" There were times when Rae appreciated having federal weight to throw around.

"I don't believe this shit, man!" Lloyd Lee stepped back away from Rae. "Wow! You mean to tell me you have that much clout?" There was a long, awkward pause as Lee stared at Rae in disbelief. Then he shook his head warily and added, "Well, if I have to put my ass on the line for you, I need to be pretty damned sure you can pull this thing off."

"You better believe I can." Dillon Rae said with some authority. "Cooperate and we'll all do well."

In twenty minutes, the party broke up. Rae realized he was running late for his meeting with Ravi Sharma, shook hands with two other men, and took the path for East Seventy-Ninth Street at a fast pace. Gavin Hart and Lloyd Lee took a different path, deep in conversation.

"So, what's the deal, man?" Lloyd said, agitated. "If our intelligence information isn't up to snuff, he'll start flexing his muscles. Then what do we do?"

"We're between the Devil and the deep blue sea. What can I say?"

"We're screwed, man."

"Have faith. It can be pulled off, my friend."

Hart parted with the detective when they reached Fifth Avenue and hailed a cab. Lee hurried to a waiting unmarked police car. They both had a funeral to attend.

Since her husband's death, Kim Wayne had spent days in a blurred haze, besieged by random relatives, old friends, flower bouquets, condolence cards, and phone calls. She had used a couple of social networking sites to inform all the people she knew of her husband's death. But the story of Howard Wayne's possible homicide had taken on a life of its own and passed from blogs to Twitter and e-mails, circulating a story that Wayne had been silenced by powerful financiers who have everything to lose if the story he was working on were published.

Information had somehow leaked out erroneously naming companies Wayne had been investigating. The named firms protested their involvement, but their stocks still plummeted. Broadcast interviews were saturated with denials, and there was a free-for-all of pointing fingers and naming names. Other unscrupulous firms saw an opportunity and had begun condemning their competitors. The frenzy had escalated to the point where the authorities were forced to intervene, squelching the unfounded rumors, condemning them as ill-informed hearsay.

The NYPD confirmed that their investigations were ongoing and not guided by the rumor mill but by actual facts. They had had to come clean in admitting that they were also getting closer to identifying the real culprits involved, none of whom were listed among the names circulating. Fortunately, much of the delirium had died down when they were ready to lay Howard Wayne to rest.

Kim left her apartment arm-in-arm with her brother for a day fated to be the most difficult she would ever face. Dressed in a black suit, with a veil set high on a short-brimmed hat, she stopped for a moment to speak with the doorman.

"All the best, Mrs. W." His voice was kind and sincere. "I'm sorry I can't be there to pay my respects to Mr. W. He was very good to me."

Kim Wayne cupped his right hand in hers and squeezed tight. "He thought the world of you. Thank you."

The trusted doorman escorted them to the waiting black Mercedes limo. Kim's brother bundled a few bills into the doorman's hand, but the man declined the offer, shaking his head sadly at Wayne's memory. Her brother grabbed his arm in respect and entered the vehicle behind Kim. The driver shut the door firmly and made himself comfortable behind the wheel for what would be a very long, harrowing day. He pulled out into traffic and headed for St. Bartholomew's Episcopal Church.

Nicholas Adams had a tough time sleeping through the night. He tossed and turned for hours, but could find no rest. Each time he awoke, everything came rushing back. When he managed to fall asleep, it was not for very long.

Luciana had spent the night, and took the morning off to accompany Nick to the funeral. Wearing dark suits, they left the apartment and made their way in Nick's BMW to the funeral service.

As they wove through Manhattan's angry, stressed traffic, Luciana took several calls. The one in Italian was from her father in Pisa. Nick didn't understand a word of the conversation; besides, he was lost in his own thoughts.

They had been dating only a short while when talk of meeting her father started. It wasn't as if he minded. Meeting the parents of a girlfriend when you were in a serious relationship was probably a necessary milestone, but Nick Adams had never had any long-term liaisons. He knew Luciana and her father had a close relationship, and phone calls between New York and a myriad of places in Italy were many, but the thought of meeting her father when he was under so much pressure was not something Adams was ready to embrace with open arms. Besides, from the sound of it, Franco Cavallini seemed rather an imposing character. And with the likes of Rae, Hart, and Detective Lee, he already had to deal with more belligerencies than he could handle. They parked a block away in one of the small off-street lots. The man tailing the couple in his Ford slowed and parked across from the church in front of an office building.

Mourners in small groups gathered as they recognized familiar faces. The previous evening's papers had been filled with articles about the murder investigation being orchestrated by the NYPD. News that investigators might have a lead on possible suspects made the day a little easier for everyone. Much gossip and many wild theories were exchanged.

St. Bartholomew's Episcopal Church is one of Manhattan's grand landmarks. The elegant church, with its Byzantine interior and complex tapestry of brick and stone, is also renowned for its choir and the largest pipe organ in New York. It was the perfect choice for a grand send-off for a man admired by so many of his peer group.

Traffic arteries around the church were clogged as the mourners were dropped off as near to the entrance as possible. Two US military buses pulled up and discharged Marines in full ceremonial uniforms. Wayne had been a hero, having served with some distinction in the first Gulf War. One Marine officer and six enlisted men emerged carrying rifles, which they held close to their bodies.

Parked away from the flock of mourners, Detective Lloyd Lee left his unmarked car and proceeded to the packed church. He and a few of his staff had turned up to monitor some of the mourners, including Nicholas Adams. They took seats toward the rear of the church.

The enormous building had drawn a near-capacity crowd. When the main doors opened, the buzz of conversation in the pews hushed as the priest followed by the pallbearers carrying the casket entered. Kim Wayne followed with a small entourage of family, a lace handkerchief dabbing at her red eyes. She was shown to her pew at the front, where she sat through the torment of her husband's funeral, oblivious of the mourners to her side and stretching to the back of the church.

Luciana squeezed Nick's arm each time the choir sang. Although she had never met Wayne, the emotion of the funeral affected her just the same.

There were many addresses and readings. Howard Wayne's retired commanding officer gave a powerful delivery without the aid of any form of notes. Leaning on an ornate brass Bible stand, the former soldier reminisced at length about their Desert Storm exploits. In the silence between his sentences a few sobs echoed around the church. Others, including two journalists, made their own contributions. Wayne had been a much-respected man of many interests. The editor-in-chief of the *Wall Street Journal* managed to bring some humor to the proceedings by telling a few jokes about Wayne. A senior official from the Securities and Exchange Commission told the congregation that Wayne was a true public servant and champion of the small shareholder, having done a great service to the financial community, and that he would be sorely missed.

A Marine band struck up a traditional marching tune as the pallbearers moved once more into position by the flag-draped casket. A picture of Howard Wayne sitting at its foot was handed to Kim, who offered a smile of gratitude to the young Marine.

Mechanically, Kim allowed herself to be led out first. As she walked down the aisle, she looked for familiar faces right and left down the church pews. Suddenly, and for no reason, she remembered her encounter that awful night at her apartment. No matter how much she tried to drive the memory from her mind she could not. That girl had left her imprint on her life forever. What would Howard have thought? She shivered and almost stumbled.

The mourners left the church and gathered outside the entrance for several minutes before moving to their various vehicles, then drove as much as possible in procession, eighteen miles north to a cemetery in Hastings-on-Hudson.

The service continued at the graveside. The military escort presented arms and held their salute while the band played the funeral dirge, Edward Elgar's *Nimrod*, and then a hymn. The undertakers removed the casket from the hearse and followed a Marine to the canopied grave. Nick and Luciana were allocated seats three rows directly behind Kim. Gavin Hart's wreath was just one of many that blanketed the gravesite.

At the conclusion of the reverend's prayers, a Marine firing troop raised their rifles, pointed them toward the sky, and fired three volleys in succession. Luciana clung to Nick's arm and shook with each discharge. The crows resting in trees struck up a chorus of angry shrieks and then fluttered away in a flurry of flapping wings. An eerie silence settled over the mourners as a bugler sounded the twenty-four-note "Taps."

Two Marines slowly folded the flag that draped the casket into a neat triangle, military style, and presented it to the widow. A solitary lament played by a sole bagpiper standing on a small raised piece of cemetery land near the assembled mourners marked the end of the committal proceedings.

As the mourners dispersed, some talked in small groups, others admired the exceptional flower tributes, and many stood in line to speak with Kim. As Nick guided Luciana toward Kim, he noticed Detective Lee speaking to Gavin Hart. Tightness gripped his throat. His heart shifted into overdrive as he watched them in trepidation. Lee nodded his head in recognition and pointed toward Nick. The two broke away, with Lee moving away down the hill. Hart walked over to someone he knew without as much as a look in Nick's direction. Then the mourners headed back to Manhattan to the 21 Club, where a reception was to be held.

# ROME, ITALY

A security guard bowed to Gerhard Liebs and held open an ornate wrought-iron gate as he left the courtyard of a small office building. It was the Italian headquarters of his *bureau de change* business. Outside, in the sunlit narrow cobbled street, a burly overweight chauffeur, his stomach bulging over his low, ill-fitting trousers, stood leaning on the hood of a black Mercedes. With a cap on his head and cigarette drooping from his lips, he was the quintessential picture of self-indulgent apathy. He had been waiting for hours. Parked in another vehicle directly in front of the Mercedes were two intimidating bodyguards. When the boss finally emerged, the chauffeur tossed his cigarette to the ground and ambled to open the rear door.

Clutching a bundle of files under his arm, Gerhard Liebs grunted, "My apartment" and slipped into the rear seat. The armor-plated Mercedes spun its wheels as the driver and the lead car accelerated into traffic, ignoring anything or anybody that had the impudence to hinder their progress.

Rome had history etched into every street. It embraced eras from ancient to Renaissance to Baroque and beyond. Treasures like the Coliseum, the Forum, and Michelangelo's Sistine Chapel bore testament to its amazing past. They crossed the Tiber river by the Ponte Umberto and turned left down Lungotevere Costello to join Via della Conciliazione that took them straight to the Vatican.

Pigeons scattered while hordes of tourists moved away from the approaching mini-motorcade as the two Mercedes swept across St. Peter's Square and entered Piazza San Pietro. As always, the journey was made in utter silence, with the great banker sitting in isolation in the rear of the Mercedes. The driver's bulky body belied the fact that he was more than just an obese chauffeur.

In fact, he was a highly trained ex-police driver who was well equipped to handle any unforeseen emergencies. Concealed under his jacket was a BFR Magnum handgun cradled within its holster. Clipped under the car's dashboard were two Heckler and Koch MP5 machine guns capable of firing eight hundred bullets per minute. Not that Liebs was expecting any trouble, but in light of how he conducted his business, his bodyguards were always present to defend him from retaliation; it was a mere consequence of his rise to power.

Liebs occasionally looked up from his files to stare at the bustling city through his tinted glasses. The dome of St. Peter's dominated the skyline, but the shadow it cast across the entrance to the Vatican added to the secrecy of the celebrated edifice. Ever observant, the Pontifical Swiss Guards, dressed in traditional uniforms, recognized the vehicles and came to attention. The barrier pole swung up, and without slowing, Liebs's mini-motorcade disappeared into a murky tunnel.

Within minutes of getting out of his car the banker was ensconced alone in his apartment. Cool within its thick, ancient walls, one could imagine what had happened over the centuries past. This very special home of his was a sinecure from a former Pontiff. Liebs would often think to himself that it was almost a gift from God Himself. The thought amused him.

Liebs awaited word on his requested audience with the current head of the Catholic Church, and he knew he would not be refused. As a previous member of the old guard, the Pontiff was fully aware of Liebs's past contributions. He had played a key role in shoring up the Vatican's finances during the days when they were laden with heavy financial burdens and scandals. Liebs had achieved many successes in the past on behalf of the Vatican. He had no problems with those that surrounded the Holy Father as they, too, had their own files securely deposited in the personal safe of this, the most frightening of men, within Bank Schreiber Liebs in Zurich.

It had been a long while since his last visit to Rome. But this was the place where he felt safe. Here he could think without distractions. Perhaps God had something to do with it. Or, perhaps not, as he was truly the servant of Lucifer himself!

In the center of the peribolos is the Clementine Chapel, the gem of the Vatican grottoes, and the precious chest protecting the sepulcher of St. Peter. Gerhard Liebs had been conducted through the underground tunnels, which were reserved only for the highest dignitaries of the Roman Catholic Church. It was an honor. He had been granted access to the secret archives, the central repository for all of the acts promulgated by the Holy See. He couldn't help thinking of his own, less-extensive vault in Zurich, which contained so many secrets as well.

While he waited for the Vatican to respond, Liebs got on with his planned work, putting in place his next investment scheme, a program promising massive returns to his loyal depositors, who would be given an opportunity to bring in new investors. Only the very wealthy and very well connected would be allowed to invest. Monthly statements showing huge profits would induce the new investors to stay through the long term. *Yes, they'll go along with it*, he thought. How could any of them possibly refuse? Some would protest. Some would say it was just another Ponzi scheme. What did he care? He had them all by the balls.

He stooped slightly as he entered the low archway that led to a high-vaulted room containing the tools of his trade. Six ultra-high-resolution monitors were embedded in a wall. Liebs powered on his multi-screen workstation system, entering passwords as each terminal came alive. There was much work to be done.

Dale Peters's office in Spain spent the entire afternoon tracking down Erich Kersch, who, being in the US, was some hours behind them.

"Not a good idea calling me on my cell phone you guys," Kersch complained. He was an early riser, but was more than irritated seeing the large number of missed calls that had come through from Spain while he was asleep. "You know the procedures." Kersch & Co. had its own e-mail server to ensure complete privacy from snooping regulators. It had long been a standing procedure. "Send me an e-mail next time." He rubbed a white freckled hand through his cropped hair, massaging his scalp, which itched. "What could be so urgent?"

The brokers asked him how they were to handle the calls they had received from Adams about his shares and his question as to whether they had been placed as promised by Kersch.

"Whatever you do, don't tell Nick anything. What we do with his shares is between me and Dale," Kersch said to the head trader. "Not even Liebs is to be informed. Got it?"

"Erich," the trader spoke in a measured tone, "I'm sorry to be the one to tell you," he hesitated, "we got a call really early this morning from Gerhard Liebs who told us that we all now work for him."

"Fucking what?" Kersch exploded. "Tell me again what that cocksucker said?"

"He has taken complete control over the company." This man was accustomed to treading on eggshells when it came to Kersch, and luckily such encounters were few. "We now report to him directly. You see, the problem is that we haven't been able to locate Dale. He's off the map. We tried everything, but there is no contact. Even his cell phones are going into voice mail. We called his house, even the boat. He's been all over the place recently. I thought he was in Switzerland. I know he's done this before, but never when we've had so much on the go."

The trader, who was completely exhausted, had been with the Peters brothers from the very beginning in Amsterdam, long before they moved to Spain. When the Dutch had gotten a little too hot on the regulatory side, they had to move their operation to a less-stringent location. He was like family.

"This is not Dale's way. Apparently Dale signed a power of attorney with Liebs the last time he decided to go missing. It stated that in the event of his absence, Liebs would take charge of the business. So my hands are tied, Erich. I can't do anything without Liebs's approval."

Kersch had reckoned that Adams's shares would have been worth some $35 million at the current stock price. Kersch and

Peters had agreed that they would share the proceeds, and string Adams along for the duration, but would settle with him only if pressured, for perhaps five million tops. But it was unlikely that Adams would have any choice. After all, he had ripped them off already, and that was painful; to them it was enough. They would sell his shares and keep the proceeds. It was, after all their game.

But with the absence of Dale Peters it looked as though the plan had blown up in his face, and if it were true that Liebs was in charge, it would be impossible for the theft to take place without him finding out. Then that venomous prick would want a share.

"Erich? Erich?" the trader asked, unnerved by the silence on the other end. "I am sorry, Erich, but you know Liebs ..."

"Where the fuck is Dale?" Kersch spluttered. "He has never gone missing like this before."

"I'm really sorry, Erich, I can't help you. We've got enough trouble as it is," he said, clearly exasperated.

"What trouble? What the hell is going on?" Kersch snapped.

"We're taking hits everywhere. Our fucking stocks are going down the toilet and we can't continue to make a market in a lot of the shares we control. Unless we get more liquidity, we are going to get some angry calls from shareholders. Mr. Liebs is just getting too greedy. He's dumping his stocks at any price; and we know it's him because of the other traders telling us from Switzerland."

"Just ask the bastard for more cash!" Kersch yelled at the line. But he knew that he also had been selling his holdings on the same basis as Liebs. He needed cash, too.

"I did ask him when he called us earlier. He turned me down flat, then he started in with the same old threats."

"Then call his bluff."

"Are you fucking crazy? If I do that, we will end up with the regulators crawling all over us. Besides, it's time for me to get out." He paused. "We've all made enough money, Erich. It's time to consider other options. I've had it. I'll go and trade in some boring Swiss bank."

"ABS is still strong. Get selling Adams's shares." Kersch lowered his voice. "I will make it worth your while! Christ, if you bail out, the game will be over. Don't forget the trail leads to you, and they'll find you in Switzerland!" Kersch almost pleaded, something that was completely out of his comfort zone. "Do it. We can talk this through in a couple of weeks when everything has stabilized. Come on."

The line went dead.

Kersch sat heavily back into Adams's old chair. He wanted to scream. Fuck, how can it have gone so wrong? His pasty, freckled face had an odd sheen as perspiration started to bubble along the recently enhanced hairline on his forehead, where the implant holes were still clearly crusted and not totally healed. His cell phone rang again. He barked, "Kersch."

"Erich Kersch, this is Marat Esdaulet."

"Ah, yes. Minister Esdaulet," Kersch answered uneasily, obviously surprised to get a call from the minister directly.

"I wanted to inform you that your associate Dale Peters has failed to live up to the terms of our arrangement." His voice was strangely muted.

"He has?" Kersch unbuttoned his collar and loosed his tie. "What happened?" He took a handkerchief from his breast pocket to wipe the ever-increasing sweat across his brow as Esdaulet spoke.

"Gerhard Liebs has telephoned advising me that Dale Peters has ceased involvement in our deal, and that the oil field project will be handled by him directly." Esdaulet sounded angry. "But not to worry, I didn't mention our own private deal with Dale. Although I presumed our deal was off since my government has received nothing, and I never received my commission, nor have I received any explanation or information from Dale."

"I thought deposit monies had already been wired to your government's account and your fee delivered personally by Dale?"

"Dale did say, given the amount, it was easier to handle my

fee transaction in cash. He was scheduled to arrive here from Switzerland, so I sent my driver to pick him up at the airport. Dale never showed, and the deposit never hit our government account either."

"I don't know what to tell you, Minister Esdaulet. Dale has gone missing, and Liebs seems to have taken over everything. I'll do what I can to locate Dale. We need to know what happened." He tried not to sound worried. "I will get him and report back today, without fail. The deal will be done. It's still on track—please."

"You have three days. If Dale doesn't resurface, I'm going with Gerhard's offer." The minister hung up.

Minister Esdaulet couldn't help himself. He was not angry. Indeed, he smiled. He just couldn't lose on the deal. They were all so stupid and greedy. It was he and he alone who would decide on who would get the huge oil deal. It was just money, after all. There was to be no emotion, and if friendships were to be lost, so be it. But if the Swiss banker didn't perform soon, then the fat American, with all of his disgusting personal predilections, would be the victor. Esdaulet just didn't care.

A thought crossed his mind: maybe he would award the contract to them both. He would get a double whammy, and they could fight it out between themselves. He doubted whether either would want a public fight. The dirty washing would provide a truly wonderful cabaret spectacle on a global stage and ruin them both. What a good idea. He would work on it. With Kersch off the line, the minister made a call to Harvey Milton.

"Fuck! Fuck you, Dale!" Kersch hollered. "You can't do this to me. We need that oil deal to happen! Dale, where the hell are you?"

Outside the Adams Banking Solutions offices, parked on the street below, occupants of a Toyota Land Cruiser were listening in. One of the men on the surveillance team picked up a cell phone and dialed Washington, DC.

After the reception following Howard Wayne's funeral, Nick dropped Luciana off at her office and returned home. He called Spain and couldn't get his trader. No one could give him any answers as to his shares. His heart sank. Could things be going pear-shaped there as well? After the long, distressing day, all Nick wanted to do was pack for his trip and get the hell out of New York. He could almost feel the hot Caribbean sun. As he became lost in thought, his cell phone rang and jolted him back to the present.

"Nick? Gavin Hart here. How's it all going?" The voice sounded friendly enough.

"Just fine."

"Saw you at Howard's funeral. Great send-off, one of the best, but a sad day nonetheless."

"Yes, it was."

"Anyhow, down to business. Do we have your commitment?"

"Listen, I've been thinking." He chose his words carefully. "I'll let you know my answer after the weekend, Gavin," he was almost brusque with his response; clearly the constant pressure irritated him.

"Damn it!" Hart raised his voice and the stakes. "We need your answer now," Hart stormed, fed up with Nick's indifference. "I don't know what your problem is, but I'll bet it's hard to pronounce."

"Hang on a minute. It's not that easy, you know. I haven't heard back from the other two guys yet," Adams lied.

"Well one's in your apartment right now and can be contacted."

"Fine, but I'll get back to you Monday. And that's my answer."

"This is not some fucking game, you dickhead." Hart couldn't believe the man's audacity and change of tone. "You need to get your ass moving on this. Don't fuck with the Government."

"Well, Ravi is being tricky. He's uneasy about the interference with his software," Adams lied.

"Then take care of it. Sort it!"

Adams resisted the impulse to hang up on Hart, but Hart saved him the trouble. He hadn't actually spoken to Sharma yet, but knew there would be no problem modifying the software to enable the incredible plan to work. He was just going to get it done in his own time and carry on with his trip as planned without committing to anything.

Adams walked out onto his small terrace to clear his head and noticed the same parked car that had been there for the past few days. Clearly he must be under surveillance, but by whom? The police? The SEC? Rae? Adams looked through the contacts on his cell phone and put a call through to the NYPD. The phone call was eventually answered. "Detective Lee, please."

After being transferred several times, a familiar voice responded, "Mr. Adams, sorry we didn't get a chance to speak at the funeral. I had to get back to the precinct."

"Are you tailing me?"

"Tailing you?" Lee laughed. "Now there's a thing."

"There's been the same car and driver outside my apartment building since Wayne's murder."

"I can assure you, Mr. Adams, that we are not sufficiently interested in you to spend taxpayers' money putting an expensive tail on an innocent man," he said, amused by the accusation.

"My apologies." Adams was relieved, as it was one less worry. "But that car is still there regardless, Detective." He asked Lee how the murder investigation was going.

It was all very complicated, Lee told him. They knew it had something to do with Wayne's exposé, but they couldn't fly to Spain to confront anyone without a solid lead or permission from the Spanish authorities. But Lee's misleading update was only to appease Adams, pure lip service. "If there is anything you can do to help, we would be very grateful." The detective paused to sip some coffee. "Is there anything else I can do for *you*?"

"Well, yes, as a matter of fact. I need your assistance. Do you know of anyone called Rae—Dillon Rae? Says he's a fed working for government in DC."

Lee paused and tried not to sound surprised at the question. After all, it was he who asked the questions. "Rings no bells with me," he lied. "Sorry, but I'll look into it sometime. Keep in touch."

Nick looked down at the car below again and swore to keep a closer eye on the occupant, whoever he might be.

# WASHINGTON

Dillon Rae and his team were busy at work. The report received from JC and Ravi Sharma was outstanding. Kersch & Co. had lately installed John Cemach, the talented software programmer who worked offsite for the Bank Schreiber Liebs in Zurich, as a consultant to Adams Banking Solutions, on Liebs's recommendation, to work closely with Ravi Sharma so the Swiss banker could keep tabs on everything that went on. But unlike Sharma, Dillon Rae found it easier to coerce John Cemach into working for his country.

Rae had pulled off a spectacular coup. It was bold and crucial to the success or failure of the plan. Rae had covertly completed the acquisition of a small Caribbean bank. Secret strategic stakes by governments were sometimes taken in private banks to keep close tabs on terrorism, drugs, arms money, and other criminal proceeds. CAY BANK Inc., domiciled in Grand Cayman in the Caribbean, fitted Dillon Rae's chosen profile ideally. And it was all thanks to the careless trip to Miami by its chairman, Dieter Gruber, and the secrets unearthed on his cherished laptop.

And what secrets. It couldn't have been better. Of course his agency had been monitoring the bank for years and knew many of the transactions carried out by many of the customers who thought they had complete anonymity. But by getting the whole database, the plans he had worked on so diligently could be enacted. He had gone out on a limb. He had faced enormous pressures in DC from many surprising quarters. It was as if they themselves were about to be implicated. He noted the opponents and would visit their interests on another occasion. There would be time enough.

CAY BANK was a typical banking institution for many who preferred complete secrecy in hiding their assets and incomes far from the regulatory authorities of their home countries. Quite sophisticated in its services for such a bank, it had excellent corresponding facilities with major international banks. And, by coincidence, it had the best possible state-of-the-art electronic payment, an anonymous online banking and credit-card system installed by none other than Adams Banking Solutions itself.

It was the first and only deal that ABS was working on. It was Gerhard Liebs who made the introduction to CAY BANK's chairman, Dieter Gruber. CAY BANK was to be the test case.

And now all that remained for Dillon Rae's dastardly plan of deception was for Nicholas Adams to agree to come on board. He was impatient to implement the next stage.

Luciana was busy. She was a hard-working lawyer, but being a junior she had a considerable workload. She needed a break, but she knew she shouldn't really be going, as she normally worked over the weekends. Anyway, she was going whatever, and she was determined to use the time away to get the space to get to know her boyfriend better. She felt so much love for him and genuinely felt for him for the entire trauma he was going through in his business life, which seemed so unbelievably complicated and distressing. She had been single for some time before Nick. It wasn't that she hadn't been inundated by offers from so many different men from all walks of life. She was always being hit upon, including by some of her own colleagues. She was a beautiful girl, and intelligent as well. Luciana Cavallini could have anyone; yet despite all of his apparent problems, Nick was the man for her. He was different from the others.

The phone vibrated on her desk. It was her father.

"Ciao, Papa."

"I've returned your call several times, *tesoro*." He sounded tired.

"I know, Papa, but I've been in court all day," she lied. Luciana hadn't mentioned Howard Wayne's murder to her father or anything about her new boyfriend. Given the circumstances, and knowing her father, she felt it would be smarter to approach her father using kid gloves.

"Everything okay?" His voice betrayed his roots that originated as a boy in Sicily. "What is it? Money?" He teased her mercilessly. Always did. For him she was just his little girl. "Or is it that you miss your neglected Papa?" Franco Cavallini laughed out loud.

"Papa, I have lots to talk about." Luciana talked with her father for some time before broaching the topic of Nicholas Adams. Although Franco Cavallini expressed pleasure in hearing of the new man in his daughter's life, he was circumspect and more than apprehensive about the news. He would have much preferred that his daughter date an Italian, a good Catholic, one who was homegrown, who could take an interest in his business and someday become a son-in-law and give him grandchildren.

"Trust me, Papa. He's a good man."

Cavallini abruptly changed the subject and offered to wire money if she wanted. But Luciana assured him that her finances were fine, that he had done more than enough as it was.

"*Arrivederci. Abbi cura di te. Dormi bene, Papa.*" She told him to get some sleep. It was well after midnight in Pisa. She missed him, but she had no illusions about her father.

While she was talking, she tidied the files and cleared her desk of the clutter. Luciana left her office. She couldn't wait to set off for her long weekend with her man. It would be a perfect break from a week of confusion and unanswered questions.

When she arrived at Adams's apartment, Ravi Sharma, clearly hassled and under pressure, helped her in with her luggage. "Going away for some time I see," he said, eyeballing the number of bags. "Or are we moving in forever?"

"Do you think I'm taking too much, Ravi?" she smiled but was concerned.

"If you ask me, it looks like you're both fleeing the country." He tried to give her a wide grin. His white teeth contrasted with his dark skin, which seemed to have developed a rash, and his normally blue eyes lacked luster and were bloodshot.

"What did you say, Ravi?" Nick suddenly appeared at the

169

doorway with packages. He had gone out to pick up some wine for dinner as an excuse to get a closer look at the car parked across from his building. When he had walked by the vehicle and peered inside, all he could see was a guy reading a newspaper that partly obscured his face. "Who's fleeing the country?"

"We are," Luciana teased, slipping an arm through Sharma's, laughing.

"If that's what you want!" He sounded petulant, but laughed at the preposterous notion of the two shacking up. "I thought we'd stay in tonight and watch an Internet movie," he said, kissing Luciana fondly. "Ravi isn't feeling very well, but still insisted on cooking us a meal."

"That's great, but you shouldn't if you're not feeling up to it, Ravi." Luciana's tender voice sounded concerned.

"It's nothing a little nourishment won't cure." Sharma stiffened, but smiled wryly.

"Well, it all sounds good to me. I'm too shagged to go out."

Nick and Luciana decided to call it a night halfway through the film. It wasn't a good movie. They had fooled around on the sofa like a couple of teenagers and lost the plot some time ago. It was going to be an early start. A limo was picking them up at the crack of dawn for their early morning flight.

The ever-vigilant observer kept watch as the lights went out in Nick's apartment. He diligently e-mailed his report.

New York never slept. Even at that time of the early morning the hustle and bustle continued. Nick and Luciana were in a limo bound for JFK. Luciana caught a few scattered moments of extra sleep, resting her head on his shoulder, while he, for most of the ride, looked vacantly out the window, lost in his thoughts. A band of bright-orange hues contrasted vividly against the darkness of the morning. He marveled at the Manhattan skyline as the car emerged from the Midtown Tunnel, travelling east into the broad thoroughfare of the Long Island Expressway. The driver thankfully was not in a chatty mood, but broke the silence by loudly announcing their arrival. The cold air that entered through the door when the driver opened it woke Luciana with a start. Their bags were unloaded and soon they were heading toward the business class check-in desk. Of course, the crap had to start again.

"Your booking has been cancelled, Mr. Adams," the agent said in an almost gleeful manner.

"Look, there is some mistake." Nick wasn't particularly concerned. "Here are the passports and the electronic tickets." He placed them on the high counter that separated them. "And you will observe," he said triumphantly, "the boarding passes I printed off last night." *That will show them*, he thought. Silly bitch—so very arrogant. The woman, large and extremely unimpressed by his protests, picked up a phone and called to double-check what was on her screen.

"Sir." There was such an attitude in the way she was dealing with him. "Your payment for the tickets was revoked by your credit card provider overnight. It seems that there was a problem with the card you used to make the booking." There, she was winning. Some of the passengers in the queue that was building up behind Nick and Luciana started to murmur their frustration at the delay.

"You have got to be joking." Nick flushed and Luciana noticed. "My card is fine. Try it again, please." He drew the card from his wallet and presented it to the woman. "Please." He almost sounded contrite.

"Okay, but I have to follow airline procedure." She took the card and put it into the reader. He put in his PIN. Declined. "I have to retain the card I am afraid. Do you have another credit card please, Mr. Adams?" Now she felt bad.

Nick nodded. He pulled out a debit card and handed it to Luciana. "Sweetheart, do me a favor and get a thousand dollars from the cash machine. We don't want to be stuck for cash. Cash machines are near Gate 7." He whispered his PIN in Luciana's ear and pointed her in the direction of the row of ATMs.

"Mr. Adams?" The ticketing agent announced louder than

he would have wished. "There seems to be the same problem. Master Card has declined your card, sir."

"Christ, this is a joke." Adams responded, startled.

"It could be a computer problem, sir. There have been a few recently, something to do with a new system to handle higher volume levels. Perhaps you have another card?"

One by one Adams handed over charge and debit cards issued through unrelated financial institutions. They were all denied authorization, and all in the presence of other travelers who bore witness to his humiliation.

Trying desperately to maintain his cool, Adams dialed AMEX from his cell. His call did not connect. Instead, a message from his network provider requested that he contact them immediately, stating that all calls with the exception of emergencies were barred. Nick stood there, stunned. The agent informed him that the airline would have to sell his tickets to someone else if he was unable to make the purchase.

He knew he shouldn't, but he did so anyway. From the back of his wallet he took out a gold card that had no name embossed upon it, only the usual numbers. It was his anonymous credit card issued in Switzerland. He had been warned not to use it in the US. He ignored the instruction—*just this once*, he told himself. It worked like a charm, much to the evident relief of himself, the check-in girl, and the irritated travelers that stood in line.

"Everything okay?" Luciana had arrived by his side as he was handed the boarding passes.

"You got the money?" He saw her nod. He released an audible sigh of relief. All was not lost. At least that card was working. They walked toward passport control.

"I tried using your card, but a message appeared saying 'refer to issuing bank.' Maybe I keyed in the wrong PIN number." Luciana shrugged her shoulders and remained silent.

"So, how did you get the cash?"

"I used my card." She smiled to hide her concern. She knew she had his correct PIN and had tried it several times with the same result. On the third attempt the card did not reappear out of the ATM.

"I'm screwed, honey. Thank God I prepaid the hotel for the weekend. All my cards have been declined."

"Declined? You're maxed out on all your cards?"

"No I can't have. It's not possible," he said visibly distraught. "I have a $100,000 spending limit with AMEX alone. Not only that, AMEX and all my other cards are up to date, and none of them is authorizing payment. I can't even call my bank because my cell has been cut off."

Luciana squeezed his hand. She was now down a thousand, and they hadn't even left New York yet.

A man sporting a black leather jacket, standing against a nearby pillar, had taken a more than casual interest in the chaos besieging Nick. But the grin on his face soon faded into a look of complete surprise when the boarding passes were handed over. That should not have happened. Now the shit would hit the fan. He had assumed Luciana would storm out of the terminal and head back to Manhattan alone. There was no contingency plan. The man could only watch as the couple disappeared through security. He took out his phone and dialed. It would not be an easy call.

Takeoff was smooth, and they were soon rising and circling over Manhattan. Nick watched as New York disappeared in the distance, and with it, he hoped, all of his tough luck.

"There must be a simple explanation," he said. "There's no valid reason why any of my cards should be declined."

"Then how did you pay?" She raised an exquisite eyebrow that arched below her luxuriant hair.

"I will explain, darling. It's okay—I hope."

"Relax, *tesoro*, or you'll ruin our vacation. We have enough cash to tide us over, and we can use my cards for any incidentals." A smile played across her lips as she tried to cheer him up. "Let's just think about getting there, going for swims, lying lazily in the sun, and fooling around. Deal?"

"Deal." Nick placed a gentle kiss on the forehead of the one woman who seemed to have stolen his heart. He raised his champagne glass. "To us."

# ANTIGUA

The plane landed ahead of schedule. First off the aircraft, Nick and Luciana were through passport control and out into the balmy heat in no time. Welcoming, soft Caribbean sounds dancing in the air affirmed they had officially arrived in paradise. The resort had sent a black Japanese SUV to get them, and within minutes they were being driven in comfort at breakneck speed to the hideaway location. The half-hour ride took them through local villages and beautiful countryside of farms and fields. Finally, the SUV turned into a palm-lined drive leading to the graceful, tropical chic of the Carlisle Bay.

Set in a sweeping bay on the unspoiled south coast of Antigua, the hotel lay on a stunning beach amid a backdrop of rolling hills and a lush rain forest. With an exceptional spa, swimming pool, tennis courts, two restaurants, three bars, a cool library, and a screening room, the trendy resort was everything the couple could wish for.

The gray wooden walkway over a lily pond led them to an open-air lobby where the general manager, who looked like he'd been on happy pills for years, personally greeted them. After being lavished with cold towels and tropical punch to refresh them from the heat, the couple were taken on a brief tour, then whisked away to their two-room suite, and from their private terrace, the stunning view of the ocean. It was timeless Caribbean beauty.

With only a long weekend ahead, the couple wasted no time, quickly undressing and heading straight for the pool. They claimed two empty sun beds and ordered drinks.

At long last, Nick switched himself off, his troubles neatly tucked away in a remote memory crypt, not to be disturbed until he resurfaced on Monday. He lay motionless on the lounger, absorbing the hypnotic heat and captivating setting. His eyes followed the trail of six black pelicans swooping down over the pool and out to within one hundred yards of the shore, before they dove vertically in unison into the blue waters. The scene was spectacular.

When he turned to lie face down, Luciana massaged sunscreen onto the perfect contours of his well-toned muscular back.

"That's just making me waste an erection," he groaned, enjoying the fondling.

"Behave." She slapped his bottom in mock admonishment. "You'll have plenty of time for that later. If you behave." She giggled.

After a while the pool waters beckoned and Luciana responded. She moved as though on a catwalk over to the edge of the free-form pool, her turquoise-and-gold bikini accentuating her curvaceous figure and small, firm breasts, and dived in without creating so much as a splash. Nick waited for her to reemerge, but couldn't see her. When he stood up, he saw her swimming the entire length of the pool underwater, gliding gracefully along the tiled bottom.

Nick dove in after her, unnoticed. When she finally broke the surface and extended her arms to climb out, Nick grabbed her from behind and pulled her back underwater. She tried to break free as she fought for air, but he placed his lips over hers and kissed her. Depleted of oxygen, they kicked their way to the surface, gasping for air, bursting out in giggles and threats of unimaginable vengeance. They played together without a care in the world. The stress had gone. Nick challenged her to a length of the pool race. He won. Once they caught their breath, they got out of the pool and made their way arm in arm, like any honeymoon couple, to the bar. Nick smiled. Luciana noticed that he looked more like the man she had met in the Hamptons, relaxed and in control.

# NEW YORK

"Shit!" Dillon Rae could hardly contain his anger as he paced around his hotel suite. The rage simmering in his gut rose to full boil. He fought to keep his mind focused on devising an alternate plan of attack. His eyes settled on a stream of sunlight that seemed to pulsate to the intensity of his determination. He had spent too much time, effort, and Bureau money at this stage to have his meticulously laid plans placed in jeopardy by Nicholas Adams. And just at a time when everything was almost set to roll. Putting a block on Adams's lines of credit was straightforward, easy, and within his powers. He ordered a temporary administrative freeze placed on Adams's US accounts. But the surprise issuance of the tickets again at the airport had come as a total shock. With Adams due back on Monday evening, Rae would effectively lose three full days, and that was unacceptable. He barked orders: "Find out from the airline how he got the tickets. And one other thing." He paused. "Get one of our local agents to make a surprise visit to Antigua." It was time for pain to be administered. "Find him and get him to call me for his instructions, and make it quick!"

Rae left his hotel room just in time for his early lunch with Gavin Hart. He leaned against the paneled elevator wall and watched the numbers count down until it arrived at the lobby level of the Four Seasons Hotel. The polished doors parted, and he stepped out into a bright, open space. He strode through the columned, grand foyer of minimalist modernism with a feeling of walking through a great temple. Impressions of grandeur were everywhere. When he entered the hotel's Fifty-Seven restaurant, Hart was seated at a table by a large window. He wearily rubbed the bridge of his nose, exhausted after a long drink-fuelled session picking the brains of a few Wall Street friends in preparation for that afternoon's booked encounter with Harvey Milton. For him to succeed in his role, Hart needed to be well briefed on virtually every possible expectation before his appointment.

"Gavin, don't worry about fucking Adams." Rae's facial expression hardened. "He'll be back sooner than you think. He's already under a great deal of duress," he continued. "He's had a lot to absorb over the past week. But he needs to appreciate that we don't have the luxury of time on our hands. And I'll be damned if I'll let the little shit screw things up. I," he paused, lowering his voice as he leaned in toward Hart, "am prepared to do whatever it takes to get him on side," he added. "I guarantee he'll come to his senses." Rae reached for the wine bottle and filled their glasses, narrowly beating the wine waiter, whose duties had been usurped.

Knowing that Rae never made empty threats, Hart stared at his glass, wondering how far Rae would take things to protect the grand plan. Then he turned the subject to Milton.

"So … I am to step carefully with Harvey?"

"Yeah. Don't antagonize the guy. The last thing we need is to have his security or bodyguards throwing you into the street. And for God's sake, dispel any notion that you're up to one of your Hart fraud exposés. Just deliver the deal of a lifetime." Rae meticulously spread butter on the perfectly baked roll lying on his plate. "You're going to have to convince Harvey Milton that it's in his best interest to take the deal. Just keep reiterating that it's a government matter and that he will have our full support, from the White House down."

"But what if he doesn't buy the proposition?"

"If offered the right incentive," he sneered, "Harvey Milton III will do whatever we want. He'll go with us when he hears what's on the table. You'll see. And if he doesn't—well, rejection has never stopped me before. We'll just have to tighten our grip around his fat neck."

"I just wish I had the book and film rights to this plan of yours." Hart smiled.

"You have all the documents?"

"Yep, they're all in my briefcase." Hart looked down the side of his chair, where a brown leather shoulder case rested. "The reports on Gerhard Liebs were pretty enlightening and ominous. He is positively the most odious man I have ever investigated."

"That's why Harvey Milton will buy the story."

"What happens if he runs a check on me? I mean, who can vouch for me? Which government agency?"

"He won't find out anything more than he already has. Besides, the deal will make him too preoccupied. It alone will render all the convincing he needs." Rae looked at his watch. "Just make sure it's a one-on-one. Don't let anyone else attend or get involved."

"So you're certain he'll go for it."

"Gavin, you must have figured out from the reports the kind of guy he is. Believe me, he won't pass this one up."

"Maybe." His mouth twisted into a sardonic smile. "I'll give it my best shot."

"Listen, Gavin," Rae assured him, "you have a better chance at persuading him than anyone in the agency. You can give him my card, and he can check through this secure number if need-be."

Rae and Hart spent the next hour going over details with military precision. When Hart finally left, a man who had been lunching on his own just a few tables away soon joined Rae.

"Sorry to have kept you," Rae said coldly, glaring at the other man. There was a definite edge of sarcasm in his voice. "Now, if it's at all possible for you to do a job properly, how about a little restitution for screwing up?"

Rae was less than pleased with the man's performance that morning. Mastering the art of thinking quickly on one's feet was a prerequisite for every one of TRU's task force members. But the man knew his boss only too well and chose not to feel in any way slighted by his irascible nature. "Sorry, but it took too long getting hold of you, and by the time I did, they were airborne," the man explained, stone-faced. His was the sort of face that wouldn't be picked out in a crowd or a line-up. That was his strength and his stock in trade.

"No excuses. You could have checked to see how he managed to get on the plane. Anyhow, I want you to go to Trump Tower and hand-deliver a document of some sensitivity to the person whose name is printed on the envelope—and to him only." Dillon Rae took a white envelope containing his ticking time bomb out of an inside pocket. "Be there as soon as possible; then call me and tell me you have done it. And don't fuck this one up."

The man left the Four Seasons and made his way down Fifth Avenue to Trump Tower. Having located the separate condominium entrance and then entered the Tower through the public entrance, he took a seat in the atrium beside the waterfall that stretched over several stories to wait for the appropriate moment of delivery. He pulled out Rae's envelope and read its explosive contents.

# MILTON GLOBAL INC. HEADQUARTERS

At a quarter to three, Milton's office had an unwelcome visitor. How he had gained access to the building was anyone's guess. It was a well-guarded fortress with an ogre of a doorman strategically placed on the sidewalk outside the smoked-glass lobby doors, allowing entrance only to those invited.

His PA did her best to turn him away, but the federal agent held a legitimate warrant. He insisted on seeing Harvey Milton himself, despite Oscar Randell's protests that the papers should be served on the company's attorneys. Also, trying to protect his employer with the greatest loyalty, Randell lied and told the agent that Milton simply wasn't in. He tried to maintain some dignity and decorum, but a shouting match ensued outside the penthouse's front door, alerting Milton's security and bodyguards. The agent stood his ground, fully aware that Milton was inside and warned Randell that he would summon the NYPD for assistance if he had to. Two security guards took their position between the two men and asked Randell for permission to escort the agent off the premises. But to avoid any undue embarrassment by getting the NYPD involved, Randell told security to hold off for a moment and asked the agent to wait while he consulted his chairman.

Milton showed no emotion or concern and agreed to meet the agent. With Milton's security remaining in the foyer, two of his bodyguards, along with Randell, escorted the agent through the circular foyer down the corridor leading to Milton's executive suite.

"What can I do for you?" Milton remained seated, not even bothering to look up from the document he was reading, while Randell hovered protectively. One bodyguard stood within his office while the other remained just outside the door. Rae's agent served Milton with the papers. Milton handed them to Randell without as much as a glance.

Randell read aloud the first page of the United States Supreme Court subpoena, drawn up against Milton Global Inc., and Harvey Milton III. Milton raised his eyebrows as Randell read the extravagant claims and accusations, charges from the IRS of tax evasion, charges from the SEC of share manipulation, to possible employment of illegal immigrants, dealings in narcotics, and smuggling charged by US Customs, along with a heap of other serious misdemeanors. The document covered every possible felony that could be committed in the US under the Racketeer Influenced and Corrupt Organizations Act known as a RICO order. There were twenty charges spread over several pages.

Describe in detail the alleged enterprise for each RICO claim. A description of the enterprise shall include the following information:

> (a) State the names of the individuals, partnerships, corporations, associations or other entities allegedly constituting the enterprise;
>
> (b) Describe the structure, purpose, roles, function and course of conduct of the enterprise;
>
> (c) State whether any defendants are employees, officers or directors of the alleged enterprise;
>
> (d) State whether any defendants are associated with the alleged enterprise, and if so, how;
>
> (e) State whether you allege that the defendants are individuals or entities separate from the alleged enterprise, or that the defendants are the enterprise itself, or members of the enterprise;
>
> (f) If you allege any defendants to be the enterprise itself, or members of the enterprise, explain whether such defendants are perpetrators, passive instruments, or victims of the alleged racketeering activity.

And so it went, on and on.

Milton let no hint of emotion cross his face, but there was a slight trembling in his demeanor, a flash of fear so swift it was barely noticeable. The American tycoon cleared his throat and smiled coldly. He lifted himself from the sofa, laughing faintly, and grabbed the subpoena from Randell to look at the ridiculous, yet dangerous accusations.

"This must be a joke. What sick bastard came up with this crap? We have done nothing to merit this extraordinary treatment," he said flatly. Randell stood frozen in disbelief. "We've paid tens of millions in taxes and given generously of our time and money to charity and worthwhile civic endeavors. We employ thousands and have helped drag America out of recession. I have even backed presidents!" his words were delivered slowly and calmly. "So why are we being penalized or singled out?" He threw the document down onto the carpeted floor. "This is a witch hunt, and I will make sure heads will roll, just watch me."

His assignment complete, the agent said nothing and turned to leave.

"Hang on there!" The controlled fury beneath the surface of Milton's face rose to his cheeks. Randell noticed him begin to sweat. His breath caught in his throat as a shadow crossed his face. "You tell your employers that, one, this is preposterous and out of order; two, there is no case to answer, and I will sue their asses; and three, I will take this straight to the White House. Then we shall see the heat redirected. Boy, you better believe me. Now get out!"

The agent nodded; his face expressionless. He was used to abuse and never took such things personally. He was simply doing his job. As he left, he took in the extraordinary opulence of Milton's penthouse and smiled. *Perhaps everything in the subpoena was true*, he thought. Security escorted him out. For him it was all in a day's work.

Milton's promise to take the accusations to the White House was not an idle threat. He had been a frequent visitor over the years and was a generous contributor to several presidential campaigns regardless of the party. Individual politics were irrelevant. It was just good business.

His PA stepped in with water and two tablets for Milton's blood pressure. She also suggested postponing the rest of the scheduled appointments. "No," he responded emphatically, "there's too much on our plate." Milton sat back down on the sofa and wiped his sweating brow with a handkerchief. The room fell silent as he gathered his composure.

"Oscar, deal with the subpoena. Get the lawyers onto it at once." He turned to his PA. "Use the usual route and get me into the White House. Listen, both of you," he clasped his hands together, "there's more to this than meets the eye. We have nothing to answer to." He paused. "At least not in the US," he smiled. "Even though we may have been somewhat economical with the truth elsewhere." He guffawed, and allowed himself a broad grin, relaxing once more. The government would not have been so heavy-handed with him just for Kersch & Co. activities, surely? There was a hidden agenda. Care would be needed. There was no need to panic.

The early sunshine had all but disappeared. Through the tinted plate glass windows of the penthouse, the New York skyline appeared shrouded in a gray, damp mist. Milton was winding up a brief meeting with two of his New York bankers and bid them farewell. The group very nearly bumped into Gavin Hart as he stepped out of the elevator.

Hart was shown through the foyer to a large reception room lavishly furnished with tapestries on three walls. A grand work of art hung at each end of the room. They looked vaguely familiar, but one thing was for sure—he knew they were priceless. Bronze statues lining the main wall diverted his attention away from the massive paintings. A girl entered with a tray of coffee and water, placing it on an exquisite seventeenth-century travelling chest positioned between giant ivory elephants that had been converted into lamps. They planned for Hart's meeting to take place in this drawing room, away from the Liebs files sprawled out all over Milton's office.

"Mr. Hart," Harvey Milton growled as he entered the room. Oscar Randell walked closely behind, having just returned from delivering the subpoena to the Milton Global attorneys a block away. Milton offered the journalist his hand and motioned toward the tray for Hart to help himself. "This is Oscar Randell," he nodded toward the younger man. "Please make yourself comfortable."

They knew all about Hart. In addition to receiving a brief bio along with a letter of introduction, they had carried out their own extensive checks and were well aware of Hart's background and notoriety as the scourge of crooked leaders of industry.

"It's good of you to see me, Mr. Milton." Gavin Hart walked uneasily across a Persian rug covering the marble floor and sat down on a sofa.

"Harvey, please." Milton's grin grew wider. "No ceremony here." Milton took a seat on a sofa across from Hart and Randell left the room. "We read your profile with great interest, Gavin."

"Ah, yes, but you know how it is—these things only say what you want people to read." He laughed nervously; although he was never normally intimidated, this large American was making him feel uneasy.

"Quite so, Gavin," Milton smiled.

Hart had also been well briefed and made aware of the man's expensive habits, his connections socially, politically, and commercially. Hart was able to engage Milton in general conversation on just about any subject. They pussyfooted around the main reason for the meeting. Phones rang continually. Decisions were made quickly and professionally. A continual flow of employees came quietly in and out of the room. Decisions were made, signatures given. Hart got caught up in the life of Harvey Milton.

Milton's PA interrupted to remind Milton of his video conference call with the Indian prime minister in forty minutes. Hearing this, Hart shifted uneasily as he sat on the edge of the sofa, coffee cup in hand. Nothing had been broached relating to the purpose of his visit.

Preempting the thought, the large American looked at Hart, and waving away another secretary, he smiled. "So, Gavin," Milton picked up a glass of water and quaffed half the glass in one gulp, "tell us your deal, because that's why you are here, surely?" His eyebrows were raised.

Hart nearly gagged. In an instant everything had progressed directly to the point. "Deal?"

"Come on, man. Spit it out!"

Gavin Hart wasn't sure where Milton was going with this, but he listened.

Milton, who was almost on the right track, quietly started to accuse his visitor of the underhanded way he had obtained material for a forthcoming exposé of Milton Global Inc. He questioned Hart's motives, although he expressed a certain admiration for how Hart had managed to get this far in seeing him. Under all normal circumstances, there was no way an interview would have been granted. But the letter received from one of the most powerful US senators had tipped the balance. Hart, too, had powerful friends, he mused. He exercised caution. He had to be careful.

"Mr. Milton … uh, Harvey." Hart sat awkwardly, but appeared more than grateful for Dillon Rae's senatorial letter. "What I have, or rather, what I am proposing, is so sensitive, I hardly know where to begin."

"Sensitive?" Milton cocked his eyebrow. A sudden guarded glint appeared in his eyes. He loathed surprises. He remembered a conversation some years back with Liebs that had begun with virtually the same line. "I am sure there can be nothing sensitive that involves me. But please," he cleared his throat, "get on with whatever you're here to propose."

"It's a business deal. Simply put, I've come as an emissary."

"Emissary? From whom? Is it the good senator to whom you owe this meeting? Well, I've met him on several occasions at the White House and he has also been my guest at several functions. Surely he could have come here himself."

"The government," Hart said firmly. "The US government."

"Is this something relating to the crap shoot subpoena I received today?" Red burned across Milton's cheeks. "I knew it. Too damned coincidental," he swore. "Well, you can take your proposition," he sneered, "and you know what you can do with it, my friend!" He called out for his PA.

Realizing Milton was no pushover, Hart decided to put an end to the potential tirade and stood up. "Just a minute, Mr. Milton. I don't know anything about any subpoena." Hart looked Milton straight in the eye. "So, please, there is no need to be offensive." Hart was a real pro, accustomed to enraged eruptions from politicians, fraudsters, and the criminals he exposed over the years, so he could pretty much handle Milton. "Please, hear me out." Hart raised his hands in mock surrender. "And, from what I've been told about you, you might even be interested in what I have to say."

"I very much doubt it." Milton waved his PA away, still clearly annoyed by Hart's intrusion.

"Well, then, let me be blunt and come straight to the point."

"Please do. You've been waffling from the moment you arrived."

Hart ignored his comments. "I am acting on behalf of various third parties who need your help and who are willing to pay handsomely for your cooperation." Hart reached into his side pocket and retrieved a rather worn black Moleskin notepad. The topstitching on its fastening strap was frayed. Hart opened to a specific page. "Let me first reemphasize that what's being put forward has nothing to do with me and has no bearing on my profession. I can also guarantee that no pressure will be put upon you in any way," he lied. "As implausible as it may seem, I am here to offer you, among other things," he paused to make his dramatic statement, "one billion dollars."

"A billion dollars?" Milton let out a harsh laugh. "Sure, and I believe in Santa Claus." In an instant his amusement abruptly vanished from his face, and he began to choke. He grabbed a glass of water from the tray and drank until his breathing became even again. He dabbed at his teary eyes with a handkerchief, and his composure returned to normal.

"Yes. Seriously. One billion dollars, tax-free. It is all yours if you cooperate. I can prove it. Do you want it or not?"

Milton nodded his head in open skepticism. "Okay, I'll hear

you out." He looked at his Patek Philippe watch and sighed. There was something wrong, and he just couldn't put his finger on it. "You have thirty minutes."

He called in one of his security guards, who walked over to Hart, mumbled a few words, and frisked him. Then he turned to his boss and nodded. Hart was clean: no weapons, no wiretaps.

"Right. I am sorry about that, but I am sure you understand? Now we can get down to real business. Explain yourself," he sounded polite and genuinely interested, "how do I get one billion dollars?"

Hart wasn't surprised that he had been frisked. It wasn't the first time. He turned over a sheet of the notebook and pulled the cradled pen from its loop. "Gerhard Liebs. You're acquainted with him?"

Harvey Milton's eyes narrowed. "Ah, it had to be!" he sat up with some difficulty and with a look of triumph on his face. He suspected Liebs was plaguing him again and would push it too far someday, but he was prepared to listen. He sat very still, his greedy business interests overriding his instinctive distrust of Hart now that he had mentioned Liebs.

It turned out it was all to do with the Swiss banker. It was not too soon. Hart had no indication that he had piqued Milton's interest and went on without interruption outlining Dillon Rae's plan. He explained that the US government had conducted an investigation with the cooperation of every foreign agency it could coerce into exposing the empire of Gerhard Liebs. Then from his capacious briefcase he produced a large dossier containing over five hundred pages.

"This report," Hart rose from the sofa and handed the tome to Milton, "will show you what's been discovered."

Milton quickly leafed through the heavy file, occasionally whistled, sighed, or laughed quietly. Now why hasn't Oscar managed to produce such a file, he thought? "Is this for me?"

"Yes." Hart's face split into a smile, the first since he had arrived. "At face value, everything seems legitimate, but it's all smoke and mirrors. As you can see, the report documents how people are being swindled, shareholders of public companies are being conned, drug barons are getting rich, arms dealers are supplying weapons to our enemies, terrorists are being funded— you name it, Gerhard Liebs has a finger in every pie. The Swiss banker believes he's beyond the law and has manipulated laws and people to such a degree that he has become a serious threat. And there lies his vulnerability." Hart paused for a moment as Milton reviewed more pages. "We," he cleared his throat, "what I mean to say is that the US government is determined to put this man out of business once and for all. But we need help."

It was veritable music to Milton's ears. The manna from heaven he had been waiting for. His heart tripped into overdrive as a rush of adrenaline consumed him, but his demeanor remained noticeably cool.

"What can *I* do?" Milton closed the file and pressed the intercom, calling for the hostess to bring in more refreshments. "One billion dollars seems a pretty fat fee." He drummed his fingers on the hardcover. "No one gives that kind of money away without guarantees." He looked at Hart across the table between them. "What have I got to do to earn this sum?"

"Every detail has already been mapped out, meticulously," Hart replied in his most compelling voice. "All you have to do is follow the plan precisely as instructed."

Milton looked intrigued. Hart had captured his complete attention.

"We will draw the sword against Liebs by adopting his own methods," Hart continued without waiting for feedback. "Our collaborators have used great ingenuity and skill at every step of the game." The hostess arrived and placed fresh coffee and water beside him. "Thank you," he said, smiling at her. "Your role will be stage-managed."

"Acting is not my strong point, Mr. Hart." Although Milton knew his whole life was one big act.

"Gavin, please."

"Yes … Gavin."

"Think of it as just another business deal." Hart stared at Milton candidly.

"Well, for such a large fee, I'm sure I can handle any task you have in mind. So, what's my role in all this?"

"You're the bait."

"Bait? I don't understand. Why me?" Milton asked inquisitively.

"We needed someone within Liebs's inner circle. We've singled you out because we believe that, more than anyone else we've identified, you have the balls to take him on. And as an added incentive to the one billion dollar fee, Milton Global Inc. will be allowed to take over all of the legitimate businesses owned by Liebs left in the aftermath."

"Fine words, Gavin. But Gerhard Liebs is a very formidable opponent and hasn't gotten to where he is without being a master at every game he plays."

"That could be said of you as well," Hart responded with cool irony.

"Hmm, maybe. Okay, so fair comment. I acknowledge that, it's a sort of compliment?"

"So, you see, we have to play you off against him."

"Play me off?" Milton shifted rigidly on the sofa and tried to mask a sudden feeling of unease.

Hart seemed unaware of the sudden coldness permeating the room. "Hear me out, Harvey."

Milton nodded once, but stared with cool, distant eyes. "Go on—tell me how this grand scheme will work."

"Well, in a nutshell," he reached for his cup and sipped at the already cold coffee, "you will need to meet first with Liebs face to face, which is vital if the plan is to succeed. Timing on this meeting is immediate. It is essential we move fast."

"Meet?" Milton laughed huskily, a laugh devoid of humor. "Easier said than done, my friend. I haven't actually seen Liebs for quite some time. We don't really communicate anymore," he took a sharp intake of breath pausing to think for a moment. Liebs was becoming a bigger pain than ever lately, interfering with many deals of Milton Global and its subsidiaries. The situation could be just the opening gambit he needed, he thought. "Perhaps a meeting could be possible. After all, our paths do cross now and then. I've got an idea as to how such a meeting could take place. Go on."

"The government will afford you immunity."

"Immunity?" Milton's voice rose as he looked at Hart with puzzled eyes. "From what, may I ask?"

"You could face a firestorm of allegations awash with exposure. That recent subpoena, the way you have described it to me, could be just a part of a domino effect. It would be a financial Armageddon, a total catastrophe."

"You can't be serious. I can fight these petty pen-pushing clerks at every level. That battle could go on forever." Milton smiled.

"Frankly, I don't think you'll last very long in the ring." Hart lowered his voice. "There's no telling what certain organizations will do if you decide not to play the game. Sorry, but I don't think you really have much of a choice. You're either with us or against us."

At that moment, Milton realized exactly where he stood. Hart had him by the balls.

"I'll give you a moment to ruminate while I stretch my legs." Hart ambled toward the plateglass window to look out onto the breathtaking panoramic views that spanned as far as the eye could see. The streets below were gridlocked, filled with toy-like stationary limos, cars, trucks, buses, and yellow cabs. He looked calm, but inside he was a maelstrom of doubt.

A few moments later, Hart turned to rejoin Milton. Getting a sense that Milton was ready to hear more, Hart outlined the details of what was being proposed to his now-intrigued and receptive audience of one.

"Firstly, a new bank account has been established for you." Gavin Hart smiled at the large perspiring American industrialist. "When you hear me out, you will know why."

"Go on," Milton said, his attention grabbed. "I'm listening."

# ZURICH

Gerhard Liebs looked strangely disheveled as he stared blankly at a wall in his office. Facing one's demons is never easy, even for Liebs. He lowered his head questioningly, a copy of a financial report in his hands. Due to various financial crises plaguing global markets, certain cash cows that generated sums that routinely came in over the years were beginning to dry up and had taken their toll on a large portion of his portfolio. Once unencumbered assets were now pledged against loans. To make matters worse, his own investigations of his staff and his field managers confirmed suspicions that many were on the take. *I've allowed them too much rope*, he thought. He pressed the Grand Cayman speed dial, wincing at the pain from his fingers.

His conversation with CAY BANK was short. "Freeze all Alpha accounts until further notice," he said in cold measured tones into the receiver. The only words the shocked Dieter Gruber could utter at the onslaught were a quivering, "Right away, sir, Mr. Liebs."

But unbeknownst to anyone but Dieter Gruber, there had been changes at the bank. There had been a recent change in ownership at CAY BANK. But he couldn't tell Liebs over an unsecured line. At the insistence of Dillon Rae, Gruber had remained with the bank, in his new role as an involuntary member of Rae's TRU task force, sworn to secrecy.

Liebs held power of attorney on CAY BANK accounts introduced through Bank Schreiber Liebs, referred to as Alpha accounts. Many Alpha account holders had built up sizeable fortunes from their work within the Liebs empire, among them Kersch & Co., Erich Kersch, and Dale Peters. Valentina Vinogradov banked there as well. Dieter Gruber knew them all intimately, and now, so did Dillon Rae. Gruber had sung like a canary when he was arrested in Miami. He was integral to the deal, but expendable in the medium term. Rae had everything from the laptop of the careless, but meticulously accurate, banker.

By cutting off access to the funds held on the accounts, Liebs got straight answers and unvarnished truths from his Alpha account holders. And should an individual be less than forthcoming, he remunerated himself by issuing a right-to-compensation from the culprit's account. It was a useful fail-safe tool, a practical supplement to blackmail.

Dieter Gruber was cleverly installed at CAY BANK by Liebs to look after his interests, with whose help he managed to pull off scores of complex frauds over the years. Liebs's exploits were done on such a scale as not to alert the international banking community, with a careful intricate network hiding all of the transactions, sometimes in Japan, sometimes in Nigeria, Russia, Hong Kong and Dubai, and several obscure locations so far unmonitored by the regulators.

The banking community was not aware of the full extent of Liebs's activities, which netted billions globally. There were suspicions, of course, but could find nothing that any one jurisdiction could put a finger on. Interpol watched and observed. But so far no one had been brave enough to blow the whistle. There was always someone at the top who called off the hounds. He was quick to take advantage of changes in technologies, and employed bright, young, highly skilled computer programmers and black hat hackers to exploit security weaknesses. From the comfort of their homes and offices, these programmers hacked into secure networks of some of the largest banks and institutions in the world. Ten of the banks they secretly hacked into did well over $500 billion in trading each day. Money would be siphoned off legitimate accounts in one country to new accounts held elsewhere. No matter how paranoid banks were about security, small errors were always made. When John Cemach and his team found the weaknesses and the flaws, Liebs pounced.

It seemed that no law enforcement agency from any country could ever crack JC's money control systems. With access to the Adams Banking Solutions platform and numerous other electronic payment systems he had helped to build with Ravi Sharma, Liebs squirreled away funds, and timed all transactions to coincide with peak banking hours at each target bank just before the weekend. JC even knew how to bypass bank "watcher" software systems that triggered compliance alarms when large sums, generally over $100,000, hit a targeted donor account. And he always left a signature gift in the form of a Trojan virus threat that popped up as a window on bank screens when investigators got too close. Few banks wanted to take the risk of a threatened meltdown because the cost and inconvenience involved could be substantial, so in the end the bank always made up the shortfalls. They would prefer to stick their heads in the sand.

Liebs had JC by the balls, just like Ravi Sharma, and neither had any choice but to do Liebs's bidding.

Liebs's hacking ventures preserved his empire's financial equilibrium. His was by any measure a criminal organization. The plates still spun, but Liebs was tiring.

# MILTON GLOBAL INC. OFFICES

Harvey Milton was conducting his fourth meeting of the day. The room was packed with Indian businessmen seeking financing to launch a major telecommunications initiative in their country and eager to sign a contract with Milton Global. Milton Global was adept at securing profitable communications deals with emerging markets well ahead of their western counterparts. But the requisite concessions and bribes always minimized his company's margins. Daunting timeframes and sufficient capital reserves were essential in ensuring that projects with real profit potential stayed afloat. He had it all. Even at this meeting he brought in the Indian prime minister on a video conference link, who made it clear to his assembled fellow countrymen that a deal had to be done with MGI. Milton was tired and nervous, for he, too, was spinning plates. But the situation might not be a problem for long if he agreed with Gavin Hart's extraordinary motion that he had to take on Liebs head to head.

Milton began to feel better and felt the excitement and daring of his involvement in being a party to snuff the financial breath out of Liebs. He had not formulated his plan yet, but he had accepted Hart's offer. How could he lose? For him a billion dollars, tax free, no more investigations or accusations, and the rich pickings left on Liebs's carcass.

The Indians left. The boardroom was empty. The video connection to New Delhi cut. He called for Randell and immediately composed a formal invitation to get the ball rolling so that he might meet with the tyrannical Liebs. Randell arranged for it to be hand-delivered to Liebs, wherever he might be at that particular moment.

# ANTIGUA

Luciana and Nick left the pool area and strolled hand in hand down to the white sandy beach below. Large waves broke fifty yards out, and frothy cappuccino water gently lapped around their feet as they walked. As the water retreated, the sand and pebbles were sucked back into the sea with a long sigh, making holes under their feet. They walked, stumbled and fell, ran, and played in the water, splashing at each other. The sun was going down, but there was still heat and a cooling breeze coming off the land. They made their way back to their villa, brushing the wet sand from their feet. For the moment their troubles were behind them.

The villa door opened with Nick's card, and they ran to the shower. Showering was a soapy mess of suds, bodies rubbing together, and sharp tingling water under high pressure. Nick pleaded with her to relieve his frustration, but Luciana refused. There would be time enough after dinner; she pushed him away, feigning irritation as she opened the glass door. Nick was having none of it and ran out of the shower behind her, cracking a soaked bath towel in the air to force her to submit. He pursued her around the suite until they fell laughing uncontrollably on the bed. He leaned over Luciana, grinning, and then lowered his head to briefly kiss the soft, flat surface of her stomach. Luciana stretched out languidly and pushed at his head, forcing him lower. But Nick moved his head away and stood up, looking down. "Let's see how you feel now." He grinned and turned away, wrapping a towel around his waist. "Come on you, let's get dressed or we'll be late."

"Just you wait, leading a poor damsel astray." She rolled onto her side and curled up laughing as she hid her head under the pillow. "You don't love me anymore!" But the words were mumbled. Nick turned and saw her naked back and almost succumbed.

As a private jet taxied to an area away from the main terminal building, a 4x4 that had been waiting on the tarmac moved slowly toward the plane. The aircraft cabin door opened, and steps were lowered. The only passenger emerged, shielding his eyes from the high-beam lights that had been negligently left on by the driver. He walked the short distance to the vehicle and slid into the rear seat. The vehicle swung around, passing through the security gates, where only a cursory glance was given to the occupant's papers. Any friend of the prime minister was obviously not to be treated with anything other than the greatest of courtesy.

At a location closer to the sea, dinner was being served in the open-air restaurant as a sultry breeze stirred the air, but not enough to blow out the candlelit lamps on the tables. Soothing music wafted across the terrace as a piano and sax softly played. Above the seated diners, the clear, pollution-free night sky was covered in stars. The Carlisle Bay was a Mecca for high-net-worth families, couples, and celebrities. The true jet setters were already honed and already bronzed, men accompanied by long-legged girls with perfect tans were mingling with others less vain who, unused to the Caribbean sun, were red-faced or sported bare shoulders showing white strap lines.

Luciana, wearing her black, plunging, backless dress, looked everything a man could desire that evening; her olive skin looked even more vibrant from the afternoon's sun. She was already deemed by staff and male guests alike the prettiest girl at the resort. Nick was dressed less formally in a white linen shirt that hung over his black Paul Smith jeans. Passing the outdoor diners, the couple walked to a set of carved wooden doors and entered the striking dark enclave of the restaurant. Air-conditioned and walled off by glass, banks of dark-framed slats lined one wall, with flickering torches lining another.

Once they were seated in the vivid fuchsia armchairs, an army of efficient staff began their descent with an eclectic mix of Japanese, Thai, and Vietnamese dishes, and of course the wine list. They talked. Held hands, touching and stroking. Halfway through the second bottle of wine, Nick waved the air for the check, which he duly signed. He stood up from the table, rather unsteadily on his feet, and moved round to Luciana reaching down to kiss her exquisite forehead. He pulled her up from her chair, and taking her by the hand he led her out past the pool and down toward the beach.

They kicked off their shoes where the grass met the sand, passed the jetty, which was lit up by candles, and wandered slowly toward the headland on the powder-soft sand. The gentlest of waves kissed the shore. The sea and the sky became one. Nick picked up a coconut lying on the beach and threw it into the sea. Its impact set off a phosphorescent pinwheel display just below the surface.

It took some skill to negotiate the rocks between the bay and the small beach beyond the headland, which even during the day was deserted. They splashed their way across the shallow water like naughty children, finally arriving at the deserted beach. Luciana lay back on the sand and watched the stars, her knees bent. A cool distant waxing moon made long shadows across the sand. She closed her eyes, allowing the light breeze to ruffle her hair and let the mist from the sea stroke her face. Nick sat running his fingers through the sand, making shapes which he brushed away lost in thought.

"Darling?" Luciana asked, arching her back while supporting herself on her elbows. "Are you okay?"

"Yeah." He murmured. "How could I not be?" He tried not to slur his words, "I have the most beautiful of girls in the most amazing setting. Isn't this just incredible?"

"Yes, I can smell Angel Lilies. It's such a sensual scent." Luciana moved her hand closer to his and played with his fingers, still toying with the sand. "It's a world away from Manhattan. Thank you my darling man."

"Thank *you*." Nick smiled faintly; his face looked relaxed and also had benefitted from the sun that day. "Thanks also for listening and putting up with all the shit."

"Forget about that, darling." Luciana gave him a long, endearing look. "The only thing that matters, *tesoro*, is that we enjoy this piece of paradise together. *Baciami*." A peculiar excitement bore down on her. Her voice became husky and much lower. "Make love to me, now. Here on the beach."

"Try and stop me!" He moved in closer. Her dress had climbed up her thighs, revealing a matching black French lace thong. Leaning over until their lips met, he kissed her, and the rest of the world melted away. His mouth enclosed hers and his teeth bit lightly on her lower lip. Nick raised his head and started to undo the strap of Luciana's dress, which slipped down, exposing her brown nipples to the moonlight. He felt a hand tug at his belt buckle and search for the hardness beneath his jeans.

Luciana quickly stripped. Nick stood up, hopping on either foot as he stripped, while his sprawled lover, her legs wide, invited him to finish what he had tried to start that afternoon. He could no longer contain himself as he lowered himself down onto her body, mouthing her nipples, enjoying the sensation of her warm skin under his moist tongue. He traced her sweet body contours, ending his short tantalizing journey between her young thighs, which made her moan as she arched her back, raising her hips off the sand to receive his tongue.

Nick's breathing quickened. He could feel every last muscle in his body tense. Luciana said something in Italian as his hardness pressed against her skin. "Oh my God," she whispered, "this is unreal. Fuck me now."

Their overheated bodies propelled into action. Nick matched Luciana's fervent Italian passion. Holding her hips, he impaled her again and again. She writhed under him, her nails digging into his back.

Luciana grabbed Nick firmly around the waist and maneuvered him onto his back. Almost in the same motion, she straddled him, as if on horseback. The pounding of the waves was hard to hear over the pounding of her heart and the panting of their breath. Her thighs grew tight under the mounting pressure in her pelvis. His body clenched around hers as she shuddered with the power of her orgasm. She called out Nick's name and Italian words he did not understand. He held her slim, smooth hips and moved her spent body up and down. Both were satiated, gasping.

Luciana rolled over and found the sand was cold. Nick gazed at the exquisite curvature of her body. Surely someone up there in the starry firmament above them had blessed him with one of the most beautiful women he had ever seen.

They made love once again, this time slowly. They peered deeply into each other's eyes, waves lapping at their feet.

A full hour had passed since they had left the hotel. Both had fallen into a deep sleep. The drop in temperature awoke Nick. He looked at his watch and gently shook Luciana's shoulder. She stirred and curled up into his arms. "God, you're shivering. Come on, let's get back." He stood up and carefully pulled at her arms, raising her from the sand. Steadying her, he picked up their discarded clothing and they dressed. They found their shoes and began to make their way back, tired but besotted with each other.

Love may be blind, but their passion had gone beyond the beach and into the sand dunes, behind which, unknown to them, a figure safely hidden in the shadows of the grasses watched. Upon turning off the video camera with night vision, the voyeur slid back and stood up. His job was done.

It was too early. Nick Adams held onto his throbbing head and slowly opened one eye. The hammering came from the front door of the villa. Nick's eyes snapped open, and he sat bolt upright. He could hear his name being called by a female voice. "Come back later! Please!" Didn't they see the *Do Not Disturb* sign on the door? But the hammering was persistent. "I'm coming. Hold on a minute," he called out irritably, while searching the room for a bathrobe. He settled for a towel.

The knocking got louder. "Go away," Luciana muttered from beneath a pillow that she had placed over her head, her shiny, black hair trailing across the edge of the bed. Adams walked barefoot across the marble floor to the small entrance hall, where he released the security chain and opened the door.

"Please, come back later, we haven't gotten up yet," he said to the woman as he opened the door. Then he saw them.

"Mr. Adams?" The resort's female assistant-manager was the first to speak. "We need to speak with you. May we come in?" A pasty-complexioned man in a crumpled cotton suit stood behind her in the corridor, with two burly uniformed Antiguan policemen on either side of him. "It would be, let's say, less public?"

"What's going on?" Nick's stomach began to turn.

The sallow-faced man stepped forward and addressed the manager. "Thank you, my dear." He turned to Adams. "Your passport, please, sir."

Nick noticed a disdainful look on the manager's face. "At this time of day?"

"Please, Mr. Adams, this need not take long. Please let us in." It sounded more like a command than a request. Nick noticed the hardness in his voice.

"Sure," he replied hesitantly. "But please wait in the living room. My girlfriend is still in bed."

"We will need her papers as well, Mr. Adams." The plainclothes policeman spoke in clipped, no-nonsense, bureaucratic tones.

Adams entered the bedroom and peered through its partially opened curtains. He noticed a couple of policemen outside on his terrace. One had his arms folded, while the other kicked idly at the grass.

"What's happening, *tesoro*?" Luciana sat up in bed, clutching her bent legs, her head resting on her knees. "Why do they want our passports?"

"Nothing darling, it's probably a formality. Maybe they think we are fugitives or even terrorists." But he didn't laugh. Clearly something was wrong. "Where is your passport?"

She motioned toward her suitcase. "My papers are in there, in the side pocket."

Adams heard a noise and turned. The man had stepped through to the entryway of the bedroom with a policeman right behind him.

"Please, gentlemen," he said, lifting his hands. "Would you

mind staying in the living room? My girlfriend is not dressed." He hoped to appease their sense of decency.

"Very well, Mr. Adams."

Luciana slipped out of the bed, wrapped in a sheet, and stood motionless as Adams padded barefoot back to the living room.

"Thank you, Mr. Adams." He took the passports and quickly flipped through them both, and then handed them to the policeman standing near the window. "And your flight tickets please?"

Adams sighed inwardly and retrieved the tickets from the top drawer of a table.

"Good," the man said, looking through the various papers. "All seems in order now."

"Why wouldn't everything be okay?" Now he was getting angry. "I don't know what this was all about, but is this the way you treat your tourists?" He paused and then, offering a hand to the two officials, added, "Anyhow, thank you, gentlemen, for dropping in. Now, if you'll excuse me, getting back to holiday mode will be the order of the day."

But the suited official was having none of this man's nonsense. "Your papers are in order, and therefore you will be able to make the flight off this island at 4:00 p.m. this afternoon." The man's brown eyes were stern, his voice cool.

"Leave? What, today?" Luciana stood by Nick's side in confusion.

"It is now eight fifteen. The hotel would like you out of here as soon as possible. We will arrange a police escort to take you to the airport at ten thirty, where you will have to wait in the departure lounge until your flight."

"What the hell is going on?" Adams demanded.

"Hush, for a second, Nico." Luciana moved forward and looked at the man. "Please explain what has happened, sir. I am sure there has been some mistake."

"Miss," the man said, looking her straight in the eyes, "you have been reported for gross public indecency and have abused our country's welcome. The law is quite clear. You are no longer welcome at the Carlisle or anywhere else on Antigua."

"You can't be serious." Nick lowered his voice, shaking his head in disbelief. Had they been observed on the beach? Surely not? Even someone watching from a hundred feet away would find it pretty hard to make out anything. And he would certainly have seen anyone closer than that. "What puritanical pervert reported us?" Luciana looked at Nick and put her finger to her lips. "Nick!" It was a gentle but emphatic warning to be cautious.

"That, I'm afraid, is our business. You will kindly vacate your room as soon as possible." The man turned and left the room, issuing instructions to the police standing there. One policeman moved across to the window and shouted at his two colleagues outside. They raised their hands in acknowledgment.

"Nico, what is going on?" She turned her attention to him in an accusatory voice. "I just can't believe this is happening." Luciana stood frozen like a sculpture of a Greek goddess, the white sheet draped about her. Her eyes, fixed on the beach in the distance, were slowly filling with tears, the feeling of crushing disappointment enveloping her.

Nick placed a comforting arm around her, as she began to sob gently. "Come on darling, we were just doing what all couples do."

"But who could have seen us?" she whimpered.

"Maybe one of the locals, or it may have been somebody from the hotel."

"I feel so dirty." She clutched the sheet tightly about her.

Nick swung her around and looked into her tear-filled eyes. "Don't ever let me hear you say that again, do you understand?" He wiped her cheeks with his thumbs.

Things went from bad to worse. Nick was a prisoner of his own making. There was another knock at the door. The assistant manager stood rigidly outside, holding an envelope. She handed it to Nick, explaining that it was their receipt, and that breakfast would be served in their room to save any more embarrassment with other guests. Her charming, welcoming beam of the day before had disappeared. Turning, the assistant manager pushed past the two policemen standing outside the door and made her way along the terrace path.

A small group of guests started to gather on the paths and lawn in front of their villa, curious at the presence of the police. Eventually bored, they shuffled off to their sun loungers and the beach beyond.

Nick and Luciana did not touch breakfast. They simply packed in silence. Luciana had regained her composure, but Nick's anger was still brewing. He remembered being in Antigua during Sailing Week two years earlier, when it was commonplace for all manner of so-called lewd acts to be carried out, as sailors of both sexes rocked and rolled for days. Nick could vouch for this from personal experience.

Elsewhere in town, the agent had completed his meeting with the chief of police. The video was clear. It was a coup. He had no idea how he was to carry out his instructions from Special Agent Rae, but shadowing the target couple and catching them having sex on the beach made his task so much easier. Had it not been for their carnal activities, he would have had to resort to other means to punish the errant Nick Adams. Not a pleasant option. The police accepted the video evidence from the strange visitor. It wasn't his place to question his superiors. Such incidents were commonplace on a holiday island. Hell, he remembered his youthful encounters and smiled, feeling young once again. But instructions had been given. The full force of the law would be used. It was a shame.

By noon Nick and Luciana had cleared customs and passport control, and were ensconced in the very basic surroundings of the airport's small departure lounge. Meanwhile, a small, white, unmarked jet taxied onto the runway from the side of the airport. After waiting ten minutes for a passenger jet to clear the runway, it took off and disappeared into the distant clouds. Job done.

"Here, sweetheart." Nick handed Luciana a bundle of bills he had retrieved from his wallet, partially repaying the money she had drawn out of the ATM in New York.

"Keep it, *tesoro*. You may need it until you sort everything out."

"Please, I insist," he said.

"No," Luciana protested. "You still have to get through the weekend. You can reimburse me when you want. Stop being so proud, Nico. *Ti amo, tesoro.*"

"Okay, but I will do that next week." He looked into her eyes. "You beautiful creature. You know, I don't care; I would do it again and again. It was the most wonderful, sensational, sensual experience of my life." He put the money carelessly into his trouser pocket.

"Oh, yes my darling." She smiled at him and stroked his cheek. "For me too." She sat back, and looking about her, she lowered her voice. "Don't you think there is a pattern emerging? It is too coincidental, Nico. I am feeling very uneasy about this ..."

"Us?" Nick looked despondent.

"Not you silly. Everything else."

The couple passed the time searching for duty free gifts, drinking at the bar, and eating tasteless sandwiches and chips. International and local flights came and went as they waited. Luciana slept on Nick's lap while he read a book on his tablet.

Hours passed before they were finally seated on a flight to San Juan, Puerto Rico, where they would catch a connection to JFK.

"Well, that's one island we can't go back to." With sarcasm, Nick smiled at Luciana, who grinned nervously.

"We don't need an island for a replay, my darling sexy boy." She winked at him. Champagne was served, and business class got into full swing for the short flight.

Nick sat lost in thought, looking preoccupied. Luciana's hands snaked across his lap to break his trance. "Come on, Nico. The nightmare is over. It happened, and tomorrow is another day."

He nodded. But he still couldn't work out their deportation from Antigua. It just didn't add up. Something was seriously amiss.

The flight from San Juan to New York touched down thirty minutes late. By the time the passengers disembarked, cleared customs, and retrieved their luggage, it was after midnight. There was little or no traffic on the roads, and they were back in

Manhattan in no time at all. A black SUV pulled out from the airport drop zone and followed their yellow cab some distance behind.

Outside Nick's apartment building the taxi driver unloaded their luggage. Nick paid the fare, and the weary couple hobbled with their bags through the building lobby to the elevators. The SUV slowly passed them and parked a little farther up the street. Awakened by the commotion of suitcases entering through the revolving doors, the snoozing night doorman tried to get a message to Nick before he caught the elevator, but failed. The doors of the elevator closed in his face.

Nick wrestled with his keys at his front door, twisting and turning each key, jiggling the locks several times, but to no avail.

"What's the problem?" Luciana asked.

"The fucking lock's jammed. I can't even get the keys to turn. Fuck." He held his hands up to his head and then noticed a slight indentation in the doorframe. "The lock's been changed. Look, it's brand new. Oh, shit, there must have been a break-in and Ravi had a new lock fitted or something. Great. That's all we need!"

"Ring the doorbell. You'll just have to get Ravi out of bed."

Nick rang the bell, but there was no answer. Meanwhile, Luciana pulled out her cell phone and called the apartment. A recorded message from the phone company informed her that the number was no longer in service.

"Oh, no." she exclaimed. "Your home phone is no longer in service."

"What? Try Ravi's cell."

"He's not picking up. Besides, he thinks we're coming back late tomorrow night, so he's probably out or decided to stay at his place on Fire Island. Come on," she said, tugging at Nick's sleeve, "let's go, we can stay at my place."

Back in the lobby, Nick searched for the night doorman to get some kind of explanation, but he was nowhere to be found. Tired and confused, they finally hailed a cab to Luciana's Soho loft. Behind them, at a discreet distance, the SUV shadowed their cab. It was a busy night for the sole occupant.

After unloading their luggage just inside the front door, they dragged their exhausted bodies to the loft apartment. Luciana's apartment mate wasn't at home. She rarely was; she was in love and had all but virtually moved out. Anyway, she was away on holiday. That would prove to be useful to them, although at that stage they didn't know why.

"Stylish" would best describe Luciana's massive loft apartment. Its modern décor was comfortably inviting, with plush furnishings, wood finishes, touches of stainless steel and an open plan layout. It was Nick's first visit to Luciana's loft, as she had spent their time together at Nick's apartment. He was impressed by her style.

An hour later they were sound asleep. A troubled, exhausted coma had swept over the couple. Tomorrow would come around all too soon.

Luciana arose early, leaving Nick sound asleep. Quietly opening the bedroom door, she tiptoed across the wooden floor to the kitchen to make herself coffee.

Luciana's refrigerator lay bare, apart from bottles of water, wine, Diet Coke and a large piece of Parmesan cheese. With no food in sight, she would wait for Nick to wake before deciding what to do about breakfast.

Nick awoke to find himself alone in a strange bed. It was, of course, not the first time he had had the same surprise. Lost for a moment, he remembered he was at Luciana's place. She didn't respond when he called out to her. He grabbed the towel she had placed on the chair beside the bedside table for him, wrapped it around his waist, and staggered into the living area. "Hi," he grunted, heavy with sleep.

"Ah, so we are awake?" She smiled at Nick and moved toward him. "Good morning my darling," she smiled back. "I'm so sorry, but the cupboards are bare. Krista and I never seem to get around to food shopping," Luciana explained, shrugging her shoulders. "Besides, thanks to you, I'm never here."

"Hey, no problem. Why don't I get dressed, go out, and get us something?" Nick suggested, leaning over to kiss the tip of her nose.

"Sounds good to me. You can get food and papers nearby. Walk north to Prince, turn right, then down two blocks."

Nick threw on a pair of jeans, a shirt, and a baseball cap. With some cash and Luciana's keys in hand, he ran down the building stairs and out onto the wet sidewalk. On a Sunday morning in Soho, the streets were particularly busy. Even though it was drizzling, pedestrians with open umbrellas were already out shopping for books, clothes, and antiques or visiting the galleries and food locations in the area. He crossed streets, weaving in and out of slow-moving traffic, but didn't notice the silent observer who watched through a half-open car window, through which wisps of exhaled smoke curled out into the morning air.

Luciana dressed and put on what little makeup she normally used. She picked up voice mail. The one from Ravi Sharma was shocking.

Twenty minutes later Nick returned with two bulky brown paper bags. The Sunday edition of the *New York Times* balanced precariously under his arm finally gave up and slipped, spewing its contents onto the kitchen floor. He called out for Luciana, but received no reply. While bent over to gather the fallen paper, he caught a brief glimpse of her rolled up in a ball on the sofa. Her face was tear-stained and expressionless.

"I got all sorts of great stuff, honey," he said, pleased with himself. He started to unpack. He waited for the return of his warm greeting, but none came. He left the unpacking, and stepping over the newspaper strewn across the floor, he moved over to the sofa where he sat alongside the prostrate Luciana.

"Nick, you've got more problems to deal with." Her words were dull. "If that were at all possible," Luciana whispered. Nick immediately grabbed hold of her arms, but she slid away from his grip. She rolled off the sofa and stood up. "Listen to this message," she said, holding the phone out to him.

"Who is it from?"

"Why don't you listen and you'll find out soon enough." There was snap to her words which he hadn't encountered before.

Ravi Sharma's voice couldn't be clearer. "Please, don't panic,

Lu, but I didn't know what to do. I thought maybe you could get this message to Nick. It's a long story, girl."

"I knew something was wrong," Nick mumbled.

"Just listen for Christ's sake!"

Sharma's voice went on. "I got back Saturday afternoon at about three o'clock, and my keys wouldn't work. Anyway, I talked to the concierge, who told me that two men had arrived at lunchtime and let themselves in with keys. Apparently they changed the locks. They told the doorman that it was on your orders."

Nick listened in silence.

"Well, I got hold of the managing agent. What an unpleasant jerk. He was so fucking rude; sorry Lu, but he made me mad. Anyway, he says there's some problem with the lease, something to do with the apartment being leased by an offshore company. I told him I'd be happy to meet with him to work things out before you guys returned. But he was adamant about speaking only to Nick, so I left for Fire Island. Please have Nick call me as soon as you get back. I'll be on my cell. Sorry darling, love you!"

"Hmm, this doesn't sound so good. Can I use your phone?"

Luciana nodded.

Nick stood in disbelief as he spoke to Sharma. There was another piece of news: his BMW had been repossessed. Apparently the concierge refused to give the recovery agents access to the garage at first, but the men presented legal ownership documents, so he had no choice. Sharma told Nick that the leasing company claimed the terms of the contract had been breached since he was no longer an officer or director of Adams Banking Solutions. The car would be sold, and Adams would be forced repay any shortfall incurred on the lease.

Adams's quiet anger flared at Sharma's words. He had suffered many ups and downs in his life; been on the brink of bankruptcy many times, and had fought his way back; and all stoically, without looking back. But his previous trials paled into insignificance compared to the current nightmare unfolding before his very eyes. It was now blatantly obvious to him that certain powers were hell-bent on either ruining him or forcing his hand. He was determined not to let their tactics rattle him. No matter how the forces at play played their cards, he resolved to have his own way in the end. Adams shook his head as he ended his call with Sharma and did not say a word.

"Do you want to talk about it?" Luciana met his silence calmly and rubbed her hands down his spine. "Sorry I sounded so bad tempered, but I worry for you, Nico."

"They will stop at nothing. First the credit cards and then my cell phone. Then we're deported from Antigua, only to arrive home to find that I've lost my home and my car as well. What more can they possibly do to me?"

"'They?'" Luciana reached up and placed a hand on his cheek, pulling his face down as she looked into his eyes. She could read his silent rage.

"Dillon Rae and Gavin Hart. That's who." But he wasn't totally convinced. He could also see Erich Kersch's hand somewhere in the nightmare. He had seen some of his tactics in the past, but chose to ignore what was plain to see. "You know, the whole fucking clown show."

"Why would anyone want to do this?" Luciana asked impatiently. "What the hell have you done?"

"What do you mean by that? I haven't done anything."

"Well, there must be something. They don't behave like this even in Sicily."

"No—they just shoot them instead," he growled.

"Well, maybe that's next. It happened to Howard Wayne."

"Okay, maybe there is a reason." Adams knew well enough that he had annoyed Dillon Rae by stalling the plan against Liebs. "I need to make a few calls," he said suddenly.

"Make the calls. I'll put breakfast together and then we'll figure out what to do."

Nick dialed Gavin Hart, but his call was diverted to voicemail. So he rang Erich Kersch, who was somewhere in Phoenix. Kersch denied having a hand in his recent misfortunes and strangely offered his help in sorting out the matter with his car. Since Kersch sounded in unusually good form, Adams couldn't detect anything underhanded in his tone. They spoke about Nick's share sale, which, according to Kersch, was on schedule. But Kersch skillfully concealed from Nick the fact that the sale had already taken place, with the proceeds already sitting in an account at CAY BANK.

Nick searched his BlackBerry for Dillon Rae's contact information even though it was still barred. When he called the Washington number using Luciana's landline, a male operator explained that he could only take messages, that if it was urgent, he would do what he could to get a message through to Rae.

Nick returned to the kitchen with a mix of trepidation and determination. Luciana saw the resolve in his eyes and made several attempts to get him to talk, but he just sat there silent, distracted, and deep in thought. Luciana began to doubt everything Nick had told her since they had met. Had he been lying to her all along? The only thing she wanted now was the truth. A fuck on the beach was all very nice, but she didn't want trouble and strife; she had her own life and ambitions.

They ate breakfast in silence. Finally a ringing phone broke the silence and Luciana went to answer it. It was someone asking for Nick, so she blankly handed him the receiver.

"Nicholas Adams." The voice of Special Agent Dillon Rae was barely controlled. "What the hell have you been doing?"

"I could ask the same of you," Adams responded acidly.

"Cut the crap," Rae fumed. "We offered you a government assignment which you agreed to get back to us on last week. But instead you frolic off to the Caribbean. I want your commitment now. Do you understand? You have no choice."

"There will be no deal until you tell me what game you're playing," Adams said boldly, a scowl darkening his features.

"Game? You know the game. Hart told you what you have to do." Rae ignored the insolence in Adams's words. "You pathetic little shit. Who's playing games here? If you don't get with the program, I can assure you that your life won't get any easier. What's happened is a mere drop in the ocean compared to what might happen to you from now on. I suggest you stop screwing your girlfriend and start delivering or you'll end up with nothing." The line went dead.

"Fuck you!" Adams shouted at the phone. Alarmed by what lay unspoken in Rae's words, Adams made a futile effort to get him back. He slammed the receiver down and swore.

"So?"

"It was nothing."

"Nothing?" Luciana screamed. She could have secured a place at the old Fulton Fish Market on pitch alone. "You say 'nothing' as though nothing has happened to us. It was supposed to have been a romantic break for us, and can you not see that something is seriously wrong here?" Her voice was cold with anger. "I thought we had more between us than this." She turned to leave the kitchen, her shoulders trembling.

"Luciana, I'm sorry …"

She spun around to face him. "Look what's happening to us! You can't take on everything singlehandedly," she cried.

"I was planning on following through with what they wanted. But I just needed time to understand fully what I was getting myself mixed up with," he said, trying to reassure her.

"'They? There we go with *they* again! Who the hell are *they*? These people you're involved with?"

"The people I told you about."

"And who exactly are these *people*?"

"I don't want to get into it right now. But what I will tell you is that they'll remove the block on my credit cards and phone, give me back my car and apartment, and then everything will be as if nothing had ever happened."

"Will it? I wonder." Luciana rushed out of the room, ignoring his outstretched arms. She went into her bedroom only to reappear wearing a shiny black raincoat.

"I'm going out for some fresh air. Perhaps when I return you'll tell me what all this is really about and where I fit in." She saw him move toward her. "Stop." She backed away from him. "And don't follow me. I mean it, Nick Adams."

Luciana was down the stairs and across the street before Adams could protest. Dodging pedestrians, she sprinted toward

Spring Street. It was still wet underfoot, although the rain had stopped.

The moment the building door swung open, the driver seated in the unmarked car started his engine to follow her. He abruptly pulled out into traffic, causing two cars to brake to a screeching halt. Horns blared. He ignored them.

Luciana had no idea where she was headed. She just needed to get away. Where had he made his money? Fraud undoubtedly. *"Merda,"* she murmured. Getting involved with anything shady was something she had reason to avoid at all cost. Suddenly Luciana was back in the past. It would be like Italy all over again when she was a child. And for a fleeting moment she considered that perhaps her father was behind it all. Franco Cavallini wasn't pleased about her dating a non-Italian, and may have resorted to creating a wedge between them. She realized that although it would have been beyond him, it was an absurd notion.

The driver followed close behind as Luciana walked along Houston Street. Deep in thought, she had wandered near Washington Square, walking along LaGuardia Place, and was about to cross Bleeker Street when suddenly a revving engine from behind jolted her from her introspection. The black Ford SUV spun its wheels. Scorching rubber, it made a sudden right turn onto Bleeker, plowing toward her. She turned and saw in absolute horror the vehicle coming straight at her. She spun around in a desperate attempt to avoid the car but it was too late. There was a heavy thump as the front fender hit her. Her body was hurled into the air and sailed over the hood of the car like a rag doll. She came down with a shuddering crash, striking the windshield of a Volvo heading south, her body form embedded in the shattered glass. She slid across the hood and in an act of self-preservation held out her arms to cushion her fall before spiraling onto the road.

The driver of the Ford knew exactly at what angle to hit his target without causing too much physical trauma, give or take a few degrees. He was confident the target would be all right, suffering only scratches and some minor bruising. Slightly impeded by the wet road, he stepped on the gas pedal and gunned the vehicle away from the scene, ripping off the side mirror of a parked car in the process. Some people ran after the vehicle waving fists, while others crowded around the girl lying in the street.

The babble of tongues confused Luciana. The blackness slowly faded, as strange faces emerged. A young, bearded man cradled her head, looking worried. Pain ran through every bone. "Are you okay?" he kept asking her. She tried to raise herself, but a sharp pain lanced through her side. The man instructed her not to move.

Two NYPD cops were the first on the scene. They took statements from those in the crowd who had witnessed the accident. No one had taken the license number of the hit-and-run vehicle; he had sped away too fast, they claimed.

As Luciana lay there, she felt the world fading in and out as if it were trying to slip away. In the distance she could hear an ambulance siren getting louder as it approached. It seemed to be in sync with the pounding in her head. When it arrived, two paramedics examined her, placed her on a stretcher, and slid it into the ambulance.

"Is she going to make it?" the young man who tended to her asked.

"Excuse me, sir." One paramedic moved him out of the way. The ambulance made off, its siren wailing until it faded in the distance.

The Ford would be taken out of service later that day. Directives not to create bad blood with the NYPD were to be followed explicitly, particularly since the NYPD was never consulted or notified about this specific operation taking place within their patch. They would get touchy. The driver headed toward the FDR Drive to the Midtown Tunnel. He telephoned his report.

Adams was alone in the loft when the phone rang. He answered, thinking it might be for him. Luciana was in tears.

"I'm sorry, *tesoro*," she sobbed. "Something awful just happened to me. My God I am so sorry!" Her voice was strange.

"Where are you? Come back home, sweetheart, everything is going to be okay, I promise."

"I've had an accident. I'm at NYU Medical Center in the ER. They're about to take X-rays."

"What?" he shouted incredulously. He could hardly believe her words. "No." A thousand voices in his head clamored to be heard. "Are you all right? Please tell me that you are." His eyes teared up. "It's all my fault."

"It was a hit and run."

"Hit and run? Oh, shit," he shouted. "I'm on my way." A cloud of suspicious thoughts enveloped him. He was completely losing it. It could have been an accident, but he just knew the pattern by now. The FBI, whose motto was Fidelity, Bravery, and Integrity, would not stoop so low, surely?

Despite his haste Adams made a call. Now was not the time to panic, but the nature of the attack on Luciana began to make horrible sense.

"Tell Dillon Rae to back off." For a brief moment he was consumed with the idea of revenge. "I'll do what he wants. And tell him to leave my girlfriend out of this. Do you hear?"

"I hear you, sir. I'll relay your message," the bored male operator responded. He was used to taking such calls for Rae.

There was no unmarked car observing Nick as he ran out of Luciana's building and hailed a cab to rush him to NYU Medical Center.

The usually meticulous Nick Adams arrived disheveled, his hair a mess, bleary-eyed, his spirit beaten. Reception directed him to the X-ray department, where he found Luciana sitting in a wheelchair, wrapped in a hospital blanket, talking to a couple of uniformed policemen who were taking notes. She looked dreadful. *What have I done?* he thought, his eyes glistening with tears. He wished he hadn't let his stubbornness get in the way. He should have been less arrogant. How could he fight the FBI?

When Luciana caught sight of Nick, the emotional floodgates opened and she cried like a child, her face naked with fear and vulnerability. He moved quickly to her and pulled her gently into his arms, tucked her head under his chin, and kissed her forehead repeatedly. Her right arm was in a sling and Luciana winced. Her eyes showed the pain as they embraced.

Luciana looked up and addressed the officers: "This is my boyfriend, Nicholas Adams"

They looked at Nick and nodded. "Well, we're done here. If there's anything you wish to add to your statement or anything else you can remember about the incident, you should contact the precinct and we'll take it from there." They smiled. "If our investigation turns up any vital information, we'll contact you at the number you've given us." The officers wished Luciana well and left the emergency room, their radios hissing as they issued new instructions.

Luciana's back hurt badly. Apparently, there were minor abrasions all over her body and bruises scarred her legs. But the X-rays found nothing wrong internally. The doctor assured Nick that Luciana would be all right, but insisted she stay at the hospital overnight for observation. Luciana refused outright to stay as advised, adamant she was going home if there wasn't anything seriously wrong. Although the doctor recommended against her leaving, he could not force her to stay. He told Nick that she needed rest and someone to look after her for the next few days, that her ribs would hurt for a while, and despite her considerable pain, in a week she would be back to normal. A checkup was scheduled for two weeks later.

He hailed a cab and gave the driver her address and the instructions to drive slowly and to avoid all of the potholes. The Sikh driver didn't understand a word and had to rely on Nick's directions and continual admonishment as the cab fell into one hole after another.

Nick put Luciana to bed immediately and sat for some time beside her, holding her hand. There was so much he wished to say, but his words seemed to dry up and crumble to dust. He kissed the bruises marring her skin until the codeine painkillers took effect. He insisted on preparing something for her to eat.

Having eaten and finally resting more comfortably, Luciana fell asleep.

Nick left the bedroom, shutting the door quietly behind him. As she had asked, he made a few calls on her behalf, contacting her office to request a few days of sick leave. Sharma was ready to assist where needed. Her father, fortunately, was unavailable. He also placed a call to Detective Lee to report the curious accident and asked if he could help with any information on the hit and run. Lee sympathized with Adams on his girlfriend's predicament, but his tone seemed surprisingly flat. There was something suspicious in Lee's manner. Adams asked whether there was progress on Howard Wayne's case. Nothing new, Lee told him, but he promised to touch base if anything developed. The more-than-brusque conversation left his stomach churning.

The phone rang. It was Dillon Rae. Before Rae had a chance to speak, Adams lashed out, "So! You got my message. You win! I knew you guys could flex your muscles when you had to, but I never knew you would resort to such evil methods! First you make me look like a real idiot at the airport, and then we get thrown off the fucking island! And …"

"Mr. Adams," Rae interrupted, raising his voice to cut short the deluge of accusations, "have you quite finished?"

"No, I haven't." Adams was too lost in the fury of his anger to listen to anything Rae had to say. "Then I'm locked out of my apartment, my car is repossessed—and I have a sneaking suspicion that you had something to do with my girl's accident!"

"Accident?"

"Yes, accident. What! You really think you were going to pull that one over on me? Am I that stupid? Do I have the word 'cunt' written all over my forehead? A hit-and-run driver deliberately struck down my girlfriend. Sound familiar?" The most compelling reason for him to assume Rae was behind all these events was that his intuition was almost always right on the money. If he had followed his nose more often, he would have avoided much trouble in his life.

"She's okay, I hope?" Rae sounded genuinely concerned.

"Luckily for you she is." The slight catch in his voice told Rae that this guy was close to a breakdown.

"Whoa, hang on now, I can understand that you're upset."

"Upset isn't even in the universe of what I'm feeling."

The indignation didn't surprise Rae at all, so he met the tirade calmly. "So Nick," he paused for a moment, "you have decided to help us? Well, it's certainly about time."

Adams felt a sudden burning resentment of the man who was hell-bent on doing whatever was necessary until he conceded. "Just tell me how I can get my fucking life back." A long breath escaped his pursed lips. Now Rae could stop riding herd on him, he thought. But this time he vowed to navigate the course by his wits without losing his ass in the process.

"I assure you that you will benefit from your decision in every way. Just think of it as doing your part for your country." Rae was deliberately short and suggested that a meeting take place the following day with all parties who were involved.

The nearly hysterical anger Adams had vented a moment earlier slowly evaporated. He informed Rae that he had already worked out a way to implement the plan.

Rae was pleased that his efforts to gain Adams's full commitment had worked after all. "Okay, then. Tomorrow you get back your apartment and car."

"That's big of you," Adams sneered.

"And your credit cards will be unblocked. But," he paused, "your bank accounts will continue to be frozen as security. You will gain access to any cash when the job is completed." He paused. "You are extremely canny, Nick. I don't know how you paid for your airline tickets, but I will find out." There was another long pause. "And I know you have squirreled away money somewhere outside your own country. This, my friend, is against the law, and you will be a criminal if I find out. Just a warning."

"There is no basis for that accusation." But he was less than convincing. And they both knew it. "If my accounts are frozen, then how do you expect me to use my cards?"

"You have credit limits. Use them. By the time your next

statements arrive, the file will be closed and all will be well. Welcome to the team. I will be in touch on your reinstated cell phone." The line went dead.

Nick sat on the sofa and began hyperventilating. Relief swiftly followed the shadow of regret that had been plaguing him. He called Sharma to give him the news that things were back on track. But his voice carried no certainty in his words.

Lloyd Lee got back to Nick with unsettling news that the car was untraceable, especially since none of the witnesses had been able to make out the license number, leading to a dead end on both the car and driver. The NYPD filed the incident as a hit and run . He was sorry, and Adams noted his evident sincerity. "Just another unfortunate accident. Thank God that it was not any worse," Lee told him.

# CYPRUS

Cyprus is a boulder in the Mediterranean, by the coastal white cliffs near Paphos; the land of gods and goddesses; the legendary birthplace of Aphrodite, the goddess of love, sex, and passion, who loved and was loved by many gods and mortals alike.

On the southwest coast, a little more than a stone's throw from Petra Tou Romiou, on the outskirts of Paphos, another goddess dwelled. Not the love goddess of antiquity, but a present-day goddess of absolute beauty, the modern personification of writer Pausanias's depiction of Aphrodite, the patroness of war and espionage, the unstoppable former special agent in the Russian Secret Service, and ingenious underground operative. A proficient assassin, a skilled marksman, an expert at stabbing, poisoning, and strangulation, a master of the martial arts, she was the best. In certain circles the unpredictability and ruthlessness of this independent operative were well known. A consummate professional, she wielded more influence than almost anyone in her field. And although she worked for the highest bidder, she had begun taking on more and more assignments from one single client, who always paid handsomely and was always generous with performance bonuses that the Swiss banker insisted upon giving her.

But her allegiance to Gerhard Liebs was temporary, to endure until she had amassed enough wealth to launch her own elite espionage syndicate, an unrivaled transnational network-for-hire, complete with a secret training facility located in Cyprus.

When the former KGB no longer needed her services, Valentina Vinogradov began a life of art theft by appointment. She knew who privately held what, and where to retrieve previously stolen pieces. Many wealthy men and women who lusted after specific works of art had been introduced to her, and she had built a solid reputation in the field, ultimately as the go-to source for stolen art. The Russian oligarchs understood her and gave her commissions and carte blanche in return for trophy art.

Sometime ago Vinogradov had carried out an assignment for someone who wished to acquire a certain Blue Period Picasso. Vinogradov had successfully located the item in a stately English home nestled in the heart of two thousand acres in Gloucestershire. An ageing pop star, who spent most of his waking hours coked up, owned the house. Although it took little time to work out the security system, Vinogradov had unintentionally tripped a laser beam. The gods protected her that night; when the alarm went off, the security company had been less than diligent. The frequency of false alarms at that manor house had become a local joke to neighbors and the police alike. She cut the canvas from its frame and made off with the painting; two Irish wolfhounds lay dead in the courtyard, a loss more important to the owner than the painting. Vingradov's ability to acquire such a rare acquisition to order had impressed and delighted Liebs.

So the Swiss banker and the Russian ex-KGB agent developed a special relationship. Vinogradov had often survived attempts to kill her, sometimes by the skin of her teeth. One day while "working" in Austria, she was disturbed in the middle of the night by a German baron brandishing a hunting rifle. The baron raised his gun and fired a shot at the intruder but missed. As he aimed again at Vinogradov, he looked down at the safety catch. In a split second, she sidestepped him with a quick, martial arts 540-degree kick, and threw the Austrian aristocrat to the ground. He landed on his gun, which went off, shooting him through the chest. Vinogradov escaped without the Fabergé egg she had been sent to get, but was not detected. The next morning German papers deemed the tragic accident a suicide. It was then that the notion of useful suicides was born. Liebs marveled at the new opportunities this extraordinary woman had opened up.

Vinogradov had just returned from a party hosted by her exclusive members-only sex club back in Europe. She had sought relief from pent-up emotions. Her club was a place where women felt liberated, its creed all about the female. Members could dance in their underwear, and drink with no pressure and no expectations. It was a playpen for the world's sexual elite where guests went for titillation and to have no-strings-attached sex with any number of men and women. Held at different mansions and palatial flats, the location of each secret event was not revealed until the day before the party.

The club accepted membership of single women and couples from only a choice group of successful, intelligent, beautiful, high-flying people. Members and guests had to be at least conventionally good-looking and arrive masked. A man could not get beyond the secure threshold unless a woman accompanied him. Drugs, cameras, and phones were not allowed. Circulating bouncers roamed the premises to ensure everyone adhered to the rules and that there were no lone males quietly acting like pervs in the shadows. The dress code was elegant attire, period costumes, über-expensive lingerie, and whatever struck your fancy or fantasy.

In Cyprus, seated at a wrought-iron table on her spacious veranda, Vinogradov threw back a shot of chilled vodka. The sun was hotter than usual, and there was little breeze, but the heat didn't faze her. Her sense of well-being was intrinsically linked to three things: the success of each assignment, her temple of promiscuity, and this secret retreat.

The villa, built on a sloping waterfront site, overlooked a pebbled beach lapped by the clear, warm seas of the bay. Intermittently looking out at the unobstructed 180-degree sea views and the two stranded Windsurfers searching for wind, she studied notes taken from an encrypted e-mail she had received earlier.

Once Vinogradov had every detail of her new assignment committed to memory, she roamed the rooms of the house barefoot. Its interiors were traditional Cypriot white walls. Raw concrete, white stucco, and glass carried the island theme both inside and out. A dramatic atrium formed by stainless-steel balustrades in the foyer led to the upper floors. She climbed the curved staircase to the mezzanine and entered her bedroom, where she packed while keeping watch from her bedroom balcony on the plight of the two sportsmen. They had given up the struggle, jumped into the sea and swum toward the shore defeated.

Vinogradov left the villa and headed for the center of Paphos Fort, the fishing harbor near her bank. Cyprus was not only the perfect spot for obscurity; it was also a highly desirable place for money launderers. And with special arrangements made on her behalf, she walked away from the foreign exchange desk with $50,000 in cash.

Back at the villa, Vinogradov took a local painting off her bedroom wall. From the hidden vault she selected three different passports and several credit cards, retrieving as well a number of metal pieces wrapped in canvas. Skillfully she assembled the pieces and fitted a silencer. Having methodically checked it, she dismantled the weapon and placed its components into a specially coated bag. X-ray machines at airports would never be able to identify any weapon she carried. She scorned the amateurs who ran security. She mused about becoming a consultant and telling them the tricks of her trade.

She had an assignment. Another plane, another continent.

# ROME

When a midnight blue Range Rover arrived at the Vatican, the Swiss guards stopped the vehicle at the gates, refusing entry, but the driver insisted that the envelope be taken to Gerhard Liebs immediately. Satisfied with the guards' guarantee, the driver reversed and headed back into the narrow streets of Rome. The guards checked the envelope through a scanner and delivered it to a member of Liebs's staff.

Liebs was manipulating his keyboard and accessing one of his many computer screens that reflected off his frameless spectacles. He barely looked up when the girl, who had been given the unenviable task of disturbing him, knocked quietly at the door. Liebs growled. She scurried in, mumbled a few words, placed the manila envelope on the left corner of his desk, and backed herself against the doorway, awaiting instructions. His gloved hands moved to an envelope opener and he slit it open, retrieved its contents with some difficulty, still wearing his gloves, and read the document. Smiling, he looked up. "This is good. Very good. Thank you, my dear." He placed the letter on the desk and stood up. The girl remained, nervously waiting. "There is no reply, you may go." A smile crossed his taut, thin-skinned face. "There is one thing: some coffee, please," he ordered. He needed to think carefully about the contents of the envelope.

Liebs paced the ancient stone floor, occasionally stopping to stare at the letter that curled along its folds. *Why?* he asked himself. Why would Harvey Milton be suggesting that the two of them meet? His last attempt at blackmailing Milton had been laid to rest, so it seemed unlikely that the invitation was in response to that. What was Milton up to? The rhythm of his pacing increased as he mentally ran through the possibilities. He wrung his gloved hands together. A damp spot of yellow stain seeped out through one of the fingers. His innate distrust of human character was always a cause for exploring the intent behind requests. He would not respond immediately, at least not until he had come up with a potential motive for the meeting. The venue choice he noticed was left up to him. The *Cerise*? Rome? Perhaps his schloss? Deep in thought, he contemplated his next move.

# NEW YORK

All was proceeding as planned as the day stretched into evening. Gavin Hart thrived on such assaults on criminals, and judging by the adrenaline that surged through his body, he knew Rae's plot would be his best battle yet, the type of assignment he dreamed of: to work hand in hand for once with law enforcement authorities on an undercover operation to snare a group of high-profile crooks. Hart was not only impressed by the complexities of Rae's operation, he had no doubts that the plan would succeed. On his word of honor Hart swore to keep his rights to exclusivity under wraps until all the arrests were made, at which point he would fill the airwaves with the biggest story he had ever broken. He would become an international celebrity overnight.

Gavin Hart had learned that Liebs received Harvey Milton's invitation, and Milton was on standby if the Swiss agreed to meet. But Milton began demanding certain assurances. He wanted his subpoena rescinded along with some verification on the billion-dollar deposit, which was a mere drop in the ocean from what he was slated to make in the overall deal.

Dillon Rae was also edgy with excitement. At least he hoped events had finally been set in motion leading to the moment of truth. What Rae initially viewed as a quick-hit mission had morphed into something far bigger, the greatest assignment of his career. There was a lot riding on the success of this operation. It could potentially catapult him into the ranks of one of the FBI's Executive Assistant Director posts, where he would rub shoulders with the Bureau's elite. His director could count on him, but he hoped inwardly that his ambitions hadn't blindsided him into triggering a downfall. He was already stretching the agency's considerable resources rather thin, and knew he would soon be put to the test.

In the hours before each project assignment, Rae would pace restlessly back and forth, with long, deliberate strides. He thought through all possible aspects not covered methodically, of everything that could go wrong, because if anything did, he'd have his head handed to him on a platter. He knew the Bureau only too well. He needed to keep to the roadmap.

Nick Adams's apartment was an inner sanctum of calm—the calm before the storm. It was a crystal-clear night, and as forecasters had predicted, the weekend rain had completely disappeared.

Earlier in the evening Adams had received a new set of keys and moved Luciana in so that he could look after her while he worked. She was recuperating upstairs in his bedroom. Nick checked on her every so often, but he was busy. He hadn't slept more than a few hours, and it showed.

In his study, hovering over his laptop, frustration clawed at him, and he acquired a knot in the pit of his stomach. *Damn you, Rae*, he cursed silently, rubbing his hands together as he stared at the screen. The cogs and gears in his brain suddenly ground to a halt as he recalled Rae's campaign against him. The anger he felt paled compared to what he had experienced en route to the hospital, the dread of losing someone he loved. It was similar to the anguish he experienced when his mother had left the family home while he was still a child.

When Nick reached the age of twelve, his mother had fallen in love with another man and subsequently lost custody of him to his father, a man of oppressive patriarchal values, who was twenty years her senior. From that point, Nick grew up between two worlds: his father's stuffy existence as a Harvard law professor and his mother's joie de vivre lifestyle during holidays in Los Angeles. But although he tried to live up to his father's expectations, he had inherited his mother's lust for life. His father was an alcoholic and took his hate of his wife out on Nick. It was not until his mother's accidental drug overdose that he began to grow serious about the direction his life should take.

Now Nick Adams forced himself to refocus, to push past his exasperation and look at his predicament rationally. Special Agent Rae had proposed an extraordinary deal. He had promised Nick all sorts of performance incentives to pave the way for an agreeable arrangement with the SEC, the result of which would ensure the future of ABS, as Adams would take back the reins. His wrongs would be overlooked. Mitigation measures would be applied toward him, and he would be able to pay his unpaid taxes with no penalties. Adams's ultimate prize of leading a normal life and enjoying the spoils of his work was tied into the ultimate success of Rae's operation. No matter how bad everything seemed, he had an opportunity to turn the ordeal around in his favor—yet again.

Ravi Sharma lay resting in his room at the rear of Adams's apartment and was very depressed. God knows he had enough to be miserable about without his health problems. Twelve months earlier he had been diagnosed with HIV AIDS. To add insult to injury, he had no idea how long he'd been infected. The social stigma associated with the disease and the fear of its outcome had made him reluctant to get tested for many years. By the time he had started the medication it was almost too late. Owing to the advanced stage of the disease, his doctor had placed him on a course of powerful drugs. They would prolong his life, but made him thoroughly sick in the process. It wasn't that he had trouble sticking to the medication schedule; it was the side effects that were a bitch to deal with.

He suffered in silence. His carefully crafted exterior looks were deceptive. His feelings of shame and unbelievable fear were carefully hidden, but on occasion the hopelessness overwhelmed him, reminding him of the folly of his past sexual liaisons, the days of his ardent promiscuity now long gone.

Support group assistance would have helped, but it was not an option for such a private person. So he sought emotional escape through his work, writing source code and creating superior software systems. Eventually the treatments began to fail, and his doctor switched him to an experimental combination of antiretroviral drugs, with hope that the new medication would successfully attack the virus at the current stage in its life cycle. It was his first day on the new drugs, though he held no illusions about his mortality.

Incense burned from a brass container. Unable to sit in the lotus position, he remained stretched, deep in prayer to his Hindu god. He wanted to help turn things around for Adams before he died. He was convinced he would not survive.

In a "Paul on the road to Damascus" moment, he was well aware of the confusing religious irony when that startling moment of brilliance gave him the solution. It was though it had crashed down from the sky onto his frail shoulders and forced his emaciated body to a sitting position. His eyes widened.

Yes, he could make certain dominoes fall quite differently. Although he could not alter the course of his demise, yet in its wake he would leave a bizarre legacy laced with his genius. Finally he had found the liberation that only absolute certainty can give.

Sharma took a deep breath and pulled himself together. In an instant he was on his feet. He shuffled painfully to one of the computers sitting on his desk. He had work to do, but he was up against God's plans for him.

# SCOTTSDALE, ARIZONA

But Erich Kersch's own God had plans for this wayward mortal who sat hunched on a sofa in his newly built, seven-bedroom mansion, trembling. Eyes closed, his head buried in his hands, a prescription bottle lay beside him. A strangled sobbing resonated throughout the living room, his chest heaving as he fought for control. An oversized flatscreen TV suspended on the wall in front of him had gone to a blank blue screen. There was no mistaking it: he was in shock, and it had swept over him in a tsunami of agony. His face was white and expressionless, his eyes red, his gut twisted into knots.

Unbeknownst to the arch stock promoter, Kersch's wife, the hard put-upon Phyllis, had earlier that afternoon received a Special Delivery package addressed to her. She had opened the parcel somewhat bemused thinking that it was an Internet purchase she had forgotten about. Certainly she had not ordered music, as she always downloaded what she wanted. The DVD was in an envelope from out of state marked confidential with a handwritten note included. Puzzled, she turned on the entertainment system and placed the disk into the player.

The DVD player whirred. At first there was just interference, then suddenly, without any warning, titles, background music or commentary, the screen burst into life of sorts. A video close-up of Erich Kersch filled the screen for thirty seconds. Not sure what to make of it, she shouted for her mother to join her from the garden. Just as her mother stepped through the arched portal, the film went straight to hardcore porn. Phyllis froze, dumbstruck. Her mother shrieked, dropping a pair of pruning shears onto the marble floor.

They saw clip after clip, scene after scene of disjointed images, stills, videos, each with one common denominator—Phyllis's husband, fully exposed. Never in her conventional life had she ever seen such incredibly detailed exhibitions of virtually every lewd sexual act imaginable, with her husband as ringleader and the main thespian on the stage of degradation. By the reflection in his eyes, Kersch was undeniably enraptured in each and every frame. There were close-ups and distant shots taken through windows, doors, from under tables, sometimes in focus, sometimes not. The sound was almost nonexistent.

Reeling, the Baptist-educated Phyllis attempted to make a mad dash for the bathroom to vomit, but she banged her shin on a glass coffee table and lost her balance. She grabbed onto a tasteless porcelain statue to steady herself, but sent it crashing to the floor, where it smashed into tiny fragments. She hollered in a rage and kicked the glass tabletop, which sent it whirling to the marble floor. Glass shattered everywhere, strewing diamonds across the hard floor. Her mother gasped and collapsed in a dead faint.

Still shaking from shock, Phyllis sprang around what was left of the table to pick up her mother, clutching her slight form. Her mother's hands and knees ran red as Phyllis half-carried, half-dragged her to a sofa trying to avoid broken glass. With her knees barely holding her up, she sat her mother down amid cushions and massaged her head. Her face was white as death, her eyes glazed. Phyllis sank into the sofa, where the two sat, unable to say or do anything for a very long while. How Phyllis, a former pageant queen and churchgoer—of all people—could be entangled in such debauchery was beyond her comprehension. She hated her husband before this, and now she knew what she had to do.

When both women finally regained composure, her mother said, "I'm sure you realize there's no way back from this. Just think of it as your long-awaited ticket to freedom." Her mother knew too well that Phyllis had never really loved Erich Kersch and had married him for the security and lifestyle he offered. "You have a chance to close this marriage chapter in an honorable way: file for divorce, then get everything." Her mother grinned cynically. "Better to be free, my dear." Not that she had fared well in her own marriage, having been through three husbands, with another in her sights. What chance did her daughter have with that example?

Phyllis raised her trembling fingers to her tear-stained face and wiped away the moisture. *You never know where a day might take you,* she thought. "Now that we've seen the truth, it makes all the sense in the world." She shook her head and added, "That sick bastard and his money will soon be parting company."

A stream of encouragements followed from her mother. "Now get ahold of yourself and start packing. Get everything you can get your hands on and put it in the car."

Phyllis dragged herself off the sofa and made for the kitchen, where she sat at the breakfast counter. She retrieved a phone book from her handbag, picked up the phone, and began dialing. Soon she had an attorney. Within minutes of speaking to him, divorce and custody proceedings were set in motion. Her next call was to the bank, where she gave orders to transfer everything in their joint account to her personal account at once. Files and financial documents she took from Kersch's study she placed into a cardboard box and gave to her mother. She took out the offending DVD, and placing it into her laptop, she made a copy for her lawyers, then replaced the original into the player.

Within the hour, Mrs. Phyllis Kersch slammed the gearshift into drive, pressed down hard on the gas pedal, and screeched her way out of the driveway, on her way to pick up her children, her mother seated alongside her. For the interim they would be taking up residence at her mother's house.

Erich Kersch needed to go to his loveless home. He hated every minute. But when Kersch returned home that evening, he noticed the house was strangely in total darkness. He left his car in the circular driveway and approached the front double doors. He was about to use his key, but the door was already open. He feared a break-in, but gingerly pushing the door, he entered. At first sight, it did appear to be a break-in. He turned on the entryway light and discovered his home in a complete shambles, mangled figurines, toppled furniture and broken glass. He ran from room to room, calling out for his wife and children. His shoes crunched on the broken glass. There was no reply. He ran upstairs.

Scrawled in lipstick on the large mirror above the dresser in the master suite was the word "Bastard" in two-foot letters scrawled in lipstick. The smashed frame of their wedding photograph lay in the center of the bedroom floor.

"Oh, God!" he yelled as he flew down the stairs. He ran into the living room and saw the lipstick again, this time smudged across the mirror above the fireplace "Watch the DVD, scumbag!" it read, underlined in vivid red slashes. The broken lipstick lay on the floor, spent.

He was confused. He looked down at the DVD machine and as instructed, the ill-fated Kersch pressed the play button. By now he was shivering uncontrollably.

The DVD played until the screen went blank once more.

Kersch slowly looked up at the screen again; then he pulled himself off the sofa and stood up to turn off the system. But there was more to come.

The bullet from the silenced pistol, a Fabrique Nationale 5.7 mm, entered the right side of his head and spiraled through his brain. The impact thrust his head and shoulders forward, then jerked his upper body backward. His eyes widened for an instant; then his eyesight faded. Brain tissue and blood and bone fragments propelled sideways and upward. A spray of blood from a carotid artery showered the room. His body jackknifed and fell to the floor with a thud. He lay there, spread-eagled, his lifeless dull eyes staring upward at the ceiling.

Valentina Vinogradov had fired the single shot, expertly and with her normal precision, from several feet away. She stared down at Erich Kersch with indifference as a pool of blood framed his lifeless body. The Kersch operation hadn't taken much planning. A courier sent the DVD for guaranteed next-day delivery from a depot in New Jersey, paid for with cash using a false identity, by the assassin's employer. She flew from Cyprus to Miami, and then caught a flight to Phoenix. When she arrived, she tracked the package online to establish the exact delivery time. The rest was clear sailing. Liebs's secretly filmed DVD was crude but effective.

Valentina had only a brief description of the contents, and even she was surprised at the filth portrayed so graphically and sourced from many venues in New York. The reaction of Kersch's wife was far better than even Vinogradov had anticipated. Her swift departure from the house eased Vinogradov's logistical maneuver considerably. It also saved her killing others on site.

She had little time to dress the stage, as the silencer had been louder due to the cavernous nature of the sitting room. She unscrewed the silencer and put the gun beside the corpse cleaning it of prints. She extracted the DVD and pocketed it. She wiped the lipstick graffiti off the mirrors, and minutes later Vinogradov was back within the confines of her rental car parked across the street. Rigging the interior lights of the vehicle to remain off at all times was a habit formed from experience. In the early hours of the next morning, by the time Kersch's body would be discovered, Valentina Vinogradov would be onboard a flight back to Cyprus, her assignment completed without a hitch.

# NEW YORK

On clear days Manhattan sunrises were special. A bright morning sun flooded the kitchen as Nick Adams prepared breakfast.

The building intercom buzzed and Adams answered. The gruff voice of the concierge declared, "Delivery, Mr. Adams. I'll have a porter bring it right up."

"Thanks," he responded, his dark hazel eyes fixed on the receiver as he replaced the handset. Minutes later a porter handed him a handwritten envelope. Inside was a set of keys to his BMW. Dillon Rae was a man of his word after all.

Nick took breakfast to Luciana, who was still resting in his bedroom. She seemed to be better, but would still cry out when touched. Bruises were visible across her body by now, and the swelling had increased, but the pain had diminished and her throbbing headaches had receded from blinding to simply annoying. Once certain that Luciana had everything she needed, he was out of the door to run a few errands before sitting down with Sharma for a hard day's work.

First stop: a cash machine. Not only was his PIN accepted, he was able to withdraw a thousand dollars. In succession, he checked his other cards. Each functioned without a hitch.

The nightmare was slowly coming to an end. Nick left the ATM, mumbling something unintelligible to those waiting behind him. Why, they asked, would getting cash out of a machine make someone so euphoric? And shit, how many cards did he have?

He had no need to try his Swiss card.

Luciana sobbed. Her head spun. The painkillers hadn't touched the sides. She moved the earpiece of her phone away from her head.

"You must end this relationship at once! This boyfriend is no good!" said Franco Cavallini. "He's not for my daughter!" He had lapsed from Italian to English and back again, reserving the translation of his anger for the more dramatic Sicilian dialect.

"But, Papa!" Luciana said emphatically, "I'm sure he's a good man, it's all been just a catalog of horrible mistakes."

"What are the police doing?"

It took Cavallini little time to get Luciana to spill the beans on what had been going on. Soon a bizarre saga unfolded. "But, my child, there are so many men for you to choose from. With beauty such as yours, you could have anyone you want. Why him? What would your mother say? I beg you, do not throw away your roots, find ..."

"... a good Italian Catholic boy. Sure, but Papa ..."

"There is only one thing to do, I will come to New York."

"No!" she responded in a burst of indignation. It was the last thing she needed. Her own feelings had lain well hidden within, demons that stemmed from the epicenter of her family, matters that for a whole host of reasons she didn't wish to be exposed. "Papa, I only needed to hear your voice and have a good cry. I feel much better now. Everything will be just fine, I promise."

Franco Cavallini scolded her for not listening, saying that she was too enthralled by whatever this American, Nicholas Adams possessed to think clearly. Then he began pleading with her, even trying to bribe her to leave New York and return to Italy. But he knew well the stubbornness of his only daughter; it was a trait she had inherited from him.

Franco Cavallini's call to his disobedient daughter distressed him and raised his blood pressure considerably. Without a moment's hesitation he dialed a New York number. The phone rang for some time before a hoarse voice answered. "Yeah!" It wasn't so much a question but a testy "Why the fuck are you disturbing me?" statement wrapped up in one word.

"Robbie?"

"Franco!" The tone in the man's voice shifted instantly. "Is that you? Ciao, Franco. How are you, you son of a bitch?" At once they were both boys playing in the streets back in Sicily, petty-thieving tourists, and chasing foreign girls.

"Robbie, I need a favor."

"Ask!" There was no other answer that could have been given. "Anything. You know that." Robbie Castalano was honored that such a powerful man as Franco Cavallini would still find the time to call him.

Cavallini truly trusted only one man: Roberto Castalano, his lifelong friend. He respected Castalano for his loyalty, wit, and brutally honest personality. A solid, burly man, Castalano exuded an air of dignity with his upright, curiously military stance and traditional manners. Cavallini spoke quietly partly in code, reverting to his native tongue where appropriate. He put his requests forward then spent the rest of the call reminiscing. The orders would be obeyed.

"Franco, it will be a pleasure, a real pleasure. Arrivederci!"

Sharma was standing in the kitchen when Adams returned home. "Did you get the car back?"

"Yep. She's back." Nick said, grinning like a real smartass.

"Now let's try and keep it this time," Sharma said. He hadn't ever driven and couldn't see the point of Nick's clear obsession with fast and expensive cars.

For a moment Nick said nothing. It was a biting comment, but he knew he had it coming. "Point well taken," he said humbly. "And I owe you big time."

"Someday, we'll look back on this, laugh at each other nervously, and then change the subject." He turned on his heel. "Come on, we have to finish what we started. Come and see where I have gotten to."

Dillon Rae dialed Gavin Hart's cell number.

"Yep?"

"It's me. It's done. The hook has just been slung. Give our man the news," Rae said in a guarded tone.

"Got it. I'll get on it right away." Hart could barely hear Rae with the traffic noise on Sixth Avenue. He was weaving his way toward CBS Studios to complete some voice-overs for his latest program. His next call would be to cancel the studio. To hell with such menial work.

"It should convince him," Rae said with confidence. He knew damn well Milton would take the bait. "All you need to do now is keep him motivated and focused. And if he asks, which he will do, the money has been transferred."

Soon Gavin Hart was back at MGI, going over the plan details with Harvey Milton. Hart confirmed that the government had paid the funds offshore to CAY BANK in Grand Cayman. Hart played along with the charade when Milton called in Oscar Randell to get verification of the wire having hit.

"Oscar, call You Know Who and check receipt. God knows how even that bank will allow a billion to be credited without an explanation ..."

"Harvey, it is in the account. There will be no questions." Hart was confident. Randell went out of the room and Hart went through the latest updates.

After a while Randell reappeared, flushed and triumphant. "The Eagle has landed."

"Believe me next time, oh ye of little faith!" Gavin Hart smiled. "All is going exactly to plan as I promised."

Within minutes of the conversation with Randell, Dieter Gruber was on a secured line to Zurich. Liebs would be more than intrigued.

Nick Adams placed yet another cup of coffee on his desk and resumed tapping on his keyboard while Sharma conducted the preliminary beta test for Rae's scheme. He had an appointment, so he checked his watch. Sharma was exhausted, but pleased with the results. *An hour's rest is all I need to recuperate*, he thought, at which time he would begin writing code for the crucial second phase of the plan.

With his life restored to some semblance of normality, Adams was also keen to get on with Rae's operation, as Rae still had him by the balls. His accounts in the States were still frozen, and the only way to buy his total freedom and have his monies released was for Rae's plan to succeed without a hiccup. Should the sting come off, he would plan Adams Banking Solutions's future, trying to isolate the company from the aftermath—and before Kersch & Co. and all its subsidiaries went south. The sale of his shares would be enough to start over and get a new venture going. Special Agent Rae had guaranteed that ABS would be fenced off and protected. At just after 11:00 a.m. he made his way out of his apartment block and onto the sidewalk.

The taxi ride to the Four Seasons took five minutes. Right on time for his 11:30 a.m. meeting with Dillon Rae and Gavin Hart, Nick Adams entered the bastion of luxury below its fan-shaped canopy, carrying a black briefcase, and made his way up to the forty-fifth floor.

"Ah, Nick. Good to see you," Rae said as he opened the door to the suite. He was smartly dressed in an open-neck shirt. He placed one hand on Adams's shoulder and shook his hand vigorously with the other. "Come on in." It was as if nothing had happened between them at all. "Right," Rae said anxiously. "Let's get down to it." He led Adams through the sleek interior to a separate living area. Having never visited a suite at the Four Seasons before, Adams was struck by the well-appointed room with its silk-covered walls and stunning views of Central Park. But every flat surface in the room was littered with documents organized by multicolored tabs. "Everything is going well. Gavin's been navigating the course, just as planned."

"Hi, Nick." Hart waved from an armchair. Dressed in chocolate-brown corduroys and a patterned sweater, he seemed relaxed. "How's it going?" Hart had a special talent for keeping the mood light and upbeat.

"As you can see, we've been putting in a lot of time on this jigsaw. Since everything's been fast-tracked, your input is needed right now." For the first time Rae sounded almost human to Adams. "Where are you with all of your stuff?"

Adams sat on the nearest sofa and opened his briefcase. "Got it all worked out. I used the data you gave me, and a hell of a lot of imagination." Adams grinned, and they all laughed. "I laid out full schematics and passed them onto Ravi who wrote code for Phase I implementation. The beta test was completed earlier this morning and Phase II system code is being written as we speak. My role from this point forward will be that of a supervisor, ensuring that each event occurs as it should."

"And on time." Rae looked straight into his eyes. They bore into Nick's and he could see that this was one time he had to deliver. "We can't afford any hiccups." Rae looked serious and ominously added, "Also be on the lookout for anything that could go wrong. One small screwup and we've blown it." Rae's voice deepened. "If this goes off-kilter, it will send ripples all the way to the White House. Doesn't matter that we're doing it for all the right reasons. The backlash would be disastrous and would have far more reaching implications than you could ever imagine." He placed his hands together against his lips as if praying. He wasn't taking the operation in his stride as effortlessly as he appeared. While the general arrangements, logistics, and skills were clearly defined, there were details that could cause significant problems. "Latest news is that Gavin here has convinced Milton to play ball. Now it's up to Milton to challenge Liebs."

"The gauntlet has already been slapped against the Swiss's face." Hart sounded more than excited. "We await Liebs's response."

"When?" Adams asked, looking baffled. From his knowledge of the man, they were mounting a campaign to double-cross someone he believed to be impervious. In his view, Rae was either completely insane to think his stark raving mad plan would come off without a hitch or he was a fucking genius and hiding something from him.

"Milton has asked to meet with Liebs this week, probably in Europe," Dillon Rae said absent-mindedly. "Now let's talk logistics."

"Once Ravi has completed the setup with JC, he flies to the Caribbean to handle the rest on site. The bank's security protocols dictate that these procedures must take place at the bank. Your turn." Nick expected a response.

Rae laughed cynically. "Yeah, sure. And the bank will allow

someone they don't know access to their system." Hart's eyes narrowed in warning and agreement with Rae.

"They know us because they are our only real client. They know Ravi, and they will welcome him with open arms. And it's already been taken care of," Adams responded, "since we, Adams Banking Solutions, that is, were the ones who installed their software in the first place, which coincidentally has been acting up recently." Hart's and Rae's faces spilled into broad smiles. "Ravi will be sent to correct the system glitches, carry out normal systems checks, and perform routine maintenance and software upgrades. In other words, he'll get in without any problem whatsoever, then will seamlessly integrate our program into the bank's current system. Call it an upgrade." Adams smiled smugly. "But really it is a Trojan virus."

"Good grief." Hart laughed breathlessly, applauded, and almost jumped out of his seat.

"Brilliant," Rae added in satisfaction. He stood up, walked over to where Adams was sitting, and shook his hand.

Adams looked skeptically at Rae, hesitating slightly. "Okay, our side of the plan will work, but will your plan succeed? From an outsider it sounds implausible. But even if I think I know the arrangement well enough; do you really believe Milton and Liebs will fall for what looks to me like an obvious swindle?"

"That we don't know, Nick," Hart cut in, pouring him a cup of coffee, "but given what we know about the two men involved, we're banking on the greed factor. Milton's got a huge lump of cash backed by the government, which puts him firmly in our court. That billion is some ten percent of my agency's budget for the year! We just hope Gerhard Liebs is greedy enough to take up the challenge. As for the double cross, we're counting on your software to perform." There was a slight flash of concern beneath the flippant remark. "I hope you've built in sufficient safeguards to guarantee that nothing goes wrong."

"You mean so that Milton wins no matter what." Adams grimaced. "Well, with the killer app we've just pulled together, you just may be able to bank on it—no pun intended." Adams took the liberty of opening a bottle of water and took a noisy slug. "So—by putting Gerhard Liebs out of business, your crew in Washington pulls off the biggest coup of their careers?" He looked at Rae, who nodded and smiled at Nick's naïveté. "But absolute success may be dicey. I see a number of flaws in the overall plan. What do you think?" Adams gestured at Rae who nodded. "The main one being security. Liebs is bound to smell a rat. I'm sure he'll suspect that Milton is setting him up to rip him off."

"Quite so," Rae responded. "But we've taken a few precautionary measures, and I've come up with a few interesting maneuvers to secure our position."

"They had better be more substantial than just interesting." Adams's lips twisted in a sardonic smile. He calmly began to brief them on the potential weak points. "CAY BANK is a respectable offshore bank. Well, respectable enough to be trusted by Liebs and Milton, who both bank there. Liebs recommended Adams Banking Solutions to CAY BANK, and Liebs is ABS's biggest shareholder. CAY BANK is our first client, and we owe Liebs for that. No one else has taken us on as yet."

"Yes, yes, of course. That's right," Rae said, irritated by Adams's apparent move to query segments of his plan. "And Liebs is the bank's biggest customer."

Searching through his notes, Adams continued. "Are the computer system specs secure as far Liebs and Milton are concerned?"

"Of course they are," Hart said. "We figure they have between them something like fifty million dollars a day passing through CAY BANK's system. If they weren't confident the bank's protocols were protected far beyond normal routine, neither of them would ever use that bank."

"It's obvious Liebs trusts CAY BANK. His *bureau de change* business is very complex and technologically sophisticated. After all, he's defied just about every tax authority around the world," Rae added.

"Okay," Adams pushed on, "let's say they're both equally canny. Maybe Harvey Milton is a worthy opponent, but we've got to be careful tackling Liebs. He's clever, shrewd, sharp as a tack, and never to be trusted. You cross that line with Liebs and he'll have your balls before you even realize they've been had."

"You got that right." Hart laughed. "That son of a bitch is unreal, but there's something else that makes my skin crawl. I wouldn't be at all surprised if his past is littered with missing persons, if you know what I mean."

Adams looked at Hart but went on. "We need the 'switch' programming sequence from you so that Ravi can install it at CAY BANK. Where do we stand on that?"

"Switch what?" Hart asked.

"The time, zero hour if you like. We have it and we'll get that to you shortly," Rae confirmed. "When we know that the duel is on, then we will have the time. We've had to take every eventuality into account. Liebs will insist on seeing how every second on the countdown is accounted for."

"Millisecond, more like," Hart intervened.

"Nanosecond," Adams corrected.

"Yes, of course." Rae paused for a moment. "It's economic warfare, and our government rarely loses those battles. He'll get just enough rope to hang himself." Looking directly at Adams, Rae asked, "Do you know how many arms deals are financed by Liebs? How many drug runs? Do you know that the money he ripped off from thousands of shareholders, including yours, goes straight to the boys in Colombia? How do you feel about Adams Banking Solutions supporting street hustlers who feed drug habits and prey on young people?" Adams shifted uncomfortably in his seat. It was quite evident he wasn't aware of the full extent of Liebs's business dealings. His chest constricted with a sense of dread until he could hardly keep his distress unnoticed.

Although Rae was hell-bent on ridding the landscape of Liebs, the maverick agent had his own agenda, and Milton, Liebs, Hart, Sharma, Cemach, and Adams were merely catalysts used for his own personal redemption. "Gerhard Liebs's empire reaches the highest echelons of corruption and threatens much more than the collapse of Adams Banking Solutions," Rae explained. "You okay with all this, Nick?"

Adams nodded unconvincingly.

"Welcome to the school of hard knocks, kid," Hart added.

The sun began to throw shafts of light into the room, as Adams calmly laid out more of his technical plans in intricate detail. A beam of light glinting off the skyscraper across the street nearly blinded Rae as he listened. Squinting into the fierce sunlight, Rae moved to another seat. What he heard from Adams was a brilliantly conceived blueprint. He listened intently to the complexity of Adams's schematics, intrigued. Although of his methods were precarious and could boomerang if Adams got it wrong, they were pure genius.

Nick couldn't believe he had it in him to concoct such a scheme, but it was a means to an end: amends for his own greed and his slate wiped clean. For the first time that day he began to believe he could actually get out of this mess with his integrity intact. It didn't make a damn bit of difference to him what ulterior motives the others may have; all he wanted was total absolution.

By 2:00 p.m., Adams, Rae, and Hart had signed off on the plans.

"Well done." Dillon Rae said as he stood up. "I know we gave you a tough time last week and I'm sure you can now appreciate why."

"Can't appreciate what happened to my girlfriend, funnily enough."

"Come on, Nick. We hit your pocket, not your girl," Rae lied.

Adams wasn't so sure of that, but decided to let it pass. "Dillon, I'll need money."

"Of course." Rae spun around and walked to the suite's bedroom. He returned within minutes holding a manila envelope and handed it to Adams.

"Thirty thousand dollars in cash." A satisfied look crossed Rae's face. Adams felt a sudden calm that replaced the tension in his body. He flashed Rae a grin. Rae also handed him a business card. "And you can reach me on this new number and BlackBerry Messenger. Ignore the DC number from now on. Everything is secure." The agent looked down at the two men and nodded. "You know what you have to do, you guys."

Adams and Hart got up to leave.

"Oh, and I'll need to see the software today. Is 4:00 pm here, okay?"

Adams left without waiting for Hart, who had to take a piss. His destination: ABS's offices.



After considerable thought, Gerhard Liebs believed his best approach would be to welcome the meeting with Harvey Milton. The informative and intriguing call from Dieter Gruber at CAY BANK made up his mind. While Liebs was quite accustomed to moving large sums of money around the globe, he was totally blindsided by the huge one-off credit now sitting on a new account set up by Milton. One billion US dollars piqued his curiosity.

It took Liebs's PA an hour to locate Milton, even though she had the number that had been given by the American in his letter. The ever-travelling Milton, like the Swiss banker, preferred not to remain in any one place for long periods, but felt secure within the safety net of exclusive hotels, palatial homes, yachts, jets, and an army of security people. Finally the cell phone number answered.

"This is an honor, Harvey," Liebs said patronizingly.

"For me as well, Gerhard." Milton oozed charm. "I take it you've received my invitation?"

"Indeed I have." Liebs picked up a glass, removed its beaded linen cover, and sipped some water. "We rarely meet face to face nowadays, Harvey, but I do keep track of your recent successes. We seem to have many things in common." Liebs was almost amiable. "Without healthy competition, the world of commerce would be a duller place. Well, for us, at least. "Why do you want to meet, and at such short notice?"

"I have a proposition for you." Milton cleared his throat.

"Ah, yes. I read your letter," Liebs said. "I am naturally well-disposed to meet with you, Harvey, but it would be helpful if you would tell me the nature of what we will discuss, if only to allow myself to prepare."

"You won't need to prepare anything." Milton was in an ebullient mood. The enormity of what he was about to undertake was staggering, a long-awaited fantasy frame-up and double cross served to him on a silver platter. It was truly mind blowing. By some act of providence, the total annihilation of the malignant cancer that was Gerhard Liebs was within in his reach. The one billion dollars secured at CAY BANK would be his ace. It was as good as his already. All he had to do now was nail the emaciated little Swiss viper. "When can we meet, and where?"

"How about tomorrow evening in Switzerland? My schloss. I do not believe you know it. My assistant will e-mail you details."

Milton had no need of the details because the dossier from special agent Rae contained everything, even down to the banker's toilet routine. "That could be arranged. Yes ... I can move a few things around." Milton spoke slowly, playing it cool. His agenda was totally empty.

"And you will stay with me as my guest ..."

"Forgive me, Gerhard," Milton interrupted, "your offer is very generous, but I will probably need to stay in Zurich. There is some additional business I could attend to while there."

"Dinner then?"

"It would be a pleasure."

The last thing he wanted was to eat with the little prick, but if he had to, he would do anything to crush him.

"I will arrange for a car to pick you up at your hotel, and my helicopter will bring you up here. It will be much more convenient for you. After dinner we can both fly back to Zurich. Should we have any unfinished business, all can be finalized the following day". It was time for him to show the American what style was about.

All was not well when Adams arrived at the ABS offices. Many of the staff in the operations area were hovering around Birdie's cubicle, speaking in hushed tones and looking agitated.

"Hi. How's it going guys?" Nick grinned.

"Actually, not good, Nick." Birdie stood up and quietly suggested that he should make his way into the boardroom. Nick was bewildered. Something must be wrong. Again. Seated around the table were his company directors. The bright light that shone through one of the windows masked the video conferencing screen.

"Please join us." He recognized the voice, and a cold hand seemed to grab his heart as if to tear it out at that very minute.

"To what do I owe the honor?" Nick asked walking toward the screen.

"Nick," the head and shoulders of Gerhard Liebs could now be seen clearly, "sit down. Please. We …" the editorial *we*, quite obviously, "We've just received some tragic news."

Nick was shocked. He lowered himself into a chair, sat down, and picking up a pencil, he began playing with it between his fingers.

Liebs continued coldly. His disdain for Nick was more than evident. He knew all the stories. "A couple of hours ago, I called Erich's Phoenix office to speak with him,"—he stopped for dramatic effect—"and I was told that Erich took his own life last night. I convened a video conference call with everyone on how we are to proceed. I did not expect an appearance by you."

"You've got to be kidding." Adams gripped the pencil in his hand. "Erich? Christ, why?" His mind began racing. He surveyed the faces of those gathered around the table, clearly upset. The effect of Kersch's loss could prove devastating to them all, its fallout potentially enormous. Adams had never liked the pugnacious little man, but had never wished him any particular harm. "What happened?" he asked. "Does anyone know why on earth he would want to kill himself?" He looked at the blank faces in the room.

"He was apparently distraught over marital problems," one director explained. "Something about a pending divorce."

"How did he do it?" Adams inquired flatly. His pencil snapped noisily into two.

"He shot himself," a director said quietly. His voice was

hoarse and tense; the muscles in his jaw twitched as he spoke. "Right in his living room. I can't believe it."

Adams shook his head emphatically and put down what was left of the pencil. He found himself caught in the grip of a sickening mixture of emotions and was unsure of how to cope with them. The staff at Adams Banking Solutions had no other details to offer him. Some sat, others stood around the table in silence for a while and then began talking about their relationships with Kersch. No one mentioned the bad temper, the insults, the shouting and screaming, the bullying, the late-night calls, or the intimidation. Those episodes remained unspoken, though they had all, at one time or other, been on the receiving end of the tirades.

Everyone by and large ignored Adams. Liebs issued instructions and ideas from the screen. Arrangements were to be made to prepare a suitable tribute to their late colleague—the man who had supplied the cash that had taken their company public.

"Now, we must talk about how to move forward from here." Liebs began; all assembled eyed each other nervously in anticipation of his plans. There was a babble of questions directed at Liebs, but it soon became clear that Kersch would be taking many answers to his grave. Gerhard Liebs knew that Kersch & Co. would have to field "God knows what" crap in the next few days. Investors that supplied the $500 million raised by Kersch & Co. the previous year for all their public shells would soon come calling. These were companies who received only ten percent of shareholder monies invested. Kersch & Co. had taken ninety percent, promising to drip feed them as each company performed according to the promises that had been made by the unfortunate entrepreneurs and management. Creative juggling would be required; Liebs would have to come up with something pretty damn fast.

But the situation did offer an opportunity to Adams. Dillon Rae would be pleased with this information.

Liebs said, "People!"

Theories as to why Kersch had killed himself were bandied about.

"People!" he repeated, now almost spluttering with rage above the chatter in the room. "I have an announcement to make." He cleared his throat. "We will need someone to take the reins. Adams's resignation, followed by Kersch's death, will cause major repercussions for you all. I am afraid to say that ABS is rudderless."

"Mr. Liebs," a curly-haired accounts guy spoke up, "the company is almost out of funds, so we're going to need all the help we can get right now. How about if you come in as acting executive director until someone is appointed? It would certainly ease market concerns." The room went quiet as the implications began to sink in.

After a brief silence, Liebs calmly responded, "You don't need me." The next few words he spoke struck a note with everyone who heard them. "All you need to do is ask Nick to come back."

All eyes turned toward Adams, who put his hands up and shook his head. "No," he said, too quickly and forcefully.

"Nick don't play politics with this," Liebs counseled. "Erich hadn't even announced your resignation yet. It was his idea to hold off on the press release because it would have caused a crisis of confidence in the market. So you see, you could return, perhaps reinvest some of your considerable wealth," he added with a glint of sarcasm.

"Let's just see how things go," Adams responded, taking offense at what Liebs inferred.

"Okay. Then you will work on a plan. There is no time to waste. Earn your money, gentlemen." Liebs then cut the connection and the screen went blank.

Nick Adams knew that before he would contemplate any reinstatement, he would need to find the whereabouts of his share sale proceeds that Kersch & Co. should have placed by then. He had been precipitated into a mad world; everything was just so surreal, and with Kersch gone, what now? The idea of dealing with the Swiss was just too horrible to contemplate. Besides, with what was going on with the extraordinary Dillon Rae plot, he just knew that he probably wouldn't retrieve any of the proceeds. He needed to bring it up with the FBI agent, and fast.

Nick Adams would try to find his money, but Erich Kersch had been dumb enough to take his Adams Banking Solutions share-sales proceeds from Kersch & Co. and place them in a CAY BANK escrow account without Adams knowing. Now that Kersch was dead, the proceeds would be transferred from that account to one held by Liebs, who had power of attorney in the event of the demise of any Kersch & Co. signatory.

The lean and lanky JC arrived early at Rae's suite, having flown in from New Jersey by helicopter. Sharma arrived soon afterward, looking drawn and the worse for wear. Rae met him at the door and ushered him into the dining area, where JC was busy setting up his computer. "You look ill, Ravi." Dillon Rae looked concerned, not necessarily for the man's well-being, but for anything that might provide a hitch. "You okay?"

Ravi Sharma gave a weak smile. "Sure, just a cold, no sweat." It was an ironic expression considering the rivulets of perspiration that were even then trickling down his spine. He needed another pill.

Hart was lounging on a sofa, reading an early edition of the *New York Evening Post*. He folded the paper and threw it onto the floor and stood up.

Rae called the meeting to order. "Okay you guys, it's show time."

JC took Rae and Hart through CAY BANK's designated transfer system, the path he and Sharma had taken to extend the existing code, and how they had redefined the programming interfaces. He showed them how to exploit the system and gain unauthorized access by hacking into the main banking systems. And although the bank's software code appeared bulletproof, Sharma had been able to get around it, since it was his design in the first place. The best hackers in the world would be awestruck by the audacity of these two software wizards.

The four men deliberated on how to go about carrying out

the bogus inspection, rig the system, and make it all look like normal maintenance checks.

"The thing is," Hart interrupted, trying to bring down the level of euphoria, "Gerhard Liebs must be led to believe that he is calling all the shots at all times. And he can never discover that he is holding diddly-squat."

There was a buzz on the intercom. Rae answered, and the front desk announced Adams's arrival. Rae went out to meet him at the elevator. Adams mumbled an innocuous greeting with a pasted-on smile, a little daunted by Special Agent Rae's over-friendliness.

"Good to see you, Nick. Now we can get down to the fundamentals. We like your ideas, by the way." He slapped Adams on the back as he led him in. "Your guys have done a fantastic job."

JC stood up to greet Adams. Hart waved an acknowledgment. Sharma gave a strained smile and raised his eyebrows.

"Sorry I'm late, but my company is in a state of turmoil, to put it mildly." Then he said wearily, "Our broker Erich Kersch committed suicide last night, causing a major organizational upheaval."

"Very sorry to hear about that, Nick," Rae said, genuinely surprised at the news.

"Fuck." Ravi looked as if he were about to vomit. "Dead?" Adams nodded and raised his eyebrows at Ravi.

"Maybe that elusive so-called venture capitalist slash arch criminal slash stock manipulator extraordinaire finally bit off more than he could chew," Hart added. "I reckon that's not so bad. Blasted promoter."

Rae interrupted him. "I'm not sure how it will affect your situation with ABS, and I hope it doesn't create too much of a ripple in your affairs, but it can't have any bearing on what we're doing here. Fortunately for us, we never included Erich Kersch in our equation," Rae said flatly. "But to be perfectly honest, without sounding callous, we really do need to move on." Ravi wanted to talk to Nick about it, but Rae waved him down.

Adams handed out reports and returned to the plan's technical details. Using his laptop, JC showed the group in beta test mode how the system would work. He demonstrated the theoretical model they had constructed. It was flawless. Both Hart and Rae were intrigued, totally enthralled by the three younger men, who were clearly in their own esoteric element. For a man plagued for days by a maelstrom of anxiety, Rae seemed content. "This software will be the property of the United States government, to ensure that it never gets into the wrong hands." Special Agent Dillon Rae already had ideas. *What an incredible potential weapon against tax evaders.* He noted the thought.

"It's quite simple, really," Adams said to Rae and Hart, who appeared to suffer from technophobia. "It's all a matter of timing—timing that requires accuracy down to nanoseconds. The only delays we can afford are those programmed deliberately by us—or the whole fucking deal will collapse. Timing is critical."

"Nanoseconds?" Gavin Hart asked.

"Fiber-optic networks have been set up by traders all over the world so that they can trade stocks and commodities at the speed of light. It's incredible technology, and really means that the likes of you and I have never a chance of doing any trading with the same advantages." Nick knew just how much stock prices could be manipulated and what fortunes were being made, sometimes bringing down major institutions and even governments through rapid naked shorting and selling on massive scales.

"Yes," JC said, "it's an electronic domino effect. Once the first transfer takes place, the next must happen, and the next, and so on." He pointed to a location on the screen. "See, it's a trigger mechanism that sets everything in motion."

"So," Rae looked at all of them in turn, "when the critical moment arrives, everything will be reliant on your software?"

"Yes," Adams nodded. "And the outcome: fiscal meltdown for Liebs." He showed them how it would unravel, pointing to the structural diagram on the table. "At zero hour, the software will instantly activate and create an electronic extraction on a massive scale, never before seen."

"And we'll all be rich." Hart laughed loudly.

"Paid, Gavin, paid." Rae corrected him. "Nobody gets rich in this deal. Everyone gets let off the hook and gets paid generously for their contribution." He tried to hold back the hint of a grin.

"What about Milton? He gets richer. As rich as Croesus," Adams said.

Rae's mouth relaxed into a crooked grin. "Sure, he's got a special deal. But after everything is said and done, who knows what might happen?" He knew what plan he had made for Harvey Milton. He would issue Ravi with his own private instruction after the meeting was over. "Now, what about the software trigger?"

"Simple matter of adaptation," JC murmured.

Ravi Sharma opened his leather backpack, took out a flash drive and handed it to JC. Once loaded, JC turned the laptop around to Sharma. "Watch this program for a minute. It needs more work, but it does most of what we've discussed today." He took them through each stage of the program, emphasizing any areas that had to be addressed.

"That's pretty damn impressive, Ravi," Rae said. "What do you think, JC?"

"Maybe I should buy some of those Adams Banking Solutions shares." JC grinned, his hands shoved deep in his pockets.

"That could be arranged," Adams responded sardonically.

"Now watch this." He moved forward pushing Ravi aside. "May I press this button Ravi?"

The screen changed. Adams and Ravi moved away, letting Hart and Rae in closer.

A look of astonishment crossed Rae's face. "Excellent," he said, looking over Adams's shoulder. "Now I really get it!" He looked at the three men who had devised the incredible software. "You guys are fucking dangerous. I can see we will have to watch you." He laughed, but he knew others were watching them as well.

As the group worked on, Rae paced the room, pleased that he had followed through when he was given his assignment by the FBI director himself. On an impulse he googled companies that might provide him with what he required. He had many false trails, but then stumbled upon the minnow Adams Banking Solutions.

He couldn't believe his luck when he learned of their connection to Kersch & Co., then painstakingly investigated Adams, who had proved to be just what he'd been looking for, someone who had skated on thin ice and who already had a history with various institutions, including the SEC and IRS. He had found Adams's Achilles heel.

As Rae grew confident that his plan might even succeed, his initial worries finally dissipated. He had given the story, or part of it, together with guarantees of victory, to the director, who had authorized the one billion dollars from the special projects account. Now his job was nearly done. There could be no screwups. If it went tits up, he would be finished in the agency, and ten generations of Raes would be paying back the billion dollars.

Gavin Hart conducted a question-and-answer session before Rae took over again. "Now that we know how everyone fits in, we have to tighten up the timetable." Thirty minutes later, having gone over individual roles and emphasizing the importance of Sharma's task at CAY BANK, he handed out a sheet of paper to all present. "These are the critical phone numbers, wiring instruction codes, and other things that might be applicable. You will use this location as your base for meetings. It's safe and is swept for devices twice a day, so at least here you can relax. Are we cool?" He smiled and handed out three encrypted BlackBerrys. "These are for our business only. You will see that in the contacts list there are numbers to contact me and each other, understood?" He also suggested that for security purposes all documented evidence to the plan should be left in the apartment, where it would be completely safe. "Each BlackBerry will be monitored at all times. This is sensitive stuff. We have to be careful."

"Remember: everything discussed must be kept under wraps," Hart added. "Never mention or discuss anything to do with the operation as things progress. However, should problems arise, we must all contact and liaise through Dillon, and no one else." Hart stood up, yawned, and stretched his legs. It was unbelievably frustrating for him to be in on the biggest scoop of his life and not be able to breathe a word about it. He guessed the compensation would make up for his silence. He just wished the whole damn Rae deal would finish so he could get back to normality. His next syndicated TV program was scheduled to start production in a few weeks.

By 5:30 p.m. the meeting broke up. Rae asked Ravi to stay behind to tie up a few loose ends. The FBI agent handed Ravi another sheet of instructions and asked him to reprogram part of the software on his computer. He made it clear that nothing should be mentioned to any of the team about this so-called update. Ravi glanced at it and almost spluttered. "But ... "

"Ravi!" Special Agent Dillon Rae had every eventuality covered. At whatever cost.

# SWITZERLAND

Liebs received a call. The caller was evidently very resourceful, as Liebs's number was not in the public domain. It was Nicholas Adams.

Liebs was not so surprised. He knew at some stage Adams would be calling to bitch about his shares having been sold or stolen and to squeal like a stuck pig. Liebs had no intention of going along with the so-called fifty-fifty deal Kersch had agreed to.

"Ah, this is a surprise. You have my number—very enterprising of you. But it is very late here, Nick." Liebs found his rimless glasses on the table beside him and put them on. "May we talk perhaps in the morning?"

"I have a concern that should be of great importance to you."

"If it's about Erich Kersch or ABS, please, let's talk when things have quieted down."

"It's to do with you, Mr. Liebs, and it's a matter of grave concern."

"I hardly think there is anything that you and I could have in common to discuss regarding my affairs." His words rasped in Nick's ear.

"Please, Mr. Liebs, just hear me out. I've uncovered something bad. All I need is thirty minutes of your time."

"Is this personal?" Liebs wasn't prepared to discuss his shares at all. "I'm sure it's something we can talk about at a more appropriate time; or better still, why don't you just send me an e-mail? I have an important series of meetings scheduled and cannot see how I could possibly ..."

"Fine," Adams interrupted, annoyed by the dismissal. Then

his voice hardened. "It's your funeral. Don't say that I didn't try to warn you, but you're about to walk into a trap."

"A trap, you say? How very bizarre, Mr. Adams." Liebs had never known Adams to be delusional, but he had to be sure. "Is this some form of fantasy on your part? A mild case of paranoia, perhaps? Because from my perspective, any connection between your reality and mine is purely coincidental."

"That's for you to judge, but you have to listen. You shouldn't deem what I've uncovered as irrelevant simply because you're ignorant of the facts, Mr. Liebs." His words had been well scripted.

"Talk to me now, boy." Liebs was rattled.

"It has got be face-to-face ..."

"Give me an indication ..."

Adams interrupted Liebs again. "It has to be face-to-face Mr. Liebs, you have got to believe me."

The man has balls, Liebs thought. There was a long silence. "On Wednesday I shall be at the New Dolder Grand in Zurich. I'll meet you there, but it can be for only thirty minutes. A New York flight should get you in around 10:00 a.m. from JFK; so let us say 11:00 a.m. at the hotel." He paused. "E-mail my secretary tomorrow with your travel information. And please, if you think we can address whatever is troubling you on the telephone rather than waste valuable time and money, do let her know."

Liebs gave the impression that he was unflustered, though he smelled blackmail. The last person he wanted to add on to his blacklist was Nicholas Adams, but that could easily be arranged if he had to. "And, Nick, please don't ring me at my residence again. Delete the number from your address book. Goodnight."

As always, the line was abruptly cut. Liebs took off his spectacles and rubbed hard at his eyes. Danger? He doubted that he could be placed in any invidious position, but he was nonetheless intrigued.

Adams's smile widened until he thought his face would crack. Despite Liebs's reluctance, Adams had managed to secure a meeting. Dillon Rae had supplied him with a collection of private numbers to Liebs's homes, cars, boat, and cell phones, so tracking him down required no effort at all. The information Rae had at his disposal was astonishing. Adams realized he had been propelled into an extraordinary plot engineered by the FBI to cause a massive double cross, all dependent upon skills that he somehow controlled. He was way out of his depth. In order to save himself from total oblivion he knew he had to go along with the plan.

Nick Adams settled back in the comfortable high-backed chair of his old office. Staying on as a consultant, on Liebs's insistence, not only maintained a sense of continuity at Adams Banking Solutions, it also allowed Adams to finalize Rae's program without any question. It was time see how Adams Banking Solutions programmers were coming along with the new changes requested by Ravi. The technicians had no idea what purposes their work would be put to, but when asked if they would mind staying on to finish modifying the code, they neither questioned him nor gave the request a second thought.

Nick arrived home to find Luciana sprawled comfortably across a sofa in the living room, her legs tucked beneath her. She looked up and moved to greet Nick, but he got to her first, slipped his arms around her, fingers curled in a gentle embrace, and sat down.

"What a fucking unbelievably surreal day I've had."

She peered into his eyes and gently stroked his forehead. "Do you want to talk about it, darling?"

"Well, if you must know, I'm a dead man walking with only hours to live. Please take some pain killers and make love to me so I can leave this realm with a grin on my face."

"Always sex on your one-track mind!" Luciana tried to hold back a giggle. "Okay, I'm a tiny bit better now. Well actually, much better. Thanks for asking." She looked at her lover and felt so much better.

"I'm so sorry that our trip was ruined. We'll go away again in a few weeks. Promise. How does Paris sound? Maybe Venice? Rome? Yes, Rome. We can visit your family."

*My family.* Inwardly Luciana cringed at the thought. She wasn't at all sure about introducing Nick to her parents, especially not her father just yet. Until her unanswered concerns were resolved, she had to keep Nick as far away from Franco Cavallini as possible.

"We'll see," she said, a little aloof. "Time to come clean, darling, now that you've obviously gotten your life back. In light of everything that has happened, don't you think it only fair for you to explain exactly what the hell is going on? You must admit these things that keep happening are pretty distressing. I even wonder if my accident has anything to do with what you're involved with. Who are you really, Mister Nicholas Adams?"

"Who am I?" Adams looked bemused; he sometimes asked himself that very same question. "You know who and what I am. And I assure you, what I have told you is the honest truth."

"Nico, don't be upset." Luciana placed a reassuring hand on his arm, but a look of worry crossed her face. "Look at things from my perspective. Any girl would be concerned."

"I guess you've got a point." Nick knew she was right. "I tell you what. Let's eat and I'll fill you in on what I have unwillingly found myself mixed up in. Is that a deal?"

"Deal." Her uniquely expressive gaze showed gratitude, her eyes sparkling. She was back to being the girl he had first met. "I will pay, and you talk. That is my deal!"

With sheer determination finally to get out of the apartment despite her aching ribs, and with painkillers in her handbag, Luciana managed to dress and endure the short taxi ride to David Burke Townhouse restaurant on East Sixty-First Street. The chic, buzzing restaurant remedied Luciana's depleted spirits, its bold colors and whimsical décor restoring her sense of fun, however briefly. It was one of Nick's favorite hangouts.

Once they were seated at a table near the large, white fireplace, Nick ordered wine and insisted on them both selecting their food and then clearing the table in front of him of cutlery, napkin and a small lit candle. He stretched his hands across to take hers and then jumped into explaining the mess he found himself in without divulging too much information. Dillon Rae would be furious that he had such a loose tongue. He told Luciana that he also had to fly to Zurich.

"When do you leave?"

"I fly out at nine something tomorrow night and get back the next afternoon."

"You'll be dead. That's a long trip."

"It won't be too bad."

"What I want to know is whether you have done anything illegal, Nico?" The candlelight reflected in her eyes. "Just give me the facts, and whatever transpires, I love you darling; and together we can make things work."

The starter arrived and Luciana released his hands and sat back. She went silent as the waiter served their plates.

"I just want you to know that I'm no criminal." Nick barely gave the waiter a second glance.

"I wouldn't have anything to do with you if you were. 'Have you done anything wrong?' was my question."

"No," he answered emphatically.

"Okay," she paused to consider her words, "then why do you have an offshore company, what's it called, Zen Holdings?"

"That was set up to get back some of the outlay I incurred setting up the company. Let's call it tax planning. Luciana, you lawyers do this for clients all the time, so don't play the innocent game with me," he snapped. Then he grinned sheepishly. "Sorry."

"Yes, but because I don't know the structure I cannot really comment; but I presume you took advice that US citizens can't have undisclosed assets. Explain about the $9.9 million." Luciana asked coolly.

"That was tax avoidance, not tax evasion. There's a fine distinction between the two, as you know. Besides, I don't have to make a decision on it until the end of the tax year."

"And what about Zen ..." she persisted.

"I choose to pay tax only on what I earn here." He made this admission grudgingly. "Anyway, darling, all of the problems stem from other things, they have nothing to do with the money. Listen, certain parties want the software I developed at ABS. It's massively clever, but in the wrong hands it could be dangerous, and they'll stoop to anything to get it."

"Certain parties? What are you saying?" Luciana stopped toying with her food.

Nick took a deep breath. "Sweetheart, I'm about to share with you something that must be kept just between the two of us. Please," he begged. "Can I trust you?" He grabbed her hand, holding it tightly. The knife on her plate slid onto the tablecloth.

"A solid relationship must be based on trust." She reached her other hand across the table and held Nick's clenched hand. "Go on then, tell me the truth."

Although about to breach a confidence, Nick knew if he didn't get it off his chest soon, he'd probably explode. He had no one else that he could talk to, not even Ravi. "In a nutshell, I'm involved in an elaborate sting, set up by Uncle Sam." Luciana leaned in closer. Nick kept his voice low, much to the annoyance of a man sitting at a table in the corner, a BlackBerry held firmly in his hand, which made eating somewhat difficult. Nick did not notice the man, even though the sole occupant of the table seemed so interested in him.

Nick hesitated slightly as he chose his words carefully. "A special task force has been set up to destroy this Swiss guy. Yours truly is only an innocent bystander caught in the middle of a raging battle between the government and this über-rich banker who's been ripping off people, companies, and institutions. He defies every international law and funds drugs and arms–and they're hell-bent on destroying him."

"So how and why are you mixed up in this?"

"I know the guy …"

"Know him?" Luciana looked at him in disbelief, released her hand from his and lowered her head.

"It's a long story. I woke up and found myself in a place where nothing is straightforward." He sat for a moment silent and distracted. "Adams Banking Solutions has AI software that can perform amazing functions for banks and institutions. The Swiss guy was the one who funded ABS."

"So if you're working with this new setup, what shall we call it, maybe a government agency, why are they giving you such a hard time?" She downed her red wine and refilled her glass. "And why would they destroy our vacation?"

"I didn't want to cooperate."

"With the US government?" she whispered, stunned.

"I was uncomfortable with the whole idea, and basically told them to take their offer and shove it up their ass. When I refused to commit, they started bullying me. I just wanted to get away to think seriously about what I was getting myself into."

"Credit cards? Getting kicked off Antigua? Phone, apartment, car? Peculiar road accidents?"

"Probably."

"And why would the government try to kill me?"

"They said your accident had nothing to do with them."

"What's next, Nick?" Luciana asked, disturbed. Her hands trembled slightly as she gripped her wineglass. "Are you seriously telling me that the US government resorts to mob tactics?" Nick just stared. Luciana paused for a moment until her pulse returned. "What about your friend, Howard Wayne?" she blurted out.

"Hmm, yep, that too." Nick filled his glass. "Howard was investigating the Swiss guy too, and his network of companies including the vehicle he used for ABS, Kersch & Co. But they said that was just a coincidence." Adams knew Wayne's death was somehow linked to the whole strange goings-on, but he couldn't tell Luciana. "The NYPD don't seem to be part of the setup."

"There's got to be more." She paused. "Why are you going to Switzerland tomorrow?"

Adams waved away the attentive waiter and spun the tale as he sketched drawings on bar napkins. Luciana occasionally repeated what he told her so details were clear in her mind. Her suspicions began to drain away as he revealed the purpose of his trip to Zurich. He shared how he now stood in Rae's good graces, having agreed to help the sting by designing the plan's essential system schematics.

"When this is all over, the freezing of my accounts in the US will be lifted. I may also decide to accept the board's offer to return as company president."

It seemed so complicated yet utterly implausible. Without

breathing a word of her intent to Nick, Luciana knew her father would be able give her some advice and confirm the validity of Nick's claims to lend some credence to his story. "I have a feeling that life with you will never be normal." Nervously, she brushed an errant strand of hair from her eyes.

"Is that the appeal I have for you?" Nick pocketed the napkin drawings, careful not to leave them behind, and ordered coffee and the check.

The single diner ordered his check, and pocketing his cell phone, left the restaurant. He had some calls to make.

On their return to Nick's apartment they heard the sound of subdued sobbing. They rushed to the kitchen, where they found a distraught Ravi sitting at the counter, his head resting on folded arms, shoulders shuddering with emotion. A bottle of cognac and a full glass perched precariously beside his head.

"Ravi?" Nick moved the glass. He hadn't noticed the presence behind him and looked up in surprise, his face wet with tears. "What's happened, Ravi?"

Luciana walked to the other side of the counter and placed her arm around Sharma to comfort him. He quickly tore off paper towels and wiped away his tears, clearly embarrassed that he had been caught in such a weak moment. "I am so sorry," he sniffed, and then coughed to cover up his emotion, "it's just so unfair ..." Then he broke down again.

"What's unfair, Ravi?" Luciana squeezed him tighter, gazing into his eyes.

"This fucking disease," he cried out with sudden alarm. Sharma grabbed the glass of cognac and downed it in one. Once the warmth had soothed his stomach, he breathed in deeply and started to take control. "It's my fucking disease, it's screwing up my life." Nick pulled up a stool, sat down, and listened. Luciana stroked Ravi's back. "I had been taking my meds religiously with no adverse reactions other than some nausea and dry mouth. They changed my HAART therapy to offset the side effects. Everything seemed to be getting better, and my doctors were pleased with my progress. But I hadn't been as diligent recently. With everything going on it was difficult to stick to the regimen.

I started getting sick again and losing weight, so I decided to have things checked out. The hospital called with my latest test results indicating ..." he swallowed, "progressive infection. They said my T-cell count has taken a huge dive and I've been diagnosed with full-blown AIDS ..." His last words trailed off as he sobbed. He lowered his head into the palms of his hands and wept a torment that he was at long last able to release.

"Oh, my God, you poor bastard." Nick felt as though he had been hit with a sledgehammer. "Isn't there anything they can do?"

Nick and Luciana shared a look of trepidation as they watched Sharma sob. Luciana's eyes brimmed with tears, but she refused to cry. Instead she continued gently rubbing his heaving back in an effort to calm him. Nick also wanted to console Sharma. The normally calm, cool, and confident Sharma he knew had become frightened and desperate. But Nick was unable to move or speak, shock and despair imprinted on his face.

"Ravi," Nick spoke quietly, letting compassion color his words, "I am so ... so sorry buddy. I don't know what we can do except offer you everything that can possibly be done to help. Just know that we'll be there for you and won't leave any stone unturned. We can get you the very best treatment. Whatever it takes, whatever it costs, money is no object. Do you hear?"

Sharma's dark, hollow eyes echoed pain as he sat up. "Thanks. That's kind. Knowing you're with me gives me strength to fight this." Sharma looked at Nick, and a weak smile spread across his face. That said it all. He wiped away his tears and the three of them stayed up and talked the rest of the night.

But Ravi had a real sense of dread and doom; he knew he had compromised his friend. He had not been straight. He vowed at that moment to make amends. And he knew just what had to be done. What a legacy he would leave.

Dillon Rae sat reclined on an agency jet, mulling over tasks, timelines, and events of the day. There was no question that

Rae's power base had risen considerably. His director was almost jocular after their debriefing session. He had always been a good snake oil salesman. Special Agent Rae had given half-truths, but for him the gamble was based on the ultimate fulfillment of his promises and assurances.

Information filtering in from the field revealed that Milton's office was all over Washington, carrying out exhaustive inquiries on Rae. Their mission only unearthed Rae's position as a special task force member within the newly formed TRU, and that if they tried to delve any deeper, their efforts would be fruitless.

On his way back to Washington for back-to-back meetings, Rae made call after call. It was like herding cats. He had scheduled sessions with TRU and presentations to members of the Bureau overseeing his operation. Everything he did or said would be called into question, since it was he who had convinced the Bureau to front the scheme, and he had to be prepared for the inevitable grilling. Well it was the director himself who had mandated Rae to come up with a way, and so he had, and in quick time, surprising his director and team.

He worked as he flew, his eidetic memory replaying the intricate details of Nick's methodology. He had to cover every potential eventuality on what could go wrong. It wasn't simply a matter of his team's technical capabilities; they had to be able to bait the hook and get the big fish. Liebs was canny and had proved to be the master of all he surveyed, surviving through every crisis and always coming out on top.

Regardless of the pressures, Rae was confident, and he marveled at the sheer scope of the operation that he led. Now it was up to Liebs to enter the ring with Milton and slug it out to the bitter end—an end Special Agent Dillon Rae had already predetermined.

High above the Atlantic, a Milton Global jet winged its way to Zurich for what was to become a truly epic battle with a fearsome adversary. In Milton's eyes it had been a long time coming. The stage had been set. The scale of the operation was staggering. Milton was certain that, given Liebs's greed and pride, he would accept the challenge. An ingenious transfer of assets from the greedy into the hands of the clever, the self-assured Milton thought. His surprising alliance with Rae had laid the groundwork for him to obliterate Liebs forever. There was no mistaking the elation he felt in anticipation of his long-overdue liberation, to be free of the arch-blackmailer thanks to the guaranteed backing of his very own government. He would surely win. And when he did take the winner's podium, he would exploit his political aspirations to the full. It was a dizzying prospect.

As the jet settled at thirty thousand feet, an even greater feeling of confidence pervaded Milton once he had digested the information handed to him by the recently recruited investigative consultant, who sat next to Oscar Randell. The hardbound asset-tracing report sat on his lap. It clearly indicated that the bulk of Liebs's fortune was well organized through a myriad of companies and trusts throughout the world and therefore ostensibly untouchable. They could only guess at the vast treasure trove that was soon to be their spoils of victory.

Randell hired the investigator specifically to enable them to get the latest on the Swiss banker. The consultant specialized in financial investigations, forensic accounting, and surveillance, and his renowned expertise was employed for the most complex of situations. Within days, the consultant had managed to provide Milton's team with timely and accurate intelligence on their mark. His report identified the types of instruments Liebs used in his schemes, gave an assessment as to the amount of assets involved, and identified relationships among a myriad of connected parties. The consultant had no loyalties to anyone, being motivated by fees alone. He had learned much from his last similar assignment in which he had carried out very similar investigations, and such was the delicacy of the operation that he had to exercise the utmost caution and stay at a different hotel from Milton and his team. He had to avoid a chance encounter with Gerhard Liebs at all costs.

The line between today and tomorrow blurred. As the clocks pressed forward, there were those who remained awake until the early hours. Franco Cavallini was at his home in Rome on a call with Robbie Castalano on Long Island, New York. Based on Castalano's information, Cavallini determined to fly to New York immediately to order his daughter to cease her liaison with this American boyfriend. If necessary, he would force her to return to Italy. Arrangements had already been made with the senior partner of Luciana's law firm, who, although disappointed in losing such an excellent member of his team, was happy to relocate her to their Milan office. For the partner, there was no favor he would not grant such an old and esteemed client as Franco Cavallini.

Cavallini replaced the handset and called his Alitalia Airlines contact in Milan. He had business in Milan late that morning, giving him plenty of time to catch a 3:30 p.m. flight, which would get him into JFK at 7:30 EST that evening. The Alitalia agent, although awakened at three in the morning, promised to carry out the request, even if it meant bumping some hapless first class passenger off the aircraft.

# SWITZERLAND

The grand drawing room of the schloss was luxurious. With its three massive bay windows, gilded decor, magnificent marble fireplace, a ceiling decorated with plaster medallions of roses, and Murano cut-glass chandeliers, it reflected the über-wealth of its owner.

Gerhard Liebs sat on an ornately carved, walnut-framed sofa upholstered in thick, slate-blue silk brocade, its long cushions and stuffed arms oozing elegant opulence. Hanging prominently on the center wall was a 1943 oil painting by Russian-born French painter Marc Chagall. A grand piano graced the room, although it had never been played. One of four drawing rooms, this one was on the second floor adjacent to a north gallery, beyond two large doors. Approaching it from the gallery, you had to climb a marble staircase.

Liebs had decided to work from home this day in anticipation of his meeting with Harvey Milton. Secure behind the castle's drawbridge, the Machiavellian puppet master rose from his seat to peer out of a window. Solid iron gates and twenty-foot-high walls left no question that uninvited visitors were not welcome. Guards carrying poorly concealed Uzi submachine guns were making rounds, an event that took place every fifteen minutes, 24/7. Even some of his staff carried handguns beneath their domestic uniforms.

Adrenaline mixed with a certain foreboding filled him as he waited in anticipation. Liebs rarely made a move without the cards being stacked in his favor, but this time he had allowed his curiosity to take over. Although informed of Milton's one-billion-dollar influx of cash, the pathetic Dieter Gruber was unable to trace its sources or pass on further information. A billion in cash was staggering. Although he knew MGI was a vast conglomerate, putting up such a sum in actual cash was impressive.

What was Harvey up to? Liebs stood for a long while peering out of the window, mining their respective pasts to uncover what could possibly be the reason behind Milton's request for a meeting. It had started to snow again, covering the wheel tracks of the vehicles that had visited the schloss that afternoon. What new ventures could bring in such funds overnight? He had to find out and get Harvey to share the wealth, or at least the source of his newfound cash cow. And did it have anything to do with the reason for Harvey's visit? Whatever the reason, he vowed to exercise his control over him. But Liebs lacked the upper hand with Milton this time and he knew it. Threatened by the unknown, the power-crazed megalomaniac vowed to gain the upper hand while on the face of it welcoming any future cooperation between them. So Liebs geared up to flaunt his wealth, clearly to establish his distinct advantage, but not before once again going through the newly updated Harvey Milton files that now contained Moroccan material that he had brought with him from the safe in his office at Bank Schreiber Liebs.

His face began to show its smug amusement. The Zurich airport staff would greet Milton and his crew on the tarmac; they would be ushered through the airport into waiting Mercedes limousines and whisked away to the New Dolder Grand Hotel. A dedicated private secretary had also been arranged to acquaint Milton with the activities organized on his behalf and to provide normal secretarial services during his stay. Everything had to be perfect; it was a matter of pride. The mystique of the master was his wealth and power, the engineered myth of his dominance, never to be shattered.

At 1:00 p.m. the jet carrying the Milton Global team landed. A thin covering of new snow lay on the ground, but overhead the sky was cloudless, and the bright sun countered the bitter cold.

The pilot switched off the engines and waved to the ground staff, who placed blocks under the aircraft's wheels. Airport staff and a minibus waited for the door of the plane to open and discharge the VIPs. They were waived through normal immigration formalities and transferred to two of Liebs's Zurich-based limos, fully equipped with bar, newspapers, and a concealed surveillance system.

Sometime after the limos had driven off, the aircraft door reopened. Shielding his eyes from the bright sunlight, Milton's turncoat consultant and erstwhile information provider to Liebs emerged. He passed through immigration along with the jet's flight crew.

# WASHINGTON

Dillon Rae was midway through a marathon meeting at agency headquarters, and the strain was beginning to show. He had faced a firing line of questions from the Bureau director. He had reminded him of their expectations, told him that his progress was being monitored closely and that intervention would be employed if necessary. His boss made it clear, in no uncertain terms, that he would be held accountable for the billion dollars he had signed off. Rae assured him that it was a risk worth taking; he had full control because the government owned the bank where it was deposited. Rae showed that all was progressing to a quick finale. After all, thanks to the geek Ravi Sharma, the money would be returned to the government treasury once Liebs's account had been bled dry.

In reality, Rae could hardly contain his excitement. His TRU group were impressed by ABS's software and the technical team of JC and Ravi Sharma, which made the job that much easier. TRU was able to monitor each account through the reluctantly recruited Dieter Gruber, but also to follow the labyrinthine trails of the financial transfers. Fortunately, they were already pretty well versed with the transaction habits of the two titans.

As Rae awaited feedback from Zurich, he contemplated his future. His body gave an uncontrolled shudder.

He was on his own. Success would change his whole life expectations. But failure? That was unthinkable; the repercussions would be devastating.

# ZURICH

Snow lay deep around the hills and trees as an Agusta A109E owned by Bank Schreiber Liebs descended onto the private schloss airstrip and discharged its lone passenger. The sheer beauty of the sprawling snow-covered estate graced the picturesque landscape, but an eerie silence loomed. A Range Rover pulled up beside Milton, its motor a quiet hum, its snow tires crunching on the hard ice. It was his host, hidden behind tinted windows, who had come to greet him. A guided tour of the sprawling property followed, giving Liebs the opportunity to show off. Considering their history, the atmosphere in the vehicle was surprisingly cordial. There was an air that something monumental was about to happen.

As the men sipped a special glühwein to warm them from the cold, the Range Rover took them along the circuitous route before eventually arriving under a covered portico. The guided tour continued inside the fifteenth-century schloss. Milton marveled at the superb works by old masters that adorned the castle's stone walls. Evidently Liebs had raided auction houses on both sides of the Atlantic. The Flemish pictures were particularly remarkable, and the Monet and Georges Seurat canvases made him catch his breath in astonishment. When Milton came face to face with a particular Gauguin, he realized who had outbid him some months ago at the Sotheby's Old Masters auction in London. The collection was outstanding, and some works, he felt certain, had been on the missing works on Art Loss Register.

The two men engaged in a stilted conversation touching on global commerce and politics, grumbled about taxes and controls, even laughed at the problems caused by increasing competition, alluding to some of their own recondite activities. After the tour, they took an elevator to the second-floor dining room, decorated with opulent eighteenth-century Russian and Bavarian furniture.

Liebs and Milton sat down for a private dinner at a long table. Twenty tall church candles in four gold candelabras cast shadows across their faces. Dinner was served, dining on Ossetra caviar and Wagyu beef. Specific instructions had been given to the chef to spare nothing in the quality or the finest delicacies, with Liebs himself personally selecting the wine from his cellars. He deliberately refrained from drinking much, though his staff was directed to keep Milton's glass full at all times. To Liebs's annoyance, the wine seemed to have no effect on his American guest.

"To business, Harvey?" Liebs questioned.

"It seems a shame to spoil such an idyllic evening." Milton picked up his glass and drained its contents. "But first, Gerhard, I must compliment you on everything; quite a show, very impressive. But I get it." He laughed heartily. "Thank you!"

"It was not intended as anything but hospitality toward a man I admire and respect." Liebs replied with smug delight.

"Respect? Hardly! You didn't seem to respect me when we had that little problem all those years ago." Milton smiled wryly.

"That book is firmly closed."

"Oh, of course it is—from your lips to God's ears."

"Harvey, it is long forgotten." Liebs changed the subject. "The purpose of this evening? You wanted to discuss something with me, I believe."

"Yes, I do ..." The American was cut short.

"Let me show you another room, where we will be more relaxed." The two men retired to the adjacent library, balloons of cognac in hand.

"Well, I am of a forgiving nature." Milton met Liebs's eyes squarely. "I'm sure that we'll never need to refer to the past again," he said with conviction. "But I am finding that your business is increasingly encroaching on mine, and frankly, Gerhard, it's becoming a bit irritating." Milton's smile had now all but disappeared. He moved to a comfortable sofa near the roaring fire that filled the enormous fireplace.

"Come, come, Harvey. Life has no rewind button!" Detecting an abrupt change in atmosphere, Liebs walked over to a sofa opposite Milton and sat down. "We may find ourselves competitors more often than not, but the spoils seem fairly evenly divided, wouldn't you say? We have both done well!"

"Not from where I'm sitting." Milton took another swig of cognac. "I hear many things through the grapevine, Gerhard. Amazing stories on how your operation conducts its business."

"No less than the stories I hear about you."

"But you've resorted to bribing my own employees, for fuck's sake!" Milton growled.

"Don't play the saint with me, Harvey," Liebs countered. "You are not disinclined to certain underhand tactics."

A chess game played between their intellects, the argument ebbed and flowed. Temperatures rose and fell, voices occasionally reaching a crescendo. Milton stood up and began pacing around the room, laughing loudly at Liebs's more-innocent-than-thou protests. He walked over to the sofa where Liebs sat, leaned across its arm, and growled, "It has to stop." His deep voice sent an undetectable chill up Liebs's spine. "Now!"

"You protest too much, sir," Liebs said quietly, but there was a hesitation in his voice. "I do not see how competition is a bad thing." There was a long pause, his eyes suddenly hard and distant, the silence heavy with matters unspoken. Secretly Liebs empathized with Milton. For some time now Milton Global Inc. had been invading his turf, and that was the very reason behind his bribing and blackmailing Milton's employees. "Well, then," Liebs continued in a calm dispassionate voice, "what do we do to change things if the current climate does not suffice? After all, it is only business."

The American sat up, put down his glass and sucked in breath. "I have a proposition. Call it the *end game*." Milton exuded confidence; Liebs noticed that he was almost gloating. "The answer to our dilemma simply calls for an arrangement that resolves our impasse. A proposal—a challenge, if you like." Milton shifted his weight nearer to the blazing fire. Arms folded, his eyes revealed nothing as they fastened on the glowing amber bed, the charred edges of burning wood, the cinders popping and exploding, sending tiny orange sparks dancing up the colossal chimney.

"A challenge?" Liebs asked bemused. "In whose favor?"

"Ours." Milton turned slowly to face Liebs.

"Ours? How very intriguing. Please, do explain."

"I plan to, but it's getting very late, Gerhard, and if you don't mind, it's better if I put forward my proposal after I've had a good night's sleep." Milton was following Rae's instructions to the letter. Gain the upper hand by prolonging Liebs's curiosity. "The evening has been nothing less than remarkable in every sense, but I would prefer to continue tomorrow with a clear head. I'm sure you understand. But what I will tell you is that *my* proposition will not disappoint."

"Intriguing. But I'm at a loss to see what we would achieve by another meeting." Liebs successfully hid the excitement he felt.

"Okay, here's something to whet your appetite." Milton studied the Swiss banker who nodded curiously. "Winner takes all. A calculated gamble, which will cause a chain reaction reaching a critical mass." Milton heaved himself up from the sofa. "The loser surrenders and the winner gains total domination."

"Winner takes all? Very enigmatic." Liebs stood up and walked toward a butler's tray, his eyes gleaming with interest. "One more drink." He poured a Pierre Fougerat Tresor de Famille hundred-year-old cognac into a clean glass and handed it to Milton. "I will get my pilot organized. We will both stay in Zurich tonight." The Swiss stabbed at a button built into a false leather bound book on the table. He would issue his instructions as soon as a servant appeared.

# MANHATTAN ISLAND

A sea of umbrellas filled the city streets as pedestrians cursed at passing cars deluging waves of dirty water over sidewalks, soaking shoes. The heavy outburst of rain poured down in a steady cascade. Nicholas Adams ran from his cab to his office building and left two angry women cat-fighting over each other's right of tenancy. When it rained in New York City, umbrella sellers did a roaring trade. When the sun came out, trucks would pull alongside, pick up the remaining merchandise, and swap the umbrellas for shades, all for a few dollars, and all controlled by the Mafia.

Adams ambled into the office suite, only to be informed of an unexpected visitor waiting in his office. He shook the rainwater from his hair, smoothing it back into some sort of style.

"Ah. Mr. Adams." The dry rasp reached Adams from behind the door and he froze. Detective Lloyd Lee extended a friendly hand. "I hope you don't mind my dropping in on you."

"No, of course not," Adams replied uneasily. "Please, have a seat." He hung his sodden raincoat behind the door. "What can I do for you?" Grabbing a visitor's chair opposite Lee, he sat down. "Coffee?"

"Thank you no. As I was just passing," Lee lied, "I thought we could talk through where we stand now since our last meeting because our conversations were somewhat confusing I think?"

"Fine by me. What's new with the Howard Wayne investigation?"

"All roads lead to Rome, as they say. But I'm beginning to think that in this case they lead to Switzerland." A blatantly contrived look of gravity descended over the detective's face.

"Switzerland?" Adams hid the sudden jolt that stabbed him in his stomach and remained silent.

"I'm told you're flying there later."

"Really. Your intelligence gathering is remarkable, detective."

"Well, actually it was your office manager, Miss Johnson, who told me." His tone was slyly smooth. "And if that's where you're going, it all seems very coincidental, wouldn't you say?"

Adams met Lee's gaze. "What are you alluding to?" Adams was furious that Birdie had told Lee his plans.

"First, Howard Wayne dies." Lee looked down at his scruffy notebook. "Forensics revealed that the person who attacked Mrs. Wayne was probably the one who murdered him. While analyzing DNA left at both scenes, we get a positive ID from central records. Then Erich Kersch, who bankrolled your business, dies of an apparent suicide. Well, we supposed that's what happened. Scottsdale police checked the DNA left at the scene." Lee's husky voice took on a slight edginess. "Afterward we find out from the autopsy report that Kersch couldn't possibly have shot himself from that angle. He would have had to be a contortionist to pull it off." Then in a voice thick with confidence he said, "The forensics results came back, and we now think we know who the murderer is."

"Who?" A look of relief slid across Adams's previously troubled face.

"The FBI and CIA know of the woman."

"Woman ..."

"She's a professional killer. We believe she left the country on Sunday; and guess where she's been? Arizona. So I got the local cops to check for fingerprints. Nothing, of course. But a neighbor noticed a rental car driven by a woman hanging around that day. We traced the rental and got a description and a name, which led nowhere. But we found a print." Lee slapped his fist into his palm. "The print matches those found in New York; it's the same woman."

"Erich was murdered?" Adams shook his head in disbelief. "Never liked the guy, but you can't help but feel sorry for the poor bastard."

"The woman fits the description on file. We've alerted

Interpol." Detective Lee shook his head. "All the deaths are linked to our investigation into Kersch & Co."

"What? You're saying that this woman is wiping out everyone connected with Kersch & Co.?" Adams was unable to mask the tremor in his voice.

"Maybe. A couple of bodies, victims of a helicopter crash, were found recently, floating in a lake in Switzerland. Nothing much to go on. Aviation authorities are still investigating reasons for the crash. But we checked some of the other prints, and guess whose we found in addition to the corpses?" Lee watched Adams's face harden. "The same woman." Lee waited and watched Adams's reactions. "And the other corpse apart from the pilot, was, guess who again?"

Tension slammed into Adams's queasy, tense gut. "You are the detective ..."

"One Dale Peters, a partner in Kersch & Co!"

"Dale too?" His voice trailed away. He sat staring at Lee open-mouthed. There was no hiding his shock. His eyes were shuttered and distant.

"Seems so. We share hefty files with the SEC on Peters over here, but he hasn't been in the US for ten years or so."

"But if there's a hit man or hit woman, whose are the orders?" Adams was struggling to calm himself. "Someone has to give the instructions."

"Exactly. You've just hit the nail on the head."

"Detective, if the deaths of Howard Wayne, Erich Kersch, and Dale Peters are linked, do you think I'm a target too?" His throat went dry.

"Could be, but I just don't know at the moment. You tell me!" Lee shifted in his seat and asked outright, "Why are you going to Switzerland, Mr. Adams?"

It hit him straight between the eyes. He knew he could not tell the detective anything and he knew by being silent he was implicating himself. The screws were being tightened. It didn't matter what respite he got, along came yet another dangerous threat. He needed Luciana. He knew what she would counsel, but he had to carry on. Tomorrow would be a tough call.

To Nick's surprise, Luciana insisted on driving him to JFK for his Zurich flight. As they pulled up at Swiss Air's terminal, an Alitalia flight from Milan was landing. Goodbyes were said, but Nick detected a certain agitation and coolness in Luciana's attitude. Once Nick was through security, Luciana quickly boarded the AirTran to Terminal 1, where someone else was patiently waiting.

In due course Luciana was on her way back to Manhattan with her new passenger. The tanned, distinguished-looking sixty-eight-year-old sat deep into the leather seat, oblivious to the surroundings he knew so well. Dressed in an expensive, hand-tailored suit, his grooming was impeccable, every strand of silver hair perfectly in place. The heavy, dark-brown-framed tinted glasses he wore made him look every inch the successful Italian businessman with an uncanny resemblance to the late Gianni Agnelli, who had been a very close friend.

Franco Cavallini was genuinely pleased to see his daughter, but his continual harping on about how it was important to hold dear the values of her birth land ate up their ride to the city. And, as far as her relationship with the American was concerned, he was very troubled. Franco's southern Italian roots originated from a place where anyone who was not a relative or friend would be deemed untrustworthy. Even if his suspicion of outsiders might be considered outdated in the twenty-first century, the family's position could never be ignored.

Greatly respected on both sides of the Atlantic by the Italian community, Don Franco Cavallini, an elder statesman of the Italian-American radical world, was semi-retired. Nowadays, most of his businesses were legitimate. Surviving many unpleasant events unscathed was testament to Cavallini's brilliance. In the eighties he had managed to escape the Maxi Trial of hundreds of Mafiosi in Palermo, Italy. In New York, he had lived to tell the tale of several assassination attempts, two car bombs, a sniper, and a machine-gun assault. "They were badly executed," he would remark with scorn. Then, as the FBI began closing its net on Mafia activities, many "old time" bosses either languished in prisons, were found dead, or sought exile. Cavallini had fled back to Italy. His trusted consigliere, Robbie Castalano, had remained in New York, trying to hold control on their fish, meat, and produce markets, having lost the refuse business. Not long after he had resettled in Italy, Cavallini redirected his focus on white-collar crime and corporate fraud. His Wall Street brokerages, media conglomerate, health-insurance racket, credit-card fraud, Internet activities, mobile phone, and phone card initiatives became huge successes.

At the same time, a new Mafia was emerging. It had become increasingly difficult for law enforcement to pinpoint who was in charge in many Mafia cities, which naturally created fresh opportunities for the mob to regroup. The new Mafia had quite a different infrastructure, one that employed the old ways on a local level, and an imposing international network on the global scene. On the down side, the new Mafia was in great need of hard cash to complete its national and global transformations, and fierce competition from other crime syndicates hadn't helped matters. Now there were the new cooperative arrangements taking place among the Mob, the Russians, the Triads and the cartels.

But things were getting still tougher. Authorities were becoming anxious about the magnitude of "dirty" Mafia money floating around the world's financial markets. As the doors of the secretive Swiss banks were gradually pried open, the Mafia was forced to find new banks and offshore tax havens. Unfortunately, these were not as secure or efficient as the Swiss banks of old, so they converted as much of their cash as was feasible into new ventures on the Internet, private equity, hedge funds, and anything that on the face of it lent legitimacy to their squalid world.

Upon Cavallini's arrival at the Palace Hotel, the front-desk attendants whisked him directly to the dedicated private elevator that led to his lavish triplex suite. The 4,000-square-foot suite felt like a home away from home to Cavallini, with its lavish décor, two-story ceilings, and rooftop terraces with iconic views of the city. Cavallini was certain to get a good night's sleep after his long trip. He would meet his daughter for breakfast in his room in the morning.

Meanwhile, Robbie Castalano was hard at work gathering pieces of the jigsaw they couldn't seem to fit into place. The fragments of Luciana's story had left out vital bits and links, so Castalano kept a vigil on Gavin Hart, whom they thought held the key to many unanswered questions.

The red autumn sunset that early evening seemed to hang in the sky, yet Hart walked with purpose in his stride, a proud lift to his head. Deep in thought, he considered his next play once he heard back from Harvey Milton in Switzerland. People passing along the quiet street off Columbus Avenue made no dent in his reflections as he approached the brownstone apartment of his girlfriend. He hadn't been able to see much of her lately. He sashayed up the steps to her building as if he had all the time in the world.

A blow came from directly behind him, a measured strike designed to stun, not kill. His attackers grabbed him, but he didn't go down. He replied with a fist, crushing the nose of one of his assailants. A strong arm seized his shoulder, pulling him backward off the doorstep. But Hart's survival instincts were astonishing. As a former member of the British Parachute Regiment special elite forces, his moves were confident. Trained in commando tactics, Hart wasn't as physically fit as he once was, but he hadn't forgotten his skills as a fighter in the Falklands, as well as the special operations assignments in Iraq and Libya. The thugs were surprised by his agility as he fought back. But before he could take them both down, a large hand clamped roughly over his mouth, his head was dragged back against a brawny chest, and fingers pressed hard beneath his chin. Hart's heels smashed into the man's shins, followed by an elbow to the gut, when a sharp, cold, metal object against his throat forced him to cease his resistance. The other man shoved a handkerchief in his mouth, bound his eyes with black tape, and tied his hands behind his back. The man on his other side took his arm, and the two of them dragged him into the back of a black Cadillac with tinted windows, which had glided up to the curb.

Hart squirmed in his seat until several blows to his head made him settle down. The car drove for about thirty minutes before stopping. Blindfolded, Hart had no idea where he was. When they removed the handkerchief from his mouth, a barrage of questions ensued. He tried to swallow to rid himself of the tightness in his throat. They raised a knife to his neck, but Hart gave nothing away, remaining silent. The pressure of the knife increased until a warm trickle hinted that the knife had drawn blood. He didn't even wince. When the blade pierced his flesh a second time, biting deeper into his pale skin, he was still defiant. They dialed a number on a cell phone, and turned on the speakerphone. An Italian-American voice answered, whereupon the room was rent by the screams of his girlfriend.

It was startling how much they knew about the Dillon Rae operation was startling. Holding back information wasn't worth risking that his girlfriend would get hurt, so he divulged just enough to protect her.

An hour later they threw Hart onto the curb several blocks from where he had been nabbed, hitting the ground with a thud. He staggered to his feet. His head felt as though someone had tried to bisect it. He rubbed his wrists, which chafed from the leather straps. The inch-long incision below his right ear burned, and a sticky trickle of blood made its way down his neck. Rae's discovery on how he had sung like a canary would surely be found out. The deal was over. The plan would fail.

# ZURICH

Nicholas Adams arrived early for his meeting with Gerhard Liebs. He was astounded by the new Dolder Grand's sheer size and elegance: a magnificent fortress-like building poised atop a hill overlooking Zurich. Adams ordered coffee as he sat in the hotel's grand foyer, waiting for Liebs to appear. Liebs arrived, obviously preoccupied, and clearly anxious to spend as little time as possible with Adams. The last thing he wanted was a cross-examination on the whereabouts of proceeds from the sale of his shares. A subject to be avoided, he engaged in pleasantries as long as he could.

"Nick," Liebs said, with hands folded, his gloved fingers resting on his thin knees, "you mentioned having important information for me?"

"As a matter of fact, I do." Adams leaned into Liebs, lowered the pitch in his voice and spoke sternly. "But you must believe what I'm about to tell you, otherwise you will end up completely wiped out."

"Wiped out?" Liebs laughed cynically at the absurd assertion. "I very much doubt that." He started to stand up. "Foolish man!"

Unflustered by the put-down, Adams countered. "Please be patient! We can play games if you want; but don't think I flew all this way to tell you something that could easily be said over the phone."

"Be quick, I am very busy." Liebs sat back into his seat. "So then, what are we talking about here? What is going on?"

"A sting operation is being engineered by FBI agents," he whispered, winning Liebs's undivided attention, "against you!" Nick leaned forward knowing that he had secured the attention. "I know because I am part of it."

"You? FBI? Is this some sort fantasy of yours?" Liebs sneered. "Federal agents? Now why would such an agency be interested in me?" He leaned back in his seat, waiting for Adams's next madness.

"You can sneer all you want when I'm done."

Liebs shrugged.

"Harvey Milton flew here yesterday to meet with you. Am I right?"

It was a statement of fact that surprised Liebs. How could Adams know of his private meeting with Milton?

"Milton is going to challenge you to a duel. One in which he is guaranteed to win. Why? Because the FBI is using him as bait to take you down."

"Bait? He is not likely to be anyone's lackey, I think." But the information made Liebs uneasy. "Go on," he said, grunting impatiently.

"As you and I know, you bank at CAY BANK?"

"Yes, one of many banks." Liebs nodded in confirmation.

"Well, that bank is caught up in an entrapment to help catch tax evaders and criminals," he hesitated, "and you've been tagged."

"And how do you know this?" Liebs gave him an incredulous look. "Why are you involved?"

"Believe it or not, I was forced to adapt one of my software programs for this undertaking."

"Why are telling me this? I can't imagine that I have earned your kindness?" His words could not be truer. There was a long silence. Then, placing his gloved fingers together, Liebs said quietly, "Let's start from the beginning." He was astute enough to know when to listen and learn. "You had better tell me everything."

The two men huddled as they sat. Adams calmly briefed Liebs, who listened intently. Half an hour had gone by. Taking a swift glance at his watch, Nick realized he had less than ninety minutes to catch his flight back to New York.

"Your flight?" Liebs asked, responding to the alarmed look on Adams's face. "Come with me." Liebs abruptly stood from his chair. "I will drop you at the airport. We can continue our talk on the way. Meet me outside when you have checked out."

Adams's story put Liebs in an upbeat mood. Thanks to Adams's surprising loyalty, Liebs was now prepared to deal with Harvey Milton. Liebs had clearly misjudged Adams and vowed to make more use of him in the future. In fact, he realized that Adams could become a threat, and he would not allow that to happen. The die was cast. Now Liebs couldn't wait to accept Milton's challenge. The game would be very different now.

The two men spoke non-stop until they reached the airport terminal. Ten minutes later, Adams was through passport control and soon on his way back to New York.

En route to his next meeting, Liebs placed a call to the States. JC confirmed Adams's story. In fact, he blurted out everything. Liebs was grateful for the painstaking protections he had built into his network of blackmail.

But JC had also followed Dillon Rae's script to the letter. He had expected the call from Liebs if all had gone well with Adams's confrontation in Zurich. Liebs had taken the bait, hook, line and sinker.

# MANHATTAN

Franco Cavallini gazed out of the eighteen-foot windows of his suite, admiring the dynamic city he had once called his own. He had already concluded his first breakfast meeting with the senior partner of Luciana's law firm, who had long since left. Now he was waiting for his daughter to arrive.

Standing at their post within the suite's entrance hall were two security men provided by Robbie Castalano. Three more were on their way. Even in New York Franco, Cavallini was a target, and many would volunteer their services. It was always the same when the Don was back in town.

Luciana arrived and kissed her father three times, smiling at his still-handsome visage. She took a place at the dining table.

"*Figlia mia*. You look tired, my little one. You are working much too hard." He paused briefly. "And perhaps, playing too hard?"

"Everything is fine, Papa, stop worrying." Luciana reached a hand across to his and squeezed it tightly.

"Well, nothing a change of environment will not cure."

"I am too busy for a holiday, papa."

"Are you sure you have fully recovered from the accident?"

"I'm still a little sore, but the bruises are fading." She showed him a bruise on her leg. "There, you see! I couldn't be seen on a beach right now, so no holiday." She poured herself fresh orange juice and picked at a croissant.

"When does your American friend come back?"

"You mean Nick," she snapped. "Call him by his name, Papa, please."

Cavallini nodded reluctantly. "Okay, Nick. Whatever." He held up a hand in resigned acknowledgment.

"Nick gets back later this afternoon, but I won't see him until tomorrow."

"There are a few things I still do not understand about your boyfriend's business. For example, this software business of his, what does it specialize in? Maybe I have contacts in that area that could be of help to him." He oozed charm.

Luciana was pleased to hear that her father might be willing to take Nick under his wing. She knew he would have to come round eventually. Perhaps he was softening toward the idea of her dating Nick after all. Cavallini asked more questions about Adams and appeared interested in meeting him. She answered his unusually deep questions as best she could, never realizing the confidences she was betraying.

An hour later Luciana left her father's suite for her office. The security guard assigned to Luciana during Cavallini's stay followed without detection.

While she was busy working at her desk, Luciana's boss stopped by, carrying a file under his arm. He looked ill at ease. With a heavy sigh, he sat down in a chair in front of her, placing the file on her desk. "Luciana," he said, straightening the knot in his silk tie, "I have an exciting new project for you, a new client who needs our help immediately."

"Of course." She sat up with interest. "I'll take some notes."

"That won't be necessary." He opened the file and pushed it toward Luciana. "Everything you need is in this file." Luciana looked down at its contents. An e-ticket confirmation lay atop the printed brief. She glanced at the flight and destination details and gagged. A vein in her right temple began to throb. She placed a hand on her chest and tried to catch her breath.

"*Pezzo di merda*," she swore under her breath, "I can't do this!" She turned and looked out of the window and muttered under her breath "I won't do this, I will not!"

# ZURICH

Lunch ended in the private dining room at the new Dolder Grand. Milton's proposal seemed outrageous and implausible in every way. It defied logic and appeared to insult the intelligence of the Swiss banker deliberately. But having been forewarned, Liebs took every part of it in his stride. Now all it would take was a little nerve and a total disregard for the truth. Thanks to Adams's heads-up on the FBI operation and JC's corroboration, Liebs knew he had the edge. But he couldn't believe how Milton presumed him to be so naïve. He went along with the charade, but had given Milton a run for his money.

"Well—, I guess the rules are established, and we are in total agreement." Milton grinned. He hoped the relief he felt had not registered on his face.

"Indeed. As you so succinctly put it: winner takes all. It will, however, require nerves of steel, you know. And I fear it will be quite a battle, my friend." Liebs looked at the face of his archrival and smiled thinly. "How much do you reckon will be in the winner's pot?"

"Now, that is for us to aspire to." Milton laughed smugly. "But we both know it will be massive, double-digit billions. Just think, Gerhard, given the magnitude of the resources available with such a fortune, nothing could ever get in the way of the victor's conquests."

"And the loser, what of him?" Liebs tried to hold back the hint of a smirk. "Bankruptcy? Skid row as you Americans say? Suicide, perhaps?"

"Total oblivion." Milton laughed with a strange glitter in his eyes. Such an option was unnecessary. He already had a billion dollars in cash safely deposited in the bank; it was a distinctly unfair starter boost to his coffers. "I will send a suitable wreath," he taunted.

"How macabre," Liebs responded. "Tell me, Harvey, just how do we protect ourselves from fraud? I need assurance that the system in place is secure. How can I know that this is not a double cross?"

"We have the very best."

"So run me through the system protocols again." Liebs was only pretending to play ball. He didn't give a damn about the system's security. After all, with the help of his own team, he would control it.

"CAY BANK will be the custodian bank." In modulated tones, Milton carefully briefed Liebs again on the inner workings of the system, concluding, "And there will be three accounts: one for you, one for me, and an empty account ready to be filled at the end of the game."

"A collection receptacle."

"Yes. Now during the game, you and I will transfer all the cash we can manage to get our hands on into our respective CAY BANK accounts." He took a sip from his glass of water and added, "The account holder with the most cash at the end wins. The system will collect and funnel the total balance of each account into the third account." Liebs's mouth twitched in a slight smile, the smile of a shark sensing blood in the water.

Milton nodded. "And the winning account draws the spoils. All the cash accumulated in both our accounts will instantly be transferred into the third account when the clock stops. The third account becomes irrevocably owned by the victor."

"Precisely. And the timing on this?"

"Allowing for the vagaries of the banking system and wire transfer hiccups, we should go for close of banking day next Monday, 5:00 p.m. New York time."

"That's less than five days! And with a weekend in between, at that." Liebs groaned. "You *really* want our alliance to be over rather quickly."

"Well, that's the challenge, isn't it? Hope it's not a case of all flash and no cash." Milton felt a flicker of amusement. "If you're as rich as you say you are, you should have no problem winning."

"Irrevocable?"

"Irrevocable. The software will control everything. It will be our virtual referee, the final electronic decision maker. But you must decide on your base of location, because the bank will need to set up a dedicated line which will remain live until next Monday and keep you in constant touch. Unfortunately, neither of us will be privy to the activity in the other's account during the game's duration."

They both laughed. As if.

"At 5:00 p.m. Monday the final true fortune will be unveiled. But how will we know which one of us has won?"

"By using your designated password. Only one of us will be able to access the winner's pot. The CAY BANK system software will determine which password is granted access to the third account. A link will be established automatically between the winner's old account and the winner's pot at 5:00 p.m. sharp on Monday." Milton took out a handkerchief and mopped at his brow. "From the start, you will be able to access your new account on the bank's online site, showing all account activity, credits posted, and the accumulating balance. You will also be able to view the winner's account standing at zero. The winner's account will remain empty until 5:00 p.m. Monday. If the screen shows a zero balance in the two accounts after that time, you will have lost. Everything."

"Very interesting, intriguing, in fact. I never knew you had this in you, Harvey."

Milton held out his hand. "Do we have a deal?"

"Of course I will want validation from CAY BANK. When I am satisfied that the transfer systems are in place, work as you have stated, and cannot be tampered with, then yes, I accept your challenge." He took Milton's hand and shook it, grimacing at the tight grip of the American. He felt the puss seeping from his fingers.

"Excellent, excellent!" Milton beamed. "By the way, we should agree that the loser gets one million dollars as compensation. The loser will need a small pension, don't you think?"

"No," Liebs replied. "The bet stands as you've stated—*winner takes all*. No compensation."

"So be it. Let the better man win. I will draw up the necessary documents for us to sign, including power-of-attorney for the winner." Milton's legal team, who was working closely with Dillon Rae, already had the paperwork ready and waiting. "I will send a PDF to you later today."

The trap was sprung. The lines were drawn. In their fight to win, Liebs and Milton would dredge up every ounce of ingenuity and wit they could muster and take the most appalling risks. They shared a craving for the power their wealth had brought, the money being just a means to an end. Everything each had learned over his long career would be put into practice to take his opponent down. Both men were renowned for using ruthless and unconventional tactics. Both would employ scheming, manipulation, deception, diversion, and distraction to win the ultimate prize.

Once Liebs had received confirmation on the details and system schematics from CAY BANK, Oscar Randell arranged for signatures, and the Liebs-Milton agreement was signed. A new offshore company had been incorporated for the contest, with each bearer share issued and held in trust by CAY BANK. Liebs set up his new CAY BANK account. At the end of the game, all proceeds from the two new accounts would be transferred into the catchments account. Whoever ended up with the winning pot would own and control the combined assets of Liebs and Milton.

On Thursday, at precisely 6:00 p.m. Swiss time, the race was on. The two men separately assembled key people and issued instructions without divulging the purpose of their directives. Asset gathering would occupy every moment of every senior executive and advisor's time, acting blindly on orders from the two contestants, for the duration of the next five and a half days. Security management teams received new briefs, new surveillance operations were set up, and the most sophisticated scanning devices were brought in at enormous expense to infiltrate the airwaves. No expense would be spared.

All over the world various parties were contacted. Directives were clear and precise: drop everything and wait for instructions. Failure to comply would have serious implications.

Millions of dollars started to flow electronically from all points of the globe. Bank facilities were negotiated and funds transferred. Assets were valued and short-term bridge loans arranged. Debts were called in, pension funds plundered, deposits sequestered. Anything that could be turned into liquid cash was seized. As a result, the global stock markets began to fall in unusual trading patterns. The only thing their respective management and staff knew was that something big was happening.

Liebs used more devious methods than Milton. He had access to vast sums through his investor organization. All he had to do was "borrow" money for the short period and replace it when he won the pot—a catastrophic move if he were to lose. But given the inside edge he had over Milton, he thought he couldn't possibly fail; therefore there would be no risk. He might even pay a dividend to those who contributed, *might* being the operative word, although they would have no knowledge of the short-term involuntary contribution they were making.

Milton, through MGI, tapped into long-standing confidential relationships he had with international banks and other institutions. The institutions relished what promised to be a major international stock play, their appetites insatiable.

By the end of the banking day, the race had netted over ten billion dollars, in almost equal proportion to both contestants, excluding Milton's head start.

# MANHATTAN

Nick sailed through customs when he arrived back in New York. In no time, he passed through to the arrivals terminal. As he searched for his pre-booked driver among the hordes of people waiting for arriving passengers, a familiar voice called his name. At first he thought he had imagined it, but the voice called out again. He looked around, probing the sea of faces, and saw Luciana.

"Lu ... sweetheart," he said, holding his arms out as she approached. "Great surprise." He embraced her tightly. "How sweet. You came all this way to pick me up."

"*Tesoro*, I'm sorry but ..." Luciana slowly pulled away from him. Nick put his hands on her cheeks and searched his lover's face. There was a profound sadness in the depths of her eyes.

"I'm being sent back to Italy."

"What? Back? When?"

"My flight leaves in two hours. I've already checked in. That's why I'm at the airport."

"For how long?" He prayed the answer would be only days.

"I don't know, *tesoro*. I'm so miserable." Luciana kissed him on both cheeks and put her arms around him again, as if never to let him go. "*Ti amo.*"

Nick picked up his carry-on bag and led her to a less hectic area of the arrivals lounge, where he found two free seats. Luciana explained that her senior partner, who informed her that she must leave that night, had given her an assignment back in the Milan office. She told Nick that the whole thing didn't add up, and that she felt her father had had something to do with it.

"Perhaps if I met your father ..."

"No. That definitely won't help matters at the moment. He is not happy with what's been going on."

"How could he possibly know?" Nick's body tensed. He felt a lump in his throat, and his eyes burned.

"My father is very persuasive. He can get anything out of anyone."

"Did you tell him?"

"Yes. Well … only some of it," she lied.

"Oh no. Not the stuff I told you in confidence!"

"He just kept grilling me!" She opened her handbag, pulled out a tissue, wiped her eyes, and tried to play innocent. "Of course I didn't go into much detail." Luciana knew she had divulged far too much to her father, especially when he seemed a bit too interested in Gavin Hart. But she didn't dare tell Nick that she actually told him everything.

"Okay, well, maybe I should have explained better. But I do assure you it will be over very soon. You'll see." He took her hands and held them tightly.

"I have no idea how long I'll be away. If it's more than a week, will you come to Italy?"

"Of course I will. Without question. Try stopping me."

As they sat talking for a while longer, an observer leaned against a wall reading a newspaper, occasionally peering over the top of it in their direction. When the time came, Nick reluctantly let Luciana walk off to the Alitalia terminal.

"Remember—don't worry about your father. He's just looking out for you. And keep away from those Italian guys." He flashed his white teeth at her.

They embraced and Nick watched her disappear through the terminal. He felt miserable. A terrible feeling of foreboding loomed.


Ravi Sharma's health was rapidly deteriorating, his body wasting away. The virus was developing resistance to his latest meds, moving to a more aggressive stage, and his T-cell count was fatally low. But his doctors were still committed to finding a course of treatment and prescribed yet another combination of drugs. Thrilled to learn they had discovered an alternate treatment, Sharma rushed out to the pharmacy to get the new pills.

On his way back to Nick's apartment, two thugs blocked his path. He stepped to one side in an attempt to pass when they grabbed him by the collar, blindfolded him, and gagged him. His abductors threw him into the back seat of a car and took off, racing through the city streets to the West Side docks. A knife at his throat kept him still. When the vehicle arrived at its destination the two men pulled him out by the shoulders, dragged him across what seemed to be uneven concrete, and unceremoniously pushed him into an empty steel shipping container. The smell of oil and rust stifled the air. Somewhere nearby a ship's horn broke the evening's silence.

The first blow hit his ribs after they had stripped him naked. Sharma screamed, doubled over and crashed to the cold metal floor. They pounded away as he crawled aimlessly, seeking safety. His wild pleas were for naught. The more they landed the toe caps of their shoes on his puny body, the farther he rolled down the twenty-foot container. He tried to protect himself with his arms, but, after a while, he just closed his eyes and prayed for the hammering to end, or for his own death. Their intent was not to kill him or beat him to a pulp, but to beat him into submission. They kicked until his groans were silenced, then the door slammed shut. From inside the dark container Sharma could hear the screech of tires as the car drove off. His entire body trembled with pain, and jabbing rushes of fear chilled his bones. Every noise echoed inside the dark metal coffin. He eventually fell asleep, but woke in fits and starts, shivering uncontrollably. A rat scurried across his body.

Sharma's unconsciousness was brief. He was woken by the grating of the container's doors and then by the sudden harsh headlights of a car beaming his shadow onto an interior wall. His blindfold had long fallen off. He pressed his face to his knees to protect his eyes from the glare and his gut from further blows.

At that moment a deluge of water from a fire hose hit him at such a velocity that it rolled him further into the metal tomb. Every limb quivered uncontrollably at the impact. "Please stop," he said feebly, arms stretched against the torrent. Suddenly the gusher stopped and the door shut again. A few moments later, the door crashed open and two men entered. He found himself gagging on the barrel of a handgun. A knee rested on his chest. His associate got down to the business in hand while another man kept watch.

The man pulled Sharma into a sitting position as if he were a rag doll. The man with the handgun took out a cell phone and made a call. After ten minutes a third man, with snowy white hair, appeared in the doorframe.

"Ravi," Robbie Castalano said, feigning anger. "I'm so sorry about your ill treatment." He shot a displeased look at the two men, whose eyes stared back in mock protest. "I promise I'll make it up to you. But you've gotta do a few things for me." Sharma shifted his emaciated frame and tried to look into the face that bore no distinguishable marks.

"What things?" Sharma's voice was hoarse and weak, his eyes red and unfocused.

"We know everything about you, Ravi. We know about your little job in the Caribbean and we know of Nick and how close you are to him." Seeing the horror on Sharma's face, Castalano said, "No need to concern yourself. He will not be hurt." Castalano walked to the back of the container. "If you help us, everything will be just fine."

"Help you?" The threatened implication in the old man's voice frightened him.

"*Smettila!*" Castalano snapped his fingers at the man on the door. "Make him comfortable and give him his clothes. What sort of people are you? Now!"

In the span of a few blurred minutes, they dragged Sharma out across the gravel-strewn concrete path into an old warehouse and up a set of wooden stairs. The warehouse was in an area of New York City where people who liked to avoid violence never ventured. Makeshift industrial lights were turned on to reveal a sparsely furnished interior. He swept the storeroom in one blurred gaze. There were a couple of tables, several chairs, and a metal-framed bed.

He was helped to the bed that smelled of cats and urine. A damp, mildewy, folded sack was propped up under his head. Castalano drew up a chair to sit next to Sharma and spoke to him in an almost conciliatory voice. Castalano explained that his expertise was needed for a special job. For this he would be rewarded with the gift of continuing life. Failure to comply would result in a reprisal against Adams and his girlfriend.

"*Capice?*"

Frightened, Sharma nodded in agreement. Castalano went on to spell out their plan. He removed an envelope from an inside pocket and handed it to Sharma. The envelope contained pages of numbers. Castalano told him that the numbers had to be guarded at all cost and destroyed after the job was done. In the wrong hands, the repercussions would be unpleasant for all concerned, especially for him and his friends.

Ravi Sharma studied the codes and numbers on the sheets. These guys were very, very smart; however, the requested additions to his work were attainable. The audacity of what they wanted led to an adrenaline rush. He assured Castalano that what they wanted could be done. It would be a tough task logistically, by virtue of the long list of numbers, but he would comply. "But, I need assurances."

"You are hardly in a position to make demands," Castalano snarled.

"I just need to know that you won't do anything to Nick, or there's no deal."

"That can be arranged."

Sharma gave Robbie Castalano a cell phone number to be used during the operation. It was not the number issued by Rae. Ravi now had many such phones, each for a different master.

"Now, just to show you that we are also players in the electronic world, here is a flash drive with all of the numbers on those sheets, do not lose it!"

Sharma remained alone in the warehouse as the three left.

The initial shock and panic he had felt disappeared, almost as though he had been an observer instead of the victim, oddly disconnected with what had really just happened.

Nicholas Adams had waited patiently at a window table in the Bice restaurant for Ravi to join him. He looked up from his BlackBerry and saw him coming toward his table. Nick put his cell down, placed his pen beside his memo pad, and got up.

"Better late than never." But he could see something was very wrong, and wished he hadn't been sarcastic. "Coffee, my friend?" He drew back a chair for Ravi.

"No, just water, if you don't mind. System can't handle the caffeine anymore." Though painfully thin, with bruises clearly visible from the previous night's ordeal, Sharma had lost neither his handsome visage nor his magnetism, which was of obvious interest to their more-than-eager-to-please waiter.

"You okay? What have you done to your face?" Nick asked, deeply shocked. "What happened to you?"

"Don't worry, I'm good." But the pain was evident as he shifted in his seat and grimaced. "It was so awful, Nick, I can hardly stop shaking."

"Tell me what's going on, in your own time. Shit, this has got to stop. When will it end?"

"God help us! Listen to me, Nick: we've got problems!" Fighting the nausea that tormented him, Sharma told Nick about his dramatic abduction. Nick listened but couldn't believe what he was hearing. The web was crawling with spiders. It was all too bizarre, how could Ravi have been kidnapped and beaten up by mobsters? It was too off the wall. Sharma then pleaded with Nick not to do or say anything, that doing so would put him in grave danger.

"I don't know what I can do to assist. We don't know who instigated this outrage, but we do know that they are on to what we are doing, which is fucking scary!" Nick now felt sick to his stomach. Had Ravi told him everything? Should he report this to Rae, who was complicit in this? They were questions with no immediate answers.

"I've come up with my own game plan to deal with all of this shit. I just need a favor."

"Whatever I can do, Ravi, just name it."

Ravi passed a note across the table. "Be there." Nick picked up the paper with an address written on it. "Come hell or high water, next Tuesday at noon. Whatever you do … do not miss this appointment. It'll be worth it," he laughed, a dry, nervous giggle. "Please, Nick, I implore you."

"What on earth? What have you done? Why?"

"Just be there! Please." Ravi leaned forward and just looked straight into Nick's eyes. "On my life, I would not ask you to do this if it would harm you in any way."

"Okay, whatever. I'll be there." Nick was intrigued. It was an address that would be difficult to find, let alone get to.

"Swear. You have got to promise me you'll show up."

"Promise. No matter what, I'll be there." Bemused, he shook Ravi's hand in agreement.

Ravi whispered, "Listen, Nick, from now on there will be no more contact between us, not by cell, e-mails, nothing."

"But, there's still shit to do …"

"Nick."

"Okay, got it." It was all very strange. He had to trust Ravi. There would be nothing without him. "God speed, my friend."

"Tuesday then."

"Good!" There were tears in his brown eyes. "We will need God now."

Franco Cavallini and Robbie Castalano were also meeting in a restaurant in New York City. They chose a small establishment off the Bowery in Little Italy. Traditionally Italian, the area had gradually become hemmed in by the Chinese. Ever-increasing numbers of defections to other areas by Italians meant they could no longer rely on protection from their own against the Triad.

"Are you sure of this guy Sharma?" Cavallini asked, tapping a cigarette on the table before lighting it with a solid gold lighter. He blended in perfectly with his surroundings. Although New

York City governance deemed smoking in restaurants unlawful, no one complained.

"He will do the job. We made a deal." Castalano moved his head to avoid the other man's exhaled smoke. "Everything has been arranged; our people are on standby. On Tuesday they will be ready. It's ingenious, Franco."

"If it works." Cavallini turned serious.

"Franco, it's a simple plan. It will cost us little. If it goes wrong, it's just a small loss!"

"It must work. *Mio Dio.* We cannot afford any more losses."

A group of men seated across the room waved. Cavallini waved back and smiled. Much homage and respect had been shown to him since his arrival back in New York.

Nick arrived at the office, still bemused by his encounter with Ravi. He was looking at Ravi's note with the address scrawled in capital letters as the elevator doors opened. Birdie looked agitated and nodded toward a man sitting in the reception area.

"Mr. Adams?" The conservatively dressed man stood up and moved in his direction, showing no expression, his eyes vacant. "Nicholas Adams? I'm here on behalf of the Securities and Exchange Commission." The man produced a card and handed it to Adams. "Could we meet privately?"

Adams offered him some refreshments, which he declined, and showed him to the conference room, shutting the door behind them.

"What can I do for you?" Adams's lips curved slightly in a ghost of a smile.

"It is my duty, Mr. Adams, to serve you with this subpoena on behalf of the United States of America Securities and Exchange Commission." He delivered the words as if making a funeral oration and pulled a sheaf of papers out of the envelope he had been carrying. Still standing, he pushed the documents across the conference table, and Adams read the first page.

"You are hereby required to appear before the undersigned and other officers of the Securities and Exchange Commission to testify in the matter of Adams Banking Solutions Inc."

The document gave a date and a location and went on to state that the investigation was pursuant to a formal order issued by the Securities and Exchange Commission under authority of various sections of the Securities Exchange Act of 1934. It stated that Adams would have to produce corporate books, papers, documents and other records, that the SEC was investigating the sale of shares in two separate lots, amounting to $6 million and $3.9 million respectively. Then his eyes caught the words:

Fail not at your peril.

Nick inwardly threw up, he gagged, his right hand started shaking, but he took control. He had to. "This looks pretty serious," he said to the man, whose face showed no emotion. He did this for a living. He had no opinions as to the rights and wrongs committed by those he visited. He cared not. It was what his job specification clearly required of him. He stood up.

"I'll have to get my attorneys on this right away."

The man turned to leave but stopped short of the door and paused. "We have bigger fish to fry than you, Mr. Adams, but your association with Kersch & Co. puts you in pretty bad company. Think carefully on how you handle this."

Then he was gone, his job done.

Less than an hour later, Detective Lloyd Lee arrived, asking to see Adams. Birdie ushered him into the conference room, and when Adams finally appeared, he entered, slamming the door behind him, clearly pissed off.

"Doesn't anyone make appointments anymore?" Ignoring Lee's proffered hand, he walked around the conference table and leaned against the back wall. "I'm really too busy for all of this, you know."

"All right if I sit?"

Adams nodded impatiently. "What is it this time?"

There was no hesitation in Lee's cool answer. "You may be a suspect in the murders of ..."

"What?" Nick had lost it. "Do you really think I have

anything to do with fucking murder? Get real, man. What sort of twisted mind came up with that idea?" He glared at Lee. "Besides, I can account for all my movements."

"Of course, you didn't kill or assault anyone, and we're well aware of your movements ..."

"Oh, so you're aware of my movements. You've been tailing me too? Well, fuck you. I've had enough! Hasn't the NYPD got more important things to do?" He glared at the detective. "Why not sort out the crime on the streets ..."

"Let me finish. You didn't kill anyone, but you may know something about things that you're just not telling us."

"Oh, really," he responded sarcastically. "And what would be my motive, detective?"

"Kersch & Co. are not your friends. They've screwed you from the very start. Howard Wayne's report gave us the full story. Admittedly, you're not the only one who suffered as a result of their schemes, but you've made millions in spite of it. Maybe you needed Wayne's research and pending expose to be, say, conveniently destroyed?"

"Absolutely absurd."

"Well, then, help me to help you. What's your take on this whole thing? It could help our investigation ... and get you off the hook." He undid his coat and relaxed a bit. "Anyway, as far as my department is concerned." He paused. "However, I can't speak on behalf of any other government agency."

Nick realized he was out of his depth. He knew he had to knuckle down and behave. He wasn't a criminal; he was an innocent caught up in a larger game into which he was being drawn increasingly and was fast becoming indispensable to a number of different parties. Adams's animosity drained away, and he began to share a few possible scenarios he had been mulling over.

Lee also exchanged information with Adams on Dale Peters's death. Adams listened intently to what Lee had uncovered. There were no easy answers, but everything led back to Kersch & Co.

"What about Gerhard Liebs?" Detective Lee changed tack. "How does he fit in? What did you get out of your trip to Zurich?"

"Fairly abortive, really," he lied.

"Is he behind Kersch & Co.?" He drummed his fingers on the tabletop. "Howard Wayne thought so."

"There is a connection. He's the banker." Nick had to be careful.

"Mr. Adams, I believe you have the answers to many questions. Can you come down to the precinct and make a statement for me?"

"Look, Detective, I've had it up to here with all this," Adams said, gesturing to his forehead. "If you want me to come down for questioning, get a fucking warrant." He stormed out of the conference room.

"I might just do that, Mr. Adams," said Detective Lee raising his eyebrows, before adding, "Oh, and by the way, our record on street crime is pretty damn good."

But his words found no audience. Nick Adams had already left the room in a tantrum—partly theatrically staged.

Ravi Sharma knew several groups in the shadows were monitoring his every move as he headed directly for the check-in desk for his flight, ostensibly bound for Grand Cayman. With boarding pass in hand, he moved quickly through the crowded terminal, ducking suddenly into the men's restroom. Reappearing wearing different clothes and a cap, Sharma sprinted to another terminal for a flight to Providenciales in the Turks and Caicos via Miami. The watchers had lost him.

Successful in giving his pursuers the slip, Sharma was well on his way to a destination that was not part of anyone else's plan. His truancy would be for only one day. By the time they noticed he was missing, he'd be at his intended and agreed destination in Grand Cayman, at a CAY BANK terminal, carrying out the final phase of Rae's operation.

Harvey Milton and Oscar Randell finally left Zurich in the MGI jet bound for the US. The private investigator had remained behind to follow a lead on Liebs's money laundering schemes and a connected third party. After a stop in New York, where the jet refueled, they picked up the ever-obliging Abigail, and took off again en route to Florida, where they landed in Miami. The trio transferred to a helicopter, flew to Milton's estate off Key Biscayne, and settled into what Randell sullenly named "the Bunker." It was a newly built, single-story building, set on a four-acre island with its own heliport and landing jetty. A Riva turbo jet speedboat and a two-hundred-foot yacht were moored in a sheltered area. Equipped with the best high-end security and communications systems available, the estate doubled as a bomb shelter, with each room fitted with storm shutters that shut instantaneously by pressing any one of thirty panic buttons, excellent for hurricanes, and very useful for anyone involved in the drug trade. Two revolving satellite dishes were capable of picking up any information Milton deemed necessary, linking with a versatile sensitive monitoring and surveillance system which would be imperative until 5:00 p.m. Monday.

Milton was delighted to learn of the significant progress being made by his staff. They were successfully moving enormous sums through the company's subsidiaries and hocking everything they could to produce any form of cash. Milton could monitor everything himself now that he was physically on site with his core crew.

He was scheduled to meet with Colombian drug barons that weekend, as he had presold sufficient kilos of cocaine and taken the cash up front. He would arrange to make payment to the suppliers seven days after they had made delivery to his people. He had credit with the Columbians. It was a simple scheme to move money into CAY BANK.

First thing Monday, he planned to divert monies from the oil-consortium deal to CAY BANK. The new pipeline funding would not suffer from a few days delay in reaching Eastern Europe. Esdaulet would wait. He had no choice.

Milton was playing Rae's game with all guns blazing.

Later that afternoon he received confirmation from a certain Saudi prince that one billion dollars was on its way to Grand Cayman as advance payment on an arms deal, the terms of which were very advantageous to the prince. This prince held a comfortable government position, but had amassed huge gambling debts in Europe. With Milton's arms deal, he would be able to settle all his debts and repay the coffers of the various chests he had robbed over the years. But there were no arms. Milton Global had never been a major supplier to the Arab Kingdom, preferring ex-Eastern bloc countries, and even Pakistan. By the end of the next week Milton would simply repay the money and cancel the contract. Other MGI negotiations were in full swing, with a number of major conglomerates surprisingly caving in to hugely discounted deals that were just too good to ignore, but completion would be subject to immediate payment. Many of MGI's banks were only too willing to cooperate by offering to bridge multi-million-dollar contracts.

Money just kept flowing into CAY BANK from the Milton Global accounts around the world.

Milton wasn't the only one being so astute and devious, milking the gullibility of the greedy. Gerhard Liebs was exercising as much ingenuity as his rival. Through his private bank that held enormous deposits of cash and equities, he prepared to "borrow" funds over the weekend, making detection highly unlikely. And, in the event discrepancies were discovered, he would easily rectify matters the following week. This afforded him vast resources. Over the years a number of his customers had reluctantly given him discretionary trust over their accounts for day-to-day management. One thirty-six-year-old individual in particular threw around billions of dollars as a currency trader, and controlled massive investments throughout the world. His cash reserves were held at Bank Schreiber Liebs, and by close of business in Zurich that day the billionaire had contributed, without his knowledge, all of his cash resources held in Switzerland. Everything had been wired to CAY BANK. It would be back by Tuesday latest, and the status quo would be reestablished.

The Vatican was also a significant contributor. Liebs had warned the Vatican that the Italian authorities were beginning to investigate the funds long hidden away from the tax gatherers. He advised them that all funds residing in any offshore accounts should find another home as soon as possible, and until such time as the a suitable solution for future deposits be made, the monies would be safer at Bank Schreiber Liebs. Liebs guaranteed that any attempts to trace the funds to Bank Schreiber Liebs would be met with overwhelming obstacles. The transfers were scheduled to take place within hours.

Another ploy Liebs used was to withhold payments from his *bureau de change* business over the weekend. Of course, any administrative screwups would be forgiven. He needed only a short-term bridge.

And with the demise of Peters and Kersch, Liebs now controlled Kersch & Co. and all its assets, including the small Eastern European oil field's millions destined to be paid.

But the master knew that to win, he couldn't just skim the surface: it had to be all or nothing. That afternoon, he arranged for an appraiser from Sotheby's Zurich to visit the schloss to value his visible art collection. The works hidden within his vault would not be valued, as their provenance would be embarrassing. A temporary bridge was arranged at several banks in Zurich and Geneva, who agreed to accept the Sotheby's valuation letter as collateral. This way Liebs could borrow cash using the same art securities many times over with each institution, resulting in another $800 million transfer to CAY BANK. Sheer genius.

Next up: the transfer of the considerable cash deposits held in trust at the bank. One exiled Libyan client, in particular, might exert just retribution should he ever find out, but it was a risk Liebs was willing to take.

As the game played on, what annoyed the two contestants more than anything was their inability to gain accurate information on the other's account. Liebs was able to hack into Milton's account and Milton had the TRU team feeding him information about Liebs's account, but neither knew what cash was in the system destined for the two protagonists' accounts. Liebs was certain he'd win come what may, but he needed to know just how much cash he had to ladle in. If he didn't have the greatest treasure trove by 5:00 p.m. on Monday, he had a contingency plan in place that would kick in automatically to ensure his win, cleverly eliminating his risk of failure.

And so the monies gushed into each account in an unstoppable torrent. It had become a swollen river of cash.

Dillon Rae was gobsmacked by the sheer magnitude of the sums involved as he scanned the accounts online. Then he realized that his work was crucial. These two fiscal megalomaniacs comprised a cancer that was spreading across the globe, and he knew his agency had to put a stop to their evil empires that heaped misery and destitution on so many, while making themselves the sole beneficiaries of the massive deception they had exercised for so many years.

At around 5:30 p.m., a woman clad in a scarf, dark glasses, and an ill-fitting coat entered the lobby of Adams's office building. She handed an envelope to the concierge, tipping him in dollar bills, and requested that he should deliver it personally to the addressee. It was urgent. The man agreed to run the errand, and the woman quickly left the building without so much as a side-glance.

Upstairs, Nick Adams was on the phone with his lawyers, discussing the SEC subpoena. They advised him that in a worst-case scenario he would have to repay the $9.9 million to the shareholders—plus a fine. He tried to get his advisors to come up with an alternate solution, but to no avail. At the end of the call, he dropped the phone onto his desk and cradled his head in his hands.

"Nick?" Birdie had entered the room, and was clearly concerned at what she saw. Where was the exuberant young man she knew so well? "I have something for you. Hand delivered."

"What now? I'm done with surprises Birdie."

Birdie handed him the small envelope and waited in front

of his desk. He read the note three times, blinking in surprise, eyes narrowing as he took in the handwritten text. "Christ!" He leaped up, causing Birdie to stagger back against the open door. "Birdie, I am so sorry, I've got to go." He moved toward her, grabbed his briefcase from the side table, emptied his desk and office safe of anything important, took his cell phone and iPad, and within ten minutes he was on Park Avenue hailing a cab. He left Birdie with instructions. She would help her friend despite his ambiguous requests.

Watching from a vehicle parked a hundred feet from the building, the sole occupant touched his earpiece and spoke. "He's on the move."

Back at his apartment, Adams packed an overnight bag and left. Three cars pulled up at about the same time and mounted their surveillance, each unaware of the other's presence. Five minutes later, Adams's BMW accelerated up the steep ramp from the parking garage of his apartment building into the street and headed out of Manhattan, zigzagging erratically through the traffic. He had noticed the tail, but he was damned if he was going to be out maneuvered. One of the cars lost him before he hit the Henry Hudson Parkway, but the other two more tenacious vehicles were still in pursuit when he reached George Washington Bridge, bound for Upstate New York. Travelling north on the New York State Thruway, Adams began driving with little concern for the other vehicles on the road. His driving was nothing short of demonic. He slammed on the brakes, causing several cars to swerve as he drove past Saw Mill River Parkway. Thumping the gas pedal, he took the BMW up to 120 mph. He looked through the rear-view mirror to see if his tails were gaining ground, and saw one driver's arm snake out the window and place a red light on its roof. The siren blared. The unmarked police SUV was bearing down quickly as it chased Adams up the Thruway. Without the cover of heavy traffic he could not escape.

It was then Nick decided to become a fugitive from justice. The van was no match for the BMW. He gritted his teeth, hit the accelerator again, and vanished. To elude capture or any potential roadblocks, he decided to leave the highway. But he saw the third vehicle, a V8 engine Audi. It was in hot pursuit. Nick accelerated down the exit ramp to an intersection, stopping short. Then he quickly backed up, heading straight for his pursuers, spun around, swerving past them, clipping the vehicle. The Audi flipped, overturned, and landed on its roof. Nick shifted gears again and sped off. A few moments later, two dazed Cavallini henchmen managed to crawl out from under the wreckage and report in to a very angry Robbie Castalano.

The detailed instructions in the letter he had received earlier led Adams to a supermarket in Washingtonville, where, as per instructions, he used the public phone outside the store to dial the number given. The phone answered, but the line oddly disconnected. He rang again and the same thing happened. Fifteen minutes later, a Mitsubishi pickup turned off the road into the parking lot. The driver flashed three times and drove slowly toward him. Shielding his eyes from the glare, Adams approached the vehicle. The driver lowered the window.

# DOWNTOWN MANHATTAN

"How could you screw this up? Get a hold of Joey now!" Robbie Castalano said, screaming down the phone line. "How could you lose the jerk?"

# CENTRAL MANHATTAN

"Find him!" Detective Lee shouted into his receiver from home. His detectives offered no rationalization for losing Adams either.

Adams left his car parked at the rendezvous point and climbed into the Mitsubishi. He and the driver did not speak. After about a ten-minute drive, the pickup slowed and turned onto a rough track. Wild beams of light from its headlamps shone through the trees, playing games with the shadows and requiring every ounce of concentration by the driver. Adams eyed the fringe of woods that ran alongside the hedgerows. The car rattled and shook as the springs tried in vain to handle the potholes. The lane led to already-opened gates and onto a smoother-surfaced driveway, which gently curved toward a large house tucked away in a wooded ravine. No lights shone.

Built in 1720 and originally a gristmill, the building was converted into an eight-bedroom house with its own water-mill-driven generator. It overlooked a large, well-stocked lake.

Adams and the driver stepped out of the car.

"My God, you are so fucking scary!" Nick slammed the door of the pickup and ran around to the driver door, which he opened.

The couple embraced. He stroked her hair; his kissing was rough and full of lust and desire. She kissed him back equally sensually and then snuggled into his chest. "I love you," Luciana whispered as he kissed her forehead.

"I love you, too," he replied softly. "I couldn't believe your note. What have you done?" he asked. "And when did you fly back?"

"I never left," she responded. "I just had to get away from you, my father, and the office. I needed time to work things out."

"What about Milan? What about your law firm?"

"To hell with the firm." Her eyes blazed. "You and I need to talk." She moved away from Nick, and taking a set of keys from under a rock near the front door, she opened it and held it open for him.

They lit a fire using logs piled in a basket beside the large, open fireplace. Nick sat in front of the fire to work off the chill while listening to Luciana as she paced.

She almost spat out the words. She was hyped up and in an obvious black mood. "I just knew my father would interfere." She stood with her hands on her slim hips and looked down at her lover. "He set me up in New York with my legal firm, but because he thought that I was involved with you and I wasn't matching up to his expectations, he persuaded the senior partner to send me back to Milan. Well, I am not having any of that, so I deliberately missed my flight and they don't know where I am."

"So it is me again?" Nick was sulky. "Always me causing the crap. Where the fuck is this going?"

"I do not know, darling! All I know is that we are now both in trouble. You don't know my father."

"Maybe I am piecing things together! God I have been so stupid!" He heaved himself off the floor and stood up and approached Luciana. "I can't believe it, but I think I am getting it."

"We have to make our plans." She pushed him away. "My father is a dangerous man."

Nick told Luciana about the three tails he had on his way to Washingtonville, one of which was a cop car. He brushed over the incident caused by him when one car had been totally wrecked. He believed the NYPD wanted him on suspicion of murder. That earlier in the day someone from the SEC had shown up at his office who issued him a subpoena that would not only bankrupt him but also imprison him if he failed to provide substantial proof of his innocence. And now, of all things, he had her irate father to contend with.

"I'm sorry, darling, but I may have even more bad news. I have to warn you that whatever game plan you are up to, you're skating on very thin ice. And I'm scared, Nico." Luciana took a deep breath. "I have a confession to make. I love my father. He's a great and wonderful man, but," she said, turning to face him, "he is not so wonderful when it comes to anyone outside the family." She walked around the wooden coffee table and sat down on the arm of the sofa. She squeezed her eyes shut. "When I say *family*, I mean the Mafiosi. My father is Don Franco Cavallini," she said, blinking back tears that seemed to come so frequently of late.

A shadow crossed Nick's face. "Don? You mean a Godfather?"

"*Si.* If you like."

His shoulders tensed. "Horse heads in beds type of guy?"

"*Si.* And I know he may make use of some of the things you told me to harm you."

"Fuuuuuuck!" Nick didn't know whether to laugh or cry. A mobster's daughter! It could only happen to him. He looked at her and saw the angst in her eyes; it mirrored his own.

A barrage of questions came fast and furious. Luciana told him the family history and that, by the time she realized who her father was, he had virtually retired. But growing up, she knew her family was far from ordinary by the way her parents and her brothers were treated. There were always truckloads of gifts, delegations of visitors, clandestine meetings, and strange goings-on in the dead of night. She recalled that once machine-gun bullets sprayed their villa in Palermo, and for weeks afterward she was kept away from school.

"Whose house is this, by the way? Is it a Mafia safe house?"

"Don't worry, it's not ours. It belongs to my tenant's parents. They're on safari in Africa until next week. She doesn't know I am here, but I had to think on my feet. I have stayed here many times, and knew where the keys are kept; I even had the alarm code on my phone. Besides, she's away in Mexico for a couple of weeks and can't be reached. So we should be okay."

"What a resourceful girl you are." Nick was amazed at her ingenuity. "I think you need to tell me more, don't you?"

Dealing with the FBI, NYPD, and the SEC was one thing, but the Mafia was an entirely different ball game. A familiar feeling of dread clenched his heart. "I don't think we should be spending too much time here. We should try to get out of the country for a while. How about it?" His voice was half-coaxing, half-determined, since he had to be in the Caribbean by Tuesday no matter what. "I can leave everything to my attorneys."

"But they'll be watching the airports."

"They?"

"Yes, 'they'—all of them. I don't care; one way or the other we are in the shit."

"Not if we are clever. We can do it; we will set up a false trail away from us. Take the heat off until the dust settles."

"Okay, Nicholas Adams, I am in your hands. We have got this far; let's not blow it. What ideas have you?" Luciana was angry. Angry with her father. How dare he!

Nick's iPad found a weak signal, and he sat down and e-mailed his attorneys. He gave them a new cell number against an assurance that they would not give it to anyone under any circumstances. He instructed them to arrange a meeting for him with the SEC at their offices the following day. A Saturday meeting would be highly unusual, but he calculated that the SEC would be anxious for swift and decisive action, and that his offer to cooperate would work in his favor. More importantly, it would at least stop them from taking too much interest in his immediate predicament. He also intimated in the e-mail that if he repaid the money and assisted them in nailing Kersch & Co., they could pull the subpoena. Fine words. He had no intention of repaying all of his money, as he would fight them when all of this was history, but it didn't matter for now because he had no intention of showing up. He was buying time. He received a lengthy reply from his lawyer begrudgingly accepting his instructions, the rest of the response he hardly looked at.

The couple planned their escape for the next day. They discussed the options available. Nick, with Luciana looking over his shoulder, searched the Web looking for the things they needed. He scribbled notes on a pad and placed his Swiss anonymous bank card on the table. He knew it would bite him in the ass at a later stage, but for now he had no choice. He knew his other cards were being monitored, and he couldn't afford a screwup at this stage. They had to get to his appointment whatever was going on.

"Will we get away with it?" Luciana asked anxiously.

"I think so. Well, it's certainly worth a try."

Luciana and Nick finalized plans for the next day's getaway and settled in front of the log fire around 2:00 a.m., surrounded by scattered plates of half-eaten food and empty glasses. They sat in silence watching the flames dance around the hissing and spitting green wood. Two candles on the coffee table flickered, throwing a ghostly light down on a loaded shotgun and a few cartridges, which Luciana had earlier retrieved from a gun cabinet in the owner's library. They were on high alert and had to be diligent, knowing they were being separately pursued by parties both known and unknown.

Luciana rose to clear their plates and headed for the kitchen. A massive bang and the sound of splintering rent the air. The front door crashed open and slammed back into the wall, almost knocking her off her feet. Plates smashed to pieces as they hit the floor. Luciana's scream echoed around the high-ceilinged room. Nick knew instinctively what had happened and grabbed the loaded but open shotgun off the floor and pocketed several cartridges. He never dreamed the skills he acquired shooting skeet all those years with his father would ever come in handy. He gripped the shotgun with both hands, closed it, took off the safety catch and moved swiftly but carefully to the entrance hall.

One of the assailants had lost his footing and tripped on the doorstep when he broke open the door. Adams charged at the man and fired a warning shot above him. Pellets of the shotgun blast hit the wooden rim of the doorframe, taking part of it away. Other pellets ricocheted and embedded in the wall. Everyone ducked. Adams fired again, trying to miss and yet frighten, but this time the blast seared the calf of the man, who screamed out in pain hurling Italian obscenities at Nick. Blood gushed out from his wounds. His trousers had been shredded by the blast.

The second intruder threw himself through the doorway, rolling on the floor, until he stood up, pointing a handgun directly at Luciana. Before Adams could respond, the man grabbed Luciana, holding her in an armlock, with his gun pointed at her temple. Nick reloaded quickly. In the next instant, Luciana, using all her strength, doubled over and drove her elbow right into her attacker's crotch. Maneuvers like that came part and parcel with growing up with older brothers.

Bent over in agony, the assailant tried to jump her again. The force of Nick's swinging of the stock of his shotgun to his arm knocked the revolver out of the man's hand. Nick swung the shotgun stock, catching the ill-fated man on the side of his nose. The man screamed and held his hands to the bloody mess that now covered his face.

With shotgun in hand, Nick grabbed Luciana and pulled her through the door. They fled to the spinning water wheel at the back of the house, crouched at the bottom of the wet stone stairs that led down to the lake, and hid in the shadows. They had to keep a watchful eye; the cascading sound of the water wheel made it difficult to hear any pursuer. Moments later, Nick could make out the silhouette of one man coming toward them. He remained still. But he didn't see it coming. All he saw was the look on Luciana's face when the other man's hand, reaching from behind, grabbed at his throat. The two men wrestled, and the shotgun fell to the water's edge.

The shorter man drew near, jumped down from the ledge, almost lost his footing on the slippery moss-covered patio stones, and barreled into Luciana. He grabbed her and then dragged her, despite his leg wound, yelling and kicking up the steps back toward the house. She jerked and wriggled, but could not break free.

The fight continued between Nick and the other assailant, whose strength was formidable. Adams more than held his own, but took a few solid punches to his gut. As they struggled, the two were hit with blasts of water from the whirling water wheel. The man, who was by now propelled toward the edge of the steps, tried to stop himself from falling beyond the water's edge. He tried to grab onto a few sodden weeds but lost his grip. He slipped and his legs became lodged in the twenty-foot diameter water wheel that dragged him one rotation, then catapulted him into the air. The man landed on the bank unconscious. Adams, too, had begun to slip, but he forced himself against the wall and held on until he reached a dry slab. From there he could see the shotgun. But his attention drew back to Luciana who was still being restrained by the other assailant high above him.

"What do you want?" Nick shouted looking up at him brushing water and dirt from his eyes. "Leave her alone, take me."

"I have orders!" Nick could barely hear him and moved nearer, away from the wheel, "I have to deliver you and the girl back to New York," the man shouted in a gruff voice. He pushed his gun into Luciana's side. "Put your hands up where I can see them," he ordered Adams.

Without the gunman noticing, Adams slowly edged his hand toward the shotgun. Feeling the stock firmly in his hand, he raised the gun and pointed it directly at man's head. "Drop your gun!" Adams shouted.

"I'll kill her!" The man shouted back.

"No you won't! Use your fucking brain!" Nick pushed the gun back into his shoulder and steadied himself. "What sense would it make to kill her? I know who you answer to." Adams aimed. It was a standoff, but a card worth playing. The attacker slowly released his grip on Luciana, who leaped so fast onto the grass and over the low wall to the waterway that the man had little chance to do anything about it. That's when Nick saw the flash. The bullet missed his head by a breath. He took cover and fired the one cartridge he had left. He thought he had missed, but hearing a deep groan, he knew he'd hit his target. He watched the man slowly disappear, staggering heavily across the lawn toward the woods.

Nick found Luciana hiding by the side of the bank holding

onto reeds, but the water was flowing fast. He kept a firm grip on a wooden post and extended the shotgun toward her. Luciana gripped the gun tightly and Nick pulled her up toward him to safety. He held her firmly in his embrace and they stood there shivering, their breaths caught in their throats. Luciana's hands hurt from the heat of the shotgun barrels that she had gripped so hard.

"Let's get out of here before someone else shows up." Nick looked around for the other assailant, but he seemed to have disappeared.

"What did you mean you knew who they worked for?" Luciana stood her ground.

"Listen, we haven't got much time, and you know as well I do!"

In the predawn hour, a plan had quickly coalesced. They managed to secure the broken front door, gather their belongings, race out of the house, and sprint hard down the path to Luciana's rental car that she had used to get to the gristmill. Luciana would have a lot of explaining to do to Michele's parents—one day.

Spending part of the night in a rental car was not what they had in mind. Nick and Luciana left Washingtonville and drove using the SatNav to a rural airfield, where they had booked a private prop plane from the Internet. They parked just outside the airfield gates, where they remained until their scheduled departure time. Dawn came. They got out of the car and stretched their painful limbs, shivering almost uncontrollably. They abandoned the car. Luciana knew her credit card would be zeroed by the charges the rental firm would levy, but she just shrugged her shoulders. It was all too much. The time would come when she would confront her father, but for now she was on a mission. To where and what, she had little idea. But she liked her man more and more, and that was sufficient. She was terrified but excited at the same time.

The engines of the Aztec twin-engine cranked noisily to life, and the old aircraft bumped forward across the short, uneven runway and turned into the wind. It quickly picked up speed, and at about eighty knots, the wheels left the ground, and it lifted into the air, heading south.

"Try catching us now, you bastards," Nick said.

"Let's hope they don't," Luciana remarked, looking distantly out the window.

Travelling at an average speed of only 225 mph, the prop plane finally touched down almost five hours later at another private airfield just south of Miami. From there, it was a quick cab ride to the marina, where the couple found the agent who handled the boat rentals. A guy in his early thirties, wearing stretch Lycra shorts and a cap barely containing his sun-bleached blond hair, ambled along the quayside toward them. The Ray Ban shades hid his weed-glazed eyes.

"Hey, you the folks who booked on the Net last night?" he drawled. His accent sounded more Australian than American. Nick nodded in response.

"The baby's over there," he said, pointing to a sleek speedboat. "How long are you guys going to need the boat for?"

"Several hours." Adams replied.

"You've driven these babies before?"

"Oh, yeah," Adams said, lying through his teeth.

Nick feigned as though he spent most of his free time on the ocean, an old sea dog. Luciana looked at him quizzically. He tried unsuccessfully to suppress a grin.

"You've gotta have her back before dark. You can keep the boat until, say, 6:00 p.m. She can be refueled anytime during daylight. Don't go out farther than one mile, which should be distance enough for your water skiing. Use the GPS system, and keep tuned into the weather channel at all times. You can reach me on my cell if you need help, and I'll be there before you break the call."

"Great. I think we're set." Nick scratched the back of his ear.

"Good luck, then. But I suggest you get to know these waters first. They can be pretty treacherous. Where's your kit?" the agent asked.

"Kit?"

"Ski kit."

"Oh. Our kit. It's at the hotel. We'll bring it down later after we've familiarized ourselves with the boat."

"Familiarize, eh?" He looked at Luciana, smiling widely. "Whatever you say. Wouldn't mind being in your shoes, dude." The agent hopped on board. "I need to take you through the radio procedures. The Coast Guard is really hot on safety."

After his lengthy orientation, the agent turned to Nick, who had booked the rental. "Sign here, there, and there," he said, handing him the clipboard.

She signed the rental agreement, smiling uncomfortably at the lanky agent.

"Guess that's it. You folks have a good time and don't forget to get her back before dark."

The area was a haven for legions of recreational boaters. The couple boarded the speedboat and set off slowly to find a small marina they had researched the previous night. Nick dropped Luciana off at the pier to stock up on food and water while he picked up as many gallons of fuel as the boat could haul. The guy at the pump didn't raise an eyebrow at the amount of fuel he purchased. He simply swiped the card, got authorization, and that was good enough for him, no questions asked.

They knew they were taking a huge risk hightailing it out of the US by boat. But how else could they get out of the country without clearing immigration first? They could feel the handcuffs tightening around their wrists. Not good.

The forecast was favorable. Luciana jumped into the boat. She had bought waterproof gear with her credit card and two thick jumpers as well as bottled water and some food. They would need it all later. Nick took in a deep breath, started the engines, put in the settings for the Bahamas, and eased the throttle pushing the boat out of the marina. They would travel from Florida, past the tip of Andros, Bahamas, and then on to Nassau at an average speed of some 20 knots. In good conditions it would take about ten hours to complete the 178-mile trip.

"Bahamas, here we come." Nick gradually pulled back on the throttle, and with a deep growl the engines pushed the boat forward, its bow rising out of the water, pointing to a place far away, where he had no clue as to what would transpire. All he knew was that he had made a solemn pledge; and he would honor it by whatever means necessary.

Ravi Sharma had been flying around the Caribbean for the past day, arriving back in Miami from the Turks and Caicos Islands, and he was now en route to Grand Cayman. He was one day late for his expected arrival at CAY BANK headquarters; they would be wondering where he was by now; the operation would be dead in the water without him.

Sharma worked throughout his flight, inputting the numbers Robbie Castalano gave him onto his laptop direct from the flash drive. He refused the meal, just took his meds, and kept typing. Extraordinary accuracy was required. One slip with any of the numbers and all would be lost in the ether when the time came to activate the program he and his unwitting software team so painstakingly built.

Special Agent Rae was not at all happy. How dare Sharma have the impudence to turn up late? The text message sent by Sharma informing him of the delay was not acceptable. Already Rae's team was putting a trace on where the SMS had been sent.

Squeezing the resources of the family on a search for his daughter might be asking too much, Cavallini reflected. He had no news as to the success of the operation. No reports had come in. He was worried, but he had the important task of putting countless men on standby, in many countries, in preparation for Wednesday morning's planned maneuver. It was proving to be a mammoth task. He was too old for all of this. Was he being pigheaded by being so against the American boyfriend? Was he just too old-fashioned? *My God, she was so like her mother,* he thought. Impetuous, but so lovely.

"We will find your daughter, Don Franco," Castalano almost whispered. They had been friends for too long to argue. "With computers, these things are easy nowadays."

"Ah. *Si.* Computers. What would we do without them, my old friend?" A hint of a smile curled at the corner of his mouth.

"Next week, we shall be singing the praises of the wonders of technology, eh?" Castalano clapped together his liver-spotted hands.

"We shall see." Franco took out a cigarette, flipped open his Dunhill lighter, and set the tip aflame.

Sharma checked into a small self-catered beachside condominium on Grand Cayman near the Hyatt. As soon as he was settled in, he made contact with everyone who needed to hear from him. Dillon Rae was relieved; he laid his concerns to rest when Sharma confirmed that he'd be at CAY BANK within the hour.

One short conversation over, Sharma called New York and checked in with his other taskmaster on a different cell phone. He informed Castalano that he had arrived at his destination and was ready.

CAY BANK was closed that day for systems maintenance, with bank managers placing staff members at Sharma's disposal. He received a briefing and was shown through to the Systems Operations Department. He was allocated his own office and terminal, and provided with all necessary codes, passwords, and PINs, giving him complete access to everything within the bank's system. It was just routine maintenance, as laid out in the terms and conditions in the Adams Banking Solutions contract.

Several calls to JC at TRU in Washington later, and all systems were operational, running as expected, and working seamlessly in sync with the add-on Trojan software performing well. Five o'clock Monday was looking good.

Sharma put down his phones, grabbed a bottle of water and chewing gum from his backpack, made himself comfortable, and settled in for the long night ahead. By 6:00 p.m. he was downloading his newly-written source code into the CAY BANK system. Finally he accessed the International Funds Transfer module from the menu and the screen blinked back at him, waiting expectantly for a command. His eyes narrowed and he bowed his head. It was a serene moment for a man who had suffered so much. No anger remained; it had transmuted into daring. A sense of purpose and resoluteness suddenly swept across his skeletal face. It would be his finest hour.

With codes in hand, Sharma carried out the final modifications and status updates on behalf of his two taskmasters. But fuck them, he was his own boss and took orders from no one from now on. He had weighed the risk factors and thrown the dice.

Lloyd Lee had lost the man he was supposed to be protecting. Reports from Washingtonville threw up evidence that Nicholas Adams and Luciana Cavallini were somewhere in the vicinity of Washingtonville, but their trail had gone cold.

He summoned his team to regroup in the meeting room. They clustered around several tables while Lee, standing in front of a white marker board, took the crew through everything they had previously covered, hoping there was something they had missed.

"Adams obviously thinks we want to arrest him, Lloyd," a detective spoke out, sipping coffee. "Am I missing something here?"

"Yeah, well, I may have implied something to that effect when I met him at his office, but I only wanted him to feel some heat. We could pull him in anytime." Lee leaned against the edge of the table, half-sitting. "I told him we didn't think he was involved in Howard Wayne's murder, but I did say that he was in a position to assist us. Maybe I pushed a little too hard. With Kersch and Peters dead, he's about the only good lead we have. And he knows it."

Detective Lee was interested only in identifying who had instructed the female hired gun to carry out the murders, and had no doubts that Adams could lead them to that person. He also had a feeling that the person involved was also heavily involved in another matter that he had been brought into. He didn't care if he got there first; justice had to be done, even if it flew in the face of the Federal Bureau of Investigation.

"Where would he go?" a female detective mused. "He hasn't been home. His girlfriend's place is clear, too. We've got his car impounded upstate where it was abandoned, and we've been in contact with rental companies."

Maybe he's skipped town. Left the country?" The coffee drinker looked at Lee searchingly.

Lee's eyes dulled. "Thought of that, too. The agencies we contacted will pick him up if he tries to leave the country."

Another detective entered the meeting room unceremoniously with a note in his hand. "Got a couple of leads, Lloyd," he said, pushing past his colleagues. "The two guys we picked up chasing Adams on the Thruway work for the Mob. One of them is not saying much, but the other guy got easily unstitched under pressure."

"Who does he work for?"

"I told you, the Mob!"

"Who's his boss?"

"Castalano." He paused to let it sink in. "Robbie Castalano."

A multitude of questions erupted in a mixture of disbelief. Lee's voice rose above the cacophony and shouted down the clamor.

"Castalano? Now that's deep." Lee looked excited as well. "Why would he be interested in Adams?"

"Word has it that he's been hot-rodding the daughter of one of the family bosses."

Ribald laughter filled the room.

"Luciana Cavallini?" the female detective questioned. "Is she a mobster's daughter?"

"She's a respectable lawyer. She doesn't work for the Mob. Did we check this out thoroughly?" Lloyd Lee asked, but he looked less sure the more he put his thoughts together. Lee started looking through his files lying on the table. "Here, see? She works for Cicogna & Partners." He picked up the telephone and dialed a number.

"Ms. Cavallini, please, Luciana Cavallini." After a few moments, he replaced the handset. "Her office says she no longer works at the New York office. She has been transferred to—listen to this," he addressed his junior colleagues in the room. "Cicogna & Partners in Milan, Italy. She left during the week."

"But she was in Washingtonville with Adams yesterday," the coffee drinker interrupted.

"What else have you uncovered?" Lee felt the adrenaline surging through his body. This was what he lived for: good detective work.

"We've picked up a trail on Cavallini's credit card activity."

"Go on."

"Looks like she rented a car at JFK." The room was set alight again. "The rental company has no idea as to where the vehicle is. They will let me know if they hear anything."

"Put a tracer on the plates and let's see where the car may be now. Let's narrow down the search. I reckon near Washingtonville?" He had a sixth sense.

"I can do that!" a voice from the back of the room spoke up. "I checked with airline schedules thinking they might flee the country, and then I had an idea." All eyes turned to him. "I thought, 'Maybe they got a small plane?'" He grinned. "Guess what, a couple chartered a small plane out of an airfield south of Washingtonville, and the description fits that of Nicholas Adams and his woman."

"Thanks for letting me know so soon," Lee said wryly.

"Sorry. I just got the flight plan. They flew to Miami, and I've got the local guys checking out airfields to see if they can find anything."

"Good work," Lee said, giving him credit. "Well, at least they're still in the country." He paused to catch his thoughts. "Being chased by the Mafia," he added sardonically.

Detective Lee was seriously contemplating whether all the trouble was worth it. Too many NYPD resources were being used on this investigation as it was. Perhaps he should take the heat off Adams for a while, let matters rest, and get him when he resurfaces. Was it really his responsibility to protect Adams from the Mob because of a girl? Looking around, the eager faces in the room helped make up his mind. Maybe he would call the FBI, much as he would hate doing so. But he would think before he made a call.

On Detective Lloyd Lee's request, the Miami Police Department eventually agreed to cooperate. They had enough on their plate without being pushed about by the NYPD. Lee had some ideas, which he thought through after getting feedback from the Aztec pilot and the cab driver that provided proof of the latest destination of the fugitives.

The Miami Police dispatched a car to the marina the boat had rented from, and they alerted the US Coast Guard about their disappearance, but Detective Lee knew that by now they had probably flown the coop and cruised outside US jurisdiction.

Miami police searched the shorelines, while two Coast Guard helicopters swept the water with searchlights bouncing off the sea, looking for any sign of the couple. They couldn't find a trace and called off the search after midnight.

*Just what are you up to, Nick?* Lee murmured to himself. He scanned the map in front of him and looked at some of the landing possibilities. Cuba and the Bahamas, seemed logical destinations. *For one who claims to be so righteous, you now have boat theft added to your list.* But he felt some sympathy as he felt that the hazardous crossing to whatever island they had chosen would most likely claim their lives.

"News?" Franco Cavallini spat the word out.
"Still no news."

"Adams." The name oozed out, slowly and contemptuously. "That young man needs to be taught a lesson. What about your men?"

"Two are back with us; one has birdshot in his leg, and the other has a sore head." He drew in breath and sighed. "The two that got caught tailing Adams ended up in hospital with a broken leg and a crushed elbow between them and are being guarded by the cops."

"Will they talk to the cops?" Franco Cavallini asked, sounding worried.

"*Si*. Maybe ..."

"Maybe?"

"*Si*. These are different times, Franco. No loyalties. You get what you pay for. With so many being picked up these days, if they talk ... they talk. They know what will happen. That's it. *Capire*?"

He yearned for his home, a magnificent villa high in the Sicilian hills with craggy mountains as a backdrop. He removed his heavy dark spectacles and wiped the corners of his eyes. The ageing process was not fair.

The darkness was all-encompassing. The sea became rougher than Adams had expected. He checked the radio and heard that the Coast Guard was issuing warnings of strong to gale force winds. Waves began rolling high above the sleek but exposed speedboat, lashing their faces with stinging sheets of spray. As he fought to elude the Coast Guard on the lookout for drug smugglers, Adams was hard pressed to bear up under the onslaught of waves pounding the small vessel. The turbo jets strained and spat as the engines rose out of the water, dipping, lurching, and sliding over dark and deep yawning black troughs of the warm Gulf Stream. Ferocious currents smashed against the boat from all directions, and it was little short of a miracle that the boat didn't capsize. Their only consolation was that the speedboat's engines hardly missed a beat. The boat always seemed to recover, steadying itself before the next blitz. Feeling queasy, Luciana took a firm grip on the safety harness and hung on for dear life. The GPS system was difficult to read in such conditions, and Nick would occasionally hand control over to Luciana and get on his knees, straining to look at their position.

"I think we're lost. Can't get a good reading on where the hell we are!"

The moon appeared from behind monstrous dark clouds, attempting to assist in lighting their way. The reluctant skipper even tried to identify the Big Dipper and other formations, but the constant movement of the boat thwarted his efforts.

They took turns controlling the boat. Having jettisoned the drums that were lashed to the stern, they were down to the last tank of fuel. One had been lost that night as it came undone and rolled into the ocean. At some point the couple had found themselves just missing a cruise ship. They were miles off course. Nick and Luciana had no chance of survival if they got anywhere near a floating hotel carrying over three thousand tourists on a cruise, or in the way of any vessel, for that matter, as they wove their way through the busy shipping lanes. Nick wiped the salt from his eyes, feeling increasingly more desperate as time passed. He had put Luciana's life at risk. Again. They had missed the Bahamas and headed southeast toward Cuba before realizing they were going in the wrong direction.

It had been a long, frightening night, but at morning break, the sea calmed and they had a chance to sort assess their situation.

The weather changed. Cumulus clouds dotted the blue sky. Shaken but safe after the past harrowing eighteen hours, Nick and Luciana had time to recover. They had experienced gale force winds and towering seas that had sent them surfing down the fronts of gigantic black waves. But the winds were now fair and manageable with a leftover swell. The GPS system had helped them get back on course. The boat was steady, taking graceful forward dips, then long rises. As they made for their intended destination, they knew they had been crazy and stupid to think they could pull it off.

But throughout the day, conditions improved, and eventually

their final destination appeared on the GPS. They may have had a tough, tumultuous passage, but the sea had also been kind to them. The weather made it impossible for the search aircraft to find them.

"Shit!" Hart shot awake from the persistent ringing of the doorbell. "What the fuck now?" He moved himself off his rumpled and messy bed and went to the hall, calling out, "Who is it?" He was now petrified of his own shadow and on his guard because of recent events.

"Open up! It's me!" This was never a very helpful answer at the best of times. "Castalano!" Gavin Hart released the chain, turned two locks, and let the mobster into his apartment.

"Sorry, can't be too cautious." Hart said with sarcasm.

"We need more information from you!"

"The kind that means I get beaten up?"

Castalano explained what was required. It was short and to the point. Hart was to ask no questions.

"So make the call!" the Italian-American rasped, clearly impatient.

"Okay, easy!" Hart went into his bedroom and retrieved his cell phone. Hart made a call to Dillon Rae.

Rae answered the phone, annoyed at the intrusion. Hart became belligerent and threatened to blow the whole fucking deal if Rae didn't tell him where everything stood, and what he was getting out of their arrangement and when. He actually didn't need Castalano to order him to make the call. He was on the verge of asking the same questions anyway. He turned on his speakerphone and moved back to where his uninvited guest stood.

"Listen Gavin, why are you going over old ground, and why the fuck are you calling me on a phone?" Dillon Rae was angry. "Everything is still on target and will definitely be over at precisely 5:00 p.m. tomorrow," Rae almost whispered. "Then we can meet and work something out. Now please—no more calls. You know how critical it is for me to keep under cover right now." Rae paused for a moment. "Are you on fucking speaker phone?"

"Sorry, I was doing something else and put it on for convenience." He lied.

"For fuck's sake, get a grip man!"

It was just the information Castalano was looking for. Hart received no thanks from the man of few words, who turned around and left.

Darkness was gathering again. Day turned to night. The calm weather of the morning transformed, and an onslaught of waves began to pound the speedboat's hull. The couple prayed the night wouldn't be a repeat of the previous day.

After many hours of constant vigilance, Nick and Luciana could see the warm, orange glow of early morning appear again on the horizon. The sky turned into a painter's palette. The air became warmer; their lips and skin were encrusted with sea salt. A vague silhouette loomed ahead on the distant horizon, and Nick could make out what appeared to be land. With the waters calmed, he had a clearer view of the GPS screen again.

"Nassau!" he exclaimed. "Wake up, sleepyhead, we made it."

"Leave me alone," Luciana snuggled back into her blanket feeling nauseous. "Tell me when we land!"

It had taken thirty-six hours, but they had made it. Nick now had to face reality. Would he pull off this stupid stunt? Would they be waiting for them on shore?

A glorious Caribbean morning greeted them, the sea a deep turquoise blue and flat calm. Lighter blues showed the sands under the water. The tireless, hot morning sun beat down on their backs. Nick eased the power throttles, scanned the shoreline, and eventually settled on where he would take the stolen boat. He made his way to a small, derelict dock well away from the main marinas. Nick needed to avoid detection. In appearance, the disheveled couple might just pass as two more tourists visiting Nassau.

Nick planned to contact the boat company in Florida sometime the next day to report the boat's whereabouts. He knew they had his Swiss card and would no doubt deduct God knows what from his Zurich account. They really could abuse his card, as he had virtually a limitless credit line guaranteed by the assets he had, and the bank would not query any payments. That was the whole point of having such a card. If his card were traced in the US he would be fucked! But with any luck, by the time anyone picked up their trail, they would be well on their way to their next refuge.

After securing the boat and double-checking that it was cleared out, Nick and Luciana, carrying their canvas bags, made for the road and hailed a taxi. An eager driver welcomed their business and found them a quiet hotel on a beach near town. They booked a one-night stay.

Luciana was utterly exhausted. She undressed, showered, and fell—naked and still wet—onto the bed. Nick pulled the sheet over her body and she fell into a deep sleep.

Nick was no less tired, but had several tasks to take care of. He showered, washed out his salt-sodden jeans, and hung them out to dry on the veranda. Once changed, he left the small boarding house to find his way to immigration at the main port. With no entry or exit customs stamps in their passports, Adams had to explain that they had arrived by boat but unintentionally missed the designated point of entry and needed a temporary visa valid for twenty-four hours. Without it, it would be difficult to pull off their next move. He prayed the officer was sympathetic.

The immigration officer reprimanded Adams for not being more diligent, that Customs and Immigration rules must be strictly followed. Since it was his first visit and first offense, the officer granted the temporary visas with a warning. Adams thanked the man for his generosity, paid the fees to clear Customs and Immigration, and headed for the center of town on foot.

After several wrong turns he located a small travel agency. He purchased two one-way tickets, again with his Swiss card, to get

Luciana and himself off the island the following day. Adams was astute enough to know that a paper trail was forming.

Then he went into a small shop that offered to unblock phones and SIM cards and bought a pay-as-you-go cell phone and put credit on it. He would need an untraceable phone from now on.

Returning to the hotel, Nick climbed into bed beside Luciana and lost consciousness the moment his head hit the pillow.

Exhausted, Sharma managed to raise his eyelids, blinking as he painfully regained consciousness. Waking was increasingly becoming more jarring, with his illness sucking the lifeblood out of him. He shifted in his chair, smothering a yawn, but refused to give in to the fatigue. It was 8:00 a.m., and he had been asleep for only about an hour. His condition was unstable. He gulped down pills with water from the bottle sitting beside his computer terminal and swung back into action.

Using one of his many cell phones, he'd had his final conference call debriefing with the TRU team, led by Dillon Rae and JC in Washington. All group members were present, but Rae and Sharma did most of the talking. Sharma delivered the preliminary progress report. It was relatively straightforward, long, and moderately boring. Things might have been easier and clearer if the TRU team had flown across to the island and been taken through procedural and program details in person, but their presence there would have attracted undue attention. They were in the hands of Ravi Sharma. He was the core to the success of the elaborate sting.

Rae had confirmed that all targeted accounts at CAY BANK were ready to be drained, and subpoenas were in the hands of process servers standing by for Tuesday's distribution to all points across the US to targeted beneficial owners. He had sought cooperation from the authorities in Switzerland, who, given the magnitude of the operation, had agreed to assist in anything to do with Liebs, but refused to allow any other inquiry into any third parties that were not connected to him. The bankers in

Switzerland would enjoy the time-honored privilege of secrecy. All but one.

Rae had built up a remarkable dossier of villains breaking the laws of the United States by secretly depositing assets into the offshore bank. So far, over ten billion dollars had been identified and earmarked from run-of-the-mill US tax evaders; they would be dealt with after the main operation was over. But TRU's main target was the Swiss banker extraordinaire, Gerhard Liebs. Thus far, according to the tally, Liebs and Harvey Milton had amassed between them well over $12 billion across their two accounts— more than the total value due from all of the other tax evaders.

"Let me confirm what will happen at 5:00 p.m. today." Sharma spoke quietly. In immense pain, he occasionally paused to take a sip of water. "Each designated delinquent account will be emptied of all its deposits and transferred to the holding account controlled by TRU. For this to work, the process must take place concurrently. The two main accounts of Liebs and Milton will also be emptied simultaneously at the agreed five o'clock limit. Reaching that precise time will cause the software to activate."

"Will we have the records of each account and the details of each transfer immediately after 5:00 p.m.?" Rae asked. "In real time?"

"Of course," Sharma lied. "CAY BANK staff will have to handle inquiries and demands made by any of the listed account holders until the agents in the field have served their subpoenas. Normal day-to-day business will cease for today, and of course at 5:00 p.m. eastern time the bank will close." Sharma's hand began to tremble and he nearly dropped the phone. "All e-banking access will be blocked. The software will trigger a transfer of the entire sum to the designated government account at Citibank New York, which will finally force CAY BANK to shut its doors. After this gets out, no one will do business with the bank."

Rae grinned and said, "Or indeed seriously consider whether to use any other offshore banking facilities in the future." He paused. "Thank you Ravi. You and I will have an accounting after this is all over!" He tried not to sound threatening.

Sharma fielded more questions and gave the answers he chose to give.

And so it was; the money just kept on flowing into the two accounts throughout the day.

The duplicitous Dieter Gruber had until now never stopped passing the account totals to Liebs. But when the first set of triggers were activated, only the TRU team were privy to or were able to access account-holder information, leaving Gruber out of the loop, meaning that he had to suffer incessant calls that day from Liebs, which he chose to ignore. So the resentful Gruber used what little charm he had left to woo the bank's systems administrator into allowing him to gain access to the latest figures. A lavish dinner and several bottles of champagne and future promises later, Gruber was able to give Liebs everything he needed to know.

The Libyan funds hit CAY BANK just after 10:00 a.m. Gerhard Liebs was only bridging as a short-term loan, and he felt it his right after all he had done for that country in those early years. Dillon Rae couldn't believe such a sum would arrive in one dollop. When another two billion dollars from Bank Schreiber Liebs followed at 11:30, the game swung dramatically in favor of Gerhard Liebs.

The TRU team watched in awe as the hours ticked by. All day long CAY BANK reported credits being posted on the two accounts ranging from $100,000 to $200 million.

Shortly afterward, Rae received a call from Harvey Milton.

"Mr. Milton?"

"How's it going with our friend Liebs?" Milton's voice sounded drained. "What's the total?"

"I would rather not have this conversation over the telephone," Rae responded, irritated. With shirtsleeves rolled up, he signaled to the team for an answer. JC slipped a piece of paper in front of Rae and gave him the thumbs-up sign.

The latest totals were $16.4 billion Liebs, $16.6 billion Milton. A staggering $33 billion, and all destined for a government account at Citibank.

"All I can say, Harvey, is that everything is going according to plan. You are leading the race, Contact me after five and we'll celebrate."

Milton grunted in response. They agreed that a celebration would be the order of the day. But Milton was at his wits' end and needed to pump in even more cash. He had taken the most appalling risks in the last few days, throwing caution to the wind, to work under duress with his government, who just wanted to beat up on a piece of Swiss shit. *But shit he will when the news comes through*, Milton mused. He shivered involuntarily and called out for his hypertension medication.

The atmosphere at TRU was electric. JC had taken a call from Gerhard Liebs, who asked much the same questions as his rival, Harvey Milton. JC responded in turn with the appropriate confidence-boosting answer. He lied through his teeth.

Calls between Washington and CAY BANK continued throughout the day. Ravi Sharma finished all pending work and needed to get some sleep. Pressing the keys on the computer keyboard was painful and fast becoming almost impossible, but he was finished. It was time to go. His eyes, bloodshot and sunken into his cadaverous skull, screamed for rest.

Sharma waited for his body to stabilize before getting up to bid farewell to the key bank staff who inadvertently assisted without an inkling as to what was being done within the secure firewalls of CAY BANK. He gave his excuses, saying he was unwell and that he needed to leave to get some rest. According to their analysis, all banking systems were working at 100 percent. Sharma smiled. He knew his greatest work was complete. It had been his best programming ever. Pure genius.

Sharma left a number where he could be contacted if there were problems. But there was no such number. He had no intention of receiving any more calls.

Back at the condo, Ravi Sharma called New York on his designated cell phone. "Mr. Castalano?"

"Mr. Sharma," the voice long ravaged by chain-smoking since the age of sixteen, growled. He had expected the call.

"It's done."

Sharma checked out of the condo, he checked his room and

paid his bill, and feeling like death, he went out into the bright sun, waved down a taxi and left for the airport. By 2:00 p.m. he was on his way to Grand Turk in the Turks and Caicos Islands onboard a small twin prop aircraft. He had to avoid the daily scheduled flights from Grand Cayman to Grand Turk via Miami. He didn't want problems with US Immigration that would jeopardize his appointment, so he had hired a small plane for the three-hour journey. During his short stay at CAY BANK, he had manipulated the bank's system to transfer sufficient funds from a third-party account to Island Air. Sure, it was theft, but after 5:00 p.m. that day it really wouldn't matter in the scheme of things.

Wrapped in two blankets, the gaunt passenger refused any refreshments except water. He reclined in his seat, feeling miserable yet satisfied that he had completed his part of the deal, even if it wasn't as Dillon Rae had originally designed. In so doing, he left behind a nest of electronic venomous snakes. At five o'clock they would all be released. Sharma fell into a deep sleep.

Just before 5:00 p.m. eastern time, an electronic clock on the wall above the rows of computer consoles indicated for a split second 16:59:59.

Dillon Rae stood as if he had an orchestral baton in hand, ready for the final movement, albeit a far-flung orchestra; his players were in Switzerland, Key Biscayne, Grand Cayman, and there in Washington, DC. He was sure they would play in perfect harmony.

At 17:00:00 eastern time he stabbed the air. "Yes!" he cried out. "Yes! Now let's see what crap hits the fan!" He could already see his promotion looming. He would become an icon within the FBI. His peers would point and whisper about his fantastic triumph for years to come, maybe generations.

He scanned the screen displaying the final account positions. The screen blinked back at him. The online feed from the bank, so cleverly linked by Ravi Sharma, showed that both accounts were drained of every cent. It had worked! Glorious day that it was! What a wizard was Ravi Sharma, and recruited by him alone.

In Zurich a different scenario was being played. Special Agent Dillon Rae had not figured the depths to which Gerhard Liebs would go to win Milton Harvey's challenge.

Liebs figured his gross take would be over $33 billion. The net, of course, depended on how much he had to repay out of his winnings to those he had fleeced, albeit on a temporary bridging basis. Some holes would need plugging immediately, but he deduced at least $14 billion of actual profit. His quest for unlimited money and power was about to accelerate. Negotiations with Milton Global receivers would begin at once. Thrilled beyond measure, he could see the greatest of futures. He was a true master, worthy of Machiavelli. The Florentine author of *The Prince* got others to do exactly what he wanted without them ever realizing they were working for his purpose. Oh, how the Swiss banker might rue that Italian comparison!

In "the Bunker" at Key Biscayne, Harvey Milton lay utterly exhausted in an untidy heap on a long sofa that groaned in protest every time he shifted his weight. Glued to a terminal in another part of the room, Oscar Randell was speaking into a headset microphone, still issuing instructions, but he was growing more anxious as the minutes passed, waiting for news from Dillon Rae of his chairman's promised victory.

Anxious eyes searched the screens located in Washington, Florida, and Switzerland, waiting for the results to be confirmed to them. Each screen was fixed on the zero funds showing, they waited for something to happen. Who had the money? This was not what was planned. The screens were frozen. Randell called Rae, who did not pick up. Both men stabbed at their respective keyboards entering the "winner's pot" passwords they had been given. They would be disappointed.

Harvey Milton only saw zero balances where he should have seen the spoils of his victory.

Gerhard Liebs only saw zero balances as well. He grabbed his phone so hard that blood seeped through the white glove on his right hand. He wanted answers. Something didn't add up. He knew he had won by hundreds of millions of dollars, but he couldn't access his account to obtain the confirmation. Something was wrong, terribly wrong.

Caribbean Trust & Bank Corporation
West Bay Road
PO Box 11354
Grand Cayman
Cayman Islands
United States Dollars

Account Summary (press enter for transaction details)

| ACCOUNT HOLDER Beneficiary/ Nominee | Credited funds as at end of business | Debited funds as at end of business | Balance Available |
|---|---|---|---|
| 0001002856 | 16,600,838,451.34 | 16,600,838,451.34 | 0.00 |
| 0001002857 | 16,492,965,763.56 | 16,492,965,763.56 | 0.00 |
| 0001002858 | 33,093,804,214.90 | 33,093,804,214.90 | 0.00 |

Special Agent Dillon Rae was quiet. He was holding his breath, saying nothing. Beads of sweat broke out across his brow. His hands were shaking. Suddenly his screen timed out. The refreshed screen were asking for his user ID and password. He was the only person who had access to the three accounts. It had worked! There it was. Zero cash in any of the accounts, just as he had planned. All of the cash had gone into the "Winner's Pot" account and debited again, en route to the US. Unbelievable! He had done it!

Thirty-three fucking billion, ninety-three fucking million and change. A vast sum. And unbeknownst to the players sucked into Rae's game, it was all on its way to a government account at Citibank in New York, a history-making triumph for Dillon Rae and his TRU team. Rae would be a hero. Ravi Sharma had carried out his instructions to the letter. He would be rewarded in time, but Special Agent Dillon knew that the man, though a proven fucking genius, was a loose cannon, and that would not be allowed. He just knew too much.

He grabbed at his notepad and reentered the requested information. The home page came up, and he stabbed at the keyboard to bring up the account statement tab.

There it was, staring him in the face. He stared and stared, stabbed and stabbed, checked and checked, again and again; but Dillon Rae could not access the Citibank account in New York, which was on a distant computer network, to see whether the $33 billion had hit.

"Call Citibank!" He shouted out. He was exuberant, yet after all of the intensity of the operation, he could feel a crushing unease in his heart. A member of his team shook his head after speaking to the bank. Rae noticed the thumbs down signal. "Then call again, and call again, until the fucking bank confirms receipt! Fuck, how hard can that be?" He turned back to his terminals. "Do I have to do everything?"

What Gerhard Liebs and Harvey Milton didn't realize was that at that moment they were both wiped out. Each thought the other had lost, but neither could get any confirmation as to the actual winner.

At 5:30 p.m. Oscar Randell received an e-mail. The stunned expression on his face said it all. After what seemed like an eternity, Randell pushed himself to his feet, dragged his lifeless form slowly down the corridor to Milton's suite of rooms, knocked on the door, and entered.

"Oscar?" Milton was in bed, resting, his hands lying flat beside him.

"An e-mail, Harvey," Randell said, dejected, handing it over.

Milton read the e-mail several times as if unable to understand its contents, hoping that the next time it would somehow read differently. "Get me that bastard Dillon Rae, and this time don't take no for an answer!"

It took thirty minutes to get the call through.

"Mr. Milton, I'm sorry, but I've been very busy ..."

"Enough of that!" Milton shouted. "Is it true what Liebs says?"

"I don't know what Liebs is saying," Rae answered coolly. "Perhaps you could enlighten me?"

Milton unfolded the crumpled e-mail he had clenched in his hand, and read its contents.

My dear Harvey,

What can I say? I salute a gallant loser! I won the match. I took up your offer and beat you fair and square. I wish you all the luck you would have wished me under similar circumstances. Gerhard

"Is this true?" Milton bellowed.

"Yes. He has won," Dillon Rae answered wryly, masking what was really taking place.

"But, we were supposed to be working together! The billion dollars ... what about my billion dollars?" Milton felt a tightening in his chest cavity. "I still have the money?" He pleaded.

"Performance related."

"You never said it was subject to anything!"

"Regrettably, you saw fit to ignore that."

"I'll be ruined. You'll pay for this, Rae. You won't get away with it. I have many friends in Washington!"

"You knew the stakes. And you were the one who approached Gerhard Liebs in Zurich. Do you think I could be blamed for that? Do you have witnesses?"

"I acted on behalf of the US government!"

"I'm afraid I don't know what you're talking about, Mr. Milton."

"I'll see you in hell, you bastard!"

A massive pain pierced Milton's chest as his heart sputtered and shorted out. The phone in his hand clattered to the floor and his face twisted in agony. He clasped his chest, gasping for air and blacked out. Randell rushed to Milton's aid and began pumping his chest with the palms of his hands, shouting desperately for help. Abigail and others came rushing in. "Get him on the floor!" someone shouted. Paramedics were called. Abigail joined Randell at Milton's side and blew air into his lungs, administering two mouth-to-mouth breaths after every twenty of Randell's chest compressions. They worked diligently to keep blood flowing to Milton's heart and brain until the crash wagon arrived. The Grim Reaper hovered at Milton's side. In a matter of minutes he started breathing again. Twenty minutes later, he was in a helicopter racing to the nearest hospital.

A call to Grand Cayman was required. At 5:55, Liebs rang Dieter Gruber for an update. Gruber's report on the latest events was as devastating as it could possibly be. Word was out that something calamitous had occurred within CAY BANK. Liebs demanded answers, but there were none to give.

On an open line to CAY BANK, JC discovered that they were in a state of hysteria.

"Is the transfer complete or not?" Rae shouted into the console. "Get Ravi on the line!" he spat.

The bank computers had frozen. CAY BANK could neither confirm nor deny that the $33 billion amassed by Milton and Liebs was on its way to Citibank. But the situation could easily be rectified. All they needed was Ravi Sharma, who had apparently gone on walkabout.

In a panicked frenzy, the TRU group was painstakingly trying to piece together their rapidly derailing situation. Rae's operation had gone disastrously wrong. The $33 billion still hadn't arrived at Citibank and there were no explanations or answers. The money was on its way *somewhere,* and only Ravi Sharma could tell them where and fix the problem. But where was he?

All resources that could be mustered by government agencies were called on to trace the whereabouts of the brilliant programmer. The cry was simple. "Find fucking Ravi Sharma, at all costs."

Immigration in Grand Cayman had no record of Sharma's departure, which was most probably due to the huge incentive he paid to the pilot. The flight plan was filed as a pleasure trip around the island. Once airborne, the pilot swung around and changed direction.

Not one member on the TRU team could look Rae straight in the eye. JC was still talking on an open line with systems personnel at CAY BANK. Where was the money? Had Dillon Rae been so blindsided by the lure of the big score that he hadn't seen the pitfalls? Was he just too clever for his own good? Had he lost the US government one billion dollars plus the extensive expenses and the whole $33 billion?

"This is not happening," Rae said, shaking his head. "This is fucking not happening!" All sorts of bells were going off in his head as he stared blankly, open mouthed, at one of the terminals. Something suddenly clicked, as an awful thought crossed his mind. Had Gerhard Liebs bribed Ravi Sharma in some way? That was it! Of course!

"I'll track down Liebs through whatever means necessary," he murmured. He would investigate Bank Schreiber Liebs and everything Liebs owned, and if Liebs was not wiped out as Milton was, he would have all the proof he needed to get the Swiss authorities to hand him over. Simple! All was not lost. A little delayed, but so what? The laurel wreath was still hovering above his head.

Rae's eyes narrowed into icy slits. It would take time, but he would find the money. It couldn't have gotten lost in the system. An electronic trail existed that would prove where the money had traveled. Pinching the bridge of his nose, Rae sat back down at his desk and picked up the telephone. "Let's keep cracking, guys." But there was a profound weariness in his voice. He needed a shot of adrenaline. "We need the wire trail, and soon. Start with CAY BANK. Get a team down there now!"

Then the team member who had been talking to Citibank shouted out. The room went silent and all eyes turned to him.

"Some money is in!" Cheers and hand shaking broke out among the team congregating around Dillon Rae, whose grin might well have split his face, it was so wide. "You can access the account now."

Special Agent Rae extracted himself from the congratulatory crowd and made his way back to the Citibank terminal and slowly, as if the keys were red hot, entered the codes.

"My God!" He almost fainted at what he saw on the screen. He staggered and swayed and eventually sank into his chair, his mind in total turmoil. "What a fucking clever genius!" He moved forward to see the large credit figure on the screen. "You complete and utter fucking brilliant bastard!"

# NASSAU

In late afternoon, the couple awakened, but said little. Much went unspoken, as if they couldn't bring themselves to mention the enormity of their situation as fugitives. They decided to spend the little time they had left walking the beach. As they walked along the sand, people were beginning to leave after a long day of swimming and sunbathing. Jet Skis that had noisily crisscrossed the water were finally still, beach umbrellas were being folded and stacked away, and vendors were gone.

They clambered from the sand onto a rock on which to chill. With waves lapping their bare feet, they sat and watched the beginning of the sunset. Sitting low over the horizon, the sun set in a blaze of fiery reds, tinting the clouds that sheltered the ocean in purple and pink hues. The couple rose from their rocky seat and strolled arm in arm back along the beach until they arrived at a small beachside restaurant.

"You okay, my darling?" Nick stopped, drew her into his arms and kissed her forehead tenderly.

"Suppose more things go wrong, *tesoro*?"

"Sweetheart, we are in the shit, and it is all down to me!" Nick turned, and taking her hand, led her to the restaurant. "We're doing this for us. And as long as we're together, anything is manageable."

Luciana looked up at his worried face. "But my father ..." Luciana closed her eyes, denying the tears that longed to stream down her face. "My father, he ..." but she couldn't tell Nick the truth.

"We'll visit your father in Italy, and I'll try to convince him that I'm right for you."

"I'm worried about what might happen tomorrow."

"Have faith in me. Trust me. Ravi demanded we turn up.

You'll see. It will all work out." But he knew he was spewing a bucket full of crap.

To Luciana's surprise, Nick started to laugh uncontrollably at the unpredictability of his predicament. Despite everything that had happened, he still believed everything would work out, just as Ravi had promised it would. How? He didn't have a clue. But there was something that made him want to trust his old friend, and he would bet his life on it. *And what of Rae, Hart, and Lee? What were they up to?* he wondered to himself. Had the sting gone to plan? What chaos had ensued? Tomorrow he would know. His whole life depended on Ravi's plans, plans that he knew little about.

Nick and Luciana checked in at Lynden Pindling International Airport in Nassau. Their flight was on time. Nick took out his newly acquired cell phone, retrieved a number from his pocket, and dialed. The marina boat rental manager answered.

"This is Nicholas Adams."

"Jesus, man! Where the Christ is my fucking boat, you schmuck? I've had the cops on my fucking neck the last couple of days. What shit are you pulling on me, man?"

"I'm in Nassau. I'm sorry."

"Fucking Nassau? How the hell am I going to get my boat back from the fucking Bahamas? What are you doing there anyway? Look, man, I'm going to have to get it shipped back at your cost. I've got your credit card info and I will fucking use it and with late penalties."

"Fine. As I said, I'm really sorry. Something came up."

"I bet it did. You guys on the run, eh? Some sort of Bonnie and Clyde deal?" The boat agent suddenly calmed down, sounding more relaxed.

"You know how it is," Adams responded wryly. Adams gave the man precise details on the whereabouts of his boat, where it was moored, and where to pick up its keys. He also reported that there had been no damage to the vessel, and that she was a beauty. "It will need a cleanup, but you can charge that to my card."

"I will," the man answered. "That I will. You have given me fucking grief, man!"

By the time the agent reported the conversation to Miami police, it was too late. Nick and Luciana left Nassau shortly afterward, flying south. It was a short flight, during which neither of them said much. Nick could hardly speak. His stomach was in knots, his throat completely dry. What the hell was he doing? Where on earth was he going?

Dillon Rae had called off the hounds. There was nothing he needed from Nick. It was Ravi to whom he dedicated his resources now.

The couple landed. Overhead, the sun blazed down. Turks and Caicos epitomized the classic image of a tropical haven, with long, sprawling stretches of creamy, white sand and clear waters ranging from azure to inky blue.

Nick and Luciana strolled along the main street of the town, oblivious to the pandemonium that was taking place outside the fantasy world they had created for themselves. It was at that moment so true that such Caribbean paradises can be illusory, offering a sanctuary for those wishing to escape from the chaos of society.

In a complex interplay of hope, nervous anticipation, and intrigue, they kept their appointment as promised. A small, brightly polished brass plate mounted on a pillar beside glass entrance doors read: International Funding Bank Limited. The doors opened automatically as the couple walked up four shallow dust-strewn steps. It was precisely 11:00 a.m. They entered and asked for the manager, as Nick had been instructed. After a short wait, the manager appeared. He walked over to where the couple was seated and smiled a wide grin that gave the very best of Caribbean welcomes. The couple stood up.

"Mr. Adams. A real honor and pleasure, sir." The deep voice oozed charm. "I understood that you would be alone?"

"This is my friend, Luciana Cavallini." Nick placed a hand on Luciana's shoulder, and she shook the manager's outstretched hand.

"A pleasure indeed. I hope you are enjoying the hospitality of our islands." The man's smile widened. He turned and walked over to the security door and punched at the buttons that released the catch. "Please—follow me." Nick looked at Luciana, who raised her eyebrows, bemused. The couple entered, followed the manager past several busy clerks, and down a short corridor. They arrived at the manager's office and followed him in.

"I think you know each other, gentlemen?" the manager beamed.

"My God! You made it! Both of you! Hey, Luciana." Ravi Sharma managed a painful smile. Nick leaped across the floor to hug him.

"We did it."

"Did what?" Luciana questioned. "What's going on?" She looked apprehensive, but strangely elated as she saw the two men so happy.

"Can we have a few minutes on our own, sir?" Sharma said, looking at the manager, who nodded.

"But of course." He walked out of his office. Pausing at the door, he said, "Some refreshments?" The trio shook their heads. He gave a short bow and closed the door behind him.

"Read this." Sharma handed a piece of paper to Nick. A look of strained triumph covered his face.

"What is it, Nick?" Luciana asked, seeing the stunned look on his face.

"I still don't get it. It's some corporate bank statement showing what looks like a credit balance of five hundred million US dollars." He shrugged his shoulders, utterly confused. "What's this about, Ravi?"

Sharma could hardly contain himself. "Half a billion dollars, for Christ's sake! Work it out, man."

"I don't get it. What does it mean?" Luciana asked.

Nick stared at Ravi's gaunt but obviously suddenly childishly happy face.

"Read the name of the account holder," Sharma urged him, stabbing at the name at the top of the statement.

Nick examined the paper and traced a finger across a name in bold print. "Bond InterContinental Establishment."

"What do the initials tell you? Come on now, think."

"B – I – C – E."

"Pronounce it."

"Bice!" Luciana cried out, grabbing the paper from Nick.

Ravi laughed. "Exactly. Your favorite New York watering hole, where we always met."

"Yeah ... and ...?" Nick responded, puzzled, almost whispering. "So what? Your point is?"

"It's your new company, buddy." Sharma sat down, exhausted and not a little dejected with his little game. "I formed this a few days ago. The company banks here, and the money is all yours."

"*What the fuck?*" A stunned look crossed Nick's face. "What the hell have you done? Five hundred million? Mine? *Oh ... myyy ... God!*" Incredulity and reservation showed all at once as he looked at Sharma. "Why?"

"Because, because, because. Just because. That's why." Ravi turned away from the two and lifted a file from the top of the manager's desk. "All you have to do is get these documents signed and notarized, give the bank a specimen of your signature, and it's all yours. Total secrecy guaranteed."

Luciana sat down. She put her head in her hands and started to rub at her eyes. She was unable to contain her incredulity.

There was a lot of hugging and laughter.

"Ravi," Nick said when he finally sat down and looked directly at the gaunt grey face of his friend, "look, it all sounds unbelievable, I mean really fucking awesome, but take me—us," he held Luciana's hand, "through the whole story. Leave nothing out, please."

Ravi explained that Zen Holdings, Adams's privately held company had received a wire credit in the sum of $10 million in Switzerland that morning.

"Use the money to pay back the cash you took from your share sale, and that will take care of your little problem with any of the shareholders and any prying Authorities, with change left over. Take over ABS, do a management buyout, and it will be yours from now on! No more Kersch & Co!"

"Unbelievable!" Nick looked at Luciana who still looked bemused. "Are you sure about this? Won't everything be traced?"

"Maybe, but I have a shrewd idea it won't be."

Sharma then proceeded to tell them in detail what had happened to Rae's entrapment scheme. It was so simple to make changes to TRU's instruction as to how he was to manipulate Adams Banking Solutions's program installed at CAY BANK. He had devised a series of domino triggers, which at 5:00 p.m. the day before drained both Liebs's and Milton's accounts into the master account. Another trigger was supposed to transfer the full amount from the master account to Citibank in New York. But Sharma reprogrammed the software to bypass the master account entirely, and split the billions into a host of smaller payments using quantum encryption to encode all the transactions, which were then wired to hundreds of accounts at banks across the globe, including the bank in which where they were now.

"And I've also left a present for JC. He'll discover my little gift soon enough. That should more than compensate for all the heat I'm sure he had to take in the last twelve hours because of me." Sharma was fiercely loyal to those he counted as friends.

"What about Dillon Rae and TRU? You can't just steal a billion from the US!"

"Ah, well I agree, but I sorted that out, trust me!" A bead of sweat trickled down the side of his face and he paused to drink out of his water bottle.

"But, Ravi, they'll trace the payments."

"I put a virus into the CAY BANK computer and destroyed the records."

"But they'll still find some of the money in the international payments system."

"By the time that happens, everything will have vanished. And that's why you need to sort things out with the bank manager ASAP. I've made certain arrangements that guarantee the authorities will come up against a brick wall."

"I knew you were a criminal, Ravi, but this is unbelievable," he said, laughing. It was extraordinary. Nick wanted to pinch himself to make sure he wasn't dreaming. He was both in shock and ecstatic at the same time over the idea of being rich beyond his wildest imaginings. But something tugging at his conscience was telling him it was wrong.

"They can check who owns the corporation. Then what happens?"

"Trust."

"I can't trust anyone. And the bank will have to disclose this transaction and the beneficial ownership."

"Not that sort of trust," Sharma said, shaking his head impatiently. "A trust has been formed behind the corporation. You're completely protected. Read the file and get your pen out."

"What on earth have you done, Ravi? And what about you? Are you going to be okay? You've opened a can of worms for yourself."

"Don't you worry for an instant about me. Anyway, you'd better pull up a chair. I've got more things to tell you." Sharma slumped back into his seat.

"Okay, so what other shit have you pulled, Ravi?"

"Let him tell his story," Luciana said, signaling almost impatiently for Nick to sit down.

"You know that I was abducted and beaten up by mobsters in New York. What you don't know was that I was forced to cooperate with them on the CAY BANK sting. I had no choice."

"How the hell did they know about Dillon Rae's operation?" Nick asked.

"Luciana was feeding them information." Sharma nodded sharply, his eyes narrowed, meeting Luciana's squarely.

Nick turned to Luciana, scanning her face anxiously. Luciana blinked back nervously. "*Si*, it's true, *tesoro*. My father was asking me so many questions about you, your reporter friend, my accident, your business, spying for the government. I thought he was just concerned about my involvement with you. I told him far more than I let on to you. I didn't realize … I'm so sorry, I had no idea." Her voice trailed off, unsure of what to say. She sat looking apprehensively at both of them.

Accepting the remorse in Luciana's voice, Sharma raised his

hands to silence her. "Fuck, Lu, you are a dark horse! Come here!" Nick opened his arms. "Listen—it's water under the bridge; you could not have known what was going on."

"And so," Ravi interrupted, "I did what I did because I had nothing to lose." There was no regret, no hesitation in his voice. "As you can see by the look of me, my body has taken a turn for the worse. My condition is deteriorating quicker than the doctors expected. I don't have long for this world, guys."

"No, no. That can't be! With all this cash we have the means to fund a cure!" Nick swallowed, resisting the wave of nausea that gripped him. The idea of losing his friend was finally hitting home.

Sharma smiled thinly, shaking his head, clearly touched by Adams's words. "I have my own plans, Nick. You really shouldn't worry about me. Anyhow, as I was saying, Luciana's father promised me a deal."

Nick leaned in closer to Sharma. "Tell us. Start from the beginning; what did happen?"

So they listened as the whole saga unfolded. It was incredible, but Nick knew what the software he and Sharma had created was capable of doing. It was, in hindsight, the best beta test ever. But the banks would never know just how well it worked, nor how dangerous it could be in the wrong hands. Luciana sobbed quietly as Sharma continued his story. It was all too plain to see how bad his health had become. But she was beside herself with rage. Her father! She never learned. Nothing surprised her anymore.

"And," Ravi announced as if awarding the Golden Globe Award, "I have another gift for you." He handed Adams a small envelope. "I've already sent instructions and the application in an encrypted file to a new secure e-mail server address I've set up for you. You'll need the file on that flash drive to install the program."

Adams opened the envelope and read the note attached to the flash drive. "Your operating system!" Adams spoke in a low tone. "You've finished it!"

"Yes. The masterpiece is complete," Sharma responded

proudly. "Do with it as you wish. Just promise to make it work, in my honor, and," he paused, looked at Nick, and said, "do good with it. You won't need to make money, so go and challenge the Big Boys and find a way to market it as a "people's software."

Sharma knew his ultimate gift to Adams would mysteriously change everything for Nick. It was Ravi's last legacy.

# ITALY

In a small mountain village just a few miles north of Naples, a feisty old witch of a woman, clad in full black mourning attire, snapped at a young bank teller. Her face was a cache of wrinkles, her white hair wisped from under a black headscarf. "Take!" she demanded. Her tone was fierce and uncompromising as she handed over a sheet of paper that showed her bank details.

"How much would you like to withdraw?" He tried hiding his incredulous look as he saw her account balance. His eyes could hardly believe her funds had grown so dramatically since her last visit.

"All of it!" she snapped, scolding the young teller for not treating her with respect when she first approached him.

Shortly afterward, the old woman approached a church in the center of her village. She shuffled up its many stone steps, through the small door within the huge main doors that led into the church, and past people lighting candles. She looked up at the face leaning down toward hers, bowed her head, and presented 100,000 euros in cash to her priest. Behind a column hidden from view there stood two of Cavallini's soldiers, several large cases bulging with cash at their feet.

Hers was only one of a multitude of such visits made in the small village that day. In similar towns throughout southern Italy and Sicily, widows and old men queued at the counters of small village banks, drawing sums in varying amounts. The network reached points all over the globe, where legitimate accounts that had either previously existed or had been recently established received substantial credits. Payments, which had initially been sent to banks in Panama, the Caribbean, Hong Kong, Mauritius, Cyprus, Dubai, and Singapore, moved onward to Swiss banks and many other Italian banks for further distribution throughout their network of branches. Each targeted account was completely emptied by customers who withdrew or transferred their funds in full by the close of business that day. By the time the more stringent governments instructed their central banks to trace the source of funds it would be too late. The task was too huge. Banks within countries that had managed to maintain their strict secrecy laws were rewarded with huge influxes of money. Monies were also wired to countries so eager for the inflow of foreign capital that their governments were happy to turn a blind eye to the money's origins. Countless numbers of securities were also quickly purchased.

Stock Exchange indices went up considerably, reflecting the large inflow of trading that day. Other monies were camouflaged as they passed through an assortment of offshore shell corporations around the world. Within days these companies would implement complex loan arrangements, use certificates of deposits as collateral, then transfer the loan proceeds back to a diverse and complex web of fiscal skulduggery.

A few of the much larger sums were apparently "lost in transit," thanks to the programming skills of Ravi Sharma. It didn't really matter what the final total received was because an amount well over thirty billion dollars had been flushed out of CAY BANK and landed, rather circuitously, in the hands of the Cosa Nostra, thus replenishing their up-until-then rapidly dwindling resources.

Thanks to Don Franco, the vast new influx of funds would enable the Mafia to confront their competitors and regain lost ground.

In small towns and villages throughout southern Italy and Sicily as well as in New York, Chicago, and Las Vegas neighborhood bars, Don Franco Cavallini was fast becoming a legend. The old personification of a true Don was clearly back and now deadlier than ever.

# WASHINGTON, DC

"Well Dillon?" The Director of the Federal Bureau of Investigation smiled at his Agent. "Not a complete failure then, by all accounts?"

Dillon Rae sat on one of the comfortable chairs opposite his boss. "It did not go as I planned, I'm afraid." He shook his head not quite believing what had really happened. "It's not over, Director, I can assure you."

"Dillon, let it rest." He leaned forward, placing his elbows on the file that was open on his desk. "We got the money back didn't we?"

"All we got was the seed capital. I failed my mission!"

"Listen, we got the billion. And what about all of the cash you siphoned out of the bank from the rest of the delinquent accounts of US citizens?" He looked straight at Rae and partially understood his sense of failure. "After all, your unit was set up to repatriate their money back to us. I understand that what happened is not as you envisaged, but shit happens in our line of work." He paused. "Had you lost our money, then we would be having a very different conversation."

Dillon Rae thought back to the moment when he had accessed the Citibank account that had been set up to be the final resting place for the $33 billion, and his horror—and admiration—at seeing only one billion. Ravi Sharma had ensured that the initial stake was repaid to minimize the collateral damage and future retribution. Rae had no idea how he had done it, but he had, and with incredible panache. Of course, the director was correct. TRU got back immense sums, and that was a win for him and his team; but now it was personal.

"Director, my job has to go on; we need to finish the mission, sir."

"No, Dillon, leave it. It was just too fanciful to succeed …"

"Sir, I have ideas …"

"Special Agent Rae." The Director closed the file on his desk and stood up and took off his spectacles. "I am standing down TRU with immediate effect. You will be promoted and we live to fight another day …"

"But the money," Rae almost whined like a spoiled child, "we must trace the money, the money must be with that bastard Liebs …"

"Dillon!" The director stood up. "Leave it! That's an order!"

"But …"

"One concession: issue an arrest warrant against Ravi Sharma." As he reached to answer his ringing desk phone, he picked up the receiver, growled, "One moment," and cupping the mouthpiece, added, "Get him. He's too dangerous to be allowed to be a free agent." He picked up the handset and cupped the mouthpiece, "He could be very useful to us!" The director quickly shook hands with Rae and took his call. But lowering the phone, he shouted out, "And get the Swiss too!"

Special Agent Dillon Rae smiled for the first time.

# SWITZERLAND

The snowfall had let up, assisting the grand escape.

On a call to Dieter Gruber at CAY BANK, Liebs learned the truth. It was over. But he conceded it was a magnificent display of ingenuity. In the final analysis, it was Harvey Milton who had been obliterated. And that alone was victory enough for Liebs.

*Clever,* he thought. Gerhard Liebs might have lost, but they had failed to complete the job. He would weather this inconvenient storm. *Absolutely brilliant,* he thought. He laughed hysterically. What amused and amazed him most was that there were others as cunning and as manipulative as he. With the files from his vault, his crates, and the last five million in cash, which he had ordered to be sent by courier from Bank Schreiber Liebs, but which had failed to be transferred in time to CAY BANK, he would consolidate and rebuild.

A flurry of activity was taking place at the schloss. Boxes were being packed. Particular paintings, Fabergé eggs, and sealed wooden crates taken from the cellars were loaded onto trucks. Filled to capacity, the vehicles left the estate en route to a secret location. Liebs's helicopter was also loaded with as much as its payload would allow. Gerhard Liebs screamed at staff to cram more into his helicopter. "Dismantle the seats!" he demanded. The pilot just shook his head in utter disbelief.

In Washington, Dillon Rae had contacted the Swiss authorities and provided sufficient information for them to react at once.

Bad weather was coming in over the mountaintops. If they were to go, they needed to leave within ten minutes. With Liebs and Valentina Vinogradov on board, the pilot started the engine. Rotor blades began to turn. Confused, the schloss staff heard police sirens in the distance, but the pilot could hear only the engine straining as it fought to take off. The pilot's face drained of color as he saw the snowstorm approaching. There was much too much weight on board. With super effort, the helicopter rose in a cloud of fresh snow, lurching and rolling as the blades struck the thin air, gaining altitude foot by foot. The pilot turned his head, looked down at the schloss, and pointed to the Swiss police cars with blue flashing lights making their way up the snowy drive leading to the Liebs mansion. The pilot raised the engine revs and slowly and laboriously banked toward the mountains.

Black snow clouds began to appear. The wind shifted, becoming stronger as it whipped around the helicopter. Its engine spluttered and suddenly cut out. Silence filled the sky, except for an awesome rushing of air whistling through the cabin. The helicopter spiraled out of control. Boxes and crates shifted and crashed about the cabin. The pilot held onto the controls as firmly as he could and tried to unbuckle his safety harness. The wind howled. Losing blade speed, the Agusta started to spin. Rotating out of control, it clipped treetops, scything branches, hit the side of the mountain slope, and plunged into deep snow. The fuel pipes burst on impact. An eerie stillness followed, broken by angry birds circling the trees. The helicopter exploded. Orange flames leaped high into the air, burning tree growth and issuing dense, oily black smoke, which fought with the wind and lost.

The next morning, the two sets of uneven footprints that had left the crash site, leading toward the thick forest that covered the mountainside, were by then covered by fresh snow.

The crash investigators would have their time cut out trying to identify the one charred corpse retrieved from the smoking debris. Witnesses, however, attested to there being two others on board, but so far the search teams had found nothing. The snow had covered what evidence there might be as to any survivors, but later when the weather permitted, they would use heat-seeking equipment to identify where any bodies or remains might be.

The time delay was fortuitous. The two severely wounded passengers who had dragged themselves painfully from the tangled wreck, and who had crawled slowly across the deep snow and into the dense woods that bordered the Schloss estate, leaving crimson streaks in the furrows their broken bodies had made, had escaped the appalling fate of the pilot. In their strange self-centered world, they both knew there would be time enough to recuperate and re-build and carry on as before. Nothing would change. They would learn from this uncharacteristic blip. They would just have to up the stakes. Revenge would be just that much sweeter.

Several global businesses collapsed, and although the mainstream banks inevitably rescued some corporations, others were conveniently allowed to fester and die, and all because of the billions the two titans had sucked out of the system for their own gratification and glorification.

Milton Global Inc. went into Chapter 11 pending reorganization. Harvey Milton was not well enough to read the appalling vitriol aimed at him in the world's financial press. He remained president in absentia. But one night at the Miami Hospital where he was incarcerated, Colombians arrived and pulled the pipes and tubes out of the orifices of the vegetable Harvey Milton III. The staff, seeing the monitors outside flatline, rushed to his room, but he was dead. A nurse screamed as she saw what had been wedged into the corpse's mouth. The severed penis of Harvey Milton lay flaccid and bleeding in his oral cavity, and an ever-increasing pool of blood formed in the middle of the white sheet that had become his shroud.

Ravi Sharma had become too ill to join Nick and Luciana in Italy. Sharma's most enduring legacy would one day take the world by storm, and Nick Adams had promised to lock it away safely until the time was right to launch a new operating system that would dominate the computer world through which ABS would one day join the ranks of and threaten the top global software system corporations.

He had spent some time on a private island, one of the smaller cays of Turks and Caicos, paid for courtesy of Dillon Rae. Sharma took a deep breath of tropical air and winced in sudden pain. He looked out onto tranquil turquoise waters and idyllic ocean views in peace.

He had rented the four-bedroom beachfront villa within a five-acre oasis on the exclusive Pirate Cay Island. It was the perfect location for his final days. His cabana sun bed was draped with sheer curtains, with an oversized parasol perched gently swaying above his head. A constant trade wind kept him as comfortable as he could be within his shelter below the blazing afternoon sun.

A young man in colorful island shorts and white shirt trotted happily across the pristine white sand, carrying a tray with a cocktail of local fruit juices and meds for his new employer. Sharma, noticing the man hurrying toward him, slid his sunglasses to his forehead and smiled in amusement as he took stock. Maybe his life was short … but it was as good as he could hope for. The clock was ticking away to the alarm time that had now been set. At that moment he doubled up and tried to vomit. He coughed and shook. Blood mixed with his saliva oozed from his mouth.

Agent Rae needed a fall guy. It had taken time, but he found one of the two on his hit list.

In the end he hadn't needed the local island police force. Observing the plain-to-see fragility of his quarry from the rear of a police Range Rover, he realized that he might be too late. He opened the rear door and walked slowly across the hot white sand.

"Ravi?"

# NEW YORK

Dillon Rae got the call, but he arrived too late. He rushed through the precinct and down a bleak corridor, waiting impatiently for the cell door to be unlocked. As it swung open, the emaciated, naked, scarred, blotched body of Ravi Sharma, his neck broken, suspended from the end of a knotted rope made from his trousers and shirt tied around the metal rungs of his window, cast a long shadow across the stone floor. Dead.

But despite the grotesque death, there was serenity in his face, as though at long last he had found peace, and no more pain would wrack through his frail, broken body.

Dillon Rae sighed heavily and knew that with this latest death, all the answers as to where the money had gone were unlikely to be revealed, and that his plans of recruiting this exceptionally bright software programmer for the FBI were thwarted.

Special Agent Rae said quietly, "Cut him down and treat him gently; he deserves respect."

He made a small bow toward the limp cadaver, acknowledging the man who had single-handedly beaten him. He turned, and without looking back into the cell, strode off down the corridor and eventually out into the street. He needed air—lots of it.

Lawyers acting on the instructions of the absent Nick Adams agreed to a deal with the SEC. All the money was repaid to the shareholders of ABS. The monies that were owed in the settlement were transferred from the Swiss accounts of Zen Holdings, which would be closed down, and as part of the deal, Adams would be free to operate in the US again, without a stain on his character. He could resume as president of ABS to complete what he had started.

But after sending his long, detailed instruction, Nick

Adams was incommunicado. Pleased with the fat fees they had received up front, the lawyers had no idea what he would do with the negotiated free amnesty they had wrested on his behalf. They awaited his further instructions with interest.

# ITALY

Nick and Luciana strolled arm in arm through the grounds of the magnificent palazzo.

"Are you absolutely sure about this, Nico?" Luciana asked.

"If I turn down your father's offer, can I still have you?"

"You know the answer." Her eyes locked onto his.

"I don't think I can refuse, Lu."

"It's your life, *tesoro.* It is for you to decide."

"The family would never accept me."

"But you are a hero. And as the future son-in-law of Don Franco Cavallini, they most surely will."

"How did I know Ravi would transfer the money to the Mafia, for fuck's sake?

"Well, he did, and that can't change. You can't pay it all back can you? Not without putting yourself in danger!"

"I suppose because the money was all black money accumulated through criminal activities, it only means it has been moved into another branch of that evil world!"

"Nico darling, don't beat yourself up!"

"I've sold my soul to the Devil before, and he has rewarded me by giving me half a billion dollars, as well as the most dazzling, beautiful woman on earth. Maybe I shouldn't turn my back on him just at this moment?" He stopped and turned toward Luciana. "You know, there's an old Chinese proverb that says the journey of a thousand miles begins with a single step. Once you take that first step and touch the first darkness there's no return."

Luciana gazed into his eyes and squeezed his arm tightly. They walked toward the main entrance of the fine palace. Nick fell silent. He turned and looked over the vineyard below, stretching far beyond, merging into the rolling Sicilian mountains. He was alone in his thoughts.

Somewhere in the distance, he heard a mule bray, a dog bark, and a distant long roll of thunder.

From the grape-decked terrace high above them stood Don Franco, watching the couple on their approach. The mirrored lenses of his sunglasses reflected the sky as he observed the searing Italian sun disappear behind an ominously dark cloud. A storm was on its way.

# THE END